As she turned over on her stomach, Roxanna had the strange feeling that someone else was in the room with her, lurking in the darkness. She had denied the feeling in recent days. But now the impression overwhelmed her. Chills shot through her body. She lay very still, held her breath and listened.

Could it be Tom, she wondered, back from the skirmishes with the Tetons? Or was it the man who had been watching her, stalking her for weeks?

"Tom?" she blurted out. Her voice sounded small and forlorn in the cool, dark room. "Tom! Is that you?"

There was no answer.

Her hand quickly found its way across the pillow and under it to the flintlock Tom had given her. The warm metal barrel and wooden handle were comforting to the touch, but the weapon seemed unbelievably large and unwieldy as she drew it out in front of her.

"I have a gun here," she warned.

The footsteps stopped.

Suddenly, a hard, icy hand came out of nowhere and grabbed her arm. Thick, powerful fingers gouged into her flesh. . . .

LEWIS & CLARK

NORTHWEST GLORY

James Raymond

A Dell/Standish Book

Published by

Miles Standish Press, Inc.
37 West Avenue
Wayne, Pennsylvania 19087

Dell ® TM 681510, Dell Publishing Co., Inc.

ISBN: 0-440-04747-1
Printed in the United States of America
First printing—September 1981

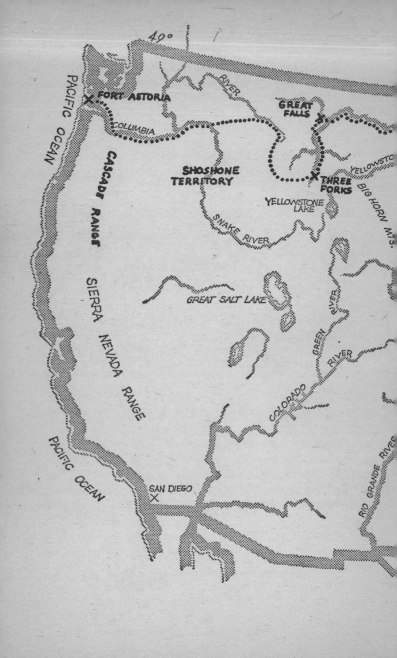

49°

FORT MANDAN

RIVER

MISSISSIPPI RIVER

BADLANDS

MISSOURI RIVER

N. PLATTE

TETON
SIOUX

COUNCIL
BLUFFS

S. PLATTE

RIVER

ARKANSAS RIVER

ST. LOUIS

MOUNTAIN

The
Lewis & Clark
EXPEDITION
1804 ~ 1805
Miles

0   50   100   150   200

PART ONE
ST. LOUIS

Chapter 1

Tom Wentworth raised his father's heavy flintlock pistol and looked down the barrel at the once-mighty horse now thrashing painfully and madly in the mud. The rain had been so heavy he had missed a turn a while ago. He was lost; he hoped he was about ten miles out of St. Louis, but he didn't know for sure.

Poor Lancer managed a last, desperate jerk of his broken leg, made a splash in a puddle, then settled down quietly. He curled his neck back, peered up through the rain at his master and awaited his fate.

Tom felt sick at having to kill the faithful old horse, but the animal was suffering. Tom knew he had to do it. He held his breath, closed his eyes and squeezed the trigger.

Although he flinched at the explosion of the powder, he placed the shot perfectly. As the ball sank cleanly into the horse's temple, his neck immediately became limber and his head dropped into the mire. Tom was relieved that there were no screams of pain. At least Lancer had died quickly.

A few minutes later, taking one last look at the

horse, he sadly shuffled wet limbs and rocks over the corpse. He wished he had time to bury him properly, but he was in a great hurry. It was May 15, 1804, and Captain Meriwether Lewis's expedition into the Northwest country would be beginning tomorrow morning. He had to get to St. Louis this night. If he missed the expedition, he would miss the thing he had come nine hundred miles to find: a fortune.

He had left Philadelphia in plenty of time eight weeks before, but he had caught the fever in Kentucky and had lost two weeks. Now, desperate to get to St. Louis and join Captain Lewis, he began walking briskly, almost running through the rain into the thick woods, hoping he was headed in the right direction.

It was ten o'clock at night when Tom arrived, footworn and weary, at an inn outside St. Louis. The inn wasn't much, just a two-story building with a battered sign that said "Lodgings" over the door. But lights gleamed in the first-story windows and the tantalizing aroma of frying bear meat came to Tom's nostrils as he stood outside the door.

Dragging his way up to the rickety, two-story house, Tom had to smile at the recollection of Ben Radcliffe's two-hundred-room Essex Inn back in Boston. The Essex was pure luxury; they even served you breakfast in bed. Just the thought of that venerable inn gave him a twinge of longing.

He had met Isabel, Radcliffe's daughter, at the Essex, and the moment he saw her playing the harpsichord, he knew that she was the one woman in the world he would be willing to die for. A month later he asked her to marry him and she accepted.

But to marry a Boston Radcliffe wasn't easy. You needed a lot of money to get into that family. To get it, he had come West. The talk back home was that on the other side of the Mississippi lay great undiscovered treasures for an adventurer. All he needed was courage—the courage to face the unknown.

The vast territory west of the river was unknown

to anyone in Philadelphia, even to William Wentworth, his father, who had fought with the army in the Northwest Territory. William had been captured and tortured by the Indians at General Joseph Harmar's defeat and had later fought with Mad Anthony Wayne at Fallen Timbers in August, 1794. But Tom's father was an adventurer only to a point; like so many others, he drew the line at the Mississippi River. Beyond that, he often said, only mad men would go.

No one answered the door, so Tom pushed it open himself and stepped inside.

He looked around the room. There were four men in dingy homespun sitting around a table, swigging ale. They were laughing loudly, sloshing their drinks on the table and floor. A fifth man who was with them—a hardbitten fellow dressed in a pair of worn horsehide trousers, looked up curiously as Tom came in. He gave the traveler a nod, then picked up his mug again and turned to his companions.

"What can I do for you, son?" said the landlord, ambling over to greet him. He was a little man with spectacles perched on his thick nose.

"I'd like a room," Tom managed. "If you don't mind."

"Don't mind at all," he said. "That's just what we've got here—rooms." He glanced at the ruff under Tom's neck. "That's a mighty fine shirt you've got there, son," he observed. "That's silk, ain't it?"

Tom was a tall, thin man of twenty-two, with a heavy shock of tawny hair, deep blue eyes and handsome, regular features. Even exhausted, he carried himself with poise and grace.

"Yes, it's silk," replied Tom. "But if you don't mind, I've been on the road for two months. I'm tired. Do you think I could have a room?"

The landlord shrugged his shoulders. "Yeah, sure you can. Like I say, rooms are what we've got plenty of around here."

"Good," Tom said wearily. "Could I have an ale first?"

"Sure thing. One ale coming up." The landlord went behind the counter and moments later shoved a tankard of ale toward Tom's hand. "There you go."

"Thank you."

"Two months, huh?" the landlord asked thoughtfully. "You from back East?"

Tom drank some of the brew. It made him feel less tired. "I'm from Philadelphia," he answered.

"Is that so? Are you here for a hanging, or what?"

"No. I'm here to join Captain Lewis's expedition."

The landlord laughed and called over to the men drinking, "Hear that, boys? He's come all the way from Philadelphia to join Captain Lewis."

The man in the hide trousers spoke: "You're going to need fins to catch up with Captain Lewis, boy. He and that red-headed William Clark took off up the Missouri yesterday."

Tom's heart sank at the news. "They couldn't have," he murmured.

The man took his words the wrong way. "You doubting my word, boy?" he growled.

Tom shook his head indifferently.

The man didn't like that either. "You listen to me when I'm talking to you, boy," he demanded.

Tom looked up. "I'm listening, and you're talking. The trouble is, you're not saying anything."

The man stood up, scraping his chair on the floor. "Now you listen here, boy—"

"Mr. Atkins—" A soft, feminine voice came from the left.

Tom wheeled at the sound of the voice and was shocked to see a beautiful young woman standing at the foot of the stairs. She was dark-haired, almost as tall as he was, thin and lithe, with high, full breasts.

She cleared her throat. "Mr. Atkins," she repeated. "You said you were going to change the linens tonight."

"What, again?" he groaned.

The man in hide laughed. "What're you doing in that bed, ma'am," he teased, "to mess up old Thurmond's linens like that?"

She stared at him, but said nothing rather than dignify his comment. She returned to the landlord. "My girl Melissa will be going back to New Orleans tomorrow. Do you think you could arrange passage for her? I really would appreciate it."

"Ma'am, I'm running an inn here, not an errand service. She's not my colored girl, she's yours. *You* arrange passage for her."

Tom stepped forth. "Excuse me," he said. "May I do that for you?"

She looked at him, pretending she hadn't known he was in the room. In truth, she'd noticed his good looks the moment she came downstairs. "I never expected to find a gentleman in St. Louis," she remarked.

"What you've got there is a momma's boy from Philly," the man in hide called out. He lumbered over to them. "I'll bet he wears satin trousers underneath his pants, to go with that silk shirt. How about it, boy? Is that true?"

"Leave him alone, Barton," the landlord interrupted.

The man was pleased that Tom hadn't chosen to answer. Growing bolder, he brushed past Tom, grinning. He focused on the woman, looking her up and down. "I'm ready and able to help you soil them new linens, ma'am," he offered. "You just say the word."

"The word is 'no,'" the woman retorted, looking him straight in the eye.

The man turned red. "I'd advise you to look before you leap, girlie—"

"She said 'no,'" Tom cut him off. "Can't you hear?"

Barton turned toward Tom, irritated. He sighed

loudly, shook his head, then ceremoniously pulled his coat open and whipped out a pistol. "Are you looking for a ball in your gut, friend?" he inquired. "Is that what you've come all this way for?"

"Barton—" the landlord tried to break in.

"You just say one more word to me, Silk Shirt," the man threatened Tom, "and they'll be hauling your carcass back to Philly in a pine box."

Tom backed up a step. "Look, I don't have any quarrel with you. Why don't we just let the lady get some new linens and go back to her room—"

"The lady is mine, friend," he said.

"Now just a minute," the woman broke in. "I'm *nobody's!*"

"Now back up, boy," Barton commanded. "Give me room to operate here." He reached out and pushed Tom with his left hand, holding the pistol back and ready in his right.

In a heartbeat, Tom's sword was out of its sheath and the light from the candle lamps overhead flashed in the gleaming blade poised against Barton's throat. The gun fell loudly to the floor.

"Hey, uh, hold it," Barton grunted. "Be careful. That's my gullet you're pressing that thing against. Don't do anything crazy."

"I ought to slit it open."

The woman's heart was beating rapidly. She swallowed hard, touched her chest with her hand. "Please," she whispered, "don't—"

Barton groaned loudly, drowning her words. "I'll leave," he said. "Just back off."

"Why should I?"

"I didn't mean the lady any harm, I swear. I was just kidding around."

"You don't kid around with a lady, Barton," Tom told him.

"Yeah, right. I know that now. Let me go home and try to remember it."

Tom withdrew, but held the saber up. He watched

Barton glance at the flintlock on the floor. "Don't even think about it," he warned him. "You'll come up with only four fingers."

Barton gritted his teeth, turned and stormed out of the house into the rain.

The landlord broke the silence. "Well," he announced, relieved, "now that that's over, the drinks are on me."

But Tom and the woman were too busy looking at each other to hear Atkins' offer.

She smiled and offered her hand to Tom. "Thank you," she said. "That was very gallant of you."

Her fingers were soft and small in his hand. He was stimulated by the touch of her. "You're welcome," he replied. "By the way, my name is Tom Wentworth, Miss—"

"Mrs.," she corrected him, drawing back her hand. "Mrs. Douglas Fairchild."

Tom's disappointment was obvious.

She looked at him for a few seconds, smiled again, then turned to the landlord, "Mr. Atkins, will you be bringing up the linens tonight?"

"Oh yes, ma'am, I'll do it. I'll bring them up first chance I get. As soon as I have a drink with my friend Tom Wentworth. We've got a cause to celebrate here, Mrs. Fairchild. It's not every day Clive Barton gets put in his place like he was tonight."

She nodded. "Then I'll say good night."

"Won't you stay for a drink, ma'am?" Atkins asked.

She shook her head graciously. "No, thank you."

Tom watched her go back up the stairs and disappear behind a door. She had stirred his feelings so much that he had forgotten for a moment all about the expedition. He drank the rest of his ale and thought about her—and Isabel—while Atkins refilled his tankard.

Atkins smiled as he poured. "Hell of a lady, huh?" he asked.

Glancing quickly toward the door at the top of the stairs, Tom nodded. "Yes she is." He turned to Atkins. "Where's her husband? Is he here, too?"

"Nah, that worthless husband of hers is why she's in St. Louis," Atkins replied. "She's looking for him. She told me they were married in New Orleans a couple of months ago. Big wedding on Canal Street, royalty there, everything. Only two days after the wedding, the rascal takes off with this character named Jean Lafitte and disappears without a word. So she traced him up the Mississippi. Now she's heard he's out west somewhere."

"I heard about Lafitte in Kentucky," Tom said. "He's a pirate, isn't he?"

"So they say," Atkins replied, pouring some ale for himself. "But *I* say, there's just no telling where in that forsaken wilderness Sir Douglas Fairchild is. If she goes out there like she says she is, she's liable to find his scalp dangling from the belt of some Teton Sioux warrior. Then where would she be?"

Tom was shocked. "You don't mean she wants to cross the river?"

"No just 'wants to,' son. She's going to. I've never seen such a determined woman in my life. Oh, she looks soft and she smells good, but there's a lot of fire in that one."

Tom's interest was piqued by what the landlord was saying. Again he stared at the door she had gone through. "Look, Atkins," he said after a minute, "I'm going to try to catch up with Captain Lewis tomorrow. If I paid you for the trouble, could you see what you could do for Mrs. Fairchild?"

"Yeah, sure, I'd be glad to. Only don't be surprised if she winds up going with you," Atkins warned. "She's already been out to Camp du Bois three or four times, trying to get the captain to let her go."

Tom was incredulous. "You're kidding. Go on the expedition?"

"That's what she wants."

"That's crazy."

"Tell her that."

"Well, Captain Lewis refused, didn't he?"

"Oh yeah, he refused all right. But that don't mean to her what it means to you and me, son. It means to her, back up and try it some other way. She's a hardheaded woman."

"But a pretty one."

"Let me tell you. Since she took that room upstairs, I've had to change her linens every single day just 'cause she likes 'em fresh to sleep on. I wouldn't change linens every day for my sainted mother. And I've gotten her black girl an extra bed. I've even gone down to the river in the rain to fetch a newspaper—" He caught himself. "Now I wouldn't do all those things for just anybody, mind you."

Tom was amused. "Then why did you do them for her?"

Atkins shrugged. "I don't know. . . . For her, you just do things."

Two hours later in her room upstairs, Roxanna Fairchild stood in front of a mirror while Melissa loosened her stays and then pulled her dress over her head. Then, while the black girl carefully laid the dress out on the washstand to be ironed, Roxanna slipped out of her underclothes. She looked at her naked body in the mirror.

Melissa came up from behind, holding Roxanna's nightgown in her hands. "Miss Roxanna," she said sadly. "Couldn't I just stay with you?"

"Melissa, we've been through this a hundred times."

"Miss Roxanna, I don't want to go back home. Who's going to take care of you if I go back home?"

Since Roxanna had heard the complaint ten times already, and answered it nine, she ignored it. "Melissa," she ordered, "just forget that. I want you to tell me something. And be honest."

"Yes ma'am. What is it?"

Roxanna examined her body from the side. "Do you think I'm beautiful?"

"Well, I know you're shameless, always standing around in the middle of a room, nekkid as a jaybird."

"Oh, Melissa, I don't care about that. Just look and answer me. Truthfully. Am I beautiful?"

"Yes ma'am, you're beautiful. All the men say so. Whenever you're walking up ahead, I hear them talking. They all say you're beautiful."

"Then I don't understand it. Why would Douglas leave me? After only two days? What could I have done wrong?"

Melissa dropped the nightgown over Roxanna's shoulders. It was full-skirted, with gathers, and a scoop neckline that exposed the cleavage of her breasts.

"If you ask me," Melissa commented, "you didn't do nothing wrong. That man is just no good."

"Melissa! Don't you dare say that!" Roxanna turned toward her angrily.

Melissa backed up. "I didn't mean nothing by it, Miss Roxanna." She paused a few seconds, then added, "He did leave you, though."

"No, he didn't. He didn't 'leave me.' He was captured. Taken away."

"Yes, ma'am," Melissa allowed, not believing it.

Roxanna faced the mirror again. "And I'm going to find him," she vowed resolutely.

Melissa crossed over to the fireplace and with a cloth pad wrapped around her hand for protection, she lifted one of the glowing red irons from the coals. She went over to the washstand and waited for the iron to cool enough to press Roxanna's dress. "I just wish we were both back in New Orleans," Melissa mused idly.

"I miss it too, Melissa," Roxanna said, picking up her hairbrush. "On the other hand, New Orleans has changed so much since Mr. Jefferson bought it from the French. The place is being fairly overrun by people from Cuba, Santo Domingo, the West Indies—"

"Coloreds, you mean," Melissa interjected.

"No, I didn't mean that," Roxanna answered, irritated. "Don't be so sensitive. You know I have nothing whatever against *gens de couleur*. It's just that the town is changing so fast. The whole country is changing fast, ever since Mr. Livingston and Mr. Monroe signed that treaty last year. Everybody's so excited over the Louisiana Purchase. They say it has doubled the size of the country."

"All I know is, it's swallowed up Master Fairchild," Melissa remarked, staring into the folds of the dress, still waiting for the iron to cool.

Roxanna brushed her dark hair and smiled in spite of herself. "Melissa, you are so blunt. Honestly."

At this point the door to the room swung open with a rush of air and clacked loudly against the wall. Roxanna's heart leaped when she saw the huge man standing menacingly on the threshold. He was dripping water, his eyes were bleary, and he held a long knife loosely in his right hand. She recognized him at once: Barton.

"Well now, isn't this a little scene," he sarcastically remarked, taking a step forward. He sized up Melissa, who was frozen in fear. Then his eyes lingered on Roxanna.

She reflexively covered her cleavage with a palm. "Get out of here!" she commanded. "This is a private room!"

He was unperturbed. "Lady," he said coldly. "If you scream, if you even breathe hard, I'll slice up this colored girl here like she was a watermelon."

"What do you want?" Roxanna demanded. "We don't have any money."

He snorted. "Money! Who needs money?" Barton walked to the washstand and with the point of his knife, lifted up a fold of the skirts Melissa was about to iron. "Not very good stuff," he observed, then stabbed a hole in the material and ripped it into two pieces.

"Oh God—" Roxanna exclaimed.

Barton laughed, and sliced another rip in the dress. "Looks like British material to me. You ought to get you some American stuff."

Roxanna clenched her fist in anger. But her exterior was cool. "Melissa," she directed calmly. "I want you to leave this room right now, do you hear me? Go get Mr. Atkins, or Mr. Wentworth."

"Now you just stay put," Barton growled at Melissa. "Tell you what I want you to do. I want you to sit down on the floor, right there." He pointed at the place. "I intend to have an audience for what I'm going to do. It's more fun that way."

"Melissa—go on. Do it!"

Barton's face flushed with anger. "You stay put, Missy," he commanded. "And get down. Now!"

Trembling with fear, Melissa scrunched down against the wall, closing her eyes tightly.

When Barton turned back to Roxanna, his cold, penetrating eyes made her shudder. There was such hatred in those eyes! She'd never seen such a man before. She had no chance against him. And if she screamed, he would kill poor Melissa.

"You shamed me out there, lady," Barton spoke contemptuously. "You made a fool out of me in front of my friends."

"No, I didn't," she protested. "And if I did, I certainly didn't mean to."

"You and that Philadelphia momma's boy. You were in it together."

"No! I don't even know him—"

"Just shut up, lady. Who knows? Seems to me a fancy woman like you might just get a kick out of doing it with a man like me."

The idea so repulsed her, Roxanna bolted toward the door. But Barton anticipated her—he reached out and snatched her arm. Melissa, hunched on the floor, drew in her elbows and covered her eyes with her hands. She began to cry loudly.

"Please," Roxanna pleaded. "For God's sake, I didn't mean to shame you."

"You've got my friends calling me a coward, lady. You figure a man can take having his friends call him a coward?"

"No, but—"

"Just shut up, lady!" he shouted, and threw her hard against the bed. Her back struck solid against the bedpost, knocking her breathless for a few seconds. But Roxanna was determined to stay on her feet.

Suddenly there was a crisp, loud knock on the door. Barton reacted quickly, lunging toward Roxanna. She recoiled from the touch of his hard, wet body against her, but he stilled her by sticking the point of his knife against her breast.

"Now you watch your mouth," he whispered. "Say one thing out of line and—" he pushed the knife hard against her.

"Mrs. Fairchild?" the voice from the door called out. "It's Tom. Tom Wentworth. Are you all right in there?"

Barton put more pressure on the tip of the knife, this time piercing the skin of her nipple.

She closed her eyes, tried to keep her chest from heaving. "I'm all right, Mr. Wentworth," she answered. Her breath quickened; her voice went higher than usual.

Melissa involuntarily let out a wail. It sounded like the cry of a beaten dog running through the woods.

"Mrs. Fairchild?" Tom repeated.

"It's all right," she answered. "It's just Melissa. She's sick. Good night, Mr. Wentworth."

There was a dead silence for a moment, then the blunt sound of Wentworth's footsteps receding down the hall. Roxanna's breathing eased, but she still felt the stinging pain in her breast. She didn't dare move; one thrust of Barton's knife and she would be dead.

"Now," Barton said to her. "It's time for you to

pay the piper, Mrs. Fairchild." He backed away from her to get a better view. "And I want payment in full," he added. "Take off that gown."

Melissa wailed again, but didn't look up.

"Please, Mr. Barton. Clive. I didn't mean to embarrass you. I didn't!"

"You look down on me, don't you, my pretty miss? You've been sneerin' at me, laughin' behind my back!"

"No!"

"Don't tell me, lady. I know."

"No. I swear!"

"Shut up!" he glared at her. "Go on, get on with it. Strip!"

Roxanna was about to touch the bodice of her nightgown when Melissa sprang up and broke for the door. But Barton was too quick for her. He seized her shoulder and pinned her hard, with a thud, against the door. She fought him, wriggled loose, yanked open the door.

And there, standing in the dim light from the hallway, was Tom Wentworth, in a military stance, sword drawn.

Barton let go of Melissa and retreated a few steps. "Well, well," he hissed nervously, "look who's come to the lady's rescue. Silk Shirt himself."

Out of the corner of his eye, Tom saw Melissa rush to embrace Roxanna. "Did he hurt you?" Tom asked the women, his eyes glued on Barton.

"No," Roxanna answered. "But he was about to."

"This is my lucky day, Silk Shirt," Barton boasted. "Now we'll see who's the coward around here."

"Don't try it, Barton," Tom warned him.

"Since when do I have to worry about a Philadelphia momma's boy swinging his daddy's old infantry sword?"

Tom took a few steps forward and nodded toward the door. "Melissa," he asked, "could you go get us some help?"

"You stay put, Missy," Barton cautioned her. "You know what I'll do to you if you move."

"Melissa, it's all right," assured Tom. "You go on. I'll keep him here. He won't harm you."

She shook her head and clung tightly to Roxanna. "I ain't going nowhere," she declared. "I'm staying here with Miss Roxanna."

Barton grinned. "So it looks like it's just you and me, Silk Shirt." He had barely said the words when he lunged forward.

Tom deftly sidestepped the blade of Barton's knife. But on a second pass he caught a nick on his left bicep. Blood began to soak his shirt red. "Give it up, Barton," he growled gamely. "I don't want to kill you."

But Barton lunged at him again, clumsily, knife up. With a lightning movement, Tom clamped down on the man's wrist and whipped his body around. Barton spun wildly and crashed against the washstand. The knife sailed across the room, landing with a clatter on the floor. Barton's upper body was curled forward. He hunched over like a cornered animal ready to spring.

But he didn't attack immediately. Instead, his hands flew to his wet coat. He snapped it open and yanked a pistol from his belt. "I wasn't planning on using this thing, Silk Shirt," he said, holding the gun out. "It makes too much noise. But it looks like you're not going to give me much of a choice."

Tom stared at the gun. Barton had him. Tom could see the gloating in the man's eyes. Barton gnashed his teeth, cocked the pistol and pointed the end of the barrel straight at Tom's heart. The instant he pulled the trigger, Barton flinched, anticipating the explosion. But there was no explosion—only a click. The hammer had snapped harmlessly against the charge. Barton cocked and pulled the trigger again, to no avail.

"That pistol won't fire, Barton," Tom told him. "You've let your powder get wet. Why don't you just lay it down on the desk and back up."

Ignoring Tom's words, Barton threw the useless pistol at his tormentor. The weapon whizzed through the air, struck a picture on the wall and sent it crashing to the floor. Barton scanned the room for another weapon, anything to fight with. Melissa's pressing iron was still heating on the coals in the fireplace. With a loud grunt, Barton grabbed up a towel, leapt to the fireplace and drew the fiery red iron from the coals.

He grinned menacingly as he held it up for Tom to see. "Now, momma's boy," he grunted, moving toward Tom, "I'm going to teach you what happens to people who make fun of Clive Barton."

Tom held his ground. "Put it down, Barton," he ordered. "I don't want to hurt you."

But Barton was determined. Stepping forward, he smiled satanically. His reddened face, reflecting the glow of the hot iron, took on a ghastly expression. "Where do you want your brand, Silk Shirt?" he inquired. "On that pretty face of yours, or between the legs? You name it."

Tom had no choice now but to defend himself. He held his breath, tightened his stomach muscles and lashed out with his saber. Surprised at his quickness, Barton blocked the blow of Tom's blade with the hot pressing iron. He had to avert his eyes as sparks broke off the metal and sprinkled down on his arm. Tom struck again, and more sparks flashed off the iron.

Tom now felt he had the advantage. He pressed forward, backing Barton across the room. Blow after jarring blow the blade slammed against the hard metal of the pressing iron. Tom forced the man back against the fireplace mantle, holding him at bay with the point of the saber. "Drop it," Tom commanded.

Barton didn't move.

"I said, drop it!" Tom repeated. He pushed the point of the blade harder for emphasis.

Barton stared coldly, hatefully into Tom's eyes as

he let the iron fall to the floor. "Don't get cocky, Wentworth," he warned. "I'm not through with you yet."

Tom backed up. "Well, I'm through with you," he replied. "Get out of here. And don't come back."

Barton grumbled something Tom couldn't understand, straightened his wet coat and cautiously moved away from the sword. He slunk slowly across the floor toward the door. But as soon as Tom turned his attention to the women, Barton bent down to the floor, scooped up the lost knife and lunged ahead with it.

"Tom! Look out!" Roxanna cried.

Tom wheeled around just in time to catch a glimpse of Barton fuming, grunting, charging like a wild bull. Instinctively Tom braced his body, and leveled the point of the infantry sword.

Barton saw the sword pointed at his midriff but already it was too late. He could not break his rush. The sharp blade sank easily and quickly into his flesh as his momentum carried him forward, all the way to the hilt of the blade. Barton was conscious only long enough to look up with a pained expression on his face. He gasped, blood spewed from his mouth and he crumpled to the floor in a bloody heap.

Barely a minute passed before the landlord Atkins appeared at the door, carrying a lantern and huffing from the dash upstairs. "What in God's name is going on here?" he bellowed. He stepped in, immediately spotting Barton's bleeding corpse on the floor. "What happened to him?" he demanded.

Tom had never killed a man before. He felt weak, shaky, sick. "It was an accident, Mr. Atkins," he explained. "He accidentally fell on my sword. I didn't mean to hurt him."

Atkins' lip curled. He knelt down to examine the body. He raised Barton's limp arm and let it fall heavily. "Well," he observed, "you didn't just hurt him, Tom. Mean it or not, you've killed him." Atkins stood up. "And," he said, "you've killed him in my house."

"Mr. Atkins—" Roxanna began.

"You'd better stay out of this, Mrs. Fairchild," the landlord advised. "A little scuffle over a lady is one thing, killing a man in my house is another."

"I didn't kill him," Tom protested. "I told you, he ran into my sword."

Atkins nodded. "All right, I believe you, son, but I'm afraid I'm going to have to let the law decide that. You're going to have to go to jail."

Chapter 2

It was early the next morning when Roxanna made her way to the jailhouse, bearing a plate of cold biscuits in her hands. St. Louis' modest prison wasn't much—just a solid set of pine boards set in log posts—but the forged iron bars on the windows looked strong enough to hold a herd of horses.

Roxanna had some difficulty explaining to the jailkeeper who she was and why she wanted to see Tom. But when the keeper saw the plate of biscuits, he realized this woman could save him the trouble of feeding the prisoner a meal. With a glance at her delicate, fine arms and well fashioned bodice, the jailer motioned Roxanna into the room in back.

Tom was in his cell, pacing back and forth. At the first sight of him in this condition, Roxanna's maternal instincts were so aroused that she wanted to go in and touch and comfort him. But for the moment, all she could do was to offer him the plate of cold biscuits. He looked under the crisp white cloth, nodded his head, but then pushed them back.

"Take them away," he requested. "I'm not hungry."

"But you have to eat," she told him. "It's not going to do you any good to starve yourself in there. Go ahead, try them; they're good. Melissa made them yesterday."

"I don't want any!" he grumbled, striking the metal bars with his fist. "I'm not interested in food. I want to get out of here. I didn't come nine hundred miles to swing at the end of a rope."

"Tom," she spoke softly, "I am sorry about this."

He relaxed a little. "Oh, never mind," he told her. "It wasn't your fault. I did it, all by myself."

"It wasn't your fault, either," she declared. "And you can be sure I'm going to tell the judge that."

Tom appreciated her interest, but he was doubtful. "I don't know if they even have judges out here, Roxanna." Her name felt strange on his lips, but he liked the sound of it.

"Of course they do," she assured him. "As a matter of fact, there's a judge on the other side of that door right now, at this minute, talking to Captain Meriwether Lewis."

"Captain Lewis!" he exclaimed. "Are you sure?"

She shrugged her shoulders, pretending to be unimpressed. "That's what he said his name was," she stated.

"But I don't understand. What is Captain Lewis doing here, in St. Louis? Why isn't he headed up the Missouri?"

"Well, he explained to me that he's been with his interpreter Mr. Drewyer, talking to the Osage Indians. He's planning on joining Captain Clark in St. Charles on the twentieth."

Tom was puzzled. "What do you mean, he explained to you?" he asked. "Why would he explain anything to you?"

"Maybe because I asked him. After all, I did spend most of the night tracking the man down—"

"*You* brought him here?"

"Well, I'd like to know who would have, if I hadn't. Melissa's on a boat to New Orleans, Mr. Atkins has washed his hands of the whole business—I'm the only witness left."

Tom tried to hide his amazement. He wondered what other surprises this woman had in store for him. For some reason, he felt a little better now. He reached out through the bars and slipped a biscuit out from under the cloth.

Roxanna smiled. "He said he knows you," she added, watching him eat.

Tom nodded as he swallowed. "Captain Lewis and my father were at Fallen Timbers together. After Mr. Jefferson gave him the job of being his private secretary, he sent him off to school in Philadelphia to prepare him for an expedition."

"Really?" she exclaimed, surprised. "Mr. Jefferson was planning an expedition even before the Louisiana Purchase?"

"Sure, that's why he made Captain Lewis his secretary—to train him for it. But anyway, while Captain Lewis was in Philadelphia he and my father met again. The captain used to come over to our house and they would drink Kentucky whiskey and play cards and then spend the rest of the night laying plans for a great exploration of the Northwest. They talked about finding a Northwest Passage, a waterway from the Mississippi to the Pacific."

"Is that why you came out here?" she ventured "To explore?"

"No," he admitted. "I came out here to make money."

"Oh," she said, disappointed. "Money for what?"

"I need it to get married."

"Oh. I see."

"But what does all that matter? How long has Captain Lewis been talking to the judge?"

"They've been in there about an hour now," she

replied. Just as she spoke, the pine door leading to the office creaked open and a man in a long gray coat walked in. He nodded, spoke to Roxanna, calling her by name, then rested his hand on one of the cell bars. "Well," he said, "I never thought I'd live long enough to see a Wentworth in jail."

Captain Meriwether Lewis was an impressive man, blond, thin and attractive, though a bit bowlegged. He looked very military and carried a mysterious-looking gun with him. It was about the size of an army musket, with a hollow steel ball the size of a grapefruit fixed beneath the breech.

Tom was too apprehensive about his situation to notice it. "Captain Lewis!" he said anxiously. "Can you get me out of here?"

Lewis leaned the strange gun carefully against the wall. "I'm working on it, Tom. I believe I've about convinced Judge Tompkins how important what we're doing is. He says he's willing to forget having a formal trial for a member of the President's expedition."

"Yes, but *when*?" Tom asked impatiently. "I hate it in here, captain. These walls are closing in on me."

"Just be patient, Tom. You'll be out as soon as Mrs. Fairchild gives her testimony to the judge."

"Thank God for that," he sighed, relieved. "I couldn't spend another hour cooped up in here."

"He's waiting for you now," Lewis told Roxanna. "If you want to go back in."

She nodded, took two steps toward the door, then hesitated and thought a minute. "Captain Lewis," she asked, "if I testify to Judge Tompkins that Tom was forced to kill Clive Barton in self-defense, they will let Tom go free. Is that what you're saying?"

"That's what the judge is saying. Fortunately."

"And if I don't say that," she continued, "he won't go free. Is that right? He'll hang?"

"Roxanna!" Tom cried from behind the bars. "What are you saying? You're not thinking of lying to him—not after I had to kill a man to save you—"

"Why wouldn't I be thinking of it?" she responded, pretending to be cool and indifferent. "I can say anything I want."

"Mrs. Fairchild," Lewis appealed in a concerned voice. "Surely you're joking—"

She shook her head. "I am most certainly not joking," she stated. "But what I *am* doing is this: I'm offering you a proposition."

"What kind of proposition?"

She looked him in the eye. "I will agree to testify for Tom Wentworth—if you let me go on your expedition."

"That's impossible," he said quickly.

"Captain Lewis, don't slough me off. I am serious about this."

Lewis sighed. "Serious or not, Mrs. Fairchild, we've been through all this before. This trip will be incredibly dangerous for trained infantrymen and skilled hunters—much less a woman! Before we get off the Missouri River we will have the Sioux to contend with. Then, once we leave the Mandans, we'll be in country no white man has ever seen—not even Mackenzie or Astor. There is no telling what will be out there—what kind of animals, natural disasters, people—I'm sorry. It's just out of the question."

"Then so is my testimony."

"Roxanna!" Tom pleaded. "Don't do this to me!"

"I'm sorry, Tom," she apologized. "Blame your beloved captain, he's the one doing it."

"Mrs. Fairchild, I promised Tom's father he would help me find the Northwest Passage some day, and this is probably the only chance we'll ever have to do it. You wouldn't make a man break a promise to an old friend, would you?"

"What do I care about one man's promise to another, captain? All I care about is going. My husband is out there somewhere in that wilderness, and I intend to find him—one way or another. If you don't let me go with you, well then Tom Wentworth will hang for murder and I'll just have to follow you and your men up the Missouri River."

Lewis crossed his arms, exasperated with her. "Mrs. Fairchild, there is something you're not thinking about here. There are other dangers. You know my men have already spent several months in camp, getting ready to go on this trip. And they may be with me another two years. The point is, having a woman along all that time would be just too tempting for them. Especially a woman as attractive as you."

She ignored the compliment. "Then I'll be unattractive," she declared.

"I don't think that's possible," he remarked.

Suddenly she thought of a way. "Then I'll dress up like a man," she decided. "In fact, I'll *be* a man, if that's what it takes to go on this expedition."

"No," Lewis shook his head, "that wouldn't work."

"Fine—then say goodbye to Tom Wentworth. I'm going in there and I'm going to tell Judge Tompkins that Tom Wentworth tried to rape me and he killed the man who was trying to save me."

"Now Mrs. Fairchild, you know you wouldn't do that. . . ."

"Oh, wouldn't I," she snapped. "Don't underestimate me, Captain Lewis. I'm desperate, and a desperate woman will do anything she has to do. I learned a month ago that my husband was seen with the Sioux Indians—so I know he's out there somewhere. And I promise you, I *will* find him, if I have to go out there myself to hunt him down."

"You know, I believe you would," agreed Lewis.

"If you think otherwise, captain," replied Roxanna, "you don't know women."

Lewis scratched his nose and deliberated. She was right, he decided: he was a bachelor, he didn't know much about women. And yet he wasn't really convinced she would lie to the judge. Still, he couldn't help but admire her spunk. He wondered if she might not survive in the wilderness, after all. Some of his *engagés* showed a lot less gumption than she did. "Tom," he said finally, "I have some urgent business north of town, so I can't spend any more time here. Why don't we let the lady have her way and let's get out of here."

"Captain, no! This is crazy, sir! You can't let her come!"

Captain Lewis shook his head. "She knows the risks, Tom. I've explained them to her often enough. Besides, she's an intelligent woman, and if she's that determined to go, she's going to go with somebody. I don't believe we have any choice in the matter." He looked at her. "Do you really think you can make forty-five men believe you're not a woman?"

"Yes I can," Roxanna stated confidently, though privately she wasn't so sure.

"All right," he decided. "We'll try it. I'll tell the men you're Spanish and don't understand any English, so you won't have to speak to them. What you will have to do is keep away from them, walk on the bank with me, stay in the shadows—"

"Anything—" she cried excitedly.

"Then let's go talk to Henry Tompkins."

"Captain," Tom said, "you can't mean this! Mr. Jefferson would court-martial all of us if he ever found out a woman was on the expedition."

"Yes, he might. But Mr. Jefferson is in Washington City, Tom, and we're out here. This is another world. The roles we all play back East, in polite society, don't mean much in a strange new place like this one we're about to see. If Mrs. Fairchild thinks she can trek through thousands of miles of wilderness to find her man, knowing of the dangers as she does, then I think she deserves a chance to come along. To show she can do it."

Three days later, on the afternoon of the nineteenth, Tom, Roxanna and Captain Lewis were riding

in a wagon, six miles north of St. Louis. While the two
men sat in front, Roxanna was being bounced around
in the bed, among hard sacks of salt and flour and
wooden cartons of weapons. But she didn't complain.
She would have died first.

"We'll be stopping at James O'Neal's place near
Coldwater Creek," Lewis told Tom, "to get some guns
and clothes. By the time Drewyer rides in, we'll have
Roxanna decked out like a man. We can try it out on
him. What do you think, Mrs. Fairchild?" he asked
her.

"Fine," replied Roxanna.

"If Drewyer doesn't notice, you're in. If he does,
that's it—you go back to St. Louis. Agreed?"

"Agreed."

"I still think it's crazy, captain," Tom remarked.

"The whole thing is crazy, Tom. We've got almost
fifty men going into a great wilderness, facing dangers
they can't even imagine. But crazy or not, it's something that has to be done. We must have control of
navigation on the western rivers, or this land, this
twelve-million-dollar 'gift' from Napoleon Bonaparte,
will wind up being a curse. It could split the country in
two."

"I thought your expedition was supposed to be
literary," Tom remarked, puzzled. "You were supposed
to keep journals on the climate, the vegetation and the
Indians, not open up waterways—"

"That's our official function, Tom. Unofficially,
we have to lay the American claim to the rivers, the
land and the Indians. And—we have to find the Northwest Passage. Mr. Jefferson has been wanting a river
route to the Pacific for thirty years. That's why he tried
to send Michaux out here in '93. And that was what
Alexander Mackenzie was looking for when he reached
the Pacific through Canada."

"Do you think there really is such a river route?"

"Mr. Jefferson does, and he's the one who appropriated the twenty-five hundred dollars to pay for all of this."

"Yes, but do you believe there is one?"

He smiled mysteriously. "I don't know, Tom. I suppose that's why explorers explore. To find out what *is* really there."

Just up ahead was a four-window shack, located on the creek bank. Lewis reined in the horses at a tree near the house, overlooking the water. He stepped down and tied the reins to a limb. "O'Neal's the best gunsmith in these parts," the captain explained. "He's an old man, but he keeps up with new developments. He knows more about the new guns than anyone west of Pennsylvania."

"That's a strange gun you're carrying," Tom observed. "I've never seen one like it before."

Lewis handled it carefully, fondly. "I bought this one out of my own pocket. I couldn't resist it. It's the newest thing."

"It's an air gun, isn't it?" Roxanna asked, straightening her dress. "I saw one in New Orleans."

"That's right. This ball here holds air, which propels the shot. It'll shoot forty times on a single load. It's a far cry from those clumsy muskets we used back in the Whiskey Rebellion." He raised the gun and ripped off three shots into a pine tree, fifty yards across the creek.

At the sound of the rifle, James O'Neal bounded out of the door of the shack onto the porch. He was bent over, a wizened man of about seventy, with long gray hair and a smooth, pink face.

"Captain Lewis!" he called happily. "I didn't know what was happening out here. Thought they'd started up the Revolution again. Welcome!"

"James—good to see you."

"Hey, that's a nice piece," O'Neal admired, squinting his eyes at the gun. "I've been hearing about Captain Lewis's famous air gun at Wood River. Come on—bring it inside, let's take a look at it."

They all went into the house, Lewis introduced Tom and Roxanna Fairchild to O'Neal. "James," Lewis said, watching with pleasure as the old man lovingly rubbed his long fingers over the glossy stock of the air gun. "We need some clothes for Mrs. Fairchild here. Men's clothes. She has to pass for a man for a while."

O'Neal rubbed his chin thoughtfully, and then nodded as if the request were nothing unusual. "You just go right back through that door, ma'am," he directed. "There's every kind of man's garment you could ask for back there."

"Thank you," she smiled. "Though I'm not sure what I would ask for."

"Now that's a pretty little thing," O'Neal remarked, after she had gone into the other room. He stared accusingly at Tom. "I'd make her stay at home if I was you, son. I wouldn't be letting her run around this place."

Tom said nothing, though he felt his anger rising. He hated even discussing the matter with anyone.

Lewis smiled at Tom's discomfort. "James, I'm going to need four more horseman's pistols. North and Cheneys, I suppose. They seem fit enough."

O'Neal nodded, drew four long pistols out of a locker. "I'd suggest you pack your powder in lead cans, captain, if you're going by water most of the way."

"I thought of that. I got Captain Clark to take care of it. And by the way, speaking of Clark, he asked me to bring him back some of your English flints. He claims that fancy fusil of his won't use any other kind."

As O'Neal filled the order, he seemed to become more and more fidgety. Finally, unable to wait any longer, he broached the subject. "Captain," he began, "I hear you're going to be using some special weapons out there."

"I wondered if you had heard about that."

"Come on, captain. Don't keep me waiting. What kind of guns do you have?"

"Rifles, James. Army prototypes. They're amazing. They're going to make muskets a thing of the past."

"Rifles! Well! Well, don't just stand there—show them, show them!"

Lewis laughed good-naturedly at the old man's enthusiasm. "They're in the wagon outside," he admitted.

After a minute, Tom was left in the room alone. He idly examined a few of the flintlocks, but his attention was focused on the room where Roxanna was dressing. He stared at the closed door, imagined her stepping out of her dress, peeling off her undergarments, yanking a pair of men's trousers up over her knees, her bare hips. . . . The idea was stirring up his lust. He felt warm, almost dizzy.

Inside the room, Roxanna was buckling a wide black belt around her tiny waist, trying to adjust the smallest pair of pants she could find to her voluptuous figure. She could make the trousers fit fairly well, but she would have to stuff cloth in the boots to make them wearable. The broad-rimmed hat was the right size, and she had even found a grey linsey-woolsey shirt that seemed adequate.

Her problem was her breasts. Standing in the trousers and boots with her chest bare, Roxanna was dismayed by the size of her bosom. Suddenly her breasts seemed huge to her—and so unmistakably movable! Who would ever take her for a man? She had to do something with them. She looked around the room, noticed a bolt of calico and got an idea. She unwrapped a few yards of the cotton cloth, circled it tightly around her chest. The trick worked: the wrapping flattened her breasts and held them secure. She tried on the shirt. It felt right now. She congratulated herself on her ingenuity. It would do.

When she came out of the room, Tom Wentworth was there waiting for her. After looking her over, he shook his head in disapproval. She tugged at the hat. "Well?" she grinned. "What do you think?"

"I still think it's crazy, that's what I think."

"You're in a rut, Tom," she teased. "You know it? Why don't you just accept the fact that I'm going to be on the expedition and let it go at that?"

"Because I think it's wrong, that's why. You're going to get hurt."

"With forty-five husky men to protect me? How can I get hurt?"

"You know what I mean."

"No I don't," she prodded. "What do you mean, Tom?"

"I mean it's dangerous for a woman to be on an expedition like this anyway, but with forty-five men along—who knows what could happen to you? It could be worse than what happened with Clive Barton."

"I'm willing to take the chance, Tom."

"Well, I'm not."

"*You're* not? Since when did you become my protector?"

"Since I saved you from Clive Barton."

She was about to dispute this, when Lewis and O'Neal entered the room again. A third man was with them, tall, dark-haired, part-Indian. His deep, cool eyes immediately fixed on her. She unconsciously lowered hers to the floor. His stare was chilling.

"George," Captain Lewis introduced, "this is Tom, I told you about him. And this fellow," he nodded at Roxanna, "is Mr. Garcia, another one of our *engagés*."

The man, George Drewyer, the interpreter, nodded at Roxanna. "Good evening," he said.

Lewis went on: "Mr. Garcia speaks only Spanish, so he won't be saying much."

"Good," Drewyer replied. "Too much said everywhere now." He looked at Roxanna. "Do you know Indian sign language?" he asked, moving his hands quickly, mysteriously in the air, to form the question.

She shrugged her shoulders, pretended not to understand him.

"He's raw right now, George," Lewis explained. "But he'll learn fast."

O'Neal smiled to himself. "Yeah, he'll learn real fast. I believe young Garcia here is up to just about anything."

Chapter 3

When the Indian came into St. Charles with the news about Clive Barton, there was only one person who seemed to care very much, and that was Private Ned Craddock. He cursed and swore so furiously that the Indian turned tail and ran, thinking Craddock's fury would be vented on him. For the rest of the day, Craddock stormed around camp like a man possessed. He took the opportunity to whip a mule that had given him a hard time the day before, and he managed to get into two fist fights.

By the middle of the afternoon, he had calmed down somewhat, but the other men kept their distance, hearing him mutter against "that swiny bastard that killed Clive Barton." No one invited Craddock to join in the poker game in John Collins' tent that evening— but he came anyway, taking a stool in front of the locker as if he belonged there. And no one dared tell him to go away.

The poker game was a usual event. The tent was big enough to hold a half-dozen men, though there wasn't much room for spectators. Collins' personal kit had been pushed over to one side, his locker set in the middle. Each of the men brought along his own three-legged stool for seating. That evening, there were five men around the locker. Beside Craddock were three men he knew well—Private John Collins from Maryland, Hugh Hall from Pennsylvania, and William Werner, a Kentucky man.

The fifth man in the group, however, was someone whom Craddock eyed with suspicion. René St. Croix was a fat, jovial-looking Frenchman who joined enthusiastically in the night's entertainment. But to Craddock's way of thinking, the Frenchman talked too fast and too much. And after a couple hours of play, Craddock was sure he detected St. Croix cheating.

The Frenchman was dealing.

"Dealer calls five-card-stud," St. Croix announced in perfect English. Everything he said pertaining to poker was spoken without an accent. "Dealer's high with an ace," St. Croix continued, looking at his cards. "Bets two dollars."

"Two dollars on one ace?" Collins groaned, then swigged some whiskey.

"Maybe two aces," St. Croix grinned.

"I'm in," Collins sighed, throwing in his money.

"Monsieur Craddock? Are you betting?" the Frenchman asked.

"Leave me alone, I'm thinking," he grumbled. He stared at his cards, a six of clubs up, a six of spades down. He put his cards on the locker, slipped his watch out of his vest pocket. "Seems to me you get an awful lot of aces, Frenchie," he complained.

"Luck of the draw, Monsieur Craddock," he demurred.

"Yeah, right, luck of the draw." Craddock flipped open the watch, looked at the picture painted on the inside of the gold lid. It depicted a reclining woman, completely naked. He rubbed the figure with his index finger, for good luck. He'd had it only a year now, but it was already fading from all his rubbing.

"What are you going to do, Ned?" Werner wondered. "Are you going to play, or drool all night?"

"Yeah, yeah, I'm going to play," he answered impatiently. "All I need is a stake. Collins? How about laying over that ten dollars you owe me?"

John Collins shook his head. "You forget that ten dollars right now, Ned," he instructed him. "I'm not about to pay any debts at a poker table."

"Now, listen here, you snipe. You owe me a whole month's pay for those French gals last Wednesday night. Three bucks apiece for you and Hall and Werner here. You're not forgetting that already, are you?"

Collins glared at him. "No, I'm not. And I'm not likely to forget it, either. I've got fifty whip lashes on my back to show for it."

"That was for insulting Captain Clark, John," Hugh Hall reminded him. "Remember, William and I had our sentences revoked."

"There you go, calling him 'Captain' Clark," Ned said derisively. "How many times do I have to tell you men, Jefferson made William Clark a lieutenant, not a captain. He's a second lieutenant, U.S. Artillery. If you don't believe me, look at his boots. It's branded in them."

"I don't care what his boots say and I don't care what his rank is," Hall declared. "He's Captain Clark to me."

"Then you're about as incompetent as a soldier, Hugh, as this two-bit Frenchman here is as a cardsharp."

"Monsieur Hall," St. Croix ignored Craddock's insult and looked impatiently at Hugh. "Are you playing?"

"No, I'm out," Hall replied.

St. Croix nodded. "*Eh bien.* Monsieur Craddock, you may draw light your two dollars. I trust you. Monsieur Werner?"

"Unh-unh," Werner shook his head, folding. "Not me. Two dollars is too rich for my blood."

"Then around we go again," the Frenchman declared. He dealt Collins, Craddock and himself another card. Collins showed two spades, Craddock got a three of hearts, and St. Croix the king of spades to go with his ace.

"Ace high, again bets two dollars," the dealer called out. He shoved out his money, lifted up a jug of whiskey, nestled it carefully on the crook of his arm and took a long swallow.

Collins watched him drink, then threw in his two dollars. "I'm crazy, but I'm sticking."

Craddock stared at his cards, then looked closely at the Frenchman, studying his every move. He hadn't seen it yet, but he was sure now that St. Croix had palmed a card. Next round, he would peg him for sure. He laid his cards on the locker and scowled at Collins. "You play cards the same way you soldier, Collins," he complained. "You close your eyes and walk straight into the fire."

"Why don't you just play, Ned, and let me worry about how I play cards or soldier."

"I'll tell you what, Collins, if a man sentenced me to fifty lashes, do you think I'd go around praising him, calling him captain when he was only a lieutenant?"

"Watch your step, Ned," Collins cautioned him. "Captain Clark is a good man. I don't want to hear any more about him, all right?"

"Fine. How would you like to hear about Captain Lewis, then? Let me ask you this: why do you think Mr. Jefferson gave those two particular men this expedition? Because they're better hunters or soldiers than you and I are, John? No. Because they're from Virginia, that's why. Just like Mr. Jefferson."

"Oh, come on, Ned—"

"Listen. Virginians fancy themselves head and shoulders above people like you and me, Collins. I know. Look at Meriwether Lewis at the Whiskey

Rebellion. While I'm standing in the ranks along with twelve thousand other nameless troops, listening to President Washington parading back and forth on his horse, charging us up, Lewis was probably lounging around in an office somewhere, waiting to be appointed ensign. By Mr. Jefferson, I'd bet a hundred dollars. And who do we poor lowlife march under when we finally get going to Pittsburgh? General Lee, that's who. Another Virginian. I tell you, it's a conspiracy."

"You're talking over your head, Craddock. I think you'd better shut up, that kind of talk's awfully close to mutiny," Werner warned him.

"Mutiny's not a word that scares me, William. I have cause to complain. Haven't you? Didn't we sit around for months, freezing our butts, waiting till it got warm so we could go on this thing? Then what do we do? We make it as far as St. Charles on Wednesday and here it is Sunday and we're still in St. Charles, waiting for Captain Lewis. We'll be on this trip for ten years at this rate."

"I suppose you'd do it different," Collins said.

"You're damned right I'd do it different. Instead of breaking our backs paddling up river with these oars, I'd be sending the whole party up in a steamboat."

"In a what?" Collins blurted, mouth open.

"A steamboat, John. Don't tell me you never heard of a steamboat in Maryland?"

"Yeah, I've heard of them all right, but they don't exist. They're nothing but a lot of talk."

"Oh, they're more than talk, Collins. I saw a steamboat in Georgia a couple of years ago, chugging up the Savannah River, big as you please. It was invented by this man named William Longstreet—"

"Monsieur Craddock, are you going to talk all day?" the Frenchman broke in.

Craddock was irritated by the interruption. "Why don't you keep your face closed until you're called on to speak, Frenchie," Craddock sneered. "You're a guest in this tent here, and don't you forget it. And while I'm talking to you, let me go ahead and tell you something—I know good and well what kind of tricks you've been playing with those cards. So understand this: if you palm another one at this table, I'm going to cut off your fingers and feed them to the fish in the Missouri River. Do you hear me?"

"Oui, Monsieur," St. Croix answered, reddening. "I hear you. But you are mistaken. I do not cheat."

Craddock flushed at the Frenchman's defiance. "I'll show you how mistaken I am," he glowered. "How much money do you have piled up in front of you there?"

The Frenchman looked down at his stakes, made a rough calculation. "I would say thirty dollars," he guessed. "Maybe thirty-one."

"All right, thirty-one dollars is the bet on this hand. I'll draw light that much."

St. Croix frowned. "I'm sorry, no—it's too much."

"No, see, you don't have any choice, man," Craddock explained patiently. "Either you play or I'm going to rip out your bowels as a cheater. Now, which will it be?"

St. Croix stared silently at his cards, then at Craddock. Suddenly there was a commotion outside the tent. Hall got to his feet and went outside. He was back in a minute. The Frenchman was still silently considering his alternatives.

Hall called out, "There's a lady outside, says she's the Frenchman's wife."

St. Croix didn't seem to hear. He was fondling his money, nervously rubbing the backs of his cards with his finger, making them damp and oily.

"What does she want?" Collins asked.

Before Hall could respond, the woman herself stepped abruptly into the tent. She was French, thirty-eight, pretty, with dark hair and eyes. She wore a black cloak that covered most of her body. *"Messieurs,"* she said.

"Go away, Celeste," the Frenchman responded in a bored voice. He was looking more at his cards than he was at her. "Leave me alone. I am working."

"Working!" she exclaimed. "Do you call gambling away all our money 'working'? How can you keep doing things like this? Don't you care what happens to us?"

He looked up at her. "I will be home later, woman. Now go away."

"Messieurs." She pleaded to the other men, her voice sounding desperate. "I haven't seen my husband in six days. Please, do something—make him come home. He *has* to come home."

"He's not going anywhere till he plays out this hand, lady," Craddock grumbled. "What do you say, Frenchie? Are you in, or are your bowels out?"

"His bowels out!" the woman shouted. *"Mon Dieu!* What is he saying?"

"Hall—take this woman out of here," Craddock ordered. "Tie her up, strangle her, do something with her. I can't stand to hear a woman's voice whining over my shoulder when I'm playing cards."

"No! I'm not going! You can't make me!"

"Celeste," St. Croix insisted, "go home. I told you, I will be there later. *Allez.* I'm ordering you."

Hall and Werner took her arms. "Come on, ma'am," Werner soothed. "We'll make sure he gets home all right. He's playing a sticky hand right now. You'd better let him see it through, all right?"

"I don't care about a poker hand—I haven't seen him in six days."

"I know, ma'am, but you'll see him later. Come on, this way—"

They took her out struggling, but neither Craddock nor St. Croix paid any attention. St. Croix loosened his collar. Beads of sweat popped out on his forehead.

"I am an honest man," he proclaimed, "but I have been in America long enough to know I can't trust men like you, Monsieur Craddock. I think if you believe I am cheating, you are as likely to kill me as not. And since Captain Lewis and Captain Clark's men stick together, there would be no justice served afterwards—"

"Look, are you in or not?" Craddock cut in. "That's all I'm interested in."

"I have to be in," the Frenchman declared. "Thirty one dollars."

"And I'm out." Collins threw his cards down. "You men are insane."

Craddock smiled. "Thirty-one dollars on the next two cards, Frenchie. No other bets. Go ahead, deal them."

St. Croix cleared his throat, loosened his cravat. The tent was charged with tension and anticipation as he rubbed his sweaty right palm on his black coat sleeve, flicked up Craddock's card and laid it on the table.

It was a three of diamonds.

St. Croix quickly dealt himself a ten of clubs.

Craddock looked at his three facing cards, flipped up the corner of the down card, to make sure of what he had. With one more card to go, he was holding a good hand already: two pair, sixes and threes. He watched St. Croix drink more whiskey, then stir around in his seat. Craddock enjoyed watching him squirm.

Suddenly the French woman outside the tent was talking to someone again, this time in her native tongue. Craddock raised his hands, covered his ears. "Get that woman out of here, Collins," he demanded. "Take her home—do something. I can't stand that noise."

St. Croix managed a smile. "Celeste is a good woman," he apologized. "But you know how women are. They try to change you, make you over."

Craddock stared at him coldly, all business. "You've got a possible straight there, Frenchie. Now if you don't have a jack or queen in the hole, you're in trouble."

St. Croix swallowed hard, tried to be professional. "It's possible I have another ace, king or ten in the hole, Monsieur Craddock."

"Yeah, it's possible, but I'm betting you don't," Craddock retorted confidently.

St. Croix sloshed down too much whiskey and coughed hard to clear his throat again. He smiled congenially at Werner, Hall and Craddock. "This is a joke, isn't it?" he tried to laugh. "You men are joking with me. All of you."

"It's no joke, St. Croix," Craddock replied. To give substance to his words, he laid a long shiny knife on the table. It looked huge and ominous next to his cards.

The presence of the knife made Werner nervous. "Why don't you call this off, Ned? I don't think René was cheating—"

"Oh, he's been cheating, all right. Only I'm giving him a chance to work his way out of it, by playing poker. All he has to do is win or lose this pot and I'll let him out of here scot free—with all his fingers intact. If he even makes a move to get up before this hand's over, though, this blade here will be gouging out his belly before his knees straighten up."

Fear blazed in St. Croix's eyes, but he tried to remain calm. "Monsieur Craddock, I will be frank with you. Gentleman to gentleman. The truth of the matter is, I cannot afford this thirty-one dollars. What I mean is, it isn't actually my money. It belongs to my wife. She brought it over from France when we came to America last year—"

"What do I care where she brought it from? Play cards."

"Monsieur Craddock, I'm asking you to be generous. She needs the money for food, for clothes—"

"Then win it back for her, Frenchie. But I'm warning you, you'd better win it fair."

The other men in the tent were excited, nervous, anxious. They leaned forward, waiting for the next card. Private Collins returned quietly to the tent, stood at Craddock's shoulder and gazed down at the stack of money on his locker. It was more than he'd ever seen on it before.

"Monsieur Craddock," St. Croix pleaded, "I am a proud man, from a proud family, but I am humbling myself to you. I am begging you, let me take my wife's money off the table here and go. I cannot afford to lose her money."

Craddock paid no attention to his plea. "I'll tell you what. Since the pot is right as is, let's turn up our hole cards." He flipped up his six.

"Two pair!" Hall declared. "Sixes and threes. I'll be!"

"Are you through yet, Frenchie?" Craddock asked, proud of his hand. "Does that do you in, or not?"

St. Croix sighed deeply, took another slug of whiskey from the jug. *"Non, monsieur."* He turned over a jack. "I am not through yet."

"He's working on a straight," Werner said. "All he needs is the ten and he's got your two pair whipped, Ned."

"Shut up, Werner." Craddock seemed worried. Then to St. Croix, "Deal, Frenchie. One more card each."

St. Croix held the deck tightly in his hand. "Monsieur Craddock, you saw my wife. She's a very fine woman, *n'est-ce pas?* She works very hard for me, she will do anything I say. Surely you wouldn't take all the money she has in the world away from her? Make her go hungry—"

"She don't look hungry to me," Craddock sneered. "At least not for food."

The Frenchman hit the whiskey jug one more

time, wiped his mouth on his coat sleeve, closed and opened his eyes several times, then gave Craddock his card.

It was a nine of hearts. That was no help to his two pair.

Hall was almost bent over the locker in anticipation. "If he gets a ten, Ned," he remarked, "you're in debt thirty-one dollars."

"Yeah, I know it. Be quiet."

"It isn't too late, monsieur," St. Croix pleaded for the last time.

"Deal yourself a card," Craddock responded.

St. Croix took a deep breath, turned up his card. At first he was the only one who could see it, as he raised it up close to his eyes. Then, slowly deliberately, he laid it down, face up.

"A ten!" Hall yelled. "He's got an ace-high straight! He wins!"

What happened then occurred so quickly that the others later remembered it as nothing but a blur. Ned Craddock scooped up his long knife from its place by his cards, brought it high over the locker table, then with incredible force, slammed the point down into the back of St. Croix's left hand, pinning it to the locker. The knife jabbed through the meat and bone, sliced down into the trunk, leaving only the horn handle showing above the skin.

St. Croix yelled a curdling scream as blood began to gush from around the handle of the knife. He frantically tried to yank his hand up from the table, but the knife held it fast. He was panicky; he pulled some of the flesh loose in the attempt, causing blood to pour out across the surface of the locker and spill over the edge onto the dirt floor.

Grimacing, mad with pain, the Frenchman tried desperately to retaliate. He crammed his free hand into his coat, came out with a pistol. He fumbled with the hammer, tried to cock it, but Craddock reached out and easily snatched the flintlock away from him.

Almost in the same motion, he swung the barrel of the fusil with all his might and struck St. Croix in the head with it. The Frenchman immediately crashed to the floor, his hand still pinned to the locker.

"Ned!" Collins hollered. "My God, man!"

"He was cheating," Ned muttered coldly. "He's been cheating all day long. I just finally caught him at it."

Collins leaned over the gambler. "He's still alive, but just barely. What is Captain Clark going to do when he hears about this?"

"You're always worried about 'Captain' Clark, Collins," Craddock complained. "What kind of loyalty do you owe a man who let you have fifty lashes?"

"I owe him the same loyalty as you do," he answered. "He's my captain."

"All right, forget that. Let's get him out of here before Clark finds him. Hugh, go get that bitchy wife of his. She can take him home. She'll probably pay us for doing this to him."

"You're an unfeeling bastard, Ned Craddock," Collins frowned, tugging St. Croix up against the locker. "I don't know why we keep covering for you."

"I keep telling you, Collins, the man was cheating us. What do you expect me to do? He was palming cards."

"Well, I guess we never will know that for sure, will we?" Collins wondered.

"Oh no?" Ned answered. "William, take my knife out of his hand and see if you don't find the card he was palming under there."

Werner frowned skeptically, looked puzzled as he stepped over to the locker. He glanced at Craddock, then Collins, who was wiping St. Croix's bloody face with his handkerchief. Werner wrapped his fist tightly around the horn handle of Craddock's knife, pressed his other fingers down on St. Croix's hand, then yanked the knife up with a grunt. It slipped easily out of the flesh.

"Now, raise his hand up," Craddock ordered.

Werner looked at him, gritted his teeth, then slowly raised the red, wet hand into the air. "There's no card here. There's nothing here, he wasn't palming."

"Let me see," Craddock growled. He looked for himself. His expression changed, his face turned blank. "I don't care if he didn't do it this time. He was still a cheat and he deserved what he got."

"I never saw him cheating," Werner countered.

"Yeah, well, that's because you were too busy mooning over his wife."

"Well, cheating or not, look what you've done, Ned. This man's dying. Let's get him out of here. Give me a hand, William."

"*Mon Dieu!*" shouted Celeste St. Croix, at the head of the tent. "What has happened to him? What have you done to him?"

"He did it to himself, lady," Craddock retorted, wiping St. Croix's blood off the barrel of the pistol.

"*Mon Dieu!*" she cried again, staring at St. Croix, pressing her hand against her breast. "Is he dead?"

"No ma'am," Collins assured her, "he's not dead. He's just knocked out. Do you have a horse outside? If we could get him up on his horse—"

"Yes, I have one. This way. Please, let me help you with him."

"We can manage him," Collins grunted, lifting him up. He and Werner dragged the heavy, unconscious body out of the tent, up to the bay gelding the woman indicated was hers. "All right," Collins sighed. "Let's see if we can get him up."

"Wait!" the woman cried out. She dropped to her knees, took his head into her hands. "René?" she whispered, then louder, "René!" She kissed him several times, caught herself, then spoke calmly. "René, listen to me. Can you hear me? Say something. *Mon Dieu! . . .*"

"Why don't you just let the poor man alone,

lady," Craddock suggested, coming up. "He's hurting enough as it is, without some broad shouting in his face." He went over to the gelding and stuffed St. Croix's pistol, butt first, into a saddlebag. "Anyway, he wasn't hit that hard. I doubt if he's going to die or anything."

"What happened to him?" she demanded.

"Excuse me, ma'am," Collins said. "If you don't mind, we really ought to get him up on the horse. William—on the count of three."

William hesitated. "Hey, Ned, can't you help us here, man?"

"Yeah, sure, why not?" Craddock stepped up, tightly clutched one of St. Croix's arms, waited for Collins to clamp down on the other, Werner on the legs. Then with a grunt, they heaved the Frenchman up and across the saddle. The horse started and snorted as the weight hit his back, but settled down when the woman yanked back the reins.

"Are you sure he isn't going to die?" she asked Craddock, since he seemed to know more about her husband than the others.

Craddock was firm. "Nah, he's not dying. He'll just have a headache when he wakes up in the morning. But I tell you what, lady—I'd keep him out of poker games, if I was you. He was in way over his head this time, and it cost him." Craddock grinned, felt the thirty-one dollars in his pocket. "It cost him in more ways than one," he added.

"Ned—" Hugh Hall tried to quiet him.

"Go on and take him home, lady," Craddock ordered, ignoring Hall. "We're through with him, he's learned his lesson. I bet you he'll be staying home now, with that bump on his egg."

"Ned—" Hall touched his shoulder.

Craddock shrugged off his hand. "What do you want, Hugh?" he grumbled. "I'm trying to talk to the lady here."

"I was going to say, Captain Clark is coming."

"Ahh—I might've known," Craddock groaned.

Werner shook his head. "Now we've really done it, John. We'll get a hundred lashes for this."

"Look, lady," Craddock lectured sternly. "What I want you to do is, back up my story, do you hear me? Anything I say, I don't care what it is, you agree with it. Do you understand?"

"I understand," Celeste responded. "But why should I? Did *you* do this to him?"

"Yeah, that's right, I did it, and if you don't back me up, I swear on my mother's grave I'll sneak into your house one night and murder this thieving bastard in his sleep. Don't you believe I won't."

She looked straight into his eyes and nodded her agreement. They stood silent and attentive as Captain Clark approached. His presence always drew strict attention from the men he commanded. The tall, red-headed William Clark was known by his troops as a natural leader, an effective, reasonable and orderly man.

He walked up to the group, his huge black servant York ambling a few feet behind, and stopped in front of the woman. "Ma'am," Clark tipped his hat to her, "what's all this noise about here? Are these men bothering you?"

She looked at Clark, then at her husband strung over the saddle on his belly, and back at Clark. "No," she answered, trying to appear calm. "They're not bothering me, they were helping me. They're trying to get my husband back on his horse."

"Private Craddock, who is this man?" Clark demanded.

Craddock cleared his throat. "Sir, we found this man wandering into camp a while ago—drunk. I guess you noticed he's a bit bloody—looks to me like some red savage got a knife after him."

Clark carefully raised St. Croix's head. "Private Collins, get him off this horse. He needs medical attention, right now."

Collins moved briskly. "Yes, sir. William—give me a hand."

"I'll take him," interrupted York, the black servant. He was over six feet tall, his body thick and rippling with muscles. He plucked St. Croix from the saddle as if he were a wet leaf on a limb and wrapped him around the back of his neck. The other men had seen York's strength before, at Wood River, but it always amazed them to see him in action.

"Take him on down to the keelboat, York," Clark instructed. "He doesn't look too bad." He tried to comfort the woman. "We'll fix him up a little before we send him back to St. Charles."

"Sir?" Hugh Hall stepped up, snapped his boot heels together, held himself stiffly at attention. "May I say something, sir?"

"What is it, Hall? What have you got to add to this?"

"Sir. . . ." he hesitated, swallowed hard.

"Well, come on, man, I don't have all day."

Hall gulped again, then promptly changed his mind. "It's . . . nothing, sir, I was mistaken. I have nothing to add."

"Then for God's sake stand back and let us get on with it," Clark snapped. He looked over at Ned. "Private Craddock?"

"Sir."

"Craddock, you seem to know more about this incident than anybody—after we patch this man back to health, I want you to give me a full report on what happened to him. And I do mean a *full* report—the whole story."

"Yes, sir."

"And I want it right, you hear? I want the simple, uncluttered truth of the thing. Which is something you don't always provide."

"Sir—"

"Don't correct me, Private Craddock." Clark suddenly lowered his voice. "Look, Ned, I know how these men follow your example. I'm trying as hard as I can to make that a good example. Do you think you could help me do that?"

"Yes sir," he answered. "I could do that."

"Good. If you don't, you may find the next two years seem awfully long." He turned to Celeste. "Ma'am, why don't you come with me. We'll see what we can do with your husband."

She smiled weakly, feeling a bit comforted by Clark's smooth manner and his warm Virginian voice. She felt relieved to be taken care of so properly.

He touched her elbow to get her started and they began tracing York's footsteps down to the keelboat.

As soon as they were out of sight, Craddock seized Hall's collar and drew him up next to his own body. He looked straight down into Hall's grey eyes. "Hugh, count yourself lucky you didn't tell Captain Clark anything about what happened." He tightened his grip on Hall's collar, squeezed it together. "Because if you had," he continued, "it probably would have been the last thing you ever did on this earth."

Hall stared at him, his face crimson from the choking, but he said nothing. A few seconds later, Craddock eased the tension, let him loose. He made a pretense of smoothing down Hall's collar. "Well, let's forget it, Hugh. No problem. The main thing is, you didn't tell him." Craddock patted him on the chest. "All right men," he called to the others, "what do you say—let's play some cards. I've got a bundle here to lose. Thirty-one dollars' worth."

Chapter 4

By the time Captain Lewis's wagon finally rolled through the mud into the camp near St. Charles, Tom Wentworth's desire for Roxanna Fairchild was feverish. When Lewis's friends and well-wishers began attaching themselves to the procession to the Missouri River, he had to sit next to Roxanna and pretend she was "Mr. Garcia." Worse than that, the bumps in the roadway occasionally threw them into each other and he felt her soft woman's flesh underneath her man's clothes. It was very difficult for him.

Fortunately, when they reached the site where the expedition was camped, his attention was diverted from Roxanna. The camp by the river suddenly came alive, as men emptied out of tents and lean-tos and gathered around Lewis's wagon. The place teemed with people, hardy-looking young men in buckskins, Indians in waistcloths and moccasins, even neatly dressed, well-scrubbed townspeople from St. Charles.

Tom stood up straight in the wagon, amazed at how many people had come to this western point, leaving civilization so far behind. But as he scanned the scene, something odd caught his eye. At the edge of the clearing, an attractive woman in a black cloak was leading a horse and rider into the woods. The rider was a portly man in a formal suit, hunched over in the saddle. They disappeared into the forest, though their image lingered awhile with Tom.

Captain Lewis pulled the horses back, locked the brake, jumped down and greeted William Clark. Smiling broadly, he introduced some of the company to Clark, a doctor, three military men and six or seven citizens from St. Louis. "And you know Auguste Chouteau," he added. Earlier, Lewis had described the austere Chouteau to Tom as "the heart, soul and bank vault of St. Louis."

Clark energetically shook Chouteau's hand. "Auguste," he said, "they told me you were coming to bid us *bon voyage* on our little expedition. I'm glad you could make it."

"I had to make it, William," he responded. "And look, let me urge you not to underestimate what you men are doing here. All of you. This is no 'little expedition.' This is a great day for America. You men are about to open up the country—after this day it will never be the same."

Lewis was warmed by Chouteau's words. He waited until there was a break, then introduced Tom and Roxanna (as Mr. Garcia) to Clark and the sergeants of the company, John Ordway, Nat Pryor and Charles Floyd. For this test, Roxanna had scuffed her face with dirt, and pulled her hat low on her forehead. She kept her eyes down as Lewis talked, no one questioned her sex. She sighed quietly when it was over, safe for the moment.

Clark welcomed the whole group, then announced publicly that the people of St. Charles were giving a party to celebrate the start of the expedition. Festivities would begin that night. At Clark's announcement, the men cheered and joyously flung their hats into the air.

In all the commotion, Tom leapt down from the

wagon, instinctively extending his hand gallantly to Roxanna. She frowned at him. "Tom—" she chastised him, trying not to be heard by the others.

"Oh," he caught himself, embarrassed at what he had done. He lowered his hand quickly. "I'm sorry."

She slid down the edge of the wagon to the ground, and whispered to him, "If you give me away with your male stupidity, Tom Wentworth, so help me. . . ."

"I won't give you away," he assured her. "I'll be careful."

"You'd better be."

"Tom?" called Lewis, approaching them. "This is Private Hugh Hall, he'll show you and Garcia around. Captain Clark and I have a few more plans to make, so I'll see you both in the village later, all right?"

Roxanna nodded, Tom thanked him.

It was dark when Hugh later escorted them down to the river, where the ten or eleven bright campfires scattered around the banks of the Missouri defined the various cliques of men in the camp. "We've got near fifty men," Hall told them as they made their way through the trees, past the fires and toward the water. "During that long winter on Wood River, we kinda broke off into groups among ourselves. Captain Clark and Captain Lewis approve of it—I guess it works out all right."

Roxanna nodded, understanding, but she wondered how on earth she would ever fit into such an arrangement. And she wondered, as they caught the curious glances of the men around the fires, were they scrutinizing her, were they guessing that she was really a woman? . . .

"This here's our keelboat," Hugh pointed to the long hull tied to the bank. Two men were loading crates on it by the light of six torches placed along the deck. "She's fifty-one feet long, has twenty-one oars," he boasted. "She's got a cabin, a sail, lockers in case of

Indian attack, swivel cannon fore and aft. She's ready for anything."

Tom wondered about all the security measures on the boat. "Just how often do the Indians attack?" he asked.

Hugh shrugged his shoulders. "I guess I don't know much about attacking Indians when you get right down to it, Tom. They just give us orders." He pointed at the open boats, continued. "We've got those two pirogues, too. Six oars in the red, seven in the white. One cannon each. That big dog sleeping on the white boat is Scannon, Captain Lewis's dog. He's coming along with us."

Tom was impressed with the keelboat and pirogues. They were much stronger, much larger than he expected. "Captain Lewis said there were also some horses," he commented.

"Yeah, that's right, we've got a couple of horses. You see, Captain Clark's the river man, so he handles the boats. Captain Lewis is the hunter, so he and Mr. Drewyer will be on shore, mostly, shooting game and such. Did Captain Lewis show you his air gun? There's nothing like that in the world."

"Yes, he showed it to us," Tom replied. "Wonder if it's everything it's cracked up to be."

"Wondered myself." Hall paused. "Well, look, do you want to go on board?"

"Yes," Tom answered. "We would like to see what we're taking up river."

Hall glanced at Roxanna, but said nothing. She kept her head low as they stepped over a landing plank onto the keelboat. The black man, York, was busy lifting crates, then easing them down into the hold.

"She's quite a boat, don't you think?" Hall boasted. "I wouldn't call her pretty, but she'll do the job."

"It looks loaded enough," Tom observed.

"Oh, she's loaded enough, all right—like a Spanish harlot. We've got two tons of pork, two tons of flour, six hundred pounds of grease, tools, rifles, muskets, blunderblusses, cannon—you name it. We even have twenty-one bales of trinkets to give to the Indians."

At the mention of Indians, Tom looked closely at Hugh.

"What *do* you know about them?" he asked.

"Not much at all," Hall shrugged. "To look at 'em, you can't tell what they're thinkin'. But once you've been around 'em a while, I hear—well, look, if you've got questions on that score, you might as well talk to Captain Clark himself or that interpreter o' his, Mr. Drewyer. The word around camp has it we'll be running into Sioux, Mandans, Shoshone, maybe a few Poncas and Omahas. Who the hell knows what else?"

"You heard-tell anything about the Welsh Indians, Hugh?" Tom tried to sound casual as he asked the question. The whole idea of Welshmen living somewhere on the Western plains sounded far-fetched. But in Philadelphia there was talk of such a tribe. And along with the talk, there was mention of a large fortune to be made."

Hall appeared puzzled. He shook his head. "Never heard of them."

"They live like Indians," Tom explained. "A fellow in Philadelphia told me there was a batch of them that might be descended from Welsh pirates."

"Well, I guess they could be that, but I don't know anything about them."

Tom tried to prompt Hall. "They say they're sitting on millions of dollars' worth of stolen British and French treasure—"

"Well, maybe so, but like I say, they don't really tell us much around here, so I wouldn't know. It's my guess, though, if your Welsh Indians are anywhere between here and the Pacific Ocean, we'll find them. Or they'll find us."

"Aren't you interested in all that money?"

"Nah—all I'm interested in is following Captain Clark and Captain Lewis. Just like I followed Captain

John Campbell in the Second Infantry Company, before I joined on here. I guess I can leave the treasure
hunting to others."

"But think what you could do with the money,
Hugh."

"I figure I'll be getting enough money the next
two years," he stated with certainty. "The captains are
generous men."

"Hey, Hall!" shouted someone from the bank.
"What're you doing loafing around on that tub? Let's
go!"

Hall squinted his eyes, made out the face of Craddock. "I'll be there in a minute," he called out. "Captain Lewis said to show these men around."

"Well, bring 'em with you," he hollered back.
"Show them around St. Charles. Tell them I've got a
French girl for each one of them. We're going to raise
a ruckus tonight, Private Hall. I've got enough money
for all of us."

"I'll be there in a minute," he yelled.

"Well, come on, Hugh, they're not going to wait
all night for us. It's spring, man, the chippies are hot."

"Go ahead, private," Tom encouraged Hall. "Don't
let us keep you."

"Now you two are welcome to throw in with us,"
he offered. "Ned Craddock is kinda rough, but he
does know how to have fun."

"No, thank you," Tom replied. "Garcia and I will
just stay in camp a while and look around."

"Are you sure about that? These folks are planning a big celebration, it should be fun."

"I'm sure—go on. But thank you."

Hall patted Tom good-naturedly on the shoulder,
then bolted across the plank and off the boat. He
quickly joined Craddock, and the two men eagerly
hustled off into the night.

"That was close," Tom said to Roxanna, relieved.

But Roxanna was red with anger. She glared at
him accusingly. "I suppose you're proud of yourself for

that, aren't you? Well, I wish you'd tell me what right you have to make my decisions for me. What right do you have to *protect* me, Tom Wentworth?"

Tom was surprised by her reaction. "Well, what would you have done," he asked defensively, "when Ned Craddock brought out his women—"

"That's not the point, Tom," she interrupted. "The point is, I have come all the way from New Orleans without any help from you, and I certainly don't need it now. I want you to just let me be, can you do that?"

"Let you be what—a woman? That's what I'm trying to keep everybody from noticing, Roxanna."

"Don't call me that," she fumed in a whisper. "My name is Garcia, God forgive Captain Lewis for ever thinking of such a name. But I'm stuck with it, so use it."

He was irritated by her haughty tone, but tried to be civil with her. "Well, anyway, I suggest we find a place to sleep tonight—"

She wasn't diverted though. "Find yourself a place to sleep, Tom Wentworth," she told him. "I've got some business to attend to. I'm going to walk around camp a while and see if I can hear anything about my husband. There has to be somebody around here that's heard of him."

"Not if everybody's like Hugh Hall."

"There's nothing wrong with him," she retorted. "Just because he isn't dedicating his life to getting rich—"

"Like me you mean?"

"Yes, like you. Why don't you go to the party without me—go ahead and drink and cavort with the local women—"

"I just may do that," he stormed.

"Go—do it."

"All right—I will!" he declared and promptly left her on the keelboat.

The next hour he wandered around the camp and

woods, fretting over his tiff with Roxanna, and thinking about his feelings for Isabel. A sharp and painful conflict had formed in his mind over the past two days: how could he be in love with Isabel and be so attracted to Roxanna at the same time? Roxanna had set him to wondering about his fortune, too. Would it be proper in Boston to finance a marriage with ill-gotten money from the wilds of western America? He'd never thought about it before. . . .

About ten o'clock he found himself in St. Charles sitting alone at the whiskey shop, drinking ale and listening to the other men carousing, singing and playing cards. But he felt like a spectator rather than a participant and he soon tired of the noise and smoke. Tom got to his feet and went outside. In the street there was some boisterous dancing to fiddle music. The men of the expedition were joined by a number of young and middle-aged French women in dark clothes, and their shrieks and hollers almost drowned out the scraping of the fiddle bow. But Tom walked around the dancers, uninterested.

Near the blacksmith's shop, he saw a clutch of important looking men standing in the shadows, talking. Drawing closer, Tom recognized Lewis and Clark, Auguste Chouteau and a Captain Stoddard, who had come by earlier to see the expedition off. Tom eased nearer, to catch what they were saying. He hoped they would be talking about money.

They were.

"Mr. Jefferson aside, William," Auguste Chouteau was saying, "what we're looking at here is an opportunity of a lifetime. With any luck at all, with what you and Meriwether will accomplish out there, we'll have an American trading company at the mouth of the Columbia in three years."

"Look, Auguste," Clark pointed out, "I understand what you're saying, and I know you've done more to build up St. Louis than any man alive—but as much as you'd like it to be, this expedition just isn't a commercial venture. It's an official government mission."

"Wait a minute now," Chouteau argued. "John Jacob Astor hasn't gotten to you first, has he? Is he footing your bill?"

"No, Auguste," Clark answered. "He's not footing our bill. As far as I know, he's not even aware of our trip. Neither are the British."

"Now there you're wrong, William. You're underestimating yourself again. Alexander Mackenzie's got himself what's called the XY Company. That's a trapping concern and likely to be *very* aware of our intentions. Not only that, but there's the Hudson's Bay Company breathin' down everyone's necks. In fact, I'd watch my men carefully, if I were you. It's always possible you have a spy with you."

"Auguste," Lewis inquired, "hasn't René Loisel set up a trading post upriver?"

"That's right, he opened one up last year, at Cedar Island."

"Was that one of your projects?"

"No, no. Loisel financed that himself. And he's losing money on it, by the way. The Sioux are stealing him blind. But I'm not interested in individual trading posts, captain. I'm interested in the same thing Astor's interested in—setting up an American fur trade. I want to beat Mackenzie and Hudson's Bay to the riches. I want an American fur trade monopoly, based on *our* lands—*our* wealth."

"There's nothing wrong with that, Auguste," Clark acknowledged. "We're not discouraging that. I'm just saying we are mostly military here, not commercial."

"All right, then let me make it commercial. I'll buy the whole expedition."

"Buy it? What do you mean?"

"I mean finance it. Pay for everything—supplies, salaries, whatever. Name your price. What could it cost—thirty, forty thousand?"

"We can't do that," Lewis protested.

"Captain Lewis," Auguste persisted, "I'll be frank with you. I'm a businessman, and I stand to gain a great deal of business if we can establish a working trade in the Northwest. But damn it, I'm also an American and I want us to claim the land Mr. Jefferson just bought from Napoleon. You both know that a piece of parchment called a treaty doesn't mean a thing to a man out here in the wilderness. We're going to have to *make* that land ours. And there's only one way to do that—we've got to control the commerce in the Louisiana Territory. There is no other way to do it."

Tom remained close by Lewis and Clark and the other two men for another half hour, but he missed most of what they were saying. The two quarts of ale he had drunk earlier now began to have their effect on him. His head was throbbing, his stomach was churning wildly, the whole world was spinning around him. With his hand clutching his belly, he stole away to a secluded place behind the blacksmith's shop.

He knew what was wrong—too much drink and too little food. But knowing the trouble didn't make him feel any better. He leaned his forehead against the clapboards of the shop, listened to the vague, confused sound of fiddles playing somewhere in the distance, then urinated against the wall. But relieving himself didn't help his nausea. Tom wobbled a few steps back toward the corner of the shop building, in the direction of the music, then stopped and braced himself against the wall. Suddenly his chest began to heave involuntarily, his throat tightened and gagged. He dipped his head down and vomited the bitter, foul-tasting ale onto the ground.

When he found a watering trough a few minutes later, he dropped to his knees and plunged his head into the water. Rinsing his mouth out and swallowing some of the cool liquid made him feel better, but he still had to sit on the ground for a while to get his bearings.

When he did at last manage to get to his feet and start back to camp, he was accosted by a woman who had burst through a gate in front of a small, white-washed house.

"Please, help me!" she pleaded, pulling his arm. "Hurry!"

He noted her French accent, then recognized her as the woman he had seen earlier in camp, leading the horse and rider.

"What is it, ma'am?" he asked.

"Oh God—help me!" she screamed excitedly, yanking at his sleeve. "You have to help me. My husband—"

"What *is* it? What's wrong with him?"

"You've got to stop him! Oh God. . . ."

Distracted, almost panicky with fear, she broke away from him and rushed through the open gate, back over the brick walkway into the house. As soon as she disappeared inside the front door, Tom ignored the nausea and pain in his stomach and sprinted after her.

He found her in a bedroom, frozen in her tracks, with her hand over her mouth. She was staring in horror at a bulky man in a cotton nightgown, on the bed. He was curled back against the headboard, looking like a frightened animal. His left hand and forehead were wrapped in blood-stained bandages, his eyes were closed, and he had the barrel of a dueling pistol stuck three inches into his mouth.

"*Mon Dieu,*" Madame St. Croix exclaimed. She was pale, faint, wobbly on her feet. She reached over and latched onto Tom's arm and pleaded with him, "Do something, do something. He's going to kill himself!"

"Sir?" Tom's voice quavered. "This woman loves you. How can you make her suffer like this? Please, now—hand me your gun."

René St. Croix shook his head slowly, deliberately. His face was dull grey. His eyes were yellow and they appeared glazed, almost vacant of expression.

"René, listen to me," Celeste pleaded. "Please— stop a minute and think about what you're doing, will you do that? Do you want to leave me out here all by myself? Is that what you want?"

Tom took the opportunity to venture a step closer to the bed. But St. Croix noticed him, recoiled, shoved the barrel farther down his throat. He grunted, warned Tom with his eyes to stay back.

The woman let go of Tom and pressed her hand to her bosom. She swallowed hard, took a deep breath. "René, I want you to stop this right now, do you hear me? Just stop it!"

"Ma'am—"

"René—for the love of God. . . ."

St. Croix moved his hand to cock the pistol.

"Oh no!" she screamed.

When St. Croix closed his eyes and began crossing himself, Tom saw his chance: he leapt to the bed, hurling his full weight against the Frenchman. Tom grabbed the butt of the pistol and the two men struggled with it. Somehow Tom managed to pry it out of St. Croix's mouth, but the Frenchman refused to relinquish his grip. They wrestled for control, twisting and turning on the bed. Suddenly both of them lost their footing and crashed to the floor. With a flash of white light and a burst of smoke, the gun went off. A ball exploded into the wall mirror next to the window.

Tom eased his hold on St. Croix, relieved that the pistol had been harmlessly discharged. But the Frenchman was not ready to give up. He bounded across the room toward the fireplace. Tom saw immediately what he wanted—the musket hanging over the mantle. St. Croix reached up, fumbled with it for a moment, then yanked the musket free from the wall hooks.

Tom drew out his sword. "Put the gun back," he commanded St. Croix.

"What will you do, monsieur, kill me?" he asked sarcastically.

"No, I won't kill you—I'm not going to do that for you. But I will lop off that good hand of yours, if you don't put that musket back where you got it."

"What do I care about a good hand, monsieur? I want to die."

"For the love of God," his wife beseeched, "why are you doing this, René? Are you trying to drive me mad?"

He looked at her pitifully. "I lost your money, Celeste," he murmured in a cold, distant voice. "I lost all of your money. I took it to the Americans' camp and lost it in a poker game."

"Oh no, René—"

"I am sorry I did it," he apologized. "I won the hand, Celeste, I swear I did. But they wouldn't let me have the money. It was your money, though. I deserve to die."

"But *why?* Why did you do it? You knew it was all the money we had in the world."

"I don't know why," he admitted. "I just did it. I saw it and I took it. I've brought too much shame to you with my years of gambling, Celeste. Too much shame to both of us—"

St. Croix cocked the hammer on the musket and swung it around. But before he could move the long barrel toward his head, Tom jumped in. The hilt of his sword crashed down swiftly on top of the Frenchman's head. St. Croix groaned loudly, dropped the musket, clutched at his head and fell over on his belly, unconscious.

"He'll never change," Celeste said later as she tucked the coverlet around his legs. "It was roulette and baccarat in Paris, here it is five-card-stud and draw poker—but it's all the same. Gambling is an obsession with him. He just can't stay away from it."

Tom laid the Frenchman's pistol inside the trunk

at the foot of the bed and eased the lid down quietly. "Did he say who he played poker with at camp?" he asked.

She smoothed out the spread with her slender, skillful fingers, then looked up at him. "No, he didn't say. And I don't want to know." She turned her attention back to the bed again. "It never does any good to know."

"But if we knew who it was," he suggested, "I could confront them and get your money back. One way or another."

She straightened up, considered the idea for a moment, then shook her head. "No," she decided, "I've been through this before. It just never seems to do any good to know . . . even if they did cheat him. And who knows if that's true? René has lied before. When it comes to gambling, you can't believe anything he says."

"Are you sure you don't want me to find out from him who it was?"

She nodded. "I'm sure, but thank you for offering." Satisfied that St. Croix was comfortably situated in bed, she picked up the lamp from the table and led Tom out of the room. They talked a few minutes more about St. Croix's gambling, then about the expedition. Tom knew it was time to go, but something about Madame St. Croix and the way she was looking at him made him linger. To his surprise, he was finding her very attractive, standing in the front room with the glow of the lamplight on her face. He realized she was much older than he was, but even so, she seemed so warm and sensual. . . .

"Tom?" she said, catching his stare. Celeste St. Croix was an intelligent woman, she recognized immediately the look in his eye. She knew what he wanted—what, she decided, he needed.

"What?" he answered abruptly, caught off guard. "Oh, I'm sorry," he apologized, then added, "I was just about to go."

"Do you want to go?"

He shrugged his shoulders. "Well, no," he admitted. "I mean, there is nothing else I can do here, so I think I should be going."

"Yes," she agreed, "I think you should."

"Yes ma'am."

"Please, monsieur—it's 'Celeste,' not 'ma'am.' I am not that old."

"Oh no! You're not old—" he spoke too quickly, then broke off.

She smiled at his awkwardness. "Would you like to stay here tonight, Tom? With me?"

He thought he felt his heart jump into his throat when he heard those words. But he tried hard to grab hold of himself and appear unrattled, as if he expected to hear them all along. "I have to go," he repeated. "We're starting up river tomorrow."

"You can get up just as early here to start up river as you can in camp, *n'est-ce pas?*"

"Well, yes, ma'am—"

"Tom—" she chastised, "what did I just ask you?"

He turned red with embarrassment. "I'm sorry. I mean 'Celeste.'"

"You know," she remarked, "if you are worried about my husband, you don't have to. He won't wake up till tomorrow morning."

He still hesitated, not sure of what he should do.

"You're not going to make me beg you, are you?" she asked.

"Oh no—"

"Well then, come with me. Please," she whispered softly, extending her hand toward him. "Stay with me—just this once."

He took her hand, felt his breath quicken at the touch of her warm, soft skin. She led him into the other bedroom, set the lamp on a table next to the bed. Without a word, she began unhesitatingly to undress. "This was my daughter's room. But you don't have to worry about her, either. She was married last summer. They're living back in Pittsburgh."

Tom waited nervously at the foot of the bed, his pulse racing, his heart thumping rapidly, nearly bursting with desire. He still could hardly believe what was happening to him. And yet it was real. He was watching her drop her blouse to the floor, step out of her skirt, unfasten her lacy undergarments, let loose her firm, round breasts. . . .

He held down his impulse to seize and hold her. Instead he waited until she had completely bared her voluptuous body and was lying on the bed linens before he hurriedly peeled off his clothes, scattering them about haphazardly on the floor.

When he slid in next to her, and as their lips met in a long, gentle kiss, he thought he would lose control of himself, that it would all end in one quick explosion of his lust. But Celeste St. Croix was an expert in the art of lovemaking. She knew instinctively how to excite a man but she had also learned how to keep him excited, and ready, until she had brought her own body to the precise point of needing him.

She took him into her body and rocked gently, then with increasing fervor until one, then another pulsating orgasm shook her body. Her pleasure increased his own excitement. Suddenly, wonderfully, there was the violent release of his own pent-up desire.

Later, he lay with his head resting luxuriously on her naked breasts, while she playfully twirled locks of his tawny hair around her fingers. "Tom," she inquired, "do you have a lover?"

He flinched at the question. Somehow, it seemed improper for her to ask him that. Almost indignantly he answered, "No, I don't have a lover."

She wasn't bothered by the tone of his voice. "You don't have to be so polite and gallant with me now, you know. I'm not foolish enough to think I am the only woman you've ever been to bed with."

Tom nestled against her breast. In truth he had

been to bed with only one woman, a whore in Kentucky, but he didn't want to admit that to Celeste. He responded to her question with a vague sound of assent.

"But you don't have a lover," she persisted.

"No."

"Now, Tom—"

"I don't, really," he assured her. He circled one of her breasts with his hand, then ran a finger lightly across her nipple, making it hard and erect. "I have a fianceé back in Boston, but I don't have a lover."

"Tom," she squirmed a little under the excitement he was renewing in her, "will you promise me something? Will you stop by St. Charles on your way back from the expedition? To see me?"

He kissed both her nipples, raised up and looked into her eyes. She was beautiful, he thought, warm, loving—and beautiful. He decided that she was someone who deserved a better fate than living with René St. Croix. "If I stop by," he asked her, "will we do this?"

She smiled and nodded. "Of course we will, monsieur," she assured him. "You're very good at it, you know."

He liked hearing the words. "Then I'll stop by," he promised.

She laughed happily. "So be it then. But let's not think about that now, Tom. That's a long time from now, *n'est-ce pas*? The important thing is, we are together now, Tom Wentworth, and we still have half a night in front of us. Don't you think we could do something about that?"

"Yes," he agreed, "I do."

"Are you up to it?" she teased.

He was excited all over again. "Oh yes," he exclaimed and hungrily covered her face, her chest, her stomach with kisses. "Oh, Celeste," he cried between kisses, "I love you, I love you."

Celeste St. Croix lay on her back, warmed by his

attention, stimulated by the touch of his lips on her skin. Soon she was burning, she had to have him again. She began to writhe and groan and dig her nails into his back. Then she could take it no more; she pulled his hard lean body upon hers, opened her arms and legs to him, and took him in.

PART TWO
THE MISSOURI

Chapter 5

As it turned out, Roxanna had not dared go ashore after Tom left her. All night she could hear the sounds of the men carousing. And the squeals of women left no doubt as to what was happening to them. But their cries wavered in meaning between hilarity and despair. Roxanna slept fitfully, sometimes wondering whether she should rush ashore with a gun to protect those being molested, and sometimes feeling as if she were the only one in camp not enjoying herself that night.

The next morning, she felt ashamed of her own cowardice and she wasted no time preparing to go out. The men were already up and about by the time she left the keelboat and went ashore. But Roxanna Fairchild meandered through the bustling camp virtually unnoticed. It was a big day for the captains, the crew and the villagers. As the men packed their gear and reloaded the boats, the French people of St. Charles offered them cheer and encouragement. Some of them sang songs to fiddle music, a few even pitched in to help the explorers break camp.

The number of dignitaries on hand to send off

the expedition had now swollen to thirty or more. Roxanna heard a few of the names of these distinguished-looking men in New England broadcloth suits, stiff collars, cravats and shiny boots. One of them was a Mr. Lansing, a Boston publisher who was trying to convince the captains to let him print their journals when they returned. Another was a Mr. Neale, a writer from Mr. Dennie's *Portfolio* in Philadelphia. A third was William Forsythe, a rich trader from New Madrid.

Roxanna hadn't seen Tom Wentworth that morning but at noon she caught sight of him a ways off from camp, busily packing a load on a horse. She had to walk close to Ned Craddock's little pack of men to reach him. As she passed by their fire, she heard one of them laugh abruptly. Resisting an impulse to turn and face them, she forced herself to ignore them completely.

Tom was standing next to the horse, tying down the edges of a stiff bundle with long rawhide strips. "Good afternoon," he greeted as she came up. "I was just about to go find you."

"Can I help you?" she asked.

He gritted his teeth. "I can manage it."

She was silent for a while, not wanting to irritate him. But she hadn't uttered a word since last night. She desperately wanted to talk. "It's an exciting day, isn't it?" she finally ventured. "All this activity everywhere. You know, some of the children from St. Charles are even playing games with the Indians. I didn't know they did that."

"It's exciting enough, I guess," he agreed. "It's a day I've come nine hundred miles to experience." He ran a rope under the horse's belly, tied the makeshift girth and patted the load to confirm that it was well lashed down. "There you are," he announced. "I think that should do it for you."

She crossed her arms, puzzled. "What do you mean, do it for me?" she asked. "Whatever you've got in there, Tom, it's not mine, I can tell you."

"What's in there is a tent, and yes it is yours. So is the horse. I was just wondering if you were satisfied with the way I fixed it."

"Now wait a minute," she objected. "I have never in my life slept in a tent, Tom Wentworth. And you know perfectly well I don't own a horse. So neither one of those could be mine."

"As of right now, they both are. Captain Lewis says you can use one of the hunting horses. This one."

"I'm not using anything of the sort. I've already told Captain Lewis, I'm not going to accept any special treatment from anybody, and that includes him. I'm going on this expedition as a man, and that's how I expect to be treated."

Tom looked at her. "Actually," he admitted, "the horse and tent were in case you refused to go back home. That's what he wanted me to get you to do."

Roxanna was indignant. "Well you can save your breath because I'm not going. There is nothing you or Captain Meriwether Lewis can say that would change my mind, either."

"Maybe not, but we have heard a couple of things about your husband you might be interested in."

"What?" she blurted. "What did you hear?"

"Yesterday a man named Cartel, a friend of Private Cruzatte's, came down the river with a load of furs he got from the Omaha Indians. He told Cruzatte he heard the Omahas talking about an Englishman living with the Arikaras—"

"Douglas? My husband?"

"He said the man had red hair and a scar across his left hand."

"Yes! That's Douglas. He got the scar at Oxford, when he was a boy. Is he all right? Can we find him? Why didn't this Cartel bring him back?"

"Just calm down, Roxanna," he said coolly. "He's not hurt. Cartel claims he's been with the Arikaras only about a month. The Omahas swear he's one of Jean Lafitte's pirates."

"He was *captured* by Jean Lafitte," she corrected him. "There's a big difference. When do you think we'll reach him, Tom? Where are these Arikaras?"

"Roxanna," he tried to calm her down, "there is something you ought to know about it before you start making plans. The Omahas told Cartel the Englishman is not a captive. He's living with the Arikaras of his own free will."

"That's absurd," she sniffed, pretending to be unaffected by the idea. "He couldn't possibly be there because he wants to be. He's a very sophisticated and cultured man—"

"I know he is, Roxanna, but I also know he's *not* being held prisoner."

"I don't believe you," she stated flatly.

"Well, I don't have any reason to lie about it," he countered. "I'm just telling you what Cartel told Cruzatte—"

"Who told Captain Clark, who told you—what kind of evidence do you call that? I'm sorry, I just don't believe it."

"You can believe it, Roxanna. It's true."

"It is *not* true," she insisted.

"Roxanna—"

"No, damn you!" she shouted. "He can't be living with a bunch of savages because he wants to be. It's ridiculous."

Tom glanced nervously back at the camp. "Roxanna, lower your voice, somebody will hear you."

She held her hand over her mouth, breathed deeply, got control of herself. "All right. I want to see for myself. I want to see Douglas and talk to him—and ask him myself. I'm not coming this far to let some fourth-hand gossip turn me back. You can go tell Captain Lewis that for me."

"I don't think your husband wants to be found, Roxanna. Look, why don't you go back to New Orleans and think about it? Mr. Chouteau could arrange a boat down the Mississippi—"

"You'd just as well forget that, Tom. I am not about to go back home."

He was irritated by her resoluteness. "Well I can tell you," he interjected harshly, "you won't like what you find, Roxanna."

"And just what does that mean? Do you or this Cartel *know* what I'll find?"

"Not for sure, no. But Cartel did say . . . there are rumors about him."

"What's that supposed to mean?"

He was put off by her persistence. "Well, I don't know," he confessed.

"I do," she said. "It doesn't mean anything."

"Roxanna—if you'd just go home."

"The only place I'm going, Tom, is up the Missouri River, with you and the rest of these . . . men. And when I find these Arikaras, whoever they are, maybe then you can be rid of me, once and for all."

She left him with the horse, made her way back through the camp. As she neared Craddock's fire, the enticing aroma of salt pork and biscuits and coffee gnawed painfully at her stomach. Having had no food today, she found herself slowing down, lingering, just to smell the meat cooking. That was when she heard Craddock yell at her.

"Hey—what's the matter, Spanish?" he called. "Did he turn you down?" The others around the fire guffawed. She stared back at them. There were three other men in buckskins, and a grey-haired man in a black suit and hat, sitting next to Craddock. For a second, she thought she had seen the man in the suit before—maybe in New Orleans. But then she decided she hadn't.

"*Ah!*" Craddock sighed loudly, mockingly, "*Mi vida, mi vida!*"

Roxanna pulled down her hat and hurried away from them, the sound of their laughing and snickering ringing in her ears.

The men were all ready to go by three o'clock. At three-thirty the pilots ceremoniously cast off the lines to the keelboat and the pirogues, and the crowd on the bank cheered wildly. Captain Clark raised his sword high, and the four swivel guns fired three shots each in salute.

The expedition was officially under way.

For the next four days Roxanna laboriously worked her way through the forest with Captain Lewis and Drewyer on shore. Lewis ordered her to hang close to the river, to keep watch on Captain Clark as he skillfully engineered the three boats up the powerful spring currents of the Missouri, dodging overhanging limbs, snags and rocks as they went.

Once she saw the keelboat flip over on its side as the pull of the swift water snapped the tow line and kicked the hull onto a sand bar. She saw the oars draw in all at once, on command, and twenty men hurl themselves into the swirling water to try to hold down the upper side of the boat. After a half hour, the sand underneath the hull washed away and the boat began to ease back upright. Then one of the men fastened a rope to the stern of the boat and they all towed it ashore. Ten minutes later, they were off again.

Evenings were hard on Roxanna. Most of her life she had been the center of attention in a crowd, noticed and admired by men wherever she went. Now, hiding her sex, she was cut off from the rest of the expedition. The men's natural prejudice against someone who looked different from them isolated her. They had no interest in taking up with the man Captain Lewis had brought in from St. Louis. Besides being Spanish, this Garcia looked frail to them—weak, silent, just not at all their kind of man.

Worst of all, she learned from Tom that some of them believed she was a sodomite. Ned Craddock had spread the rumor around camp that Mr. Garcia was a freak, not to be trusted in a company of men. Tom himself avoided her too, for reasons she couldn't understand.

On the twenty-fifth, the expedition camped at La Charette, a few miles east of St. Charles, where the La Charette River flowed into the Missouri. At four in the afternoon, Roxanna was on the ground, on her knees, unfolding the tent she had eventually agreed to accept from Captain Lewis, when Tom Wentworth appeared.

"*Buenos tardes, Señor Garcia,*" he teased her.

"Oh shut up," she said, restraining a smile. She fumbled with a mass of tangled rope.

"Captain Lewis wants to see you."

She looked up at him. "Why would he want to see me?"

Her response made him angry. "Doesn't it ever occur to you just to follow orders, Roxanna, like everybody else? All I know is, Captain Lewis ordered me to get you. We're going down to Femme Osage Creek. You, me, Captain Lewis and Captain Clark and Mr. Drewyer."

She got to her feet. "Is it Douglas?" she asked excitedly. "Have you heard something else?"

"No, you can relax. This isn't about your husband. Nobody's heard another word about him. We're all going down to see Mr. Boone."

"Who?"

"Mr. Boone: Daniel Boone."

Roxanna dropped the rope and eagerly went with him to meet the famous Indian fighter. She had heard of him in New Orleans; even in the elite parlor rooms on St. Charles Avenue, men indulged themselves after dinner by telling tales of Daniel Boone fighting the bloodthirsty Cherokee Indians, blazing dangerous trails in the Cumberland Gap, and leading the first white settlers into wild and treacherous Kentucky. Daniel Boone was always a good subject of conversation, one of America's great pioneers. Roxanna's only regret was that as Mr. Garcia, she wouldn't be able to speak to him.

But Captain Lewis eliminated that problem on the way to Boone's eight-hundred-acre estate. A half a mile out, he told Roxanna that he had revealed her secret to Clark and Drewyer, so she didn't have to pretend to be Garcia while they were away from the other men.

"Well, thank goodness somebody else knows." She yanked off her hat, shaking her hair down. The sudden change in her appearance was startling, the men in the wagon now looked at her so closely that she felt embarrassed. She unconsciously smiled at Drewyer, who abruptly turned his head to the side. "Up until now, there's been nobody to talk to, but Tom."

"Mrs. Fairchild," Captain Clark faced her from the front bench. "I think I ought to tell you that while we do know who you are, we don't really approve of your being on this expedition. I for one think you ought to turn around here and now, before we get into Indian country."

"Captain Lewis has been through all that with me."

"Well, I haven't been through it," he told her. "I don't think you understand the dangers ahead of us, Mrs. Fairchild. Which is why I wanted you to make this trip with us to see Mr. Boone. There's not another man alive who knows more about what we'll be facing in the wilderness than he does. If anybody can make you listen to reason, he can."

"I'm always willing to listen to reason, Captain Clark," she pointed out. "But you may as well know right now, I'm not empty-headed."

"I know that," Clark allowed. "You're a courageous woman, or you wouldn't have made it this far. I'm not questioning your mettle. But try to see it from our point of view. We are on an official mission, sanctioned and paid for by the United States Congress. We're representing the government here—Mr. Jefferson's government."

"And Mr. Jefferson wouldn't want a woman on his mission—is that what you're saying?"

"No. What I'm saying is, try to imagine what would happen to this country if you were hurt while you were on the expedition. Mr. Jefferson's detractors would pounce on the incident like a pack of wolves. A *woman*—injured, or captured by Indians—on the President's mission. It would have half the nation up in arms."

Clark's political argument had little effect on her. "Perhaps what you should do, then, is see to it that nothing happens to me," she suggested.

"I can't," he replied. "Neither can Captain Lewis or Mr. Drewyer here. We're all too busy trying to take fifty men into a hostile country."

Lewis cleared his throat. "Tom Wentworth has the time, William," he offered. "Maybe he can take care of Mrs. Fairchild."

"I beg your pardon," Roxanna spoke indignantly.

"Good," Clark replied. "Tom, she's your responsibility."

"Sir—" Tom began.

"Captain Clark," Roxanna protested. "I don't need anyone to look after me. I can take care of myself."

"Nobody can take care of himself out here, Mrs. Fairchild," Clark told her. "But we can wait on that until you've heard Mr. Boone. Who knows—all this fretting over your presence on the expedition may not even be necessary."

Roxanna was silent and angry for the rest of the two miles. She sat rigidly, with her arms crossed, next to Tom Wentworth. She looked idly at the scenery and half-listened to Lewis and Clark and Drewyer discussing their endless collection of maps and charts of the Upper Missouri. They compared James MacKay's drawings of the river with a number of others Lewis had bought in St. Louis, talked about the differences in the map by John Evans which Mr. Jefferson had given to Lewis before he left Washington City. They discussed questions to ask Mr. Boone about the accuracy of their papers.

When they reached the house, an old black man hoeing in the yard told them in a raspy, unconcerned voice that Boone wasn't at home. After some aimless talk, he directed the party to a point on the river, a mile away. They walked across a rolling field and located him on a hill near the river. A gray, balding man of seventy, he was leaning on his long rifle, staring, shaking his head at a commotion occurring near the edge of the water.

Roxanna was surprised to discover the old pioneer dressed in neat clothes, instead of rough buckskins. He was older and more wrinkled than she expected, too, but his bearing was still good, his back and shoulders straight and true. As she drew close, she took note of his lean body, his clear face, his sharp, alert eyes.

She and Tom and Drewyer hung back a ways while the captains walked up to Boone, introduced themselves and shook hands with him. After a few minutes, the old man glanced back at Roxanna, turned, and nodded to Lewis. Then he motioned with his hand for them to come over.

He was polite and gracious when Tom and Roxanna were presented to him, but then suddenly his face took on a very serious look as he turned his attention back to the river bank. There were three men next to the water, digging around in the mud.

They all watched as one of the men threw a blanket over a large object they managed to tug out of the mire.

"What is it?" Roxanna asked.

"It's a man," Boone answered, straightening up. " 'Least it *was* a man," he corrected himself. "Ain't much left to him now."

"What happened to him?" Lewis asked.

"Able found 'im a while ago, 'neath a bunch of

weeds. Looks to me like he ain't been there long. Maybe two, three hours."

The three men struggled up the bank with the body, now wrapped loosely in a gray wool blanket. As they reached the others, Lewis stopped them, lifted up the blanket, and looked under it. Instantly he grimaced, shook his head in disgust.

"God in Heaven," he cried. "What did they do to him?"

"They skint 'im," Boone answered. "Just like you'd skin a rabbit, captain. They pulled 'is skin up over 'is neck."

Roxanna couldn't believe what she was hearing. She felt compelled to see for herself. She took a step toward the body.

"Roxanna, no—" Tom shouted, grabbing her arm.

Daniel Boone put his hand on Tom's shoulder. "Go ahead and let 'er look, son," he offered. "If she wants to."

She wriggled loose from Tom's hold and knelt next to the body. Taking a long, deliberate breath, she carefully gripped the edge of the blanket between her fingers and slowly pulled up the cloth. Her stomach turned at the ghastly sight underneath: what once had been a man's body was now nothing but a mangled mass of blood, skin, exposed meat and muscle, black mud and wadded grass. A sharp pain suddenly seized her chest and her throat tightened. She had to turn away from it.

"Roxanna?" Tom helped her stand up.

"I'm all right," she insisted. But she was lying to him. She felt ill—woozy, weak at the knees. She had to take hold of his arm to steady herself. And then, just as she thought she was in control of her senses, the image of the mutilated corpse flashed in her mind and her knees buckled under her. She tried desperately to cling to Tom's wrist, but it was too late. Her mind was spinning around and around, growing darker and darker. . . .

When she woke up, she found herself inside a small room in a soft feather bed, under a quilted coverlet. Gazing down at her was an old woman with a severe but kind face, dark straining eyes behind dim spectacles, and thin, straight white hair twisted into a bun on top of her head.

The woman smiled warmly as Roxanna began to stir in the bed. "Hello," she spoke in a soft, clear voice. "How're you feeling?"

"I don't know—what happened?" Roxanna asked, rising up. Then she remembered. "Oh no—I didn't faint, did I?"

"Yes, you did," she nodded.

"Wouldn't you know it," she groaned. "Just when I was gaining some ground, I faint, like some silly little bridesmaid. The men must have loved it."

"What do you mean, 'loved it'?" the woman asked, puzzled.

Roxanna let the question pass, as she only now noticed that her chest was nude. She dropped the coverlet to her waist, revealing her naked breasts. "Could I have my shirt, please?" she asked.

The old woman lifted the shirt off the back of a rocking chair and handed it to her. "I guess you'll want this, too," she said, holding up the cloth Roxanna used to bind her breasts. "Whatever it is, it was choking you, so I took it off."

"Thank you." Roxanna took it from her. She sat next to the headrail of the bed and began wrapping the cloth around her chest.

The woman crossed her arms and looked at Roxanna with wonder. "A girl as beautiful as you ought not be wearing men's clothes," she observed kindly. "It ain't proper."

"Are you Mr. Boone's wife?" she asked, adjusting

the cloth over her breasts, and loosening it a bit so the binding wouldn't hurt.

"Yes," she nodded, "for more years than I can count."

Roxanna stopped, looked at her. "Then you can understand why I have to go on this expedition. Why I have to wear these clothes."

She shrugged her shoulders. "All I know is, wearing clothes like that ain't proper."

"Well, no, it's not 'proper,' Mrs. Boone," Roxanna agreed. "I'm not saying it is." She tucked in the cloth, swung her legs over the edge of the mattress. "But of all the people in the world, you ought to be the one who could understand why I have to do this. You were the first white woman in Kentucky, you know better than anyone what it's like for a woman in the wilderness."

"Yes, I do know what it's like," she agreed. She took off her spectacles, wiped them on her apron, then put them back on. "And believe me, it's a thousand times harder than you'd ever imagine. Roxanna, my own son James was taken by the Indians and tortured and killed. It was brutal. If you thought seeing that man's body was hard, imagine how it would be if it was your own son you were looking at. Someone you'd nursed with your own milk. That's something you don't forget, even after thirty years."

Roxanna lowered her head, suddenly ashamed of her inexperience, her weakness. "I don't know if I could take anything like that," she admitted. "It must have been awful."

Mrs. Boone rubbed her arm nervously. "Two years after James died," she went on, "Daniel brought us to Boonesborough, to the fort he'd built. Me and my daughter were nothing but the men's squaws back there, Roxanna. I never told it to Daniel, and I wouldn't tell it to him now, but that's what we were: squaws. We cooked their food, washed their dirty britches, mended their smelly socks, mopped their

brows and fed them broth when they had the fever.
And nobody even so much as thanked us."

Roxanna nodded, but said nothing.

Mrs. Boone continued: "Then one day my daughter was jerked up off the ground by some awful Cherokee brave and carried off into the woods screaming. Right in front of my eyes. It was too much—I lost control and wrecked everything in the cabin. And Daniel—he almost went crazy."

"What happened to her? Was she hurt?"

"No, praise the Lord. We got her back before anything else happened to her. We were lucky."

Mrs. Boone walked over to the window, looked out through the open shutters at the fresh new green grass and trees. "You may as well know I was attacked, too, Roxanna. Twice. Once by a half-breed Shawnee, once by a mountainman. Daniel don't know about either one. Men don't want to know about such things. But you might as well go ahead and expect it to happen, 'cause it will."

Roxanna wanted to know what 'attacked' meant, exactly, but she didn't dare ask. She stood up, shoved her shirttails into her trousers. "That won't happen to me," she asserted. "I've got fifty men to protect me."

Mrs. Boone looked at her with pleading eyes. "Roxanna," she warned, "you're a fine, cultured girl. A lady. You don't have any business being out here in this terrible place."

"But I do have some 'business,' Mrs. Boone. I'm looking for my husband."

"Well, I'm sorry, but you'll never find him, child," she predicted. "Not out there. You'll die first. If it's not Indians, it'll be a fever, a bear, a snake—something. Please, go back home, Roxanna. Leave the exploring to men."

"Did *you* leave it to the men?"

Mrs. Boone paused, surprised at the question. She considered it for a few moments. "That was different," she concluded. "I was a poor North Carolina farm girl. I didn't have near as much to lose as you do."

"I have a husband to lose."

"Then lose him. Captain Lewis said you barely knew him. Let him go. It's not worth it. You were born for the finer things of life, Roxanna, not binding your breasts up in that thing and heading into the wilderness. Let Captain Lewis and Captain Clark do it. Let that young Tom Wentworth do it. It's their job. It's not a woman's."

Roxanna reached for her boots. "I don't want to sound disrespectful, Mrs. Boone, because I admire you very much. To me you're a great person. You're as much a hero as your husband is. But things change. I just refuse to be a squaw, here, New Orleans, or anywhere else. And I don't care if going on this expedition is a man's job, I'm on it, and that's all that matters to me." She yanked on a boot with a grunt. "And Mrs. Boone, no matter what those men say to me, no matter what they do to me, I'm going to stay on it," Roxanna vowed.

A few minutes later Roxanna located the men standing near the barn. There were ten or so others around them now, hanging close, mumbling, mulling over the situation. They all became quiet, turned and watched her closely as she walked up to them.

"Roxanna," Meriwether Lewis was the one who greeted her.

"Captain Lewis," she warned him, "don't you dare ask me if I'm all right—"

"I wasn't going to," he half-smiled. "By now, I know better than that."

Boone laughed. "You're a spirited little heifer, ain't you? Rebeccah fix you up in there?" he asked.

"Yes, she did, Mr. Boone. Thank you. She's a wonderful person."

Boone nodded. "Yep. She is that."

There was an awkward silence for a few moments. Then Captain Lewis broke it to resume their conversation. "Back to this business, Daniel. What makes you think it wasn't an Indian? Would a white man do something like that?"

"Captain," Boone answered, "you got good white men and bad white men, just like you got good Indians and bad Indians. But I tell you, I know a few white men born right here in these United States that'll make savages look like European royalty. Anyhow, this skinning trick ain't Indian style. Looks to me like it was a mountainman done it."

"Why would a mountainman do such an ungodly thing?" Clark asked.

"I don't rightly know, Captain," he answered. "I reckon being out there in the wilds with nothing but low life around you does something to you. Makes you ungodly. I do know I seen a man skint alive when I was living with the Shawnees in '78. And it was a mountainman did it. Worse thing I ever saw a human being do."

Roxanna looked over at the covered body, then at Boone. "Was he a white man?" she asked.

"Yes ma'am, he was white all right," he replied. "I figure he must've been that Hudson's Bay Company agent that's been snooping around here the last week or so. All these trading company men are starting to get edgy nowadays. They're all snarling around each other's throats, itching to start a war. I hate to say it, captains, but Mr. Jefferson buying all this land, and then this expedition of yours is what's got 'em all stirred up."

Lewis nodded. "That's what Auguste Chouteau told us back in St. Charles."

"Well, it makes sense, I reckon," Boone concluded. "There's a fortune in fur and hides out there, and everybody wants it—the French, the British, the Canadians, the Americans, everybody. They're all saying, who gets control of the waterways, gets control of the fur trade."

"But we're not after fur trade," Clark reminded

him. "We're here to lay a rightful American claim to the land—"

"I know. What I'm saying is, if you men find that passage Mr. Jefferson has been looking for ever since he sent that renegade Michaux out to look for it, you'll be finding something else, too—the North West Company, the Hudson's Bay, Great Pacific Fur, XY Company and every last French trapper that wants to call 'isself a trading company. You'll have 'em all breathing down your necks, ready to reach out and take what they want. That's what happened to this fella here. I reckon since he was Hudson's Bay he was British, so you can figure the French or the Canadians, or somebody else hired theirselves a mountainman to kill 'im and fix 'im up like that."

"What can we do about something like this, Mr. Boone?" Tom asked.

"Ain't much we can do about it, son," he confessed. "I'm magistrate here, and this is my responsibility, but mountainmen sneak in and out of here like catamounts. You can't go out there after 'em. Wouldn't do you no good if you tried."

"That doesn't seem right," Tom observed.

"Well, it wouldn't be right back in Philadelphia," Boone countered. "But this ain't Philadelphia." He motioned at a tall man with a reddish beard nearby. "Able," he ordered, "take 'im up to La Charette and turn 'im over to Seth Taylor. I'll pay for it."

"Yes sir."

They watched Able and two other men load the body onto a wagon and drive off with it. Daniel Boone threw his rifle over his shoulder, began walking back to the house. The others followed.

"Things was a lot simpler back in Kentucky," he explained to Lewis. "Before I took Trudeau up on 'is offer and come out here, I could pretty much count on knowing what I was up against all the time. Out here, though, it's like with that fella Able's taking in to Taylor. Ain't no way of telling what he was up to. What's happening is, you got some sly folks with big money coming out here now, wanting to make even bigger money. Folks like them trading companies. And we're just seeing the first of 'em, captain. I tell you, it'll get a lot worse after you men cross the mountains to the Pacific. The place will be swarming with 'em."

"What about the Indians?" Captain Clark asked. "What should we expect from them?"

Boone rubbed his chin. "Well, I reckon your first problem's going to be the Sioux. At least the Teton Sioux. They're the ones controlling the Missouri. They're not going to just let you pass by 'cause you're coming to 'em from President Jefferson."

"We ran into René Loisel this morning," Clark said, "coming down from his trading post at Cedar Island. He says the Tetons gave him a hard time last winter."

"Yeah, the Tetons are a rough bunch, all right," Boone acknowledged. "What you want to do is talk to old Pierre Dorion about 'em. Some folks'll tell you he's a cutthroat 'isself, but one thing's for sure, he knows his Sioux. At least he knows the Yankton Sioux. He's been trading with 'em for twenty years. 'Matter of fact, he's married to one of 'em."

"We'll look him up," Clark promised.

"In the meantime," Boone told Lewis, "they tell me you got this fancy rifle that works on air. Is that true?"

"It's true."

"You don't reckon an old man could take a look at it, do you?"

"I just happened to have brought it, Daniel," Lewis smiled. "It's in the wagon. And you can take as many looks at it as you want."

Chapter 6

After the stop at La Charrette, the expedition was on the move again, westward up the Missouri. As the days and weeks passed by, Roxanna gradually became lonely. Since she wasn't strong enough to wield a pirogue oar or handle a keelboat sail, and since she couldn't take the chance of being recognized by the men, she stayed off the boats and on the shore with the hunting party. They settled into a routine: Lewis, Drewyer, and Tom killed the deer, elk or bear, she cleaned and dressed the meat and prepared the hide for later use.

Being away from the others sometimes made her depressed. Often at night she would pitch her tent by herself on the outskirts of camp, crawl under her bed roll, and lie awake for hours, listening to the sounds of the woods, remembering her soft canopied bed at home, and aching to feel the strong, firm touch of a man next to her. But ultimately those feelings made her stronger. They made her all the more determined to find her husband.

As spring became summer, the Missouri River

grew hot and steamy. Now that the spring turbulence was gone, the three boats could navigate westward over calmer waters, but there were always other obstacles. The heat and humidity were almost unbearable. On land and water insects abounded. Mosquitoes followed the boats and swooped down on the men in great clouds. Ticks and flies infested the evening camps. There were also the usual stomach ailments, sunstrokes, and cases of boredom and fatigue expected on such long and tedious journeys.

And there were the inevitable dangers of the wilderness. On June 26, 1804, the expedition reached the junction of the Kansas River, where the Missouri changed its course to almost due north. On that day, Roxanna and Tom Wentworth were out on the starboard side, walking slowly through the timber, looking for deer, when Tom's foot slipped off a rock and landed on a rattlesnake. The rattler quickly snapped out at his leg, but Tom dodged its fangs, then reacted sharply by ramming his heel into its head and grinding it into the dirt. After a few minutes, he kicked at the snake with his toe to make sure it was dead, then picked it up for Roxanna to see.

"Look at the size of this thing," he said. "It must be seven feet long."

Roxanna was about ten feet away, but that distance wasn't far enough for her. "Tom," she commanded, "put that thing down."

"Why? It's dead."

"I know it's dead, but I don't like it any better dead than alive. Would you please put it down. I hate snakes."

Tom drew the head up close to his face, to get a close look at the fangs. "It's too bad I crushed the head. We could have kept this one to send back to Mr. Jefferson."

"I'm sure Mr. Jefferson would be just overjoyed to get it," she replied sarcastically.

"I don't know. If—" he broke off his sentence.
"Oh my God," Tom cried.

"What is it?" Roxanna asked.

"Shh—" Tom quieted her. He held his body stiff,
inhaled a long easy breath, and listened. Suddenly he
heard it: the eerie, terrifying clacking of rattlesnake
rings. He slowly looked down, and there, ten inches
from his foot, was another snake, coiled and vibrating
its tail. Tom now realized that he didn't have his rifle.
He had leaned it against a tree to pick up the dead
snake. But his flintlock was behind his belt—perhaps he
could ease it out before the second snake attacked.

"Tom—" Roxanna whispered. She didn't dare
move, she might startle the snake.

"Don't say anything, Roxanna. I'm going to try to
get out my pistol. Now don't move, I think I can get it,
if I do it very slowly."

"Tom, there are more of them!" she exclaimed.

Wentworth heard the chilling sound of another
rattle behind him. He knew now his one-shot pistol
was useless. He was standing in a bed of snakes. What
he needed was his sword. "All right," he tried not to
panic, "just stay there, Roxanna. Don't even breathe."
Without bending over, he let the dead snake slip
through his fingers and fall to the ground. Moving his
right hand across his waist, he cautiously wrapped his
fingers around the hilt of his sword.

The snakes hissed noisily at him, and shook their
rattles wildly as he slid the blade slowly out of its
sheath. He had the sword up, now, ready to lash out
with it, but as soon as his muscles flexed, one of the
snakes behind him darted its head forward and sank
its fangs into his left leg. He yelled out in pain,
whipped around with his sword and sliced the rattler in
two. In a rage he swished the sword about, severing the
head of one, then another.

Roxanna screamed again. "Tom!" she yelled,
"turn around—quick!"

But by the time he turned his head around, he

was feeling a sting, then a searing pain behind his knee. The snake retreated and, with lightning speed, recoiled and struck his leg again, in nearly the same place. It was ready for a third attack when Roxanna rushed up with a stone and smashed it into the ground.

"Roxanna—watch out!" Tom called out, discovering another snake near his foot. He slammed down the edge of the sword and opened its skull. He swung around again but there was nothing to strike at—just snakes writhing in their death agony. "Come on," he panted. "Let's get out of here!"

As they hurried into the woods, leaving the horrid carnage behind, the poison quickly began to burn Tom's leg. He began to limp. Then he lost control. He had to sit down. The pale, drawn look on his face frightened Roxanna. She knelt in front of him. "Tom," she cried. "What do you want me to do? Captain Lewis is out on the prairie, the boats are miles away, I don't know where Mr. Drewyer is."

He smiled weakly, ripped open his trouser leg and looked at the damage. "Three hits." He spoke with detachment, examining the punctures. "That's enough to kill me, Roxanna."

"Oh God, no, Tom. No!"

"Look, Roxanna," he concluded. "I don't think I'm going to make it. All you can do now is to leave me here and go get help."

"I'm not going to leave you here to die, Tom."

"Just go get somebody, damn it. That's all you can do."

"I can do more than that!" Roxanna ripped off her hat, shook her hair loose, drew out her knife. "If I can dress deer," she reasoned, "I can fix a snake bite. I'll do it just like Mr. Drewyer said to."

"Roxanna, please," he pleaded with her. "My only chance is for you to go get Captain Lewis. Oh, Lord—my leg's already getting numb."

"See there?" she asked, with tears in her eyes. "I have to do something now." She drew out her shirttail and tore it apart, made a tourniquet, and bound his thigh with it, to keep the poison from reaching the rest of his body. Then she brought the knife down slowly to his calf. With a careful, light touch, she lay the sharp point on the punctures, then carved an 'x' in his flesh across the bites, to open it up.

Tom grimaced in pain as the knife cut into his skin, but he said nothing. He watched Roxanna press her mouth against his leg and begin to suck the blood from his wound. When she spit out the first mouthful, his heart almost stopped at a sound he thought he heard. It was near them, almost under them. He grabbed her shoulder and squeezed it. "Roxanna, wait," he whispered. "Listen!"

She stopped, listened, but heard nothing. It was strange. She couldn't even hear the usual sound of birds, or the roar of the river; the woods were as silent as a grave. Then, out of the darkness, came that terrifying sound again.

"Oh no—" she cried, looking around. She immediately spotted the snake, lying on a fallen tree, two feet away. Its long tan, diamond-back body was wrapped into a compact coil. At her movement it hissed, writhed, tongue out, ready to kill. Roxanna instinctively reached toward the ground for Tom's sword, but the spring of the rattler was too quick for her.

It catapulted itself off the dead tree toward its moving prey and clamped its poisonous fangs deep into the soft flesh of her arm. Screaming madly, Roxanna jumped up and frantically slung the snake off her arm, hurling it against a tree. But the snake seemed unshaken; it unhesitatingly turned her way, curled toward her through the grass, slid over a rock, and coiled itself, ready for a second strike. When Roxanna heard the frightful rattling sound again, she froze. Out of the corner of her eye she could tell that Tom had passed out. She was on her own. But no matter how hard she tried, she couldn't make her muscles move. All she could do was stand there, helpless and vulnerable, waiting . . . waiting. . . .

Suddenly a knife whizzed through the air, hitting the snake with a muffled thump. The snake whipped around, writhing helplessly, pinned to the ground by the knife. Roxanna wheeled around, saw a rough, ugly giant of a man standing twenty feet from her. He was bearded, clothed in worn buckskins. He had a buffalo robe slung over his shoulder and there was a long rifle strapped tightly to his back. He looked at her curiously, scratching his thick black beard with his thumb and forefinger. When he moved, she automatically took a step back.

"Did he get you?" the man asked, coming her way.

Roxanna knew instantly that he was a mountainman, the kind of man, she remembered, who could skin another human being alive. What would such a man do to her? Although she was afraid, she knew she had to trust him. She would die if she hesitated. "Tom was bitten in three places," she told him. "He's dying."

The man walked over to her, threw off his robe, and looked down at Tom. Even five feet away, she was affected by the appalling odor of his body. It was a thick, musky, dead smell that almost overpowered her. But her disgust turned to fear when he turned to face her and shoved out his huge hand toward her chest.

"What do you want?" she asked desperately.

"Give me your knife," he demanded. "Mine's in that rattler's head, so it's got poison on it." He took the blood-stained knife from her shaking hands, dropped down to his knees next to Tom, and began working on his leg.

A minute later Roxanna felt nauseated, then faint. She sat down on the ground, tried to watch the mountainman gouge the blade of her knife mercilessly into Tom's wounds. But her pain was too strong, too hot, too intense. . . . She looked drowsily at her arm, at the two fang marks, and ran her fingers over the puffy

flesh until the powerful venom took hold of her consciousness and she fell to the ground.

The mountainman knew from years of experience
exactly how to treat rattlesnake bites. He drew out
Tom's poisoned blood slowly and continuously, making
sure to check the tourniquet frequently to prevent the
blood from being cut off completely. After that, he
took out of his sack a mixture of powdered tobacco and
crushed leaves from certain rare mountain weeds,
packed it into his wounds and bound the leg with a
stiff, used bandage he always had with him.

When Tom was taken care of, and he had finished
with Roxanna, he leaned her against the fallen tree and
looked admiringly at her unconscious body. He concluded that he had never seen such a beautiful woman.
He felt her silky dark hair, ran his hand down her neck
and into her shirt. He was surprised to find a cloth
binding her chest, but it didn't bother him any: he
squeezed each of her breasts through it, to check their
size, and how soft they were. He had had only Indian
women lately, and their bosoms were harder. . . .

"All right, mister—back up!" someone shouted
out to him. "Get away from her."

He got to his feet, turned slowly around to see a
man in a gray cloak, holding a strange-looking rifle
pressed against his shoulder. "Easy now, soldier," the
mountainman cautioned him. "You just watch what
you're doing with that thing, whatever it is."

"What did you do to them?" Captain Lewis demanded, cocking the hammer on his air gun. He aimed
the point of the barrel directly at the man's chest.

"Hey, wait now, ease up there," he responded
quickly. "I ain't done nothing to 'em. See for yourself.
I swear—all I been doing is treating their wounds.
They flopped down in a nest of hungry rattlers back
there a ways."

Lewis noticed the bandages now, and felt relieved.
He lowered his gun. "Are they all right?" he asked.

"Now that I don't know, general. All I know is, I

done what I could to 'em. It's up to the Good Lord now. You know these folks?"

Lewis eyed him cautiously as he drew closer. "Yes, I know them. You're the one I don't know."

He laughed. "No, I reckon you don't. Buck Brussard's the name, general. I'm on my way back to the Big Belly Region. And you look like an army man to me," he guessed.

Lewis uncocked the rifle. "Captain Meriwether Lewis, United States Army." He squatted down to see to Roxanna and Tom. He touched the black mixture on Roxanna's arm. "What's this?"

"That's just something to draw out the poison," Brussard explained.

"Well," Lewis replied, standing up, "it looks like you did a good job with them. But Roxanna's looking too pale to suit me. We'd better get them back to the boat as fast as we can."

Brussard rubbed his beard. "Where's your boat, cap'n?" he asked.

"Four or five miles." Lewis put Roxanna's hat back on her head, tucked her hair under, raised her up. "Come on," he urged, "get him up, let's get going, I don't like the way she looks."

Brussard retrieved his knife and robe, jerked up Tom and threw him easily over his shoulder. He looked down at Roxanna and grinned. "Now me, on the other hand, I like the way she looks. Best looking woman I ever seen."

Lewis leaned her over on his back and stood up. "She's trying to keep that hidden. We don't allow women on this expedition, so she's passing for a man," Lewis explained, starting toward the river.

"Is that a fact," he said, following behind. "What expedition would that be, cap'n? You doing some work for Astor or Mackenzie, or somebody like that? This a company boat we're going to?"

Lewis was too worried about Roxanna to answer. He remained silent as they made their way back through the trees to the banks of the river. Once along the way Roxanna came to, but Lewis assured her in a quiet voice that she would be fine if she kept sleeping. She nodded vaguely and drifted off again. After twenty minutes, she began to feel heavy on his back, after thirty minutes, she was a burden. But he pressed on, anyway, with big Buck Brussard breathing hard, smelling bad, close on his heels.

When they finally reached the keelboat, Captain Clark met them, laid out his medical tools and potions and took over the care of Tom and Roxanna. Lewis and Brussard went on shore to wait. They drank whiskey while the other men stood around, curious to know who Buck Brussard was, and what had happened to the two men, Wentworth and Garcia.

Lewis explained the situation to the men, then turned to Brussard, "If they live, we have you to thank for it."

"I don't care about thanks, cap'n," he responded, "but there is something you could do for me."

"What's that?"

"Well, I could use a ride up to Big Belly."

Lewis considered the idea. "I'm grateful to you for saving my men. *If* they have been saved—"

"I know all about the Sioux Indians," he interrupted.

"What makes you such an expert?" asked one of the men. It was Ned Craddock, standing back with his arms crossed, scowling at Brussard.

"Like I told you, cap'n," Brussard continued, ignoring Craddock, "I got a home up that way, and I got to get through the Sioux to get to it."

"That don't mean you know anything about 'em," Craddock pointed out.

"Private Craddock, let me handle this," Lewis cut off Craddock.

But Ned persisted. "Well, what I want to know is, how come this mountainman's not living in the mountains? And how come he wants to ride with us? I thought mountainmen traveled alone. It sounds fishy to me, captain."

Brussard stared at Craddock with cool, penetrating eyes. "I reckon you must be the company ass, Craddock. Every company I ever saw had one, always hollering, bellowing like some dumb stupid mule—"

"Now you listen to me, you foul-smelling bastard—"

"Private Craddock!" Lewis shouted. "Back off!"

"Well, the stinking cur insulted me—"

"Craddock—leave it be. You asked for it."

Ned gnashed his teeth, glared at the mountainman, then looked at Lewis. "Sorry, sir," he apologized reluctantly. "I got carried away."

"Well get away from here and go back to whatever it was you were doing, Craddock, while you still can."

"Captain Lewis, I'm not afraid of this guy. What's more, I don't think a man who smells like a crap heap ought to be going on our expedition—"

"All right, Private Craddock, that's enough!"

He hesitated, mumbled, "Yes sir," and turned to go.

"Hey, Craddock," Brussard called after him. When Ned looked his way, Buck whipped out a hairy object from behind his belt and flipped it toward him. Craddock instinctively caught it.

"It's a scalp!" one of the men cried.

Ned turned it over nervously in his hands, trying not to look at it. "All right," he growled, "just what is this supposed to mean?"

"It don't mean anything, it's just a scalp, like the man says. Only it's a white man's scalp."

"So?" Craddock spoke defiantly. "Red savages take scalps. So what?"

"So a red savage didn't take that one, Craddock. A mountainman took it. You think about that tonight when you're trying to sleep."

Captain Lewis watched Craddock clench his fist in

anger, turn red, then storm off, with several of the men following. Minutes later he glanced over at the keelboat, hoping to learn the fate of Tom and Roxanna, but Clark was still busy attending to them. He downed a slug of warm Kentucky whiskey from his cup and led Brussard by the elbow away from the other men. "Buck, we already have a Sioux interpreter, this man Dorion we picked up a while back. What good do you figure you could do us up there?"

"I know Pierre Dorion, cap'n. He's a good man, but he lives with the Sioux. That ain't what you need here. What you need to survive up there is somebody that hates the Sioux. Somebody who can guess what their next move's going to be."

"Meaning you."

"That's right, me. I may live up there, cap'n, but I don't like the Sioux Indians one little bit. It ain't Indians in general I hate, it's the Sioux. This buffalo robe here, for instance. A Shawnee chief give it to me fifteen years ago, back before Wayne broke 'em up at Fallen Timbers—"

"I remember," Lewis replied. "I was there."

"Yeah, I figured you was," he grinned. "I ain't met a white man yet who didn't claim he was at Fallen Timbers. But anyhow, if you ever did fight around the Ohio, you know all such Indians as the Shawnees want is freedom, cap'n. All they want's to roam around and hunt their game, just like a trapper or anybody else. What they *don't* want to do is take over other Indians' land, like the Sioux done to the Arikaras. Or they want to sit down by a river and make white people pay tribute to 'em for the right to take the water—which is what these Tetons are doing on the Missouri now."

Lewis looked closely at this big, curious man. "Why do you hate them? What'd they do to you?"

"Well—what they done to me is my business, cap'n. All I'm saying is, the Teton Sioux ain't like your Shawnees or Kickapoos—they're not going anywhere. They're sitting up there on that river, waiting for you.

And they'd just as soon massacre this whole expedition as they would pee in the river. So you'd best have somebody like me around to keep you alive."

Lewis paused. "Do you stay in touch with the Shawnees now? With Tecumseh and that group?"

"Well now, I don't figure that's any of your business, cap'n. All I'm doing is heading home, no more to it than that. My problem is, I got to get through the Sioux Indians to do it. So the long and the short of it is: I need you, and you need me."

Lewis nodded. "It looks like that's the case, Buck," he agreed. "All right," he added, extending his hand. "You're on."

"Good. It's always a pleasure, riding with a man of reason, cap'n."

Lewis winced at the mountainman's odor as he stepped close, but he held his breath and gave him a hearty handshake. "Why don't you get settled, Buck?" he suggested congenially. "We'll talk about the Sioux later. Since they seem to be our chief enemy at the moment, I want to learn everything I can about them. Right now, though, I'm going to have to go find out about my men."

Brussard's eye gleamed. "One of your 'men' ain't much of a man, cap'n. Not from what I saw of 'er."

Lewis was irritated by the statement. "I hope you keep that to yourself. I don't want anybody taking advantage of her because she's a woman."

"Don't worry, cap'n," Brussard laughed. "I'll keep it to myself." He walked off, laughed again and muttered, "I'll keep it *all* to myself."

On the keelboat, Roxanna was awake and up, leaning against the mast, her right arm wrapped and held in a sling. Captain Clark was on his knees near Tom, worriedly running his fingers through his red hair. "He's awfully weak, Meriwether. It's a miracle he's made it this far. Three rattlesnake bites should've killed him. It may be that concoction the mountainman put on him saved his life. It's drawing out an awful lot of that poisoned blood."

Lewis stood tall and erect, with the butt of his long rifle resting on the deck next to Tom's shoulder. "Is he going to make it, William?"

Clark stood up. "I don't know if he will or not," he confessed. "He's young and tough, he might pull through. But I have no way of knowing. I've done all I can."

"He doesn't look any better," Roxanna observed. "His face looks horrible. It has no color at all."

"That's the fever," Clark responded.

"He looks worse than when we brought him in," Lewis worried.

An idea suddenly came to Clark. He began to see Roxanna not as a recovered patient, but as a nurse. "Mrs. Fairchild, do you have any experience taking care of the sick?"

She understood immediately what he was getting at. "Well, yes," she admitted, "but not a young man— "

"Good," he cut her off. "Nobody else around here has that experience, and somebody has to take care of him for the next few weeks. It looks like you're the natural choice."

"Now just a minute, captain—"

"He's a sick man, Mrs. Fairchild," Clark reminded her. "He needs looking after."

"But you—or Captain Lewis—"

"We don't have time, Mrs. Fairchild. We have fifty other men to see to."

She looked down at Tom. His face seemed twenty years older than yesterday. His cheeks were sunken, his eye sockets black, his lips a thin blue. "If he wasn't so irritating. And so protective. He acts like I'm a little girl sometimes, Captain Lewis. You've seen him."

"He gets that from his father, Roxanna. When Tom's mother died with the fever in '86, William decided that it was his fault. He decided if he had looked after Maria properly, if he hadn't let her leave the city, she would never have caught the fever. Tom probably took over that sentiment himself," Lewis explained.

"I just wish he could look at me like a man," she complained. "The way you do, Captain Lewis."

Lewis couldn't help but smile at the idea, but he didn't correct her. "Don't be too hard on him, Roxanna. Tom is a little impulsive at times, but anybody in Pennsylvania will tell you, with his background at Yale and Tapping Reeve's law school, he's destined to be one of the best lawyers in Philadelphia. Maybe even the country. Don't sell him short."

Roxanna nodded. She wasn't selling him short: she was trying to defy a strong attachment she had for Tom Wentworth—an attachment that was slowly growing, despite her wishes. She knew that as a married woman, she shouldn't be having such feelings about a man. She was well aware that while Tom did sometimes irritate her, still she missed him terribly when he wasn't with her. At the same time she knew she had to go on pretending to be a man, she wanted so very much to prove to Tom Wentworth that she was a woman. A fully grown woman. . . .

Tom groaned and stirred under the deerskin blanket. Clark bent down and wiped his wet face with a cotton cloth. "He's burning up," he said. "Damn this heat—it's not helping any."

"Roxanna—" Tom mumbled, opening his eyes. When he saw Roxanna, he reached out his hand.

She took it. "Hush now," she murmured softly. "Go back to sleep. You need to rest."

"Where are they, Roxanna?" he asked trying to get up.

She pushed him down gently. "They're gone, Tom," she assured him. "Just relax. Go back to sleep. It's all right."

He smiled weakly, breathed haltingly for a few seconds, then drifted back into unconsciousness. Roxanna pried his fingers off her hand, looked up at Captain Lewis, slightly embarrassed. She stood up.

"I'm sorry," she announced to Clark. "I can't take care of him."

Clark wrinkled his brow. "Why can't you?"

"I just can't." She couldn't very well tell him she was trying not to fall in love with this man. That was her business. They would just have to accept her decision.

But William Clark wasn't that easily swayed. "Mrs. Fairchild," he looked at her intently, "whatever your objection to doing this is, I can't afford to indulge it. What we need here and now is someone to look after this man. That's all. Someone who'll watch his fever and see to it he's fed and kept cool as possible in this terrible heat. Is that so much to ask?"

"I would just rather not, Captain Clark."

"I was beginning to think I was wrong, not wanting you on this trip. Now, I'm not so sure."

"Captain—"

"All right, Mrs. Fairchild, if it'll make it any easier for you, I'm ordering you: take care of this man. Stay with him and tend him until he's either standing up on the ground himself, or buried six feet under it. Is that clear?"

She closed her eyes, took a deep breath. "Yes sir," she assented. "It's clear."

"Good. Now you're making sense. Joseph Fields will take your place on shore."

Roxanna resigned herself to Clark's orders. She reached down and straightened Tom's blanket and pushed a lock of his hair off his sweaty forehead. "He's so hot. I'm going to wet this cloth, maybe I can keep his face cool."

Tom moved when she left his side. He opened his eyes, looked drowsily about for a few minutes and tried to speak, but his tongue wouldn't form the words. By the time Roxanna returned with the wet cloth, he was asleep again.

Spending the next two weeks so close to Tom was

a trial to Roxanna; meanwhile, despite the intense heat on the river, the men went about their work. The hunting parties shot deer, elk and geese for meat, trapped beaver for the hides, while the boatmen dragged huge catches of catfish out of the water. Sometimes Captain Lewis would return from an exploration with a pack horse loaded with plums, raspberries, currants and grapes, and the men would stop everything to eat them.

Even with hunting and fighting the Missouri River and suffering the relentless heat, Lewis and Clark found time to catch a number of curious looking animals, which they described in their journals. One day Joseph Fields killed a strange little animal none of the men had seen before. Private Cuzatte said it was what the French called a *brarow,* the Pawnee Indians a *chocartooch.* Ned Craddock proclaimed loudly that it was properly called a *badger.* Whatever they called it, Captain Clark had its carcass cleaned and stuffed for presentation to President Jefferson, along with other specimens he would like, such as one of the *barking squirrels,* which was what Clark called the prairie dogs that lived in the open fields near the Platte River and Council Bluffs.

All this time Roxanna did nothing but attend to Tom Wentworth, who seemed to be getting worse by the hour. During the days, while each man was conscientiously doing his own particular job, she felt secure, if not happy. But at night, when she had put out her lamp and had crawled naked under her wool blanket, she shivered with fear. Without Tom nearby, she felt alone and scared. The big smelly mountainman always seemed to be near her, watching her, ogling her body, undressing her with his eyes. She lived in terror of the day when he would reveal her to the others. Or when he would do something even worse.

And Ned Craddock was as bad, in another way. He used every opportunity he could find to ridicule her, and to goad the other men into making fun of her. She had learned to hate him.

"I'll tell you, if I ever get as sick as Tom Wentworth," Craddock told Hugh Hall one evening, "do me a favor, all right? Whatever you do, keep that Spanish sodomite away from my body. I'd rather be pushing up flowers out there on that prairie than to have one of those heathen creatures fawning over me."

It was late at night, and the other men in camp were asleep or lounging lazily around low fires, reluctant to move about in the heat. Craddock was leading Hall down through the darkness, to where John Collins was standing guard behind the torches on the keelboat.

"Good evening, John," Craddock sung out goodnaturedly as they reached the boat. "You got it ready for us, there?"

"Look, Ned," Collins answered in a concerned voice, "I changed my mind. Why don't we forget it? If Captain Clark ever finds out I let you and Hugh steal whiskey off this keelboat, he'll run us all through the gauntlet. He may even throw us off the expedition."

Craddock dismissed the idea. "So what if he does throw us off? What have we lost?" He climbed aboard the boat. "Besides, you worry too much, John, my friend. We can always say the Omahas took it. You know the red savages—they'd rather steal whiskey than eat."

Hugh Hall stepped onto the boat. "Is anybody else on board, John?" he asked Collins.

"No, they got Tom Wentworth with Captain Clark, so it's empty. Here it is," he lifted up a hide cover, exposing six bottles of liquor. "Just take it and go, before someone sees you."

Craddock smiled gleefully as he reached down for the bottle of liquor. "Ah—this is what we need to put away the gloom, Hugh." He uncorked one with his teeth and guzzled it. The liquid burned his throat and stomach, but he liked that hot, excited feeling, even on a warm night. He handed Hall a bottle and held out another one for Collins.

The sentry shook his head, declining the bottle. "I can't drink, I'm on duty."

"Look," Craddock told him, "the only duty you've got in life is to yourself, son. So drink. Go on, drink!"

"No, Ned—"

"Drink it, Private Collins."

"I don't *want* it!"

"Damn it, John, you drink this, or I'll start hollering out your name as loud as I can. Right now. In ten minutes that beloved 'Captain' Clark of yours will be laying fifty more lashes on your back. Are you ready for that?"

Collins looked at him for a minute, remembering the pain of his last beating. Ned Craddock had been responsible for that one, too. He thought a minute, then silently took hold of the bottle and let a big swallow slide down his throat. It was too much: he coughed it up.

Craddock guffawed approvingly. "Hey, there you go, John. The only way to beat this stinking heat is to soak your gullet in a pot of old Kaintuck."

Three hours later, the night was still warm, the torches were low and the three men on the keelboat were sprawled out on the deck, drunk. Craddock was allowing the others to examine his watch with the nude picture in it. "That's no chippie you're looking at there, men," he told them confidentially. "That's a genuine English lady. Every bit of her's the real thing. I never told anybody that before, but it's the truth. A real live English lady. Married to a duke, no less."

Hall was dubious. "I never heard of an English lady sitting around on a stool naked."

"There's a lot you've never heard of, Hall, but that doesn't mean it don't exist."

"How come she's English, Ned?" Collins wondered, looking closely at the picture. "Were you ever in England?"

Craddock snapped the watch away from him. "It's none of your business where I've been," he growled.

"I was just asking," Collins defended himself.

"Well, don't ask," he ordered firmly. "If you want to ask about somebody, ask about Tom Wentworth. Find out about him. I figure a man who'd wear fancy clothes like his out here in the woods has got to be British. You know how the limeys are, all proper and everything—"

"That naked lady of yours isn't very proper," Hall observed.

"That lady's worth ten Tom Wentworths," Craddock proclaimed. He slugged down a long shot of whiskey, wiped his mouth on his sleeve. "As a matter of fact," he told them, "every man on this boat's worth ten Tom Wentworths. The only difference between us and him is, your daddy and mine were never bosom buddies with Captain Meriwether Lewis. They didn't fight the red savages together on the Ohio River."

"You're wrong about that, Ned," Collins corrected. "Captain Lewis isn't partial to Wentworth. And when Tom's not sick, he does his job, just like the rest of us. He's all right."

"Ah—Tom Wentworth is nothing but a fortune hunter," Craddock grumbled. "Ask him, if you don't believe it. He'll tell you, the only reason he's out here is so he can make enough money to go back East and marry this high-class wench in Boston."

"What's wrong with that?" Hall asked.

"What's wrong, Hugh, is Tom Wentworth never bothered paying his dues for this expedition. How come he didn't spend that cold winter with us on Wood River, hunh? While we're freezing our butts off, he's back in Philadelphia, toasting his buns in front of some cozy fire."

"Oh, come on, Ned," Collins groaned. "Tom

Wentworth's as good as any man on this expedition and you know it."

"All right, what about that mountainman? Where was *he* last winter? And how is it he's got Captain Lewis's ear and you and I haven't, John? You tell me that. What makes this Buck Brussard so special?"

"Well, he knows the Upper Missouri, for one thing," Collins offered.

"I'd be surprised if he knew any more about the Missouri River than I do," Craddock said and drank more whiskey. "As a matter of fact, I figure Buck Brussard's in cahoots with these river savages. I'm guessing he's a spy for the Sioux Indians."

"I doubt that," Collins responded.

"Well, one thing you can't doubt, John—a man who scalps human beings like Brussard does is not a normal man. He's either a red savage himself, or he's low enough to work for them. Either way, he's not somebody Captain Lewis ought to be listening to when we go into Sioux country."

"Captain Lewis knows what he's doing," Hugh Hall declared. "Anyway," he added, "I wouldn't be bothering Buck Brussard if I was you. They say mountainmen can break a man's back just by hugging him."

Craddock was exasperated with the company he had to keep. "They also say there are two-headed monsters out there in the mountains, too, Hugh. Are you going to believe that, too? Damn, Hall, you're a bigger fool than I thought you were."

Hall bristled. "Now look here, Ned—" he began.

"Forget it."

"Well, I don't like being called a fool."

"Then stop acting like one," Craddock told him. He paused, took note of Hall's frown, then gave him a friendly slap on the shoulder. "Forget it. Look, I'll tell you what," he announced. "I figure this is as good a time as any to do something I've been wanting to do since St. Charles. Let's get up from here right now and go over and have a few words with our Spanish friend, Garcia—how about that, Hugh?"

"Why would we want to go see Garcia, Ned?" Hall asked, surprised. "He can't even speak English."

"So we'll speak Spanish. I knew a few words: *Buenos noches, adiós, gracias*—whatever."

Craddock struggled to his feet, steadied himself against the side of the boat. The deck whirled under his feet for a second, and the torches on the boat spun around his head, but finally he gained his equilibrium. He felt a wave of nausea for a second, but it passed. He looked down at the others. "I want to have a man-to-man talk with this fellow," he decided.

"Why would you want to do that?" Collins asked.

"Because I want to, that's why. And because I want to tell him how it looks for the rest of us on this government expedition to have a freak like him along. It makes us all look bad. I'm going to tell him to pack his gear and get lost. Got any messages you want delivered, John?"

"Why don't you leave him alone, Ned," Collins remarked. "Nobody cares how he acts."

"Well, I care and so do most of the other men. It's time somebody said something to him."

Collins stood up, faced Craddock. "Leave the poor man alone, Ned. I mean it."

"Don't you figure he has a right to know how the men feel about him, John? Well, I do, and it looks like I'm the only one around here man enough to tell him."

"You're headed for trouble, Ned. If Captain Clark finds out what you're doing—"

"Yeah, I know, the great Lieutenant Clark and his fifty lashes again. Well let me tell you both, I'm not afraid of William Clark or any other man. Hugh, get up. Let's go find Garcia."

Hall sat up, but stayed down on the deck. "I don't want to go bothering Garcia this time of night," he stated. "And you shouldn't, either. He hasn't done anything to you."

"The man offends me, all right? I'm sick of looking at him, and I want to tell him that, face to face. No big deal, just we're sick of looking at him. Now get up from there." He clamped his hand on Hall's arm and yanked him to his feet. "We'll need a torch. He always pitches his tent way across camp, the freak."

"He's not a freak, Ned," Collins objected.

"Call him what you want to, John, in my book, a sodomite's a freak."

"Ned—"

"Shut up, John. Hugh, get up and grab a torch."

Hall obeyed reluctantly. He took one of the torches from the bow of the boat and held the flame over his head. In the dim light from the torch he watched Craddock quaff the rest of his whiskey and heave the empty bottle into the darkness. They listened to the invisible bottle plop into the water, then Hall and Craddock left the boat.

They meandered slowly through the woods, among the dying campfires, out into a clearing, beyond the grove where the horses were tied. "That's his tent," Craddock pointed. They were looking at a place right at the edge of the tree line. "His lantern's still on— maybe he's up waiting for us, Hugh," Ned teased him.

But Hugh wasn't in the swing of this particular antic. "Ned," he begged, "let's go back. I don't want to do this."

"Damn it, Hugh. I don't want to hear any more, all right? All I want's a few words with this joker, that's all."

"Ned, I've got a headache, maybe we should go back to camp."

"All you've got to do is hold the torch, Hugh. Is that so hard? I'll do the rest."

"He's probably asleep, Ned."

"I don't care if he is asleep. I want to talk to him, so I'll wake him up."

Craddock started off, looked back at Hugh.

"Come on, Hall," he ordered. "Unless you want that fire stuck up your butt."

Hall hesitated, then joined Craddock, and the two men moved stealthily across the clearing, toward the tent. The night had cooled off some, but it was still warm enough for Craddock to sweat. He wiped his face with a handkerchief and stuffed it back into his pocket.

Thirty feet from Roxanna's tent, Hall pulled up. Craddock took three steps further, then turned around. "Now what?" he groaned impatiently.

"I'm not going, Ned."

"Your gut must be made of mush, Hugh. Come on."

But Hall was firm. "No," he insisted. "Go on without me. I'm not going."

"All right, don't go," Ned sighed wearily. "Stay here. I'll rouse him up myself." He stepped lightly through the tall grass toward the tent, lit up by a dim lantern within. He was almost sober now, but light-headed enough to be bolder than usual. He came to the closed doorway of the tent and was just about to go in, when he heard a snap behind him, the sound of a dry twig cracking under a foot. He turned around slowly.

There was nothing in front of him but darkness, and Hall, thirty feet away, standing stiffly under the torchlight. Craddock held his breath and waited for a minute. He heard no sound except the roar of the river. He sighed, satisfied that there was nothing to worry about, and grasped the folds of the doorway between his fingers. . . .

"Craddock!" called a voice behind him.

The abrupt sound sent an icy shock through his body. He spun around, but saw nothing but blackness again. He waited breathless as he heard another twig break, then the rustle of grass. Suddenly, out of the dark, a giant figure appeared, a monstrous shape partially cloaked in buffalo robe: Buck Brussard. Craddock felt his whole body shiver.

"Draw your knife, Craddock!" the mountainman said coldly, taking a step closer.

"Get out of here, Brussard!" Craddock growled. "This is none of your business."

"Draw your knife," he repeated.

"Draw your own knife," Craddock mocked him. "Go fight a bear. We don't hanker after your kind around here."

Brussard was unruffled. He stared straight at him. "You're on my turf, Craddock. I ought to slit your throat without saying a word. But since I've heard so much about you, I'm going to give you a chance to fight."

"I'm not fighting you, Brussard. This isn't your turf. You don't own anything out here."

Craddock saw the torch move, come bumping his way. "Ned!" Hall cried out, puffing. He pulled to a sharp stop five feet away. "I didn't see him," he admitted. "He slipped past me."

"Hugh, go get my gun. It's on my locker. Hurry!"

"He's got a rifle on his back, Ned."

"I don't care what he's got. Do what I say—go get my gun. Get me something to kill this bastard with, once and for all."

"Why don't you kill me with your knife, Craddock," Brussard suggested. "I heard that was your trademark."

"I don't fight with knives," Craddock replied.

Brussard began walking toward him. "That's not what I heard. I heard you used a knife on a Frenchman back in St. Charles." He wiped his palm across the front of his buckskin shirt. Craddock paled. Someone at the card game that night had betrayed him. Was it Collins? Or that upstart Wentworth—who had saved St. Croix from suicide?

"You heard wrong," Craddock growled. "I don't believe in fighting with knives or anything else. Ask Hugh there, he'll tell you."

Brussard flashed his white teeth in his beard as he

unsheathed his sixteen-inch, bone-handled hunting knife. "That don't matter, Craddock," he insisted, coming still closer. " 'Long as I believe in it, that's all that matters."

Craddock was no longer drunk. His mind was sharp now, he was acutely aware of what was happening. He knew that he was in the middle of a situation he couldn't control and it terrified him. "Look, Brussard," he spoke in a shaky, raspy voice, "I'm not bothering you, so why don't we just forget it? I just strayed off the path here, all right? No harm done. I'll go back to bed."

"Hey, Craddock!" someone yelled. "What're you doing, backing down?"

Ned nervously glanced around at the voice. His heart sank when he saw that several of the men had gathered around to see what was going on.

"Show him who's boss, Ned!" another of the men called out. "Don't let him talk to you like that!"

"Watch that knife, Ned, he's mean with it," a third man warned him.

Craddock recognized this last voice; it belonged to his friend William Werner. He took heart—maybe Werner would help him.

"William!" Craddock called out. "This bastard's gone crazy. Shoot him!"

"Stand up to him, Ned!" Werner responded.

"William, damn it!" Craddock could feel cold sweat dripping down his neck as Brussard came closer. He wiped off his forehead with his sleeve, but it didn't help. Pouring down his face now was the sweat of fear, not heat.

As the mountainman slowly drew to within a few feet of him, Craddock knew he had to act quickly. As he reluctantly slipped out his knife, an idea came to him. Brussard was such a large target, lumbering toward him, maybe he could stop him before he had a chance to attack. He held his knife by the blade, waited until Brussard was six feet away, then he swiftly cocked his arm and with all his strength flung the knife toward the man's heart.

He missed. The blade caromed off Brussard's left shoulder and disappeared into the tall grass. Now Craddock was defenseless against the mountainman. And Brussard was so close that Craddock could see his terrible black eyes, burning like the eyes of some huge animal stalking its prey.

"Hugh!" he called out frantically, not daring to take his eyes off Brussard. "Damn it, Hugh, where are you?" Craddock stole a quick glance around. It looked as if the whole camp was out now, watching him. Without a weapon, he had only one chance. He knew they would call him a coward for doing it, but at least he would be alive. . . .

In a frenzy, he bolted toward the woods. After a few steps he felt confident again, but then his boot banged up against a hidden tree stump. He stumbled and fell over into the grass. Craddock sprang quickly to his feet, but his motion was blunted abruptly by a crushing blow. A hard fist smashed into his chest. He staggered back, reeling from the impact, and tried to get away. A massive arm crooked tightly around his throat. And suddenly Craddock was being dragged violently over the ground. A minute later, Brussard was slinging his victim down to his knees. Grabbing a handful of hair, Brussard yanked back the head of the cowering man.

The long blade of Brussard's knife felt cool against Craddock's throat. He tried not to breathe. Just one slip, one cough and his own blood would be warming that cold steel.

The men reacted to the scene with alarm. "Hey, let him go, Brussard!" one of them hollered.

The others called out to him the same thing, as if only now believing what Brussard was about to do. "All right, man," Werner yelled. "He's had enough! Turn him loose!"

Buck Brussard acted as if he didn't hear them. He

pressed his bearded chin against Craddock's head and pushed the blade tighter against the skin. "How would you like it, Craddock?" he whispered. "You want it across the throat, or over the scalp? Which way would your friends prefer?"

Craddock was too scared to speak. He could only manage a few gutteral croaks from deep in his throat.

Brussard wasn't really interested in how Craddock answered his question, though. He knew what he was going to do. He brought the gleaming blade up in front of Craddock's face and laid its sharp edge on his forehead, at the hairline. He breathed heavily against Craddock's back. "All I have to do," Brussard panted, "is tilt 'er like this. Once the skin's broken, your scalp'll peel off your skull like a onion skin."

Panicked, Craddock suddenly grunted and struggled to get loose, but Brussard was too strong; he slapped Craddock's head roughly back against his own chest and held it there. "Be still, Ned," he ordered him. "I'm not through with you yet. This'll only take a second. A slice and a jerk and it's all over."

"Buck, don't do it," Craddock gulped. "For God's sake, man, I don't want to die!"

"Well, you're just one swipe away from dying, Craddock. Think about that."

"Please, don't," he whispered meekly, for only Brussard to hear.

Brussard grinned. "What's that, Craddock? What'd you say?"

"Please—don't kill me," Craddock begged.

"One more time, for your buddies out there."

"Please!" Craddock screamed.

Brussard let out a big belly laugh, released Craddock's hair, and drew back the knife. As he stood up, he ceremoniously sheathed it and looked down at the man on his knees. "From now on, Craddock," he warned, "you watch where I am. Watch where I am all the time."

Then as quickly as he had appeared, he vanished

into the dark woods. As soon as he was gone, the men hurried around Craddock. Werner reached down to help him up, but Craddock knocked his hand away. "Leave me alone, I don't need any help."

"Are you all right, Ned?" Werner asked.

"Yeah I'm all right, why shouldn't I be?" he snapped back, getting to his feet. "I guess now you'll believe he's a red savage." He searched through the faces of the men. "Where's Hugh?"

Werner shrugged his shoulders. "I haven't seen him, Ned."

Craddock made a show of brushing the dirt off his clothes. "Look at that," he stared back at Roxanna, who was standing outside her tent, watching them. "He never even bothered to step in and stop it," he complained. "Freak!" He gestured obscenely in her direction.

"Hey, come on, Ned, you know it wasn't Garcia's fault," William Werner protested. "All he was doing was sleeping."

"Look at him," Craddock pointed, ignoring Werner's words. "Just standing there, taking it all in."

"Here comes Hugh," one of the men announced. "You men better straighten up; he's got Ordway and Pryor with him."

Moments later, the three men came up to the group, Hugh still carrying the keelboat torch. "Are you all right, Ned?" Hall asked him.

"I wish everybody would stop asking me that," he bellowed. "I'm fine, there's not a thing wrong with me, all right?"

"I was scared there for a minute."

"Yeah, well, you didn't have to be; the big ape wasn't going to do anything." Craddock was trying to save face, but he suspected it wasn't going to work. Not now. The men had seen too much. They had seen him run, they all knew he was a coward.

"What happened to Buck Brussard?" Hugh asked.

"I don't know, he took off into the woods, I

guess. I don't care what happened to him. All I want to do is go get in my bed and sleep."

He started to go, but John Ordway stepped out in front of him. "I'm afraid you won't be doing that tonight."

Craddock looked at the top sergeant. He didn't like Ordway because of a run-in they had had back at Camp du Bois. "What do you mean by that?" he asked him.

"I mean you're going back to camp with me, Private Craddock. You're under arrest."

"Under arrest! For what? For defending myself against the heathen?"

"For stealing whiskey from the keelboat."

"Stealing whiskey!" Craddock feigned surprise. "What kind of trumped-up charge is that? I haven't been anywhere near that keelboat. Ask Hugh Hall, he's been with me all night."

Ordway ignored his protests. "Come with me, Craddock," he ordered. "Captain Clark already knows about it. He's talking to John Collins now. We've got a court-martial set for first thing in the morning."

Ordway took his arm, Craddock looked over at Hall. "You keep your mouth shut, Hall, you hear me? I don't want you telling Clark and Ordway lies."

"He won't be doing that, Ned," Ordway commented. "Private Hall's on trial, too. We know all about it."

Craddock twisted his arm loose, looked defiantly into Ordway's eyes. "You think because you're a sergeant and make eight dollars a month to my five, you're a better man than I am?"

"I don't think anything of the sort, Ned. I'm just doing my job. Let's go."

Craddock felt his right arm snatched by Ordway, his left by Pryor, the other sergeant. As they tugged him away, he shot Hall a venemous look. "You heard what I said, Hall," he scowled. "One word out of you, and you're a dead man."

He spit out the threat with the same harsh, ominous tone as usual, but the words now had a hollow, weak sound to them. They had lost their power. They were nothing but air to the other men.

And he knew why: a few minutes ago, he had shamed himself in their eyes.

Chapter 7

"I'm telling you the truth," Tom insisted. "An Indian warrior stood right here on deck, right where you're sitting, and looked down at me. It sent chills up my spine."

Roxanna could not help smiling at his words. Since first light that morning, she had been sitting by his pallet on the keelboat. Though the cotton cloth was nearby in a bucket of cool water, she didn't need to press it to his forehead any more. The fever was broken. His features were pale and drawn, almost grey, but the glazed expression had vanished from his eyes and the perspiration had dried from his forehead. And he was talking, making sense at last!

"It was only a dream, Tom," she answered him gently.

"No, it wasn't a dream," he asserted. "It was real. He was about five-feet-six, bare-chested, except for a string of yellow beads around his neck, and he was wearing a thin breechcloth and muddy moccasins."

"I doubt if Indians can come and go around here without anybody knowing it." Roxanna smiled at him, but her emotions were being pulled in another direction, even as she tended to him. She had been saddened by what she had heard at the court-martial a while ago. Hugh Hall and Ned Craddock were going to be publicly whipped. The sergeants were considering John Collins' case now.

"That could've been a Sioux warrior," Tom suggested, rising up. "Are we in Sioux country yet?"

"Not yet," she answered, pushing him down. "Now don't get up, Tom. You're still sick."

"I'm not sick, I feel fine."

"I don't believe you. People with a fever don't feel fine. You're going to have to stay put until the fever goes down."

"You're an awfully bossy Spaniard, Garcia," he pointed out.

"Be still. You're just not strong enough to get up yet. Besides—" She was about to say something else when she heard Captain Lewis return to the boat. He walked over and smiled down at Tom.

"You're looking better than you did an hour ago," he greeted cheerfully.

"I'm fine, captain, really. It's just that Roxanna is treating me like a prisoner."

"Well, she has the final word on your condition, Tom. She's the one who pulled you through. We're relying on her to tell us when you're well."

Roxanna looked up at him. "How is the court-martial going, captain?"

"It's over, Roxanna. That's why I'm here."

She knew what he meant. "Captain Lewis, I don't want to see it."

He shook his head and his tone was cold. "I'm sorry. All members of the expedition are obliged to witness punishment."

Roxanna began to protest, then pursed her lips. The implication was clear. She had chosen to come on the expedition and now she had no alternative but to accept the captain's decision. She had to witness punishment, even if her personal feelings ran against it; she had no right to protest.

A few minutes later Roxanna left the boat and walked with Lewis through the trees to the designated punishment area near the clearing. Captain Clark was there already, standing alone, rocking nervously back and forth on his heels, with his hands behind his back. They joined him and silently waited for one of the sergeants to bring John Collins forward.

Roxanna began to feel very uncomfortable when Sergeant Nat Pryor and Collins moved past them on the way to the oak tree twenty feet away. When she saw someone binding Collins' wrists to a stake in the tree, she couldn't keep still any longer. "Captain Clark!" she spoke anxiously. "Can't you do something to stop this?"

"What do you mean?" He looked at her grimly.

"This . . . cruelty. You're not actually going to let them beat him, are you?"

"I can't do anything about it, Mrs. Fairchild." He looked straight ahead; his face was rigid, his expression blank. "This was the court-martial's decision."

"But to give a man a hundred lashes just for being drunk—"

"That's enough, Mrs. Fairchild," Clark silenced her. "John Collins was drunk on the watch, which is a very serious offense."

"But a hundred lashes!"

Clark turned on her. "We don't have a police force out here, Mrs. Fairchild. We have to depend on the watch to keep us alive. When a sentry gets himself drunk, he puts all in jeopardy."

"Yes, but surely you agree to beat him publicly is inhuman?" she persisted. "Nobody in New Orleans is flogged in public—"

"You have jails in New Orleans," Clark countered. "On this expedition we don't have the luxury of locking up our offenders. If this mission is to succeed, Mrs. Fairchild, every man will have to do the job he was recruited for. But none of us can do our jobs if we're wondering if someone's going to slip past a drunk sentry and cut our throats while we sleep."

Roxanna said nothing. She could see she wasn't going to change Captain Clark's mind about anything. She turned away from him and looked at the fifty men who had dutifully gathered to watch the beatings. They were standing in a large semi-circle, gathered around the tree. Each face was grim, frozen in a kind of sad, distant stare. They seemed to stiffen as a dark-haired man in buckskins stepped up. In response to Pryor's command, the man unrolled a lash of knotted rawhide and began systematically popping it across Collins' bare back. The men watched his motions closely, transfixed, mesmerized by the swoop of the leather up through the air and down across Collins' white skin.

Roxanna was repulsed. She could hardly stand to watch. After twenty whacks of the lash, the relentless beating of rawhide had drawn crimson tracks all over Collins' exposed body. After forty, the red marks began to deepen and look like a network of bloody ravines. By the time the counter had droned out, "Eighty-one. . . . Eighty-two. . . . Eighty-three . . . ," Collins' body was wet and limp. His knees wobbled. Then, with a loud sigh, he dropped to the ground and passed out.

The lashing continued: "Eighty-four. . . . Eighty-five. . . ."

"Captain Clark!" Roxanna implored. "For God's sake, he's killing him!"

Clark stood fast, pretended not to hear her. It was his duty not to be affected by the spectacle. Though he couldn't show it, he despised any kind of corporal punishment. Even now, watching one of his men being whipped, he felt each lash as if it were being laid across his own back. But he had to appear firm, strong and disinterested if he were to maintain order among fifty potentially rebellious and dangerous men.

"Eighty-seven . . . Eighty-eight . . . ," the counter rang out.

Roxanna felt such an aversion to the beating that she had to turn her head away. But then the monotonous sounding of numbers and the cruel, squishing sound of leather slapping against bloody skin now became louder, almost deafening to her. "Ninety!" the counter seemed to shout. "Ninety-one!" She closed her eyes.

The lashing seemed to go on for another hour. Finally the counter cried, "One hundred!" It was over. Roxanna looked up to see Sergeant Pryor whip out his knife and cut Collins down from the tree. Pryor and two others lifted the punished man up and began to carry him off. As they dragged his unconscious body past the captains, Roxanna felt pity for the beaten man. And she felt anger at everyone else for allowing such a thing to happen.

Meanwhile Sergeant John Ordway and Private Patrick Gass were waiting with Ned Craddock at the white pirogue on the river. Gass was nervously flicking his hunting knife up into the air, watching it stick up in the ground, and picking it up again, when he happened to notice a curl of white smoke rising up over the trees a few miles off. He put up his knife, studied it for a few minutes, then asked Ordway, "John, who do you reckon that is? Think it could be Tetons?"

Ordway had already seen the smoke. "Not this far down, Pat. Trappers maybe, or Omahas."

"No, I don't think so. I've had this feeling all morning, somebody's been watching us, John. You remember when we were in the First, back at Kaskaskia, that Ottawa camp we stumbled on? I had the same feeling then, remember?"

Ordway nodded. "Yeah, I remember. If the captain had listened to you then, John Milnor'd still be alive today."

"Well, I don't blame the captain for that. Who's going to listen to a private, anyway?"

"Nobody, I guess," Ordway admitted. "But then

you're not always going to be a private, Patrick. Who knows? Maybe you'll be an author. You keep filling that journal of yours up, and who knows?"

"Right now all I'm concerned about is that smoke, John."

Ned Craddock spit on the ground. He'd had enough. "All right, Ordway," he grumbled. "I may have to stand here and wait for my whipping, but nobody says I have to listen to you two jaybirds squawking over a bunch of smoke. Why don't you shut up, both of you."

"Somebody ought to know about that smoke, Ned," Gass advised. "I have a feeling it's important."

"Well, I don't happen to see how some red savage's campfire's so important, Gass, so save it, all right?"

Gass bristled, gnashed his teeth. "Sometimes, Ned, I think you deserve just what you're going to get today."

"Do you, now. So the little Irish fella's a judge now, is he?" Craddock's voice turned nasty. "Go back home to Pennsylvania, Gass, I think you left your brains cooking in a pot on the stove."

"You're always trying to stir up trouble, Ned," Ordway remarked. "Why don't you just take your punishment like a man, like Collins and Hall, and just straighten up for a change."

Craddock stifled his response when he saw Buck Brussard walking their way. Just seeing the mountainman sent an uncontrollable rage through him. For a second, all he wanted to do was kill him. He jumped on Gass, tried to tear his pistol from his belt, but Gass reacted sharply, knocking his hand aside. Ordway quickly pounced on Craddock and pinned his arms back.

"Tie his hands, Pat!" Ordway commanded.

"Be still, Ned!" Gass grunted, reaching for a rope.

"Leave me alone, Ordway. Let me go."

"We're going to have to tie you up, Ned," he told him.

"Gass, damn you, don't you touch me. . . ."

But Gass managed to bind Craddock's hands together as Ordway held them, and the sergeant was able to release him. He and Gass eased back and watched Craddock apprehensively for a moment. They relaxed when it appeared that he was calm and in control of himself again.

"Well, good morning, men," Brussard greeted cheerfully, coming up to them. "Nice day for a beating, ain't it, Ned?"

"You son of a bitch—" he started for Brussard, but Ordway held him back.

Buck grinned broadly. "Why don't you go ahead and cut 'im loose, sergeant," he suggested. "I'd be glad to kill 'im for you. Save you the trouble of a flogging."

"I'm going to get you alone some day, Brussard," Craddock vowed. "And when I do, you're a dead man."

"Patrick," Ordway commanded, "go ahead and take Ned to the tree. I'll be there in a minute."

Gass touched Craddock's shoulder and Ned kicked viciously at him with his boot. "Get your hands off me," he snapped.

"Well then, come on," Gass said. "Unless you want us to carry you."

"I'm coming," Craddock snarled. He paused to glare at Brussard. "Some day, mountainman. . . ."

"Ornery fella, ain't 'e?" Brussard asked Ordway. "That's what I like about these things, sergeant. You learn a lot about folks, watching them being beaten. Take Ned there, for instance. He's acting just like the coward he is, ain't 'e? Mad at everybody because he's nothing."

Ordway nodded, watched them move toward the other men. When Craddock was a safe distance away, the sergeant broached the subject of the campfire to

Brussard. "We were talking about that smoke up in the hills. Patrick's been worrying about it."

Brussard didn't bother to look. "Don't know why he'd be worried, sergeant. Nobody seems worried about them two Teton bucks that's been following us for three days."

"Two Teton warriors! Are you sure?"

"Yeah, I'm sure. I know a Teton Sioux when I see one. So I reckon with them two bucks hanging close, you don't need to worry about a little smoke, do you?"

"I knew it! Someday I'll learn—Patrick's instinct about things like this is never wrong." He looked up at the swirling smoke. "What do you think they want?" he asked.

"All they want to do is watch, sergeant. And wait. They got the river locked up where they're sitting, so they're curious about who's headed their way."

"I guess I ought to tell the captains about those Teton warriors."

"They know about 'em already. They're keeping an eye out. I don't reckon there's anything to get worked up over. Not yet, anyway."

"Well, it still makes me shiver, thinking of some Sioux war party following us and watching us all the time."

As Ordway and Brussard were talking, Craddock was walking slowly ahead of Patrick Gass in the direction of the fifty men congregated around the flogging tree. On the way he paused in front of Roxanna, who was sandwiched between Lewis and Clark. He stared at her accusingly, made her lower her head and keep her eyes glued to the ground. "You freak," he maligned her. "You're the cause of this." Roxanna almost blurted out a response, but she caught herself in time.

"Go on, Ned," Gass pushed his back.

Craddock scowled but said nothing. At the oak tree two other men peeled off his shirt and stood back and waited at attention for Ordway to arrive. Gass took two strings of rope out of his pocket and tied Craddock's wrists to the stake.

"The captains are watching, Craddock," he whispered behind Ned's ear. "Try to take it like a man."

"Untie me, coward. I'll show you who's a man."

Gass shrugged his shoulders and backed off.

A few minutes later Ordway was standing erect in front of the men, announcing the sentence to the captains. He stated that Craddock was to receive fifty lashes for stealing whiskey from the keelboat, the same as Hugh Hall had gotten earlier.

Craddock felt a chill grip his body when he heard the sentence. He'd seen floggings before, but he hadn't paid much attention to them. Now, it seemed like a terrible thing to do to a person. He closed his eyes, gritted his teeth, and waited.

The first few lashes across his lower back merely stung, but then suddenly they became very painful. Craddock wrenched his back around to divert the blows, but moving only made it hurt more. Soon the leather was cutting into his flesh, and he could feel his skin opening up, becoming drenched with blood. As each lash struck his body, his anger increased.

By the time the count reached twenty strokes, Craddock couldn't restrain himself any more. He shouted, "Stop it! That's enough, damn it!" But no one seemed to hear. The blows kept coming, each one more painful than the last. "Stop it!" he yelled. "Hit me one more time and I'll kill you, you bastard!"

And still the leather popped.

The men stood silently around him. But each man, to himself, compared the valiant way Collins and Hall had taken their punishment to the way Craddock was now losing control and becoming enraged. He jerked madly at the ropes that bound him, kicking wildly at the tree trunk, twisting his body, yelling obscenities at the tormentor he could not see.

Meanwhile the counter tolled out the numbers: "Thirty-nine. . . . Forty. . . ."

"Stop it!" Craddock screamed. "What do you want? I'll pay you—"

"Forty-one. . . . Forty-two. . . ."

"No! Don't do it any more—please!"

"Forty-three. . . . Forty-four."

At the count of forty-five, Craddock let out a terrible shriek of pain and buckled under. The next thing he knew Ordway was cutting his ropes and he was crumbling to the ground. He looked up at the sergeant through bleary eyes. "I'll get you for this," he vowed. "I'll get all of you. Every last one of you."

Then he passed out.

After the flogging, there was a marked change in Ned Craddock's behavior. He began to keep to himself, to say almost nothing to anyone, to turn down card games. He didn't even drink much. Some of the men decided among themselves that at long last Private Ned Craddock had finally been set straight. Others were more apprehensive about it. They watched him staring blankly ahead as he pulled an oar on the pirogue, or trimmed a sail on the keelboat, and wondered if perhaps he wasn't merely sitting back and waiting for his chance—to get even.

But as the expedition gradually moved closer to Teton Sioux country, they paid him very little attention. Each man began to do his work with particular care, with an eye out for a Teton warrior and an ear tuned to the strange animal cries of the invisible war parties which followed the boats from the shore line.

"We can't let the Sioux bully us the way they do the French and Spanish," Captain Lewis told Tom Wentworth one evening. They were drinking whiskey after supper, around Wentworth's fire. "We've got to show the Sioux that Americans mean business. We have to get through their lock on the river and reach the Mandan village by late fall."

"What's so special about the Mandans, captain?" Tom asked. He stretched out his aching leg. He was well now, but he still had some pain in his knee. "Are they supposed to be rich? They say back in Philadelphia some of these tribes out here drink water out of goblets made of gold."

"Maybe some of them do. But not the Mandans. They're as poor as most other Indians. The point is, Tom, the British traders around Lake Winnipeg have a monopoly going with the Mandans, and it's the British grip on the American Indians that Mr. Jefferson is trying to break. It's important to undermine British support of Tecumseh in the Indiana Territory, but here it's more than important—it's vital. If we're going to lay claim to the Louisiana Territory for the United States, we first have to establish contact with the Mandans."

"And the Sioux are blocking us from the Mandans."

Lewis nodded, took a drink of whiskey. "I'm not saying this to the other men, but our whole domestic and foreign policy is at stake here, Tom. Either we control the territorial United States here and now, or what Napoleon feared would happen will—the British will have eight hundred and thirty thousand square miles of land next door to us. We can't let that happen. The future of the country depends on our controlling the commerce of the rivers of the west."

"But the Teton Sioux are only one tribe," Tom observed.

"That's true, they are," Lewis agreed. "But they're the strongest river pirates on the Missouri. Buck Brussard tells me all the other tribes are waiting to see how they handle us. He claims if we can control the Sioux, most of the others will lie down for us all the way to the Pacific."

"So we use what Mr. Reeve back at law school used to call an *argumentum baculinum,* an 'argument of force.'"

"We'll use force, diplomacy, trickery—anything we have to use to lay our claim to this land and make the Missouri safe for American trade."

"Then my father was right," Tom mused. "This is a lot more than a trip to explore the West."

Lewis smiled. "It's that, too. In fact, by the time we reach the Mandans, we should have enough plant and animal specimens to send one of the pirogues back to Mr. Jefferson. You can be sure with his curious mind, he's pacing the floor, waiting to hear from us."

Tom took a drink of whiskey. "Captain—" he said thoughtfully. "What about Roxanna? Couldn't you send her back on the pirogue when we reach the Mandans?"

"Well, yes, I could do that, but I'm not sure I should. She's pulling her weight."

"Yes, but someday somebody's going to find out—"

"We'll worry about that when it happens, Tom. Right now why don't you concentrate on the Tetons? Stop thinking about Roxanna Fairchild."

"Oh I try, believe me," Tom sighed. "But sometimes, just the thought of her almost drives me crazy. And I find myself thinking about her more and more."

"She's a married woman, Tom," he reminded him. "And I believe you're still engaged to Miss Radcliffe—"

"I know," Tom interrupted. "That's the part that's driving me crazy."

Lewis laughed, but then snatched up his gun as a short, dark man in buckskins stepped out of the darkness into the circle of light made by the campfire. But he relaxed when he recognized the man. It was Patrick Gass, wearing a pained, worried expression on his face. "Captain," he spoke softly. "Excuse me."

"Private Gass, don't you know better than to sneak up on people? What is it?"

"I'm sorry, sir, Captain Clark sent me to get you. It's Sergeant Floyd, he's taken a turn for the worse.

They got him over at Captain Clark's tent, tending to him, but he looks real bad to me. Like he's about to go, any minute."

Lewis stood up. "I hoped he was getting better."

"He was better this morning, sir," Gass explained. "He just got worse all of a sudden."

"All right, look. I want you to go find Garcia and bring him to the tent. He's the best nurse we have around here. He pulled Wentworth through, maybe he can help Floyd."

"Yes sir."

"And get the mountainman too. I don't know if it'll do any good, but it's possible he knows an Indian remedy or something."

"Yes sir. Where'll I find him?"

"Just start looking for him. He'll find you."

A few minutes later Captain Lewis and Tom Wentworth entered the tent. Charles Floyd was lying on Clark's cot, sweating and writhing under a fever. Lewis stepped over and looked down at him. "Still got that pain in your belly, Charles?" he inquired, trying to calm him down a little.

Floyd held his stomach with his hands. "I hate to be a bother, captain. I thought I had it beat. I guess I didn't."

"Well, stay with it, sergeant," Lewis said. "Maybe we can get you some relief."

Clark took Lewis aside. "I gave him some laudanum this morning, but it's worn off. He's in pain, but I thought he should be aware of what was happening to him when the end came."

Lewis nodded. "Then you don't think he'll make it."

Clark shook his head. "I don't think so." He went over to the cot and knelt down next to Floyd, propped up his head to give him a drink of water. But as soon as his lips touched the liquid, Floyd jumped back and gripped his stomach tightly with both hands. "Oh— God!" he groaned.

The pain got worse in the next quarter hour and all the men could do was to stand by and watch him twist and turn on the cot, moaning incoherently, gripping tightly the leather bag Clark had given him to hold onto. By the time Gass brought Roxanna into the tent, Floyd was desperately ill, sinking fast.

Roxanna didn't even notice who else was there. She went straight to the cot and dropped to her knees beside the patient. While Lewis, Clark, Wentworth and Gass looked on, she lifted the blanket and examined his naked stomach. She touched it lightly, and Floyd flinched, stifling a scream. He reached out and grabbed her hand and clenched it with all his strength.

Grimacing, he blew through his teeth. "This pain's terrible," he whispered to her. "Please, get me something to kill the pain."

At that point Buck Brussard entered the tent. He glanced over at Floyd, then faced Captain Lewis. "What'd you call me for, cap'n?" he asked him. "Look at the man's face. Anybody can see he's got both knees in the grave."

Floyd looked up at Roxanna. "Couldn't you please do something to get rid of this pain?" he pleaded.

Before Roxanna realized it, her pity for Floyd broke through her silence. "I can't," she apologized in her soft, feminine voice. "There's nothing I can do."

As soon as Floyd heard her voice, a puzzled look crossed his face. He almost smiled as he motioned to Roxanna to bend closer to him. With difficulty he reached up and yanked off her hat. Her dark hair was let loose and fell freely about her shoulders. "I knew it," he proclaimed.

"Damn!" Gass blurted out. "Look at that! Garcia's a woman!"

Roxanna didn't hear Gass. She gently touched Floyd's face, looked at him with pity in her eyes.

"There's nothing I can do for you, sergeant. I'd give anything I have to help you, but I can't."

"There is something you can do," he managed to say. "If . . . you would."

"Anything. Just name it."

"Well, ma'am," he murmured, "it has been a long winter and summer—" his voice was cut off as his body convulsed through a series of painful spasms. A few minutes later he gasped, caught his breath, and continued. "What I meant was, could you . . . kiss me? Just once?"

She smiled, wiped a tear from her eye. "Of course I could," she replied. "I'd love to kiss you." She leaned over him, took his face in her hands, and touched her lips to his. His skin felt cold and clammy to the touch, but it didn't bother her.

When she had pulled away, Floyd swallowed hard, then held himself in check as another wave of pain swept over his lower abdomen. Then, catching his breath, he asked her, "What's your name?"

"Roxanna," she answered.

"Roxanna," he repeated. "I like that. It's . . . poetic. You're a beautiful woman, Roxanna."

She smiled tearfully again and brought his right hand up to her bosom. She felt the easy pressure of his fingers grasping weakly through the cloth binding, then felt a sudden violent grip on her breast as his body arched up into the air. This last convulsion was a death blow to him. Suddenly his face turned a bluish color, his eyes became dilated and dazed. He emitted one last terrible groan and sank back onto the cot, at peace at last.

Roxanna had to pry his dead hand off her breast. She looked at him for a while, then took a deep, halting breath and cried for him. After a minute she collected herself, stood up and turned around. The men in the tent were staring at her, as silent and still as statues. She reached down for her hat. "He was too far gone," she intoned.

"Roxanna," Clark whispered, "thank you." It was the first time he had called her by her first name.

But Roxanna didn't notice. Her mind was totally on the man, a stranger to her, who had just died. "Thank me for what?" she asked, looking back at the body. "I couldn't do anything to help him. What good was I?"

"You're wrong about that," he corrected her. "You did a great deal for him. More than any man could do."

She nodded, understanding what he meant. "He seemed like a very nice man," she murmured.

"He was," Clark agreed.

Roxanna nodded helplessly again, then without another word, she left the tent.

There was a continued, heavy silence around the cot for a while, until Clark covered Floyd's head with the blanket. "Roxanna's a tougher woman than I thought," he admitted to Lewis. "I'm glad she was here, to give him some comfort. The kind only a woman can give."

Private Gass was relieved that the subject had finally been introduced. He took the occasion to ask excitedly, "Did *you* know she was a woman, Captain Clark?"

Clark stared at him coolly for a few moments. "Private Gass, I want you to forget what you just saw. Pretend you never saw it. It never happened. All you know is Sergeant Charles Floyd is dead of a stomach ailment."

"But sir—"

"Gass, you're a good woodsman and a good carpenter. They tell me you've also won the respect of the other men. I think it's pretty safe to say they would want you to take Charles Floyd's place as sergeant."

"Me, sir?"

"Sergeant Ordway says you can handle responsibility. He says you can be trusted with confidential information."

Gass caught his meaning. "Oh—I see," he comprehended. "You mean if I don't stir up things by telling folks Garcia is a woman, you'll make me sergeant—"

"I didn't say that. That's blackmail. What I will say, though, is I wouldn't want a man as sergeant who couldn't keep his counsel."

Gass thought it over and nodded his agreement. "What about him?" he nodded toward the mountainman. Brussard was standing with his arms crossed, watching him.

"Brussard knows about it already," Clark explained.

"Well, I'll be. There was a little conspiracy going on here all the time. I had a feeling something strange was going on around here—"

"That's enough, Gass."

"Yes sir. I'm sorry, captain. Look, I promise you I'm not going to cause any trouble. I won't tell a soul. But who on earth is the woman? And what's she doing on this expedition?"

"I don't see how that would matter to you," Clark answered.

"Well now, the man has a point here, cap'n," Brussard broke in. "I figure it's about time I found out who the lady is, too. That is, unless you're planning on making me a sergeant, too."

Captain Lewis looked at Clark for a moment, read the expression on his face. Then he looked back at Brussard. "Her name is Roxanna Fairchild," Lewis told him.

"Fairchild!" Brussard exclaimed.

"You know the name?"

"Nah," Brussard replied quickly. "I don't know it. Just sounded kind of funny. Tell me, cap'n, what's a fine looking woman like her doing traipsing around in the woods with fifty strong men—every one of 'em hungry for some taste of her kind."

"She's looking for her husband. He was in New

Orleans the last time she saw him, but she's heard he's out here somewhere."

"Well, I'll be damned," Brussard declared.

Lewis looked at the mountainman quizzically. He thought he saw a flash of recognition on his face. "What do you know about this, Buck?" he asked him.

"Hey, cap'n, I don't know a thing about it. All I know is what you military men tell me. Well, look, I don't want to spoil your wake here, but I was cutting up a hide when this little fella came after me. I'll see you men in the morning."

After he and Gass were gone, Lewis looked at Clark. "There's something strange here, William. I'm sure Brussard recognized Roxanna's name when I said it. Could that be?"

"With Buck Brussard, anything's possible," Clark admitted. "Your friend's a mysterious man."

Chapter 8

A few weeks later, the expedition had reached the mouth of the Teton River. After some consultation, Lewis and Clark ordered a keelboat and one of the pirogues to anchor about seventy yards offshore. Just before dawn, six men climbed into the other pirogue with enough poles and canvas to set up a lean-to on shore. Representing the expedition were Lewis, Clark, Drewyer, Brussard, Gass and the French interpreter Pierre Dorion. The men on the anchored craft were all awake, watching as the pirogue pulled toward shore. They avoided each other's eyes. All knew that the fate of the expedition rested in the hands and ingenuity of that small group of envoys pulling slowly toward the dark embankment.

In the dim predawn light, the pirogue pulled up to a sandbar and Captain Clark leapt out of the bow. He pulled the boat up on the sand and the other men followed, clutching their rifles tightly. Captain Lewis kept his air gun trained on the shore as the others set about erecting the lean-to. When the first rays of the sun crested the low rise beyond the river, the men were standing under the canvas with an American flag planted deeply in the sandbar.

And the Sioux were there. More than a hundred warriors lined the shore. All had their bows unstrung, but it would only take a signal for them to attack.

Captain Lewis tightened his grip on the barrel of his air gun as five Teton Sioux, breaking away from the group, moved lightly over the sand toward the representatives of the expedition.

Lewis allowed himself only one quick glance over his shoulder. On the boats seventy yards offshore, the men waited expectantly, every man with his rifle ready. They were able to defend themselves. But for the six men on the sandbar there would be no escape if the Indians chose to attack.

Lewis turned to face the Indians again. Buck Brussard came up alongside him and nodded toward the approaching Tetons.

"That's three chiefs coming there, cap'n," he revealed. "The two in front are young bucks along for the ride."

"Which is the grand chief?" Lewis asked.

"The tallest one, Black Buffalo. Untongarsarbar, they call 'im. The one on his right's Tartongawaker. The one next to him is the one you have to worry about, cap'n. The one with the red eyes. They call 'im Partisan."

The six men under the lean-to braced themselves for the arrival. The men on the keelboat and the other pirogue waited quietly, breathlessly following each footstep across the gray sand. Every man had his rifle nearby, in case one of the captains gave the signal to shoot.

Suddenly, the three chiefs stopped. A second later, they began to talk to each other. They laughed and pointed at the boats on the water, then at the lean-to.

"What are they doing, Buck?" Lewis asked the mountainman. "Why have they stopped?"

"It's an old Sioux trick," he answered. "They're testing us. The Sioux are big actors, cap'n. They're pretending they're on their way to supper or something and not concerned about all this business. But don't you believe it—them Teton bucks we can see around us now ain't a fourth of the number they got. And they're waiting to see what we're going to do."

"We're not afraid of them, Brussard," Clark declared.

"Well now, I'm glad to hear that, cap'n," Brussard responded. " 'Cause that's the only chance we got here. We got to pretend, too. We can't let 'em think we're even giving them a second thought. It ain't enough not to be afraid, cap'n. The Sioux make you show you ain't."

Sergeant Gass called out from behind, "Captain Lewis, do you want me to go out and meet them?"

"No, be still, sergeant. They know we've set up this awning for a council. Let's let them come to us."

"Cap'n," Brussard said to Lewis. "If you do send somebody out there, we'll all wind up being scrap for their dogs tomorrow. Wait 'em out. Make them make the moves."

The small clutch of Indians waited a few minutes longer, then mumbled something among themselves, and proceeded deliberately toward the lean-to. Each of them was smeared with bear grease, wore hawk feathers on his head, and had a buffalo robe drooped over his shoulders. They came to a stop near the flag, made a show of examining the white men's clothes and weapons. The second chief, Partisan, spoke loudly to the others for a while, nodding emphatically when one of them responded to him. Then he stepped forward and pointed at Lewis's air gun.

"Pierre?" Lewis asked the old Frenchman, keeping his eye on the Indian. "What does he want?"

Dorion took a step forward. "I think he wants you to give him your rifle, captain," he answered.

"*Give* it to him?" Lewis wondered.

"Yes sir. He expects it."

"Well, tell him to expect something else. I'm not about to turn over my rifle to him. Tell him we've brought other things for them."

"Captain, he—"

"No!" the Indian interrupted, holding up his hand. He stared at Lewis with penetrating eyes and made a gesture with his hands toward his chest. "Give," he demanded.

Lewis shook his head. "No," he answered. "This is my weapon. I can't give you my weapon."

"Give!" Partisan repeated.

Lewis stood firm while the Indian clenched his fist. His face became distorted with anger. Just as he was about to make a move toward the captain, Black Buffalo reached out, clasped Partisan's arm and shook it.

The head chief turned to Lewis. *"Kinnikinnick,"* he growled. He untied a pouch made of skunk fur from his belt. *"Kinnikinnick,"* he repeated holding out the pouch.

"He wants us to smoke the pipe with him, captain," Dorion interpreted.

Lewis nodded agreeably to Black Buffalo and watched him carefully take a pipe from one of the braves and load it with the mixture from his pouch. The eleven men then passed around the pipe and smoked it twice each, without saying a word. Lewis hated the taste of the tobacco, but he smiled diplomatically as he smoked it.

After they had finished the tobacco, and the peace-making ceremony was over, the Indians relaxed and stood ready to receive their gifts of jewelry, knives and clothes. In exchange for the white men's tribute, they brought forth great quantities of buffalo meat. Most of it was gray and rancid, smelling sickeningly of decayed flesh, but Lewis accepted the barter graciously, pretending to be grateful.

The Indians had examined their presents only a

short time when Black Buffalo announced in sign language that he wanted to visit the keelboat.

Lewis and Clark considered his request for a few minutes before deciding that they should give in to it. Lewis instructed Gass to get the pirogue ready, and the council walked down to the river. Captain Lewis was the last man off the boat. But as he set his foot on the pirogue, Partisan jumped forward from his seat and grabbed the stock of Lewis's air gun.

"Give!" he grunted, pulling at the air gun.

Lewis instinctively twisted the barrel and jerked the gun loose. The Indian glared at him with vicious eyes for a moment, then sat back down in the boat. He kept his eyes glued on Lewis's gun as the pirogue eased across the river to the keelboat. When the party climbed aboard, Partisan pretended to stumble across the deck and bumped into Lewis, almost knocking him over into the water. Lewis nearly retaliated but in the very act of raising his rifle, he restrained himself. He endured Partisan's derisive laugh silently.

Partisan was dressed in the red coat and cocked hat Clark had given him, and the costume made him bold. On the deck of the keelboat, while the other Indians watched, Partisan pulled his hat low on his forehead and began to swagger about, looking at the crew as if he were a general inspecting his troops. As he passed each man, he made obscene gestures of disapproval and ridicule for the benefit of the other Tetons. When he reached Roxanna, though, he stopped. He looked at her curiously, threw back his hat, then reached out and touched her face.

Lewis immediately took a step toward him and called out Partisan's Indian name: *"Tortohongar!"* he called out. At the sound of his own name pronounced so distinctly in the Sioux language, Partisan wheeled toward Lewis, grinning broadly. He ceremoniously cupped his hands, touched them to his chest and laughed heartily.

Captain Lewis paid no attention to the Indian's

signs. "*Tortohongar*—keep your hands off my man," he commanded him.

"Captain—" Drewyer cautioned him. "Watch him. He's crazy."

But Lewis continued to stare at the second chief. Partisan's grin swiftly turned into a frown. He scowled at Lewis with his hard, burning eyes. In bold defiance, he lifted his hand toward Roxanna, held his fingers out a few inches from her face and moved them up and down.

Lewis held his breath, said nothing.

Partisan moved his outstretched fingers closer to Roxanna's face, an inch away from her skin—then, abruptly, he dropped his hand. "Whiskey!" he grinned. "Whiskey!"

Trying not to show his relief, Lewis called out to Patrick Gass, "Give them each a shot of whiskey, sergeant. About a fourth of a glass—we don't want them drunk."

"Yes sir."

Later Gass handed the chiefs each a bottle containing a few ounces of Kentucky whiskey. Partisan grabbed his bottle, raised it quickly to his lips, and slugged down his portion in one swallow. Then, suddenly, as if he had been seized by a fit, he began to swagger wildly around the boat, laughing madly. With so many men on the keelboat, there wasn't room to move aside for the staggering chief. He bumped into one of the warriors, struck him playfully, knocked up hard against the mast, and came a few inches from crashing into Roxanna.

Lewis flexed his fingers on the barrel of his rifle.

"He's just acting, cap'n," Brussard whispered. "Ignore 'im."

Lewis shook his head. "I can't ignore him if he does anything to my men."

The Sioux chieftain didn't seem to notice the explosive tension about him. He went ahead with his act, swaggered about noisily on the deck of the keelboat while the others watched. After a while he became bored with his routine and marched up to one of the warriors and swiped his bottle from him. He cocked his head back and took a long pull. When he had sucked the bottle dry, he flung it with a grunt out into the water.

Turning toward Lewis, Partisan glowered at him indignantly, as if daring the captain to interfere. When Lewis didn't respond, Partisan pretended to be violently sick, distracting everyone. Then, with amazing quickness, he lunged across the deck at Roxanna, grabbed the rim of her hat, and yanked it off her head.

The men on the keelboat were startled and for a few seconds struck dumb to see Roxanna's hair fall down to her shoulders. Then they began talking, mumbling their surprise to each other. The Indian pointed at Roxanna, laughed aloud and slapped his thighs gleefully.

To add to their surprise, Roxanna spoke: "Captain Lewis," she said stiffly, her eyes fixed on Partisan. "Can you do something with this man? I don't like the way he's looking at me."

"Just stay calm, Roxanna," Lewis advised. "We've got more than a hundred Indian braves out there watching every move we make. We have to be careful."

"Captain—" Tom Wentworth began. He stepped up, ready to volunteer to yank Roxanna away from the Teton chief.

"Not now," Lewis told him.

"But sir—"

"Stay out of this, Tom," Lewis commanded.

"Captain Lewis," Roxanna insisted, "either you do something right now, or I'm going to have to. . . ."

Partisan paid no attention to her words. He looked her body up and down, grinning broadly, shaking his head approvingly. He turned to Lewis. "Give," he repeated.

"Is that the only word he knows?" Lewis muttered. *"Tortohongar,"* he called out. "I'm going to ask you once: back off. Leave . . . the . . . woman . . . alone!"

But Partisan wasn't fazed by the threat. He shrugged his shoulders, pointed at Roxanna, then bellowed out a few emphatic words in Sioux as he tapped his fingers on his bare chest.

"What does he want, Dorion?" Lewis asked.

"He wants *her,* captain," Pierre answered. "For his squaw."

"Captain Lewis—" Roxanna spoke up.

"Just be still, Roxanna. Dorion—tell him Americans don't give people away."

Brussard broke in: "He knows that, cap'n. He's just testing you."

"Well, I've had just about enough of his testing," Lewis replied impatiently.

"He thinks you were playing tricks on 'im cap'n, hiding the girl from 'im. He's mad."

"Well, I'm mad too," Lewis declared. He turned to the grand chief. "Untongarsarbar, I want you to take your men and go. Do you understand me?"

But Black Buffalo stood erect with his arms crossed and shook his head. "Woman," he grunted accusingly.

"I don't care—" Lewis's words were cut off by a surprised shriek from Roxanna. He looked around to see Partisan hanging onto her wrist. Roxanna struggled, but the Indian somehow managed to reach out and clutch one of her breasts. Lewis reacted instantly; he leapt toward the chief, latched onto his shoulder, and spun the Indian around.

Fire in his eyes, Partisan backed up a step and wrapped his long fingers around the handle of the knife in his belt. The men on the boat promptly tightened their muscles, ready to spring into action on a cue from either captain.

Meriwether Lewis stood steadfast between Partisan and Roxanna. "William," he called out in an authoritative, confident voice. "If we don't get these Indians off this boat, we're going to have a massacre here."

Captain Clark drew Dorion aside and instructed the Frenchman to tell Black Buffalo they were going back now. The chiefs were hesitant at first, but since they too could feel the tension and fear on the boat, they agreed. A few minutes later Black Buffalo had called Partisan. The Indians clambered aboard the pirogue and pushed off for the sandbar.

Sitting at the stern of the pirogue, Clark kept his eye on the shoreline as they eased closer to the sand. The Teton warriors were more visible, their number had doubled. There were more than two hundred now, he guessed, all of them standing next to the water, waiting for their chiefs to return. He glanced back at the keelboat. Lewis was on the foredeck, with the butt of his air gun resting on the floor next to his leg. Even from a distance of thirty yards, Clark could see on the face of his old friend an anxious, apprehensive look.

When the pirogue struck sand, Clark stood up and silently watched the Indians as they stepped softly out into the shallow water. But when Partisan's time came, the chieftain boldly stood up and barked out a command to the two Teton warriors. At once they grabbed the tow line of the pirogue and held it taut.

"What do you think you're doing?" Clark exclaimed.

"Woman!" Partisan growled fiercely and spit into the water. "Want woman!"

"Let the line go," Clark ordered.

"You give woman," Partisan demanded.

"Tell your men to drop the line, chief," Clark warned him again.

But Partisan didn't hear him. He was determined to push the situation as far as he could. Without warning, his hand shot forth and he struck Clark's shoulder with the heel of his palm.

"Damn you!" Clark shouted, but held onto his

temper. He knew if he drew his sword, the whole tribe of Sioux could come down on them within seconds. And since the Indians outnumbered them four to one, a show of force could end in a bloody slaughter on the Missouri River.

On the other hand, there was a point of no return. If he were weak and indecisive and let the Indians continue to threaten him, then he was conceding that the Americans were as weak as the French or Spanish and could be bullied by anyone who chose to do it.

He resolved to be firm, to show the Indians on the river that he and Meriwether Lewis represented Thomas Jefferson's America—a country that was strong enough to stand up for itself, no matter what the cost.

"Woman!" Partisan yelled, his face burning. He felt confident now, superior to his foe. "Woman, woman!" He stepped up to Clark and boldly tapped his fingers into the captain's chest. "Give woman!" he shouted.

That was when Clark drew his sword.

The flash of the swooping blade in the bright sunlight had an immediate effect. There was instant motion everywhere. The two hundred warriors on both sides of the river in unison bent down and strung their bows and stood up with them held high and ready. On the keelboat Captain Clark raised his air gun to his waist and sounded out a command to arms. There was a loud clicking of rifle hammers as barrels came up and sights were leveled toward the Indians on shore. The three swivel guns, loaded with musket balls and buckshot, swung toward the chiefs on the sandbar.

On the pirogue Clark stood poised with his sword in a position to slash into the Indian chief at the slightest hint of aggression. But he saw quickly that Partisan was not going to fight. He backed up a step and silently slid down from the boat into the water and took his place beside Black Buffalo.

The grand chief cleared his throat and said something in an oratorial voice. Dorion translated. "He wants us to make peace, captain."

"Well, he has a strange way of showing it," Clark fumed, his attention riveted on the chiefs standing knee-deep in the water. "Tell him to release the tow line and we'll make peace with him."

After Dorion spoke, Black Buffalo launched into a five-minute speech, gestured with his hands at the sky, the water and at his warriors on the banks of the river.

After he had finished, Dorion put his words into English: "The chief says his people are hungry and naked and they need more presents from us. More clothes and food. He says he can let us go now if we want to, but if we do, his warriors will follow us up the river and murder us in our sleep."

"What does he want besides more presents?" Clark asked.

"He wants to sleep on board the big boat tonight."

Clark considered the situation for a moment. "All right, Pierre," he agreed finally, "explain to him I'll bring him and Tartongarwaker on board, but not Partisan."

Dorion relayed the information. Black Buffalo looked at Partisan, nodded back to Clark. "*Warzingo*," he uttered. "*Matocoquepar*."

"He agrees," Dorion translated, "but he wants two warriors on board with him to give him comfort."

"Fine. I don't care if he brings his child bride with him, as long as he leaves Partisan behind. Tell Black Buffalo we'll shake hands on it."

"They won't shake hands, captain."

"Well, whatever—just invite them aboard, then. Let's see if we can get ourselves out of this without losing our scalps."

That evening everyone remained on the boats. Though Black Buffalo and his warriors seemed to rest easily on their pallets near the bow of the keelboat, most of the white men had trouble sleeping. At three o'clock in the morning, Ned Craddock called out to John Ordway, who was leaning under a low-burning torch, next to the rail of the boat. He was eating a raw potato. Ordway looked around for the owner of the voice. Seeing Craddock, he went back to his potato.

"Hey, Ordway," Craddock approached him. "How about cutting loose a round of whiskey for us, my friend? This waiting around to be killed by a bunch of red savages is getting a little hard to take."

"You heard Captain Clark, Craddock. No whiskey until we get out of here."

Craddock grumbled something, then was silent for a while as he gazed over in the direction of the Indians on the boat. Except for one warrior, the watch, they were all asleep. "You ever slept with Indians before, Ordway?" he asked.

"Those Indians aren't bothering you, Ned," Ordway argued in a low voice. "Why don't you just go back to sleep and forget they're on board?"

"Because I don't want my throat slit open, that's why. Nobody else around here does, either. That's why nobody's closing his eyes tonight. Look around you. Even the great Lieutenant Clark has been walking up and down all night."

Ordway bit a chunk out of his potato, chewed, and swallowed. "Don't make trouble, Craddock," he warned. "God knows we've got enough of that already. We're all losing our heads wondering what those Indians are doing out there in the dark. Don't make it worse."

Craddock ignored his words. "Are you planning on writing this up in your journal, Ordway? How your great captains sneaked in a woman on this expedition and nearly got us all killed on account of it?"

"That's not what happened and you know it, Ned. It was that crazy Sioux chief that nearly got us killed. And he may do it yet."

"I wonder what Mr. Jefferson is going to think about Lewis and Clark letting a woman go along on this trip with fifty men? I wonder what the Federalists back East could do with that?"

"I don't know. I don't keep up with politics. Maybe Mr. Jefferson won't even know she was on it," Ordway retorted. "Maybe nobody'll ever say she was."

"Well, I'll say it, you can count on that, sergeant."

"Yeah, I figured you would."

"I told all of you there was something strange about that Garcia. I told you he wasn't normal. Look at what they did, Ordway. They let *me* get flogged because of some woman."

"Garcia didn't have a thing to do with that, Ned."

"They just stood by and watched, both of them. Lewis and Clark. They let me take fifty lashes on my back, just so they could keep her little secret for her."

"Look, Ned," Ordway said to him, "I don't know any more than anybody else why that woman's on this expedition, but I do know if Captain Clark says it's all right for her to be here, it's fine with me."

"Yeah, sure, you'll do anything Clark tells you, won't you? You and Pryor and Gass lie around like three sick dogs and wait for him to tell you when to sit up and beg or when to roll over and play dead. Well, let me tell you something, 'sergeant': that woman's going to get us killed if we don't do something right now."

"Oh, I doubt that, Craddock," Ordway replied. "Whatever she's doing here, it's for sure she's not hurting anything."

"She's here, that's enough," Craddock told him. "Where are your brains, Ordway? You saw what happened this morning. You saw that Teton chief. He wants her, man. And you know as well as I do, a red savage'll give his teeth and five squaws for a white woman."

"Maybe so, but they won't get this one."

"You won't be stopping them with that rifle, Ordway. They got us outnumbered four to one. Tell me, are you willing to stand here and let a thousand Indians slaughter fifty men, just to save one woman?"

"Why don't you go talk to Captain Clark or Captain Lewis about it, Craddock?" Ordway inquired. "They're the ones in control here, not me."

"Yeah, some control. They got us all in hand— that's why we're all sitting wide awake waiting for those heathens to come peel off our hair. I'll tell you what—we'd be long gone up the river by now if it hadn't been for that woman. That Teton chief wants her bad, Ordway, and he's willing to murder us all to get her."

"He won't do that," Ordway disputed weakly.

"You're damned right he won't. Not if I can help it."

"Just what does that mean?"

"One thing's for sure, sergeant, it doesn't mean anything to you. You just stand around here like a fool, like you always do. I'll do it myself."

Ordway was skeptical. "What on earth do you think you could do about it, Ned? Are you going to handle Partisan the way you handled Buck Brussard?" he chided him.

Craddock flared up in anger at Ordway's comment, but managed to cool himself down. "You just don't worry about it, sergeant," he glowered. "You just keep eating your potato and let me do my work."

Craddock left Ordway at the rail, walked over to the starboard side of the boat and found Hugh Hall curled up on a blanket on the deck. He kicked him sharply in the side, Hugh grunted loudly. Craddock turned him over with his foot. "Wake up, Hall," he said.

"I'm not asleep," Hall stood up, irritated. "Nobody's asleep tonight."

"Well, get up, then," Craddock told him. "Come

over here a minute." He took Hall's arm and led him back to the rudder oar, away from the other men.

"What's this all about, Ned?" Hall grumbled. "Couldn't you wait till morning?"

"We've got work to do tonight, Hugh. I've got a little job for you and Collins."

"What kind of job?" Hall asked suspiciously.

"Nothing much. It's simple. I want you to sneak off this tub and go ashore and steal an Indian canoe. Do you think you can do that?"

"Yeah I can do it, but why would I want to steal a canoe?"

"You're going to use that canoe to deliver a nice, neat little present to a Teton Sioux chief. Then maybe we'll be able to get out of here in one piece."

Hall shook his head doubtfully. "Captain Clark already gave them an armload of presents, Ned. It didn't do no good. They just want to keep us here."

"They don't want to *keep* us, Hall, they want to *kill* us. And they're going to—tonight. Unless we give them what they want."

Hall was puzzled. "What are you talking about?"

"I'm talking about Garcia, Hall. Partisan wants Garcia, and we're going to give her to him. It's the only way we'll ever get out of here alive."

"Just 'give' her to him? That's crazy."

"No, I'll tell you what's crazy, Hugh. What's crazy is sitting around here all night waiting to be butchered by a bunch of red savages. I for one have a gut full of it. Think about it. What's worse—having Garcia, or whatever her name is, shack up with a Teton chief, or having your skull ripped off by a Sioux knife?"

Hall thought about it for a moment. "I can't do it, Ned. We can't go against Captain Clark."

Craddock grabbed his collar and pulled it tight around his neck. "Look, Hall, I'm not kidding about this. You don't have any choice, you little toad. You and Collins are going to do this, and you're going to do it right."

"No I'm not, either. I'm not afraid of you any more, Ned."

Craddock let go of the man's collar and held up his hands. "Fine," he agreed. "Don't be. That's good. Now why don't you and I go see Captain Clark? How about that? Let's tell him who stole that tobacco off the pirogue last week. And that whiskey the week before."

"You stole it, too," Hall reminded him.

"Yeah, that's right, I stole it too. The difference is, Hall, I got only one offense. You and Collins have two. Next time you don't get fifty lashes, you get your butts thrown off the expedition and into the wilderness."

"You wouldn't tell Captain Clark on us, Ned, would you? We used to be good friends."

"Friends don't matter when life is at stake, Hugh. Listen to me, man. I'm trying to save our skins here. If we don't get this woman to Partisan before sunup, we're all going to be dead before breakfast. I mean it."

"I don't know. If Captain Clark finds out about this, Ned, he's going to line us up in front of a firing squad."

"Well, that's better than being scalped, isn't it? Anyway, it's not like they're going to hurt her or anything, Hugh. All Partisan'll do is take her to bed a few times, till he gets tired of her. That's all a woman's good for anyway. Right?"

Hall swallowed hard. "I guess so."

"All right. Now go get Collins. And be quiet about it."

"Ned—"

"Damn it, Hall, get moving."

"I'll get him, but I don't like it, Ned."

"You don't have to like it, Hugh. Just do it."

Fifteen minutes later John Collins and Hugh Hall slipped barechested into the black water and began to swim toward the shore in smooth, powerful strokes. The main current was swift and they had to maneuver themselves through a couple of strong whirlpools, but each man made his way through the river with no difficulty. When they reached the bank, they slid quietly out of the water and lay on their bellies in the weeds, keeping their heads low.

"Coulter said their village was north of here," Collins whispered. "There's bound to be a canoe hidden somewhere between here and there."

"I just hope they've all gone back to the village," Hall stammered nervously. "Otherwise—"

"Shhh—be quiet. I hear something."

They held their breaths and listened, but all they could hear was the rush of the river and the low, muffled voices rolling over the water from the keelboat.

"What was it, John?" Hall asked shakily.

"Shhh—listen."

A while later Collins decided it was all right to move. He got to his knees and was about to stand up when out of the darkness a booted foot crashed into his chin and sent him backwards into the water. Hall heard the splash and was confused by the noise. He tried to scramble to his feet, but the foot banged solidly into his temple and rattled his entire body. As he fell, a heel slammed down on the back of his head and mashed his skull into the soggy bank.

Collins pulled himself out of the water and staggered toward Hall to help him, but something clamped down hard on his neck and yanked him forward with incredible strength. Helpless, he felt himself being flung face down into the mud.

When the men managed to raise their heads out of the mire, their eyes fell on a huge man wearing a buffalo robe draped over his shoulders. Crossing his massive arms, the mountainman looked down scornfully at his victims. "You men're lucky I ain't a Teton buck," Brussard told them. "I'd have a couple of new skullcaps hanging on my belt now."

Collins stood up, rubbed his aching chin and shook water out of his hair. He was angry and his head hurt, but he knew the mountainman wasn't a critter to tangle with. "You didn't have to kick us," he complained.

"I'd just as soon drown you," Brussard growled.

"Look, Brussard," Collins protested. "All we're doing is trying to get ourselves out of the clutches of these Indians, all right?" He scooped some mud off his pants leg. "Which is more than anybody else is doing," he added. The man suddenly groaned as a massive paw clamped down on the nape of his neck. Suddenly he found himself looking up into the face of the mountainman and felt the greasy breath smash into his face.

"You lookin' at me, Collins?" demanded Brussard.

"I'm—yeah."

"Then you look 'nd listen at the same time, 'cause I've got somethin' to tell you. If these Tetons catch you on their land when you ain't been invited on it, they'll pull the hide off your worthless body and use it for their women's gaiters."

"Why—why?" Hall managed, getting up. He didn't like the angle of Collins' head, and the stutter in his own voice betrayed his nervousness. Slowly, as if it bothered him, Brussard turned his massive head to make an assessment of the speaker.

"Call it Indian policy, Hall. The only reason you're alive right now is 'cause of their hospitality. If you break it, you're insulting 'em, and they don't take well to insult." Brussard loosed his hold on Collins and the man fell to his seat in the mud. He sat there rubbing his neck and the sight seemed to do Brussard some good. "I told Lewis to keep you swine on the boats," the mountainman grumbled.

"Captain Lewis didn't send us," Collins interrupted. "Ned Craddock sent us."

Brussard spat. "You're listening to the wrong man, Collins. You two ought to know by now what kind of man Craddock is."

"Ah—he's not bad," Collins whined.

"He's a coward," replied Brussard. "Out here, a coward will get you killed, Collins. That would be a favor to me, but not to the expedition."

"All he's doing is trying to do something about the situation." Collins picked himself up from the mud.

"Fine. Just don't ask me to stay patient when Craddock starts doing something about his situation."

"Well, it's better than just sitting and waiting, isn't it?"

"Sure—if you think bein' scalped is better than dyin' natural. When the man that's giving the orders is out for his own self, you better hide. A coward'll let everybody else take the chances, but when it comes to a fight, watch 'im. He'll back down every time, just like that Teton chief Partisan."

They were beginning to see that Brussard was making sense. Hall looked at Collins, then at the mountainman. "The captains aren't *doing* anything, Buck," he tried.

"It ain't for you to wonder what they're doing, private," he told him. "This here's been my home for twenty years, Hall. I'm beginning to get picky about my visitors. Craddock ain't invited, but he happens to be in the tow of a couple men that are. I ain't never seen a better man than Cap'n Lewis. You can trust 'im. Both of 'em. Him and Clark."

Collins looked at Brussard distrustfully. "All right," he said, rubbing his neck, "tell me this, then: how come it's all right for you to be here and not us?"

"It's all right for me 'cause I ain't part of your filthy crew, Collins," Brussard muttered. "The Tetons know me. I got a house up river a couple of miles."

His tone of voice suddenly changed. "Used to have one, anyway. It ain't there any more."

"Why not?" Hall asked.

"Some renegade Indians burned it down last spring."

"You mean the Tetons?"

"Unh-uhn, I mean renegades. 'Misfits' the British call 'em. While I was out West trapping, they come up and set fire to the house and lit out with my wife and daughter. I followed 'em south a week or two, then one day I found my wife's body under a clump of bushes. She was nekkid and all mashed up. Looked like she'd been there a month or more."

"Damn!" Hall exclaimed. "Did they kill her?"

"Couldn't tell what killed her," Buck answered. "All I know was, she was dead. The thing was, she was Shawnee, but they didn't bury her up high, Indian-like. They just chunked her in the bushes, like she was a dead rat or something."

"What about your daughter?" Hall asked. "What happened to her?"

"I reckon they still got 'er. I don't know, maybe they throwed her away, too. This bunch is a pack of young bucks so bad they were kicked out of their own tribes. They've all banded together like wolves. The Tetons told me a few minutes ago they got a white man leading them."

"I don't understand," Collins said. "What kind of white man would do something like that?"

"There ain't no difference between white men and Indians, Collins. Some are good, some bad. That Teton chief Partisan's bad all right, but when you get right down to it, he ain't no different from Ned Craddock. White men and Indians just don't understand each other's laws, is all."

"But this white man that killed your wife—"

"You never mind him, Collins. I'll take care of 'im, sooner or later. And I'll take care of 'im Indian-style."

"Do you know where he is?" Hall asked.

"You just let me worry about where he is. That's my problem. Yours is worrying about following the cap'n's orders, instead of Craddock's."

Hall decided it was time to tell Brussard why they were there. "Ned had this plan, Buck. We were going to turn over Garcia to that Teton chief. We were supposed to steal a canoe so we could take her to him."

Brussard nodded. "It figures," he shook his head. "And you ain't got the brains o' ground hogs. Tell me—where's Ned Craddock in all this?"

"I guess he's back on the keelboat," Hall ventured.

"Safe on his butt while you're out here taking the risks, right?"

"Well, yes—"

"Let me tell you something, son," he lectured Hall. "If you had took that woman in to Partisan, you would have caused the massacre of every white man on this river. You've got to understand the man. He's playing a game here. He's trying to prove he's stronger than you are. He knows how much white men take stock in their women. He figures if he can get Cap'n Lewis to give that woman to him, in front of everybody, then he's won. He controls the river. But if you was to sneak her to 'im in the middle of the night, he'd think you were insulting 'im."

"And he'd kill us," Hall guessed.

"*He* wouldn't. He ain't going to do anything hisself, no more than Craddock is. But he'd sure as hell order somebody else to do it for 'im."

"I can't take the waitin'," Collins complained. "I can't take it. It's gettin' on my nerves. I'm gonna go off my rocker."

"You do that. We'll tie you to a barrel and you can scream your loony lungs out." Brussard approached Collins threateningly and the man backed off. "Mebbe I should do it right now and save us the trouble later."

"What about Ned?" Hall cut in.

Brussard smiled. "You let me talk to Ned Craddock. I figure I've got a power of conviction such as other men don't have."

Chapter 9

Late that afternoon, in front of Captain Clark and a Teton Sioux brave, Roxanna Fairchild sat rapping her fingers on the rim of an Indian canoe. They were skimming rapidly over the river currents, headed toward a greeting party of Teton warriors waiting for them on the sandbar.

"I don't understand why the Sioux Indians want me to go with you," Roxanna was saying to Clark. "Why not one of the men?"

"Meriwether thinks they want you where they can see you, Mrs. Fairchild," he explained. "To make sure we're not using you to deceive them again. Brussard claims what we'll see all day today is the second step for the Sioux. Their threats and bluster didn't work, so now they'll try diplomacy. He says they'll pretend to be honoring us, but what they'll really be doing is trying to figure out how we're planning to trick them, and how they can trick us."

"Well," she sighed, "I did want to be a woman again. I guess it has its hazards."

"I'm afraid it does," Clark spoke apprehensively.

He wondered, if Roxanna survived the Tetons, what would his men do to her on the expedition, now that they knew she was a woman? Could he trust them any more than the Indians to control their passion, after doing without women for so long? He didn't know. He lowered his head, massaged his eyes thoughtfully. He was tired and weary, he hadn't slept at all last night. And he knew he wouldn't sleep tonight, either—not until every man on the expedition was safely out of the clutches of the Tetons.

As the canoe knifed through the water and drew closer to the bank, Roxanna grew more nervous. Peering through the haze that hung over the river, she could see that all the Teton warriors were staring at her. Their lusty looks made her draw her arms around herself and shudder. One of them yelled out something at her while the others laughed devilishly. Roxanna felt her heart beat faster. She knew what they wanted; the greed was radiant in their eyes. It was the same expression she saw in men's faces every time she'd walked in a strange bar or dance hall in New Orleans. Another risque guffaw and an obscene gesture irritated her even further. She crossed her arms over her breasts in defiance.

Clark took note of what the Tetons were doing. "Don't let them get to you, Mrs. Fairchild," he warned her. "Let them act however they want to act. Ignore them. Think of something else."

"That's easy for you to say, Captain Clark," she retorted. "It's not you they're gaping at."

When the canoe scraped ground, the eight Indians stepped forward and rolled out two brightly painted buffalo robes on the sand. With gestures they politely invited Clark and Roxanna to sit down on the robes. As Roxanna eased to her seat, one of the braves spoke in a low voice and the others broke into raucous laughter. A few minutes later the Indians hoisted them up on the blankets and carted them through a path in the woods to the village. On the perimeter of the camp, they set them down carefully on the grass and began to lead them to the council house where the chiefs were waiting.

Roxanna gazed around her at the village. It was much smaller than she expected. There were about a hundred lodges, each housing ten or eleven people. Each one was almost exactly like the others, round, made of buffalo skins sewn together and stretched across ten foot poles. The only difference among them was the pattern of red, blue, white, and yellow colors painted on the skins.

In front of the houses the women of the village sat on their haunches stripping or scraping hides, pounding meat, sewing skins, or stirring grease. The children and young men, on the other hand, were trailing along beside the procession, anxious and excited to see what the white men from the big boats looked like up close.

The Indian women were small in stature and they dressed themselves unattractively in loose-fitting skins and heavy robes. They sat as if in a trance in front of their lodges, watching the trespassers steadily. Roxanna returned their stares as she and Clark walked. When she caught the glance of a woman who was pounding a hunk of dried meat with a stone, Roxanna stopped to talk to her. But the woman quickly and very purposefully turned her attention back to her work and Roxanna decided to go on.

The eight warriors led them to the large council house where seventy stalwart men sat crosslegged in a circle. Roxanna recognized instantly that these men were older, wiser, more serious than the men who had brought them to the council house. She thought she should feel more secure with them, but she was still apprehensive. Their hard, wrinkled faces seemed so cold, so forbidding.

The chief Black Buffalo motioned for her and Clark to sit down. The other chiefs watched them obey, then suddenly fell into a profound silence and began staring fixedly at the hide walls. Roxanna took the chance to look about the room. It had been neatly and ceremoniously prepared for their visit. There were several long peace pipes resting on sticks raised over a bed of soft white swan's down. On one side of a white-line circle were a couple of worn and faded Spanish flags stuck at an angle in the ground. On the other side was the crisp new American flag Lewis and Clark had given them the day before when there was the conference on the sandbar. In the center of another circle three pots of meat were cooking over a large fire. Stacked nearby were about four hundred pounds of fresh buffalo meat, meant as a present to the visitors.

They waited in the big room for an hour, doing nothing, hearing nothing but the subdued sounds of the people of the village outside the doorway of the council house. At one point a squaw stole quietly into the lodge and stirred a pot on the fire, then left. Roxanna kept her eyes on her, hoping she would look up, but the Indian's eyes were down the whole time.

The cold heavy silence in the council house was finally broken by the abrupt entrance of Captain Lewis, who had been sent for by the chiefs. He stepped confidently into the lodge and promptly sat down on the other side of Roxanna and nodded to the chiefs.

Black Buffalo glanced around at the other chiefs, stood up, cleared his throat, and delivered a blustery five-minute speech. Neither Roxanna nor the captains understood a word of it, since Pierre Dorion had returned to his wife and wasn't around to translate. But Black Buffalo went through it anyway. After he had sat down, he had one of the younger chiefs pass the peace pipe around.

Captain Clark took it first, then handed it to Roxanna. She lifted it up toward her mouth. "It's an honor, Roxanna," Captain Lewis explained. "Women aren't usually given the privilege."

She smiled ironically. "Well, I'm very flattered, I assure you." She touched the rough carved wood to her lips, then sucked in deeply. The hot smoke rushed around her mouth like a brush fire. It burned her tongue and throat, threw her body into a deep cough. As soon as she caught her breath, she glanced up in embarrassment at the Teton chiefs. To her surprise, their expressions hadn't changed. Their high-cheeked faces appeared to her to be set in stone, their dark eyesockets burnt into their faces. They stared at her coldly, dispassionately, as likely to condemn her to death as not.

After the grand chief directed a meat sacrifice to the American flag as a tribute to the visitors, two old and stooped squaws shuffled in, dipping up the meat from the cooking pots, and doled it out carefully into eight separate platters at the visitors' feet.

"Eat!" Black Buffalo encouraged them.

Roxanna started cautiously. The first platter she tried contained *pemmican,* a mixture of pounded buffalo meat and grease. It surprised her. It was tasty, as good as some expensive delicacies she had had in restaurants back home in New Orleans. She tried the ground potato, found the bland, musky taste tolerable, but she had to struggle to get through two strings of dry, tough jerky.

One particular dish, however, the main course, sent waves of shock throughout her entire body.

"You have to eat it, Roxanna," Lewis insisted when he saw her pausing with a chunk of the hot dry meat between her fingers.

"What is it?" she asked in a low voice. "Pork? Oh God, it's not horse, is it?"

"No, it's not horse. Or pork, either," he answered. "It's roasted dog."

"Oh, captain—" she groaned.

"Don't put it back!" he scolded under his breath. "They would consider it a terrible insult."

"But Captain Lewis," she pleaded, trying to keep a blank face, to hide her distaste. I couldn't possibly—"

"Don't think about it, Roxanna," he ordered. "Just eat it. And pretend you like it."

She sighed, raised her eyebrows, stole a glance at the chiefs, who were watching her closely. They were waiting for her to insult them. She knew she had no choice. The lives of the men on the expedition could depend on her at this moment. She had to do it.

She took a deep breath and placed the morsel in her mouth and chewed it. The taste wasn't as bad as she expected, but the thought of it almost made her ill. Somehow, though, she managed to eat it without gagging.

After they had finished eating, ten thin, good-looking warriors with tambourines and clackers made of deer hooves appeared through the doorway. They walked around the circle, then danced and sang around the fire for an hour or so. Then a parade of women burst into the council house and performed a lively, ceremonious war dance. With enemy scalps dangling from their belts, they vigorously re-created the great battles their husbands had fought in, and paid them homage as their great masters on earth.

At midnight the singers and dancers filed quickly out of the council house and Black Buffalo stood up and signaled with a wide sweep of his hand that he was calling a halt to the festivities. Lewis and Clark and Roxanna got to their feet, thanked the grand chief in sign language, and he nodded at them appreciatively. At a couple of minutes past twelve, Black Buffalo appointed four of the minor chiefs to lead them out of the hut into the camp.

The village grounds were dark, with only a few lighted torches stuck in the earth here and there, but it was light enough for them to see two Indian women treading slowly up from the river, with large wooden bowls of water balanced precariously on their shoulders. When the women confronted the procession of three white people and four chiefs, they instantly backed out of the way and lowered their eyes and let the others pass.

Roxanna was becoming more and more upset by

the Sioux women's behavior. She looked back at the squaws as they resumed their walk, then turned back to Captain Lewis.

"I wish to hell I had kept my disguise," Roxanna complained bitterly.

"Beg pardon?" The man who had impassively witnessed flogging, killing and the worse kind of sickness seemed shocked by her words. "What are you talking about?"

"Look," Roxanna nodded. "These women are bartered. They're horses, goats, sheep. And I'm one of them."

"On the contrary, Roxanna. . . ." Lewis started to laugh.

"It's not funny," she cut in harshly.

He looked at her closely, a puzzled expression on his face. And for an instant, she was almost sorry she had hurt his feelings. She did not dare give vent to the doubts that were beginning to grow in her. Ever since she had been discovered, forced to resume her identity as a woman, it seemed as if she were no longer a participant in the expedition but some kind of pack or burden that the men carried along. And now, she was sure, she had become an object of trade, even though Captain Lewis gallantly denied it. Hadn't Partisan asked for her? And what did he want, if not a woman to pound hides and stir the grease for him?

Her thoughts were cut short as the chiefs leading Lewis and his band came to an abrupt stop. Roxanna caught sight of a tall, muscular Teton warrior wearing a white feather in his headband. He wore a loincloth and no robe, and there was a British cutlass hanging from his belt, slapping against his naked thighs as he walked. The chiefs made obvious their respect to the man, as they halted the group.

"That's a Teton 'soldier,' " Lewis told Roxanna in a low voice. "Be careful. They're dangerous."

Roxanna saw immediately that even the chiefs were afraid of this man. The closer he got to them, the closer together they huddled. By the time the man reached them, the warriors were packed together like frightened animals. The soldier slowed down, uttered a few brisk words to the warriors, looked straight past the white people and moved on.

Roxanna turned to watch him. The two squaws they had just met suddenly disappeared. In fact, the whole village seemed to be recoiling in terror from this man. The chiefs motioned for them to go on, but Roxanna wouldn't move.

"Where's he going?" she asked.

"I don't know," Lewis replied. "If a soldier has business with someone, you probably don't want to see it."

"What's so special about a soldier?"

"The soldiers keep order in the camp," Captain Clark told her. "They belong to a secret Teton military society that nobody can touch. Not even the chiefs. They're allowed all the power they need to police the tribe."

Roxanna ignored another command by the chiefs to move on. Her eyes were fixed on the tall soldier as he marched confidently up to a red and white painted hut about forty feet away. Without announcing himself, he lowered his head and entered the tent. A few seconds later, the soldier came out dragging a woman by the hair. The squaw's furious husband burst out of the lodge, pursuing them, with his hand poised to grab the knife in his belt. But as soon as he realized who the intruder was, he backed up meekly.

The soldier threw the woman down to the ground, flipped her over on her back, and slammed his moccasined foot into her neck. She gasped and wriggled wildly, but her frantic movements only made the soldier push down harder with his foot.

"Captain—" Roxanna objected excitedly.

Lewis grabbed her wrist. "Roxanna," he warned her.

"Please—no!" She tried to jerk her arm loose.

She was angry, afraid that the woman was going to die right there in front of everyone with not one person lifting a finger to save her.

The soldier slid his foot off the squaw's neck, grasped her hair again and yanked her up. The husband flinched, but said nothing. The soldier twisted the black hair around his hand, pulled her face tight, and bent her neck back so far that Roxanna expected to hear it snap at any moment.

When he drew out his cutlass, Roxanna could imagine the sharp blade slicing open the woman's throat, with a rush of blood spewing out onto her chest. Roxanna couldn't stand by and let it happen. She wrestled her arm free from Captain Lewis, sprinted out across the village ground toward the soldier and the woman, yelling, "No! No!"

The surprised Teton turned toward Roxanna, and when his grip on the squaw relaxed, the Indian woman broke loose and frantically squirmed through the dirt a few feet toward the edge of the camp. Then she gave up. She drew her body into a crouch and began shaking with fear. Roxanna rushed to her, fell to her knees and took the woman into her arms.

"Leave her alone!" she shouted at the soldier.

The Teton said something in Sioux, brandished his cutlass through the air for a minute or more. Then with a deadly half-smile on his face, he slowly raised his left hand to show it to Roxanna. He held it up high, made a fist with it, then pushed up two fingers for her to see.

She got his message and it made her blood run cold. Because of her interference, he was going to kill *two* women! She pressed the Indian woman closer against her body, looked around quickly for help. There were numbers of Sioux Indians around her now, standing quietly at a distance, but they were all cowering under their dreaded fear of the soldier. She knew Lewis and Clark couldn't save her. If they interfered with a member of the secret police, the men on the boats were as good as dead. They were too far away, anyway; if they moved, the Indian would kill them both.

The soldier moved his left hand about in the air, so that everyone could see the two fingers. The other Indians knew what the sign meant, but they didn't move. Suddenly the soldier had another thought. He flung his cutlass down to the ground and drew out a long narrow blade. It was dangerous-looking, more like a dagger than the usual Indian hunting knife.

Roxanna felt a wave of cold take over her body. She drew the woman closer to her breasts, but it didn't help. She was scared. What did the soldier intend to do with such a weapon? Scalp her? Disembowel her?

When he took a step toward her, she thought her heart would stop. What could she do? She knew it would be impossible to jump up and outrun such a person—he was too quick and strong. And even if she could, she would be leaving the squaw behind to die.

Roxanna had no choice but to wait for her fate.

Just as she closed her eyes, a deep, low voice behind her bellowed, "You'd best let the squaw go, ma'am."

It was Buck Brussard, striding forward with a flaming, smoking torch in his hand. He held it like a spear, tilted forward. Coming alongside the two women, he raised the butt end of the torch and slammed it into the ground.

The Teton brave stood with his knife in front of him, completely unmoved by the mountainman's appearance. He stared at the torch for a second, then turned to Brussard and spoke to him in Sioux.

Brussard listened to him, nodding occasionally, saying nothing. When the Indian had finished, Brussard spoke to Roxanna, without taking his eyes off the soldier. "He tells me the squaw's a traitor."

Roxanna crouched closely alongside the woman, clinging to her, hoping her fear would not show. "I don't believe it! Make him stop!" she demanded.

"Best leave it alone, ma'am," Brussard replied. "This here's Sioux business. I wouldn't meddle in it."

"I don't believe she's a traitor," Roxanna insisted.

Brussard clucked his tongue. "To him she is, and that's what counts. It's his village." He waited a second, then added, "He just learned she's been sleeping with a Omaha buck."

Roxanna swallowed with difficulty. "I don't care about that."

"Maybe you don't care about it, but these Teton Sioux do."

"They can't just—"

"Now you'd best listen to me a minute, lady," he ordered her. "Ever since the Teton Sioux took over this river from the Omahas, back when Blackbird was still alive, the Omahas have been doing everything they can to get it back. Now that squaw you're coddling there has been slipping off and bedding down with a Omaha warrior. That means to them she's a traitor. She's a threat to all of 'em."

Roxanna began to realize that she had thrown herself into a situation she should have left alone. But she felt strangely sympathetic and committed to this poor woman and couldn't leave her yet. "What does he want to do with her?" she asked Brussard, less defiantly than before.

"Just what he was doing before you came along—he wants to shame 'er in front of the others and make 'er leave the village."

"Good. Let her leave. I'll take her with me."

"Now you can't do that," Brussard objected, shaking his head. "You'd be insulting 'im if you did that. Making 'im look bad. He'd kill you before he'd let you do that to 'im."

"I didn't mean to make him look bad," she said, almost apologetically. "But he was abusing her."

Brussard glanced at the soldier, then at Roxanna. "I'd say he's being damn patient here, Mrs. Fairchild, but you best back off while your head's still on your shoulders. For what you did to 'im, he's got the right to lop it off."

"What I did to him!" she repeated indignantly.

"Let the squaw go," he ordered, ignoring her outburst. "When this Teton buck starts slinging that knife of his around, there won't be anything anybody can do for you. He can carve a person into little pieces before you or I could swat a fly. That squaw there'll be the first to go, too. And it'll be your fault."

Roxanna felt utterly defeated. Her eyes darted as she looked around frantically one more time. But Brussard was right. She had to do as he commanded. "Tell me what to do," she requested softly.

Brussard barked a single order: "Back off!" Then he added, "Raise your hands up in the air and back off. Slow and easy. He'll get the idea."

"Will he let me do that?" she asked tentatively.

"I don't know if he will or not. But you might as well try it. I don't see you have any other choice."

Roxanna took a deep breath, separated herself from the Indian woman and lifted up her hands. She could see the Indian's eyes following her as she got to her feet and took a step backwards. "What now?" she asked.

"Keep backing up. Don't stop."

She began stepping backwards, but stopped when the soldier came forward and snatched up the squaw by the hair. Roxanna nearly screamed as the Indian swished his blade through the air, leaving a jagged gash in the side of the squaw's face.

Roxanna turned her head away from the blood, but Brussard quickly cautioned her: "Be still! He's just marking 'er."

The squaw cried out, clutched her bloody face with both hands. She knew now it was over, that the man was through with her. She struggled to her feet and stumbled out of the village into the woods. All eyes turned to the soldier now, who stood straight and tall, coldly, dispassionately watching the wailing woman scramble out of sight.

The Teton bent down, slowly wiped his bloody blade on the grass, then stuffed it back behind his belt. Casting a quick accusing glance at Brussard, he flicked up the mountainman's torch and heaved it disgustedly onto the ground. Then without another word, he picked up his cutlass, turned his back to Roxanna and Brussard, and ceremoniously strode through the camp toward the council house.

"Are you all right?" Lewis asked Roxanna as he and Clark hurried up to her.

Roxanna had her hand on her chest. She could feel her heart pounding inside. "I'm fine," she muttered shakily. She was still frightened, but seeing the squaw's husband return to his tent made her angry again.

"I'd say you were lucky," Brussard offered. "That Teton buck could've killed you and nobody would've said a word about it. Soldiers don't allow women folk to interfere."

"They treat their dogs with more respect," Roxanna retorted vehemently.

"Could be," Brussard granted. "But that's their way, and if you want to live long enough to get on up the river, you'd best not try to change it."

Roxanna said nothing. She was thinking of the Indian woman the soldier had disfigured and exiled. She looked up at the huge mountainman and fixed her eyes on his. "What will happen to her now?" she wondered.

Brussard rubbed his bearded chin, pursed his lips. "Well, she's got his mark on 'er, so she won't be living with any Indians, I don't reckon. And she ain't likely to take up with the white folks, either. So, I guess she'll just go off somewhere and die. That's what they usually do."

"Couldn't we go find her?" she asked sadly.

"Even looking for 'er would be a violation of their way. You don't do that. That soldier would find you both. He'd dedicate his life to it."

"Come on, Roxanna," Lewis called. "Let's get back to the boat. I don't like the mood of these people right now."

"But there must be something we can do," she protested.

"There is," he replied seriously. "We can stay alive. Which means letting the Teton Sioux work out their own problems."

"But Captain Lewis—"

"There's nothing we can do, Roxanna. Come on."

That evening no one slept. As Roxanna walked on the deck of the keelboat, she could detect an apprehension hanging over her like a thick cloud. The men on the boats were restless and irritable. They were discursive in their talk, bored with their card games and meals. Late in the night, some of them, led by Ned Craddock, began to intimate to the others that perhaps their leaders weren't being as efficient as they might be. Perhaps, they suggested, the captains were willing to sacrifice the lives of their men just to keep a boat load of trinkets, journals and animal specimens out of the hands of the Sioux. The talk ran from general discontent to what Roxanna concluded was dangerously close to mutiny. But Craddock always pulled up short of talking rebellion, so nothing came of it.

Even so, nerves were rattled, and the cold dull fear the men were experiencing was honed sharp by the mysterious conduct of the Indians the next day. The captains and Roxanna were forced to attend another council and dance, so they had to go into the village again. They discovered there a tension like the one on the boats. The Sioux hung around their lodges and looked concerned and nervous as Partisan, the second chief, moved about from one tent to another, talking in a low voice to the warriors and other chiefs. At noon Roxanna saw him in the company of six tall muscular soldiers, walking into the priest's lodge for a private meeting.

"Partisan worries me," Captain Clark confessed as he looked around the village. "It looks like he's planning something big."

"Well," Lewis assured him, "whatever he's planning, we can still back him down." He paused. "If we stick together," he added.

Roxanna wondered whether to mention to Lewis the growing discontent of the men, but decided that it wouldn't help any. Perhaps by morning, when they were scheduled to leave, they would all be behind the captains again.

But at dawn on the fourth day, the twenty-eighth of September, after another sleepless night, tempers on the boats were strung like tight springs, ready to snap at any moment. At first light, hundreds of Sioux Indians began to gather quietly on the banks. The warriors and old men were armed with various kinds of pistols, rifles, spears, cutlasses and bows. Even the women, who hung back behind the front lines, looked as if they were poised for battle.

"Captain Lewis!" Sergeant Gass called out toward the bow of the keelboat. "What do you want us to do about the anchor?"

Lewis turned away from the shore, walked back to Gass. "Why don't we let the anchor go, Pat. It's gone, we can make one out of stone later. Right now, I think we'd better get ourselves out of here while we can."

"They're going to kill us, aren't they, captain?" Gass asked helplessly.

"Not if I can help it," he patted Gass on the shoulder. "William?" he called out to Captain Clark. "Let's move out."

Clark came forward. "It's too late, Meriwether," he said. "Partisan's on the bank with six soldiers. Whatever he wants, he looks like he means business."

"I'm not going to try to anticipate anyone that crazy," Lewis responded. "Let's get ready to shove off. I'm tired, William—I've had enough of this."

"Hall!" Clark called out. "Bring in the cable, we're pushing off!"

"What about the anchor, captain?" Hall asked.

"Forget the anchor, private, we're leaving. Bring in the cable."

"Yes sir."

"Mrs. Fairchild," Clark turned to Roxanna, "I want you to stay out of sight for a while, until we're a mile or two upriver. Can you do that?"

"Why should I stay out of sight?"

"Don't question my orders, Fairchild, just do what I say!"

"Yes sir," she answered meekly.

"Captain—" Hugh called out.

"What is it now, Hall?" Clark asked. But then he looked out and saw for himself what the trouble was. The Teton chief Partisan was standing on shore with his arms folded across his chest. The two soldiers on his left were wrapping their hands tightly around the two lines to the keelboat.

Clark felt the men stir nervously around him. He could almost feel their despair. Four long days of anxiety had taken their toll on morale. The men were losing their sense of purpose. The bond that held them together had been slashed at for so long by the Tetons' capricious control of them, it was starting to give way. He knew they were thinking that this bold act by the Teton chief could mean, finally, the beginning of the end for all of them.

Clark felt Captain Lewis at his side. "We need an interpreter," Clark told him. "Where's Brussard?"

"Brussard's gone," Lewis answered, his eyes glued on Partisan and the soldiers. "He took off yesterday. He said he was picking up a trail of some kind."

"Just when we need him!"

"I don't know, William, I have a feeling Partisan is going to make it clear enough for us, all by himself."

At that moment Partisan called out to them, *"Kinnikinnick! To-bacco!"*

"Tobacco," Clark repeated derisively. "Listen to him. I doubt if that crazy Indian even smokes tobacco. What do you think he's up to?"

"To-bacco!" Partisan demanded.

Lewis took a quick look around at the men in the three boats. Their faces worried him. They seemed tentative, unsure of themselves. He wondered if they were also unsure of him. He turned back to Clark. "William, if I thought a case of tobacco was all he wanted. . . ."

"Maybe it is all he wants," Clark suggested hopefully.

Lewis watched Partisan for a moment. "I doubt it," he replied. "But right now it looks like we have to play his game for a while. Let's give it to him and see what happens."

Lewis ordered Tom Wentworth to get a case of Virginia tobacco and turn it over to Partisan. Tom retrieved the tightly wrapped bundle out of the hold, walked over to the edge of the boat and heaved it out with a grunt. One of the soldiers reached out with his long muscular arms and caught it easily.

The chief snapped the parcel away from the soldier, flung it disdainfully to the ground. He kicked it, shook his head vigorously, and held up two fingers for the captains to see.

"Looks like he wants another case of tobacco," Clark observed.

Lewis crashed his fist against the side of the boat. "Damn him!" he cried. "He just won't let it go, will he?" He sighed deeply, thought a minute, then looked over at Wentworth. "Tom, tell me what's going on with the men."

"Sir?"

"The men, Wentworth," he prodded impatiently. "What's the problem? They look like they've been lost in the woods for weeks."

"I don't understand what—"

"Don't play games with me, Wentworth. Damn it,

we don't have time for that. Look at them. They're about ready to turn tail and run."

Tom shrugged his shoulders. "I did hear something," he admitted. "I heard some of the men say they thought maybe we should be giving the Indians what they want, so we can get out of here."

Lewis shook his head dejectedly. "Don't they realize we can't let these Indians intimidate us like that? If we give in to the Tetons—even an inch—then every hostile Indian tribe from here to the Pacific will think they can take whatever they want from us."

"I'm ready to fight," Tom volunteered, patting the pistol in his belt. "Just say the word."

"Good," Lewis nodded. "I thought maybe you were that much like your father."

"To-bacco, to-bacco!" Partisan yelled out. The soldiers picked it up, began chanting, *"To-bacco, to-bacco!"*

Lewis quickly surveyed the men again. They were still hanging back, wearing worried looks, waiting nervously to see what was going to happen. He knew he couldn't hope to scare Partisan with men who looked like that. On the other hand, calling them to arms could start a war. "Tom," he decided, "throw him out another bundle."

"Yes sir." Tom did as he was ordered. He pitched another case of tobacco over the edge, but Partisan let it fall to the ground untouched. He laughed, shook his head again, and cupped his hands and beat his chest with his fingers.

Lewis recognized the sign. "Well, there it is," he sighed. "Just what I was afraid of."

"What is it, Captain Lewis?" Tom asked. "What does he want?"

"Simple—he wants Roxanna."

"Woman, woman, woman!" Partisan called out in a singsong voice. The soldiers chimed in eagerly.

"He's been leading up to this for four days,"

Clark related. "He figures if we give him our woman, he can make us do anything else he wants, too."

"Well he's about to learn once and for all that Americans can't be intimidated," Lewis resolved. "If we give in now, we may as well have stayed in St. Louis."

"Captain Lewis—"

"Tom," he broke in, "make sure that flintlock of yours has a ball in it. You may need it in a few minutes."

"Captain Lewis, I'm not sure the men will. . . ." he hesitated.

"Will what?" Lewis asked. "Back me up?"

"I don't know if they would," Tom cautioned.

"Well, I know," Lewis told him confidently. "Captain Clark and I chose these men ourselves. Every one of them is a good man. They'll stand behind us."

"Woman!" Partisan shouted, waving his fist at Captain Lewis. "Give woman!"

Suddenly, responding to an unseen cue, the warriors on shore took a few silent steps forward, holding their weapons menacingly in front of their bodies. Lewis wiped his palms on his shirt. "They look deadly, William," he observed. "I wonder where Black Buffalo is? He could put a stop to this."

"I don't see him out there," Clark said. "It looks like he's letting Partisan have his way this morning."

"Tom," Lewis requested, "I want you to climb up on the bow very casually and get behind the swivel gun. Easy now—don't let them think you're standing ready."

"Yes sir," Tom obeyed, slowly climbing up to man the gun on the bow.

"Sergeant Gass?" Lewis called back. "Pass the word to the men to get ready to stand at arms at my signal."

"Yes sir," Gass returned, but he was doubtful whether he would be able to rally them. The men

seemed tired and defeated to him and unable to decide
what to do.

Roxanna Fairchild, on the other hand, didn't happen to share their feelings at the moment. She stepped
forward, put her hand on Lewis's forearm, and said his
name softly.

"Roxanna!" Tom cried. "Get back."

"No. He's talking about me, isn't he?"

"Roxanna," Lewis commanded her, "get out of
sight."

"But it's me he wants, captain," she insisted.

"It's *us* he wants."

She let go of his arm. "But if you don't give me to
him. . . ."

"If you persist in disputing my command, Mrs.
Fairchild, I can have you gagged."

She stood back utterly silenced. Never had Captain Lewis spoken to her in this way before. She
wanted to rebel. She would *insist* on being heard, she
thought angrily.

But one look around at the anxious faces of
Lewis's men and the hostility in the eyes of the Indians
made her surrender all protest.

"Woman!" Partisan screamed, his voice filled with
anger and impatience. "Woman! Give!"

Lewis looked over at Partisan and the soldiers.
"Tortohongar!" he yelled at the chief. "No! Do you
hear me? No! No woman!"

Partisan spat out something in Sioux, shaking his
fist angrily at Lewis. Then he raised his hand up into
the air.

"He's going to make an attack sign!" Clark muttered quickly.

"Give the word, William," Lewis directed.

"Wentworth?" Clark called out. "Are you ready?"

"Yes sir. I'm ready."

"All right, then. Fire one shot, twenty feet over
their heads. Now!"

Tom let the swivel gun expode and a mass of

musket balls sprayed out over Partisan's head into the trees. The soldiers dropped to their knees at the sound and, for a moment, loosened their hold on the tow line. But the chief barked something at them, exhorting them to hold fast.

From behind the white smoke of the gun's discharge, Tom hollered, "It didn't do any good, Captain Lewis. They didn't pay any attention to it."

"Load up again, Wentworth," Clark commanded.

"Captain Lewis," Collins urged. "Couldn't you just cut the cable?"

"Cutting the cable wouldn't do any good," Lewis answered. "They'd only come after us. We have to show them we mean business, Collins. We have to make them drop the tow line." He looked back. "Sergeant Gass!" he called out.

"Sir!" Patrick Gass stood at attention.

"Stand ready," Lewis instructed him.

"Yes sir," he stiffened.

"Captain Lewis—" Tom warned, his eyes riveted to the Indians.

"I see them," Lewis responded. He watched the Indians string their bows, make a show of cocking their rifles and pistols. He tightened his grip on the barrel of his gun as he saw them slowly, deliberately raise their weapons to eye level.

"Gass! Ordway!" Captain Clark ordered sharply. "Stand at arms!"

From the red pirogue Ordway shouted out a command and the men on the three boats snapped to attention. But when he ordered them to raise their rifles, they hesitated. Ordway directed them to arms again, in a louder, firmer voice, and the men stirred—but they kept the butts of their rifles on the floor.

As Partisan and the soldiers commenced their way into the river with their bows and cutlasses ready, Roxanna looked up at Tom loading the swivel gun on the bow. Her heart jumped as she realized how vulnerable his position was. If the Indians loosed their arrows, Tom would go down in the first volley.

She started to go to him, but Captain Lewis held her back. "Don't move, Roxanna," he warned her. "Stay right there."

She stood quiet, watching Tom out of the corner of her eye as Partisan stopped knee-deep in the water and signaled to the soldiers for a weapon. He brusquely seized a bow and arrow from one of them, rebuking the man for his slowness. Then, locking his angry red eyes on Captain Lewis, Partisan carefully notched the feathered end of the arrow onto the taut string of the bow.

Watching him from the portside of the boat, Hugh Hall said to Collins, "That Indian's going to shoot Captain Lewis, John!"

"I'll tell you what," Collins decided, angry and insulted to see his captain threatened. "He'd better not aim that thing at anybody. I'll kill him myself."

"But look at him, John—he's going to do it."

Partisan raised the long bow parallel to his body, turned it directly at Captain Lewis who stood with his air gun drawn across his chest.

Wentworth slowly swung the swivel gun around in the direction of the Teton chief. "Just say the word, Captain Lewis, I've got him in my sights."

Lewis remembered Tom's impulsiveness. "No, now take it easy, Tom," he cautioned him. "If you shoot him, we're all dead."

"But he's going to kill you!" Tom protested.

"Stand firm, Wentworth," Lewis ordered. "Don't shoot until they do. That's an order."

"But you'll be the first one to die—"

"You heard what I said. Stand firm!"

"Yes sir."

Partisan pulled the string back next to his ear. The powerful bow was curled toward his chest, the arrow aimed at Lewis's heart. All he had to do now was release his fingers and a Teton arrow would be whizzing through the air toward its target.

But then there was movement on the keelboat. John Collins promptly took a step forward on the deck, advanced his rifle, pressed the smooth wooden stock against his face, and peered down the sights at Partisan. "I'm behind you, captain!" he called out. "One more flick of his finger and he's gone!"

Startled by his friend's move, Hugh Hall suddenly remembered what the mountainman said about following Captain Lewis. If they ever were going to get out of Sioux country, they would have to trust him to do it. He moved out and took aim. "I'm behind you too, captain!" he announced. "Just give us the order. Whatever it is, we'll do it!"

Hall's words brought instant motion to the other men. Guns quickly swished up into the air, long barrels leveled out at the Indians on shore. Within seconds fifty hard men stood fast on the boats, ready to fire on command.

Partisan's eyes burned with fury when he witnessed the unified show of force of the white men. The feathered arrow was against his cheek, but he didn't let it go. He held it still until the muscles in his arm started to quiver and the bow began to waver in his left hand. He turned his head slightly to compare the Tetons on shore with the lines of armed men on the boats. His shoulder shook, the arrow vibrated. When he heard the noisome clicking of rifle hammers coming over the water, he released some of the tension on the bow.

"He's backing down," Tom noticed.

"He *is*, Captain Lewis!" Roxanna agreed excitedly.

Partisan heard nothing. He lowered his eyes and let up on the string. He knew he had been beaten. He flung the bow into the river, turned his back to Lewis, and climbed back ashore. He paused when he saw the other Indians relax and lower their weapons, but he didn't say anything to them. He merely cast his eyes to the ground and headed toward the village. The soldiers were confused for a moment. They held the tow line taut while they watched Partisan leave.

Finally, mumbling among themselves, they decided it was over and cast the line out into the river, freeing the boat. As soon as the keelboat was loose, its sail popped out, billowed and fluttered against a southern breeze. The wind grew strong all of a sudden and began shoving the boat quickly up the river.

The men held their firing positions, but as the Indians on the banks began to grow smaller, they began to breathe easier. Once they were out of sight of the Tetons and ordered at ease, they immediately sent up a rousing cheer and commenced patting each other on the back, laughing and reviewing the crisis, over and over.

Lewis laid his gun down and watched the men carrying on. He looked at Captain Clark and Roxanna with a slight smile on his face. "We've come together now, William. I think you can forget stolen whiskey and court-martials and flogging from now on. Now we're able to do what Mr. Jefferson sent us out here to do. We can make the Louisiana Territory a part of America."

"The men did prove themselves, just as you said they would," Clark admitted. "And you were right not to force them—to let *them* decide to follow you. I believe we can handle anything this wilderness has to throw up against us now. These men were brave."

"Well I for one was terrified, Captain Clark," Roxanna confessed. "If it had been left up to me, I would've cut the cable and run."

Clark shook his head and smiled. "Oh no you wouldn't, Roxanna," he touched her shoulder good-naturedly. "I know you well enough by now. You have as much courage as any man here."

Warmed by Clark's words, Lewis looked up at Wentworth. "Tom, why don't you fire that thing once for me? I need everybody's attention for a few minutes. Sergeant?" he addressed Gass, "bring the pirogues in close. I've got a few words to say to the men. And," he added, acknowledging Roxanna, "the woman."

"Yes sir!" Gass answered joyously.

Later, Ned Craddock leaned against the sail mast on the keelboat, whittling on a block of wood with his hunting knife. He was listening to Captain Meriwether Lewis make a speech on the foredeck. Unlike Clark, Captain Lewis always seemed slightly distant and aloof from the men, but he was an unusually effective speaker, as Craddock was learning.

In simple, clear words Lewis praised the men for their patience, forebearance, courage, and loyalty. Each member of the expedition had proven himself in terrible circumstances, he commended them, and that had made him very proud. They had shown the western Indians just how strong and determined and resolute a country America was. In doing that, he told them, they had accomplished the first of Mr. Jefferson's great objectives: they had won control of the Missouri River.

Amidst enthusiastic, responsive cheers and loud exuberant applause, he continued his praise. The expedition was now solid, unified. Because of their strength and perserverance, Lewis declared the way was now clear for the expedition to stretch beyond the bounds of the Louisiana Purchase—all the way to the Pacific Ocean!

These last words brought even louder cheers.

"That was a close call we had back there, wasn't it, Ned?" William Werner asked Craddock as the speech ended and the audience began to break up, each man going off to attend to his regular duties. "I guess Captain Lewis proved well enough he knows how to handle these Indians."

"Yeah, our captain's a real expert on the red savages all right," Ned replied wearily. "I figured the Tetons would stop him."

Werner looked at him, surprised. "What do you mean, 'stop him'?"

"Nothing." Craddock sounded mysterious. He let a sliver of wood fall to the deck.

Werner looked at the wood chip, then at Craddock. "You sound like you're disappointed," he said, puzzled at Craddock's tone of voice.

"Nah, I'm not disappointed," Craddock replied. "Why should I be disappointed? Lewis did all right, great. He handled the Indians, fine. Why don't we pin one of Jefferson's medals on him and make him a governor somewhere."

Werner shook his head. "I don't understand you, Ned. I would've thought you'd be grateful to Captain Lewis, like the rest of us. The man stood up to the Tetons. He saved our lives."

"Yeah, right. Maybe he did. But then we still got a long way to go, don't we, Werner?"

"Just what does that mean?"

"To a man like you, it doesn't mean anything, Werner. Nothing at all. Forget it." He patted Werner's cheek condescendingly and walked off, dropping shavings of wood as he went.

Werner was fuming when Hugh Hall came up. "That man's never satisfied," he complained, watching Craddock amble back toward the rudder.

"What's wrong with Ned?" Hugh asked.

"I don't know what's wrong with him, Hugh. I do know, though, he's got something on his mind. If I didn't know better, I'd think he wanted the Tetons to turn us back."

"Ah, that's crazy."

"Well, that was the way he was acting."

Hugh laughed. "He's just mad about that flogging."

"I don't think so, Hugh. I don't think it's the flogging that's bothering him."

"Well, don't think about it, William," Hugh told him. "Captain Clark's got us some whiskey, let's go get ourselves drunk. Then maybe we can get some sleep around here. I bet there ain't a man on this expedition that's closed his eyes for four days."

PART THREE

FORT MANDAN

Chapter 10

Tom Wentworth noticed the change in the attitude of the men in the days after they'd left Sioux country. They had become, as Lewis had said in his speech, of one purpose. There were none of the little cliques that had kept the men apart during the winter on the Wood River. For the first time they worked, drank and sang together in true harmony. And the expedition moved inexorably up the river toward the land of the Mandans, the Arikaras and the Minnetarees, the Indians the mountainman called the "Big Bellies."

Wentworth felt the change in himself, too. Throughout his sickness and during the four terrifying days with the Tetons, he had finally come to think of himself as a bona fide member of the expedition. He realized now that his desire to plunder the great wealth of the wilderness, the reason he came West, had slowly been replaced by a need to do his part in Lewis and Clark's great adventure.

His desire for Isabel Radcliffe, too, had faded with that other desire into nothing more than a fond memory. He was absolutely certain now that there was only one woman in the world he could ever love, only one woman he could ever take as a wife: Roxanna Fairchild. But knowing that gave him frustration, not peace, because there was nothing he could do about it. Roxanna was, after all, a married woman.

Roxanna, meanwhile, kept herself occupied during the next few weeks and made it her business not to think about Tom Wentworth very often. She found it very difficult to maintain a place in the company of fifty men without offending them. She had to make sure not to lead on any man who happened to smile at her, or accidentally touch her, or glance lustily in her direction while someone was telling an off-color joke. She had to be friendly, but not seductive, warm, but not provocative. It was a strain.

Fortunately there was a lot of work to occupy the men's attention. The weather was turning cool, so they had to begin to prepare the hides and skins for making winter clothes. And there was a great deal to see. The look of the land changed as they moved north. They began to see black earth, level land punctuated by short hills, fiery red clay bluffs along the banks, islands on the river covered with tangled dry weeds and wild rye.

They found the Indians living along the Upper Missouri very different from the Teton Sioux. For one thing, they were sedentary. The Arikaras built round, fire-heated houses of timber, earth and grass. The huts were large enough to hold whole families and horses, strong enough to repel the Tetons who occasionally came up river to steal their horses or women. The Arikaras were poor, but they were stable. The men hunted elk, deer and buffalo; the women grew corn, tobacco, squash and beans.

In their contact with the Americans, the Indians were calm, friendly and inquisitive. They were noticeably astonished by the color of York's skin. One of the old chiefs daringly reached out and touched York's arm with his fingertips to see if the black would rub off.

He broke into laughter when he looked at his fingers and discovered it wouldn't.

One of their friendly customs took Captain Lewis by surprise. On a cold, rainy evening in mid-October, Lewis was sitting comfortably inside his tent, drinking whiskey and talking with two men the expedition had met a few days before, Pierre-Antoine Tabeau, and Joseph Gravelines. Both men worked for Régis Loisel as agents with the Mandans. The Frenchmen were looking at Lewis's map drawn by the Welsh explorer John Evans when he visited the Mandans.

"This is good," Tabeau acknowledged, tapping the map with his fingernail. "Evans was wrong about a lot of things. He thought, for instance, that the Mandans were those Welsh Indians people have been talking about for centuries. But this is right. This is the Knife River here," he pointed. "Here are the two main Mandan villages. Right above them are the Minnetarees—"

They were interrupted by the appearance of an Arikara chief in the doorway of the tent. Lewis automatically stood up, invited the young man in, and extended a cup of Kentucky whiskey to him.

The chief took the cup, smelled the liquid, then handed it back, shaking his head politely.

"They don't drink whiskey," Gravelines explained, "because it makes them sick. They're smarter than we are about things like that."

"Then what does he want?" Lewis asked.

Gravelines got up and conversed with the Indian for a while. The chief was animated; he gestured vigorously with his hands toward the outside, at Lewis, then touched his hands to his chest lightly. Gravelines nodded, spoke a few words and opened the doorway for the chief to leave. A minute later the chief returned leading a small, attractive Indian woman who was almost completely enveloped by an old, balding buffalo robe.

The chief was obviously proud of his woman. He ceremoniously lifted away the robe, unveiling a buxom woman of about twenty, dressed in a tight buckskin dress. In guttural tones, with descriptive gestures, he pointed out to the three men the best of her physical features.

"I'm afraid to ask what he wants," Lewis told Tabeau.

"He wants you to have her," Tabeau explained. "He's offering her to you."

"What do you mean, 'offering'?" Lewis asked suspiciously. "As a slave? A wife?"

"No, no, Captain Lewis," Gravelines replied. "He's offering her to you for the night. It's the chief's way of showing his friendship. Not everybody can do it."

Lewis wrinkled his brow in surprise. "Are you saying he means for me to sleep with the lady?"

Tabeau laughed. "That's exactly what he means, captain. Personally, I think it's one of the Arikara's most endearing habits."

Lewis was extremely stimulated by the idea; he found the woman alluring. Her breasts were full and high, her waist small, her hips round and sensual. . . . And when she looked up from the floor and smiled softly and seductively at him with her romantically dark eyes, Lewis had to call on his reserves to resist her. Suppressing a sigh of regret, he shook his head at the chief.

Tabeau scratched his chest. "You're not turning down his offer, are you, captain?" he asked incredulously.

"Monsieur Tabeau," Lewis answered, "if I take this woman to bed, I'd be giving my men license to do the same. Which is one thing Mr. Jefferson doesn't want."

"It's only for one night, captain," Tabeau pointed out. "He'll come get her in the morning. And it's only you, it's not your men."

Lewis was thoughtful. "Whatever goes for me, goes for my men. As much as I'm tempted, I can't start something like this. I can't have my men leaving a trail of half-breeds throughout the Northwest. This is an official government expedition—we represent the United States. We can't stain its accomplishments with this kind of conduct."

"It's a harmless custom with them, captain." Tabeau admired the woman. "They don't look upon it as 'staining' anything."

"I'm sure they don't, and they certainly have a right to practice their customs. But as long as I'm leading this expedition, we have to practice ours, too."

"*Eh bien, monsieur,*" Tabeau shrugged. "It's your loss."

"Yes," Lewis sighed, gazing at the woman. "It is. But I'd like for you to explain to him why I have to refuse."

Gravelines talked with the chief for a few minutes. He and the woman accepted the decision without appearing to be offended, but both their faces showed their puzzlement. The chief took the woman by the hand and led her out of the tent, shaking his head.

That night, after the Frenchmen had gone, Captain Meriwether Lewis paced back and forth in his tent until the candle on his locker had burned down to darkness. Then he lay on his back and listened to the rain and thought about the Indian woman. Come dawn, he hadn't slept a minute.

Lewis had other visitors during the fall of 1804, as the news of the American expedition reached the fur-trading establishments around Lake Winnipeg and on the Assinboine and Qu'Appelle Rivers. One day a delegation from the three dominant trading companies in the Northwest came to see him.

The expedition was camped a mile north of an old deserted Mandan village. At three o'clock in the afternoon, Lewis and Clark were standing on a bluff, discussing their plans for winter quarters. As they talked, they gazed idly down at the river at a light snow powdering down over twenty or thirty buffaloes wading quietly in the cold, clear water. In the woods and plains around them herds of elk and deer, goats and bears ran unseen; below them, on the river banks, packs of hungry wolves sat out in the open, staring at the wading buffalo, ready to attack a weak or injured calf at any moment.

As the captains were watching the buffalo move about in the currents, they saw four men in a circular Mandan canoe pull up on the shore. Each was dressed in a European-cut beaver coat and matching hat. Sergeant Ordway met them, pointed up toward the bluff, then led them to the camp.

Later, inside Lewis's tent, the men identified themselves; two of them were from the North West Company's trading post on the Assinboine, the tall, thin man in the corner was from Hudson's Bay Company's post on the Red River. The other two were high-ranking representatives of the Great Pacific Fur Company on the Souris. The short, fat man from this company, Morton McKain, assumed the position of leader of the group. He stood up and began to pace while the others exchanged pleasantries. Finally he looked directly at Captain Lewis, unbuttoned his great coat, and locked his hands behind his back. "I see no sense in prolonging this, captain," he declared. "We're all busy men. We may as well speak directly. I believe you know why we're here this afternoon."

"Well, as a matter of fact, I don't know why you're here," Lewis admitted politely. "Unless it's to introduce us to the Mandans."

McKain, round with a reddish beard and practically no eyebrows, cleared his throat. "Well, we sent an Indian down here to tell you why we were coming, but no matter. I'm sure we'd be happy to introduce you to the Mandans, captain. But we all know you can handle Indians well enough yourself, you don't need us. We were impressed with the way you dealt with the Tetons downstream. You know you're the first American expedition to make it this far."

"We know," Lewis replied, waiting.

"Yes, well, if you know that, then perhaps you also know this area has been a British and Canadian trading territory for many years. Anderson's company," he nodded at the Hudson's Bay man, "has been trading up this way for a hundred and forty years, Laroque's company has been around ever since Mackenzie crossed the Chippewayan Mountains and made it to the Pacific. My own humble organization has been thriving ever since Colonel Bedford Styles opened up trade with the Mandans in '97."

"Sounds like you have a commercial triumvirate going up here," Captain Clark offered suspiciously. "Which is strange—Auguste Chouteau told us your three companies were constantly at each other's throats."

McKain forced a smile. "Well it is true we get a trifle agitated at each other at times," he admitted.

"But only a trifle," Francois Laroque added ironically.

McKain stared him down. "But that's only because we find the cold up here so irritating," he explained to Clark. "We have to let our tempers flare up once in a while to keep ourselves warm." He waited for a response to his joke, but got none. He went on: "We manage to settle our differences, though. We get along."

"But now," Lewis anticipated him, "we arrive on the scene. And when we find a passage to the Pacific, there goes your monopoly of the fur trade in the Northwest."

McKain was put off slightly. "I would say you're putting it rather bluntly, captain."

"But I am putting it correctly. You're all afraid of American competition. I can think of no other reason for three companies that are constantly at war with each other to band together to come to see us."

Anderson, the Hudson's Bay man, saw the handwriting on the wall. He started to get up. "I knew this would do no good, McKain," he snapped. "Let's get out of here. I've got better things to do than to waste my time here—"

"Now just a minute," McKain stopped him. "Before anybody goes anywhere, we deserve to know the captain's position here."

"There's no secret about our position, Mr. McKain," Clark told him. "We're here to establish the American claim to the Louisiana Territory. We're certainly not traders—"

"Yes, but you see, the traders will follow after you," McKain interrupted. "Let's face it, gentlemen. We all know as soon as the results of your expedition are published, the Northwest is going to be overrun with Americans trying to horn in on the fur trade."

"One American in particular," Laroque added. "A very rich and powerful one: John Jacob Astor. He has been waiting for this chance for years. Once you've completed your expedition, he'll break away from the North West Company and set up his own American business. He has the ability to control the fur market, captain."

"Look, men," Lewis said. "You should realize that neither one of us here is a businessman. We're both soldiers, we're not interested in fur trade."

"I'm afraid we're talking about more than 'fur trade,' Captain Lewis," Laroque argued. "We're talking about the possibility of a full-scale war up here."

"This is American soil now, Monsieur Laroque," Lewis declared. "There won't be any war."

"I admire your confidence, captain, but this is Canadian and British territory to the people who live up here. The Louisiana Purchase won't change that overnight."

"Then it'll have to change it gradually," Lewis told him.

"You're talking about violence, captain," McKain

nervously popped his knuckles. "Whether you care or not, people are going to lose their lives because of this expedition of yours."

Lewis was irritated by McKain's manner. "Look, why don't you just go ahead and tell us what you want? Maybe we can help you."

"Good, I'd be happy to tell you what we want," McKain answered. He glanced around at the others, then looked back at Lewis. "We have just one request," he held up one stubby finger. "We wish to accompany you on your expedition."

"You wish what!" Lewis cried, unable to contain his surprise.

"One representative per company," McKain went on. "Until you reach the Pacific."

"I'm sorry, we can't do that. That's impossible."

"It's not only possible," McKain insinuated smoothly, "it's necessary. If you don't want to start another war."

"I don't respond to threats, Mr. McKain," Lewis said simply.

"As much as I hate to admit it," Anderson broke in, "the man's right, captain. I have never approved of the Great Pacific's methods, but McKain is making sense here. If you allowed each of us to send a representative on your expedition—"

"So that you could learn what we learn, see what we see, make the contacts with the Indians we make?" Lewis shook his head. "No, William and I are explorers; we're not soldiers of fortune. We're not up here to promote anybody's business, and we're not going to be forced into treasure hunting with threats of violence."

"Then let us go as private citizens," McKain suggested. "Interested Canadians, perhaps. No one would be the wiser."

"No," Lewis stated. "I'm sorry. I'm not going to twist words around like that. I'll tell you the situation exactly as I see it, and exactly as I will enforce it: This is a government venture—we cannot allow any commercial enterprise on it."

McKain looked at Lewis for a moment, sizing him up. He took a deep breath, whipped out a purse from behind his coat. "Then we'll get down to the hard matters. How much money do you want, captain?"

"McKain!" Laroque exclaimed.

"Oh wake up, Laroque. All they are doing is playing with us, trying to raise the ante." He looked at Lewis solicitously. "How much, captain? Name it."

"Keep your money, Mr. McKain," Lewis muttered.

"Ten thousand dollars?" McKain looked at Clark. "Twenty? The three of us in this tent could raise twice that amount. What would you say to that, Captain Clark? Twenty thousand dollars for each of you. I can write out a company draft for you right now."

"I think you'd better leave, Mr. McKain."

"Ah, Captain Clark—even your almighty Mr. Jefferson has his price. What's yours? Fifty? Sixty thousand?"

Laroque got to his feet. "Put up your money, McKain. Can't you see you're not dealing with that kind of man?"

"Sit down, Laroque," McKain growled. "You're ruining the deal."

"There is no 'deal.'" He turned to Captain Lewis. "I am sorry, captain," he apologized. "I certainly didn't think we would be trying to bribe you into letting us go along. But Monsieur McKain doesn't seem to know any other way of conducting business—"

"I say, just a minute, Laroque—"

"Let it drop, monsieur. It's all over. You may as well give it up."

"That's the trouble with the North West Company, Laroque," he continued. "You give up too easily. You're willing to sit back and let these Americans have their way."

"Mr. McKain," Captain Clark stood up. "If you're finished—"

McKain looked up at Clark, who towered over him. "Yes, I'm finished," he grunted, gritting his teeth. He shot one more glance at Laroque, turned and stormed out of the tent. His clerk, Miflin, trailed after him.

"Morton McKain is an ambitious man," Laroque told Captain Lewis after he had gone. "And sometimes he can be a very persuasive one."

"He must be persuasive," Anderson agreed. "He talked us into this nonsense."

A heavy silence fell over them. Then Laroque broke it. "Captain Lewis, Captain Clark, I imagine we will see you again. I hear you're spending the winter with the Mandans."

"We hope to," Lewis responded. "If they don't object. That snow outside, though, makes me wonder if we're not already too late to start building our quarters."

"You still have plenty of time for that," Laroque assured him. "But if you need any help with the building, please contact the North West Company. We can provide you with tools, clothes—anything you need. It would be our pleasure."

"We have all we need, Monsieur Laroque," Lewis said. "But thank you."

"At least remember this: If you do need help, there is always one of our representatives around who can relay the message. If," he added, looking at Anderson, "someone from Hudson's Bay doesn't stop him."

"Thank you," Lewis said. "I'll remember that."

At that moment, outside Lewis's tent, Morton McKain looked at Miflin, flipped his fur collar up against the wind. "All right," he conceded, "it didn't work. Now I have no other choice. I have to talk to our man here in camp." He glanced back at tent. "Right now," he added.

Miflin, a medium-sized man of about forty, with hard, dark features, shook his head dubiously. "Don't you think it would be better if you waited until dark, Morton?"

"No," McKain shook his head, "it's better now. If somebody sees us together today, I have a reason for being here."

"Well, yes," Miflin agreed, "but it's still pretty risky."

"Of course it's risky, but what else can I do? Do you have any ideas?"

"No."

"Then keep your opinions to yourself and let me do this my way. I want you to stay here and make sure nobody in that tent sees me."

"I'll take care of them, Morton," Miflin assured him. "You go ahead. But hurry."

"I'll be back in ten minutes."

McKain quickly left and began meandering slowly and purposefully through the camp grounds, nodding "Good afternoon" and tipping his hat to the men as he walked through. But annoyance came into his face as he reached the edge of the campground without finding the man he was looking for. He stopped a young man who was coming into camp and asked him a question in a low voice.

"Who? Craddock?" the man asked. "Him 'nd Collins are out in the woods there, maybe a half-mile." The man jerked his thumb over his shoulder. "Skinnin' a buck and keepin' half of it fer themselves, no doubt." The young man shook his head and, at McKain's word of thanks, he strode away quickly. It was obvious to McKain that Craddock wasn't well liked here.

The snowfall was spotty now, too sparse and too fluffy to accumulate on the grass. In the shelter of the oak trees, there was little sound except the crackle of McKain's footsteps on the fallen, frozen leaves and the sighing of a harsh wind. But eventually he heard voices and, turning into the wind, he approached two men who were cleaning a deer under an oak tree.

The animal, a young buck, was hanging head down from a limb, Ned Craddock was slicing and peeling its skin off with his hunting knife. Hugh Hall was standing next to him, yawning, waiting for the hide.

"Well, good afternoon men," the man from Great Pacific greeted. "My name's McKain. Morton McKain."

"Afternoon," Hugh responded.

But Craddock didn't bother to turn around. He went on with the skinning; he jerked his blade down through the fat next to the inner skin and yanked off a strip of hide and flung it over to Hall.

"That's a nice buck you have there," McKain feigned an admiring voice. "What is it, six-point?"

"Yeah," Craddock answered coolly, "six-point." Then he turned to Hall. "Take that hide to Collins, Hugh," he ordered.

Hugh was puzzled. Craddock was only three-fourths of the way through skinning the deer. "Don't you want me to wait for the rest of it?" he asked.

Craddock was firm. He waved him off with his bloody knife. "Take it to him, Hall," he growled. "He's waiting for it."

Hugh raised his eyebrows questioningly, shrugged his shoulders and walked off carrying the skin over his shoulder.

As soon as Hall was out of earshot, McKain made a show of brushing snow off his sleeves. "Nice young man," he remarked in a cold voice.

Ned continued to work on the carcass. "Just what in the hell are you doing here, McKain?" he asked angrily. "You trying to screw everything up?"

"I am here doing what I'm paid to do, Craddock," McKain answered stiffly. "Which is something you might not understand. I was sent up here to try to salvage something out of the mess you're making of your assignment. Now correct me if I'm wrong, Mr.

Craddock, but wasn't the Lewis and Clark expedition supposed to have ceased to exist by now? Isn't that correct? Or am I confused about your duties for the Great Pacific Fur Company?"

"I figured the Tetons would turn us back," Craddock groused defensively.

"Well, you didn't 'figure' correctly, did you?— Damn you, Craddock, look at me when I'm speaking to you!"

Craddock faced him. "All right! I figured it wrong!" He tightened his grip on the handle of his knife. "Lewis pulled off some heroics and got us past the Tetons. What am I supposed to do about something like that? Anyway, it's not important, McKain."

The other man looked at Craddock with contempt. "I'll tell you what *is* important, Craddock. If this expedition makes it to the Pacific, the gate is open for American trading companies in the Northwest. Do you realize what that means? London will withdraw its money, our backers will call in our debts—Great Pacific Fur will collapse in less than a year. We must have the trade in this territory to survive, Craddock. If the Americans take it over, the company goes under."

"You worry too much, McKain." Craddock's voice was sarcastic. "I said I'd see to it they don't succeed, and I will."

"You still don't understand what I'm saying, do you? Every single thing I own in this world is tied up in this company. If it goes, I go with it. And so do Hollis, Carpenter and all the others."

"I understand that, McKain," Craddock returned defiantly. "I'm not stupid."

"Good. Then perhaps you don't mind racking that fertile brain of yours and telling me just how you've been earning the money we're paying you."

"All right, I'll tell you, but stay off my back, all right? I was working the men up to a mutiny—"

"Good. A mutiny sounds fine. What went wrong?"

"That damned Meriwether Lewis went wrong, McKain. He pulled everybody together when he brought us through the Tetons. Never seen anything like it."

"And you just stood and watched!"

"No, McKain, I didn't just 'stand and watch,' " he hissed bitterly. "I was putting a plan into operation when this mountainman stuck his big nose in—"

"Do me a favor, Craddock," he cut him off. "Spare me all your excuses—please. What you're saying is, you haven't done a thing."

"I'm saying I'm working on it, McKain. There's a long way to go yet."

"Not for you there isn't."

"Just what is that supposed to mean?"

"It means things are tighter than they were six months ago when we hired you to, do this job. The situation's critical now. Great Pacific is in trouble—"

"I told you I'd take care of it," Craddock promised him.

"Will you indeed?" McKain asked scornfully. "The way you 'took care' of your friend Clive Barton back in St. Louis? Is that the kind of behavior we can hope for?"

The mention of Barton's name puzzled and angered Craddock. "What's he got to do with this?" he shot back. "Clive Barton's dead and buried."

"Wasn't he supposed to be working for you on this assignment?" McKain wondered.

"That's right, he was. So what?"

"So I believe the man went and got himself killed last May, didn't he?"

"He didn't get himself killed," Craddock corrected him. "He was murdered. He got into a fight over some chippie in a St. Louis tavern."

"Yes, and you've done nothing whatever about his killer, have you? That's what I'm talking about, Ned. That kind of inaction is what makes the company wonder if they haven't overestimated you—"

"Now hold on a minute here. I'd like to know just what Great Pacific Fur Company expects me to do about Clive Barton when I'm out here knocking around in the wilderness for them? You tell them for me—I'll take care of whoever killed him as soon as I take care of this Lewis and Clark business."

"Why wait, Ned?" McKain coaxed. "The man who killed your friend is right here, on the expedition."

Craddock studied him silently, then objected, "He couldn't be. Everybody was in camp the day Clive was killed."

"Everybody but Lewis. And Drewyer. And . . . Tom Wentworth."

"Wentworth! Lewis's Philadelphia puppy? Come on—"

"I was in St. Louis when it happened," McKain told him. "I saw them take Wentworth to jail. And he would have had a trial, too, if Captain Meriwether Lewis hadn't stepped in. The good captain talked the judge into letting him go."

"Wentworth!" Craddock slapped the flat side of his knife against his leg. "I'll kill the bastard!"

"Good, Ned, kill him. Do something finally. I've had it with your excuses."

Craddock wiped his bloody blade on his trousers. "I'll do something, McKain," he retorted thoughtfully. "Clive Barton was an old friend. We grew up down in Georgia together."

"Well, I'm glad to know there is something that can move you to action."

Craddock raised his eyebrows. "You'd better not be lying about this, man. If you are—"

"For God's sake, Craddock, why should I lie?" he asked wearily. "It's a fact: Wentworth and Barton got into a fight over a woman. Of course the woman was hardly a 'chippie'—you're wrong about that. As a matter of fact, she was a lady, from New Orleans. And a rather mysterious one at that. As soon as Wentworth got out of jail, she disappeared from sight."

"Well, well," Craddock nodded, a glint of recognition in his eye. "A mysterious lady from New Orleans, hunh? You're talking about a good-looking woman with long dark hair, right?"

"Yes. That's right—"

"What was her name?"

"I don't know her name. What difference does it make? You don't know her, do you?"

"Oh yeah, I know her. I know her real well." Craddock's expression hardened at the thought of Roxanna Fairchild. "Only I never figured her for sleeping with the likes of Clive Barton."

McKain was amused. "I don't believe that was precisely how it was."

"Well, I don't care how it was—she's responsible, that's enough for me. She and that hothead Wentworth. I'll tell you something you can be sure of, friend—that pair will get what's coming to them."

"What do you mean, 'that pair'? The woman isn't here, is she?"

"I didn't say she was here. But you can go back to those folks in Montreal and tell them not to worry about the Lewis and Clark expedition. I guarantee you it'll never reach the Pacific."

"Good. I'm relieved to hear it."

"Now if you're satisfied, I've got work to do." Ned turned back to the deer.

"As a matter of fact, Ned," McKain insinuated casually. "There is one other thing. A rather large thing really."

"Whatever it is, I don't want to hear it," he said, cutting the deer's skin loose from its left hind foot.

"I imagine you'll want to hear this: we've hired somebody else."

"Good for you," Ned replied sarcastically. "Hire somebody else. Hire a hundred other people, I don't care. They'll all do their jobs, I'll do mine."

McKain watched Craddock make a long slit in the skin from the foot to the flank. "The reason we hired someone else is the other trading companies are getting suspicious of our operations south of Assiniboine. They've been poking their noses around where they don't belong."

"That's your business, friend, not mine."

McKain paid no attention to him. "You may have heard about some of this man's work. Last spring an investigator from Hudson's Bay Company was getting a little too close to your assignment, so we had our man take care of it for you. That was down at La Charrette."

Craddock stopped his knife. "I heard about it. The body turned up on Daniel Boone's place."

McKain grinned. "That's the one."

Craddock shook his head, surprised. "I sure didn't know it had anything to do with me. How would a Hudson's Bay man know anything about my assignment?"

"Who knows? It's possible your friend Barton let it slip to one of those drinking companions of his. Whatever—our man put an end to it."

"Just who the hell is this 'our man' you keep talking about, anyway?" he asked, resuming the skinning of the deer. "Jim Butler? Jean Lagrange?"

McKain was silent as he watched Craddock slice and tug the deerskin loose. "It's interesting how that comes off." He observed the action of the knife closely. "You know it's not that easy with human skin. Humans have too much fat, their skins and tissues are too closely bound together. It takes a real expert to skin a human being."

"You've got a sick mind, McKain," Craddock spat disdainfully.

"You know the Hudson's Bay man they found on Boone's place was skinned. They tell me he looked like a peeled grape. His whole body resembled the inside of your mouth—"

"All right, McKain!" Craddock interrupted him. "You've said your piece. Why don't you go?"

"Don't you imagine that is probably the worst way to die?" he continued. "He was skinned *alive,* you know. The killer first made a neat slit around the ankles, just like you've done there—"

Craddock had had enough. He turned around, held his bloody knife in front of McKain's face. "Shut up, man," he growled. "I'm tired of hearing you talk."

But McKain persisted. "I want you to think about that Hudson's Bay man," he said, looking directly up at Craddock. "I want you to imagine him screaming, kicking, squirming around in the wet green grass while his skin's being ripped off his bloody body—"

"Don't you threaten me, McKain," Craddock growled defiantly. "My knife is about ten inches away from that fat belly of yours. I'd think about *that,* if I were you."

"All right, Craddock. Listen to me. The man who skinned the Hudson's Bay investigator has been ordered to do the same thing to you."

"You little bastard!" Ned snarled. He grabbed McKain's collar, touched the point of his knife to his throat. "Say your prayers."

"Kill me and you'll end up inside out, Craddock," McKain warned. "I promise you that."

Ned glared hatefully at him. "You make me sick," he snapped.

"Get your bloody hands off me," McKain ordered him. He breathed easier when Craddock relaxed his hold a few moments later. "Get them off!" he yelled. "Now!"

Craddock released the collar, lowered his knife. His body was suddenly trembling with fear. His eyes instinctively searched around him for a glimpse of his potential killer. There was nothing. No sign of his killer.

"Who is he!" he demanded. "Tell me—who is he!"

"Never mind who he is," McKain answered coyly, straightening his coat with deliberation. "Just remember that he's around, watching every move you make. If you fail in this assignment, he'll do what he has to for us."

"At least tell me if he's one of Lewis's men," Craddock demanded desperately.

"Well I don't know—perhaps he is, perhaps he isn't," McKain answered vaguely. He always enjoyed having the upper hand. "You can never tell about things like this. He could be the man sleeping next to you—"

"Damn it, man!"

McKain held up a finger. "Don't touch me again, Craddock," he warned him. "I mean it."

Craddock showed him his palms. "All right," he muttered. "I'm not going to touch you. But this is sick, McKain. This man's got to be inhuman to do something like that."

"Then one morning you may wake up to find an inhuman man looking down at you," he sneered.

Ned felt a chill sinking into his bones. He shivered, trying to shake it off, but the cold gripped him tightly.

The little man from Great Pacific Fur Company shifted his beaver cap to its proper position on his head and rubbed his hands together briskly. "Nippy weather we're having. It looks like it's going to be an early winter this year."

"At least tell me *where* he is," Craddock begged. "Is that too much to ask? Is he here now? I can't go through every day waiting for him to show up—waiting for him to decide when he's going to come after me. I'll go crazy, man!"

"Go ahead, go crazy. We don't mind. Just make sure you do your job first."

"You're a cold bastard, McKain."

"And you're a coward, Craddock. I think we understand each other."

"I ought to kill you, right here and now."

"But that wouldn't be underhanded enough for you, would it? You're too gutless to do anything out in the open. You want to lie back and have other people do your dirty work. Well now, for once you're going to be forced to act, Ned. If you don't, count on it—you'll die a squalling, shrieking death in a god-forsaken place where not a living soul will hear your voice."

Craddock stood next to the hanging carcass and watched the other man tip his hat, utter a cheerful "Good morning," and walk away. He was furious with McKain and horrified at what he had said. Suddenly rage and panic seized him. He raised his knife into the air and began stabbing wildly, blindly into the deer's flesh. Five, ten, fifteen times he shoved the blade in and out of the mass of muscle, fat and bone—until finally, exhausted, he stopped and threw his body against the mangled deer. His face fell into its soft flanks as he panted rapidly.

Then he heard a sound behind him. A rustling of leaves sent waves of icy dread through his body. Was it the killer? he wondered. He held his breath and raised himself up. Was he here already, ready to make that neat slit around his ankles? Was he about to sling him down into the cold, snowy grass and skin him alive?

Terrified of what he was about to see, Craddock dropped his knife to the ground and turned slowly around, holding his hands in front of his chest, in a praying position, ready to beg for his life.

But there was no killer behind him. Not yet. The rustling sound in the leaves had been made by Private Hugh Hall, coming back for the rest of the deerskin.

Chapter 11

The cold, bright days of late autumn were stimulating and exciting times for the men of the Lewis and Clark expedition. The Mandan men they found on the Knife and Missouri Rivers were handsome, warm and generous; the women were temptingly attractive and lively. The maidens of both villages were inflamed almost into a fever by the presence of the young, bearded American men staying near their lodges.

Where there were Americans, there were Mandan girls. They hung close by, tittering, making jokes among themselves, teasing each other with sensual movements of their slender bodies in front of the men. When Fort Mandan, the winter quarters, began to go up three miles downstream, the Mandan girls came in parties to watch the work. And many of them offered to help prepare meals for the men.

Before long a few of the men gave in to their long pent-up desires, and, against the advice of Lewis and Clark, took some of the most willing maidens to bed with them.

"It's an easy thing to understand, Captain Clark,"

the new interpreter, Jessaume, tried to explain. "The Mandan girls aren't interested in men—they're interested in husbands. They consider it an honor to be taken as a wife by a white man. So, they're merely hoping. . . ."

"Even so, it's unhealthy," Clark observed.

"Yes, it is unhealthy. But Chief Shahaka looks the other way, and since they're his responsibility, maybe you should try to look the other way, too."

Despite the temptations, though, most of the men remained chaste. The captains themselves politely resisted the teasing of the Mandan women, as an example to the others. Tom Wentworth hardly paid them any attention at all—his eyes were blinded by one particular woman. The Mandan squaws seemed like pale shadows to him, when he compared them to Roxanna Fairchild. She had taken over his heart. Some part of him was far away, traveling with her everywhere she went.

But Roxanna had her own life and seemed to pay no attention to Tom. Within days of their arrival at the Mandan villages, she was right at home. Inside the stockaded walls; she shuttled back and forth from one dome-shaped house to another, as if she had lived there for years. She attended to sick babies, helped old women grind their corn, showed the young married squaws how to fix pumpkin and beans, New Orleans-style.

Tom worked, too. He chopped cottonwood trees, split logs, stacked timber, but always he kept an eye out for Roxanna. He was befuddled by her as she walked so obliviously among the men, her flowing hair as long and black as an Indian maiden's, her soft, curvaceous body accented by her close-fitting buckskin shirt and trousers. Sometimes all he could do was lean absent-mindedly on his ax and imagine making love to her.

More frustrating than this unsatisfied desire, though, was the fact that she consciously avoided him.

Whenever he got close to her, she turned her eyes away. At meals with the captains, she didn't talk to him. He tried hard to be near her, when he could, but the closer he got to her, the further away she seemed to be.

One day in November at the building site on the east side of the Missouri, he stopped by the storehouse for a new ax, and for the first time in weeks, he found her—alone. She was picking up a wooden bowl from a shelf as he stepped through the doorway into the dim cabin. As soon as she heard the sound of someone coming in, she instinctively turned, but when she saw who it was, she lowered her eyes.

"Hello," he greeted in a warm voice. This close to her, he felt a hollowness in his chest, a dryness in his throat.

"Hello, Tom," she tried to sound indifferent. She started to move past him.

He quickly placed his body between her and the open door. She stopped, and looked straight at him. In spite of herself, she wanted to touch him. He had changed since last spring, he seemed older, more mature. He was wearing a beard now, and buckskins, and he had gained solid weight. She found him more attractive than ever and that scared her.

"Could you stay a minute, Roxanna?" he asked her.

"No, I can't," she tried to put him off. "I'm supposed to be taking John Collins some clay."

"John Collins can wait," he pointed out.

"But the building can't," she insisted. "This cabin is the only one we've finished—we're running behind schedule."

"Oh, hang the schedule, Roxanna. Can't you just give me a minute? *One* minute? Don't I deserve that much, anyway?"

She paused, looked at him, nodded, and backed up. "You deserve a great deal, Tom," she said formally. "I want to thank you for keeping my secret all those months. I know it was difficult."

"It wasn't difficult, Roxanna," he replied. "As long as you were Garcia to everybody else, I didn't have to share you. What's difficult is now—knowing the other men are looking at you and feeling exactly the same way I do—"

"Tom, please," she stopped him. "Don't start anything." She looked at him with pleading eyes. "Just . . . don't start anything. I'm looking for my husband, you're looking for your money—"

"I don't care about that any more," he told her. "All I care about is you."

"Don't *talk* that way," she responded nervously. "We're friends, Tom Wentworth, nothing more. And I wish you could stop trying to protect me all the time—it's embarrassing."

He kicked the door closed behind him and stepped toward her. But he came to a halt when he saw her backing up again. "All right, Roxanna, answer me this: if we're just friends, why do you keep avoiding me? Every time I come anywhere around you, you find an excuse to leave."

"Do I?" she countered.

"You know damned well you do."

"All right, Tom, I'm avoiding you because I'm *married*. I should think it'd be pretty obvious. What do you want me to say?"

"You could say you cared. That would make the long nights a bit easier to take anyway."

She swallowed, closed her eyes, opened them again. "Well, I'm sorry," she responded. "I can't say that because I don't care." The lie hurt when she said it, but she couldn't think of another way to discourage this. She tried to be casual about it: "I don't want to sound callous, Tom, but I just don't care. Are you satisfied? Now if you don't mind, I'd like to go back to work."

He looked at her longingly for a moment, his emotions stirred by her presence. Then he nodded, sighed, and stood aside to let her pass. To his surprise, she didn't move. She stood clinging to the wooden bowl and staring at the black dirt floor. He thought he had never seen anything so incredibly beautiful as she was at this moment, with the autumn sunlight pouring through the window onto her glossy black hair. . . .

"Did you mean that?" she inquired finally. "What you said about not caring about the money?"

"Yes!" he cried. "God, yes, I meant it! I don't want any money, Roxanna. I only came out here to get enough to marry Isabel. Now that I've met you, she doesn't matter. I don't want to marry her—and I don't want the money."

"I don't believe you," she replied, searching his face. "When it comes down to it, you're only out to make your fortune. Everybody else is." Her words were heavy with resentment. She started to go, but he reached out and grabbed her arm. "I told you all I want is you. Damn the money! I don't care if I never have another penny as long as I live."

She didn't struggle when he spun her around and looked deep into her eyes, or when he pulled her body tight against his hard, muscular frame. A dull, aching desire was beginning to well up inside her and make her feel warm and womanly. She could feel her face flush with blood as she placed it against his firm shoulder and closed her eyes.

Tom ran his fingers through her hair and breathed uneasily for a few seconds. "Roxanna?" he murmured.

"Shh—" she whispered, clinging to him. "Don't say anything. Just hold me a minute." She wanted to savor that moment, hang onto it for as long as she could.

But he made her look at him. "Roxanna, I want to hold you more than a minute. I want to hold you forever. I love you."

She looked away. "Oh, Tom—no. You can't love me."

He gently turned her face toward him again. "But

I do," he drew close to her, touching his lips to hers. "I do love you," he repeated softly.

For a moment her emotions took over her reason. The natural passion she had held down for so long was violently awakened by his kiss. The dull desire now became a sharp craving, a powerful compulsion. She gave in to it; she wrapped her arms around him, kissed him eagerly, lovingly.

But then almost immediately the cool touch of his hand on her skin jolted her back to reality. She recoiled as his cold fingers groped at her beneath her shirt, slid over her chest, encircled her naked breast. "Tom—" she pleaded softly, trying to back away from him. "Don't—"

But he held her fast, pressing her breast with his fingers, and he tried to kiss her again. "Roxanna, I love you."

"Tom, stop! I'm married, damn it!"

"I don't care," he cried frantically. "It doesn't matter."

"Well, it matters to me," she insisted, attempting to wriggle loose from his grip. But she couldn't do it. She clutched his steely arm and tried to pry his hand off her breast, but he wanted her and she was no match against him. For the first time in her life she realized just how weak she was in a man's hands. The thought scared her: Tom Wentworth could do anything he wanted to with her and she would be unable to stop him.

His lips found hers again and he kissed her hungrily, pressing hard, hurting her. "You're so beautiful," he whispered between kisses, "so beautiful."

He would stop, she decided. He had to. But now there was the slow, steady pressure of his powerful body, of the man pressing against her, backing her up, forcing her to obey. She knew now what he wanted. He was going to rip off her clothes, throw her down and make love to her on the filth of the cabin floor. She looked up at him to beg him to stop, but what she saw frightened her. His eyes seemed hungry, loving her, but loving too much, almost mad with desire.

Somehow she managed to break loose from his hold. But his body blocked her. His need was inexorable. She had nowhere to go. She backed up slowly, covered her chest with her arms, shuddered—whether with fear or some craven longing, she did not know.

Tom looked at her with desperate eyes. "Roxanna," he sighed in an easy, distant voice. "I loved you the first moment I saw you coming down the stairs in that tavern, I haven't been able to think of anybody else since."

"Tom," she replied, anxiously, "if you really love me, please—let me go. Will you do that? Just let me go? Please don't do this to me."

"Do what?" he asked, surprised.

Her back was against the shelves in the cabin. "For God's sake, Tom."

"What are you talking about? Do *what?*"

"Do . . . this."

"Roxanna—" He almost moved toward her, but the terrified expression on her face made him freeze. "Dear God, Roxanna," he said, "I wasn't going to rape you. Didn't you hear what I said? I love you!" Without thinking, he took a step. "Your beauty—" he paused, reached out a hand to her. At a look, his hand fell. "I would never have done that, believe me—"

She didn't hear him. Her fingers searched blindly over the shelves behind her, located a hand ax. She snapped it up, held it out in front of her. "Get away!" she warned him.

"You are so wrong." There was real sadness in his voice. "I swear I would never hurt you, Roxanna. I would rather die."

The ax shook in her trembling hand. "Tom, if you don't want to hurt me, you'll let me go. Right now."

He shook his head dejectedly and moved aside. "Go," he told her.

She studied his face for a moment before she decided it was safe to move. Then she quickly darted past him, out into the bright sunlight that surrounded the cabin. It was ten minutes before she could drop the ax to the ground. And yet she could not say who or what she feared. Was it Tom, only Tom? Or something strange, wild and unknown?

For the rest of the day Roxanna Fairchild wrestled painfully with her emotions. Her feelings seemed to be twisted around each other, her conscience torn in different directions. She knew now without doubt that she was in love with Tom Wentworth—but she knew too that was wrong. She was a married woman. Added to that conflict was her confusion and guilt. Was the man she loved really going to rape her—or had he just been following *her* lead, responding to *her* desires? Either way she decided, she knew she would end up a loser. She was bewildered, angry and frightened by her conflicting emotions.

Two days after the incident in the storehouse Roxanna was daubing clay in the chinks between logs in one of the half-completed cabins at Fort Mandan when someone appeared in her life that took her mind off Tom Wentworth, at least for a while. She was working alone, oblivious to anything around her, unaware that the men had already paused for lunch nearby. Suddenly, she heard a calm, gentle sound behind her. "Ma'am?" a feminine voice called out.

Roxanna turned to see a pretty Indian girl of slight, delicate features, dressed in fringed deerskin decorated with blue, red and white beads. Her copper-toned skin and dark eyes seemed to make her radiant. "Good morning," Roxanna said, scraping the wet clay from her fingers into the bowl.

"You look sad, ma'am," the girl observed. Her clear English speech startled Roxanna and she quickly wiped the tears from her eyes with the back of her hand. "As a matter of fact," she admitted, "I am sad."

She noted that the girl was pregnant, but she mentioned nothing about it.

"You are too pretty to be sad," the girl replied softly.

The Indian had a curious, sweet expression on her face. She made Roxanna's problem with Tom Wentworth all of a sudden seem far away. "You're not Mandan, are you?" Roxanna asked. "I haven't seen you around here before."

"I am Minnetaree," she answered. "Born Shoshone." She smiled warmly. "My husband," she pointed toward the cluster of men next to the river. "Charbonneau."

Roxanna saw who she meant. The men were talking to a paunchy, middle-aged Frenchman with sagging skin and a scraggly beard, dressed in a poorly sewn, worn-out old beaver coat. She was appalled at the idea that such an innocent-looking girl, sixteen years old at the most, could be married to such a disreputable old man. On closer look, she noticed another Indian woman standing close to Charbonneau.

The girl noted her look. "Otter Woman," she explained simply. "Charbonneau's other wife."

"Oh."

"Here," the girl removed a bead necklace from around her neck and handed it to Roxanna. "You take it. It will make you smile."

Roxanna took the trinket automatically, then caught herself. "No, I couldn't—" she objected.

"Take it," she nodded.

"Sacajawea!" boomed out a voice from the river bank. "Come back here, damn you!"

The girl waved enthusiastically down at Charbonneau, smiled again and touched Roxanna's hand. "Goodbye. We will see your captain. We will go to the Shoshones together."

Roxanna stood in front of the half-built hut, holding the blue and white necklace as the girl scurried back to her husband. She was stunned by Sacajawea's brightness, her natural beauty and her poise. How, she wondered, could such a graceful person emerge out of a rude wilderness?

The others on the expedition were taken with Sacajawea, too. Meriwether Lewis admitted to Roxanna over a meal in the captains' cabin at Fort Mandan one evening, that it was because of the Indian girl that Charbonneau was hired as a guide to take them to the Shoshones next spring.

"Shahaka warned us that Charbonneau isn't much of an interpreter, or guide either," he told her. "But the men wanted him because they like Sacajawea. She has a strange effect on them."

"Oh really? What effect does she have on them?" Roxanna asked warily, curious to hear his account of her.

"Not the one you have, Roxanna," he smiled. He thought a minute. "I suppose it isn't strange either. She's just the kind of girl a man wants to take care of. Especially when you see how Charbonneau treats her."

"Just . . . 'take care of,' captain?" she teased him.

He shrugged his shoulders. "Don't get me wrong—I'm not denying the men see her as a woman, too. She is very pretty. But, I don't know, she's young, excitable, pregnant—she just looks like she needs protecting." He stopped, decided that he had gone far enough. "Besides," he added, "she can speak English."

"And how do you imagine one little girl ever came to know so much, Captain Lewis?"

"She knows a great deal because she's been around a great deal, I guess. She was born into one of the wandering Shoshone clans, but the Minnetarees took her captive a few years back. That old trader Charbonneau found her there, taught her English and married her. Minnetarees don't usually master our language, but she picked it up right away. I'd have to say she is a very intelligent young woman, besides everything else."

But Roxanna soon discovered that Sacajawea was also courageous and compassionate. Unlike any other woman she had seen in the wilderness, she was naturally independent. Charbonneau treated her and Otter Woman like cattle, but his treatment seemed to have no effect on her. Sacajawea was her own woman.

She demonstrated that three weeks after she arrived. On a crisp, clear November night after all the cabins of Fort Mandan were up and inhabited, a single Mandan brave stole past the fort sentinel and located the Charbonneau lodge, a couple of hundred feet from the fort. He lay on his belly in the grass outside the lodge for an hour, listening to the sounds of the night, waiting until the time was right.

At about ten o'clock, he decided to move. Jumping up silently, the brave crept into the lodge with fire in his eyes. Finding everyone asleep, he snarled loudly, whipped the hide blankets off the interpreter and his two squaws, shouted wildly and drew his knife.

But these were not the people he had come for. The woman he was hunting was cowering under a buffalo robe a few feet away. And when he spotted the squaw, he lunged toward her as if she were his only prey. But Sacajawea recognized the man. Instantly she leaped up from her bed and hurled herself in front of the squaw. "No!" she forbade him, shielding the woman with her body. "Go away! Leave her alone!"

"Ah, let him have her, Sacajawea," Charbonneau replied nonchalantly. He yawned and scratched his chest. "It's his wife. He's got the right to kill her if he wants to."

"No!" Sacajawea insisted boldly. "It's not right—it's wrong!"

"Damn you, woman!"

The Mandan cocked his head, raised his knife for Sacajawea to see. But she wasn't frightened by it. "No!" she repeated.

He curled up his nose at her and spit disgustedly on the floor.

Sacajawea rose up slowly, holding the Mandan's wife behind her. The woman looked desperately weak—her face was blue and puffy from being beaten regularly, her shoulders and arms had been lacerated by her husband's knife two days before. But Sacajawea managed to back herself and the woman out of the house.

The brave flashed his teeth furiously as Sacajawea moved past him, keeping her body between him and his wife. He followed them outside, uttering obscenities as he went. At that moment, a sentinel was passing by the lodge: "Get Captain Clark!" Sacajawea called out to him.

The sentinel, William Bratton, saw the Indian's knife, nodded and burst out across the yard toward Clark's hut. A few minutes after he left, the Mandan brave tired of waiting. Without warning, he leaped forward, pounced on the two women, grabbed Sacajawea's dress and threw her back toward the lodge. He kneeled down and pulled the head of the shivering woman and laid his knife against her throat.

Sacajawea lay curled up in pain on the ground, clutching her swollen belly, groaning in a small, low voice. Charbonneau remained still standing next to the lodge beside Otter Woman. He was simply observing, his face blank, apparently unmoved by what was happening in front of him.

"You with the knife—hold it!" Captain Clark called out. He and six other men came hurrying toward Charbonneau's lodge, guns in hand.

The brave's knife-hand stayed firm as he watched the white men gather around him. He looked at Clark and uttered a few short words the captain failed to understand.

"That's his wife he's holding, captain," Jessaume explained. "He says he's going to have to kill her because she ran away from him. He's warning us not to interfere."

Clark was irritated. "Well, you tell him I will interfere as much as I like, as long as he's on these grounds," he commanded Jessaume. "If he wants to kill his wife, that's his affair. But I'll be damned if he's going to do it here, on this property."

As the interpreter was relaying Clark's comment to the Mandan, Captain Lewis, with Roxanna and a handful of the men, rushed down the hill to join the others. As soon as Roxanna saw the Indian girl coiled on the ground next to the lodge, she raced over to her and fell down to her knees. "Sacajawea?" she asked excitedly, "did he hurt you?"

The Indian girl put her hand on Roxanna's shoulder. "No," she answered softly. "But my stomach. . . ."

"Oh Lord. Sacajawea—is it the baby?" Roxanna asked anxiously.

"No. Just my stomach," she slid her hand over her belly.

"Well, you just lean on me—that's right. It'll be just fine, just don't move for a minute or two."

Captain Lewis was standing next to the interpreter. "What's this man saying, Jessaume?" he demanded. "Has he explained why he's washing his linen on our doorstep?"

"He claims his squaw's been running off and sleeping with white men, Captain Lewis," Jessaume answered. "He says she's a disgrace both to him and his other wife."

The Indian grunted, nodded, and pointed an accusing finger at a tall man hanging back in the crowd, away from the captains.

Clark saw where the Mandan was looking. "Sergeant Ordway!" he called out. "Step out here!"

Ordway responded sharply, took six steps forward. "It's true I spent the night with her, captain," he confessed guiltily. "But he knows that. He offered her to me himself—we even used his bed. But that was all, I swear. One night, and I never saw her again till this minute."

Clark was piqued. "Damn it, sergeant. If you'd leave the wives of other men alone, we wouldn't be standing out here on a freezing night trying to reason with a jealous husband."

"He offered her to me, captain," Ordway insisted.

"I know he offered her; that's their way around here. But damn it, man, that doesn't mean you have to oblige them. They're not offended if you don't." He turned to the interpreter. "Jessaume, tell this Mandan he's mistaken. The men on this expedition do not sleep with Mandan wives unless their husbands ask them to."

The interpreter's translation didn't faze the Indian. He spat contemptuously on the ground, shook his head vehemently and promptly smashed his right foot into the woman's ribs. The white men flinched at the muffled sound his foot made in her chest, but they didn't dare move. The Indian glared at them, slammed his left foot into her and muttered something to the interpreter.

Jessaume nodded at his words, looked anxiously over at Captain Lewis. "He wants to give her to Sergeant Ordway."

"Sounds right to me," Lewis responded ironically. "Ordway deserves her."

"Now wait a minute—" the sergeant protested.

"You just hold it right there, sergeant," Clark ordered. "Stay out of this, you've caused enough trouble already. I hope you realize Sacajawea over there may lose her baby because you let your lust get the best of you—"

"Captain Clark! I told you it was only one night. I swear!"

Clark looked at him a minute, then glanced over at the lodge. "Mrs. Fairchild, how is Sacajawea?"

"I can't tell for sure, captain," Roxanna answered. "But I don't think she's hurt badly."

"Then take her into the lodge," he ordered, "I don't trust this brave."

They kept their eyes on the Mandan as Roxanna eased the Indian girl inside the lodge.

"William," Lewis suggested, "why don't we try to bargain with him? Sergeant?" he addressed Ordway, "you seem to be the main event here—what do you have on you that has any value?"

"I don't have anything of value, Captain Lewis—nothing but my old fusil."

"The fusil's fine. Give it to him."

"But it's still a good pistol, captain," he reminded him.

"Good—give it to him. Maybe he'll back up if we give him a way of saving face."

"Yes sir," Ordway obeyed reluctantly, easing out his pistol. He handed it butt first to the Mandan. The brave stared at it blankly for a few moments, then snatched it away, looked it over closely, all the time glancing suspiciously at Ordway out of the corner of his eye. Finally, satisfied with it, he placed his foot on the woman's back and pushed her toward Ordway.

The sergeant looked at her sympathetically as she groveled toward him, but he held up his palms, shook his head. "You keep her. Keep both of them."

The interpreter translated Ordway's words, the Mandan wrinkled his brow quizzically.

"Explain to him," Captain Lewis urged, "that she has not disgraced him. Nobody in this camp has slept with his wife without his permission. And while you're at it, tell him no man in this fort will sleep with *any* Mandan wife, from this second on. Not even if he's asked to by the husband."

The brave ruminated on these words for a while, then kicked the ground angrily with each foot.

The men stirred. "Better watch that red savage," a voice in the crowd rang out. "He'll kill her anyway. That's the way they do it."

"Shut up, Craddock," another voice sneered.

"The squaw's a whore—what do you expect him

to do? You want him to give Ordway a medal for bedding his wife?"

"That's enough, Private Craddock," Lewis commanded. He looked at the sergeant. "Give him your powder pouch, Ordway. Maybe that will satisfy him."

" Captain—"

"Sergeant Ordway," Clark pressed firmly. "Do you want this woman's blood on your hands? Do you want us to write that in our journals?"

"No sir."

"Then do as Captain Lewis says and give him the powder pouch. Then maybe he'll go and we can all go back to sleep."

Ordway nodded his agreement, slowly untied the pouch and handed it over. The Mandan took it, bellowed out a few words at him, then abruptly turned his back to the assembly and left. The squaw slowly got to her feet, gazed around with her dark eyes while she brushed off her dress. After casting one look at Sergeant Ordway, she lowered her eyes to the ground and hurried back into the darkness to find her husband.

A few minutes later the captains and most of the other men were crowding into Charbonneau's lodge, solicitiously trying to attend to Sacajawea while she sat up on a blanket and protested to all of them that there was no need for concern for her baby—everything was all right.

After this incident Sacajawea and Roxanna became friends. For a while, the Indian girl made it a habit to come by Roxanna's one-room cabin daily for a visit. She usually appeared early in the morning, with a bowl of colored beads and rawhide strips. Then she spent the next two hours talking to Roxanna about the life of Indian women while she made decorations for herself and her friends. Roxanna always found her fresh, vibrant and easy to talk to. Sacajawea possessed the ease and grace of a New Orleans lady—something she missed out here in the wilderness.

But as the weather turned colder and activity around the fort slowed down, Sacajawea appeared at Roxanna's cabin less and less. By late November, when the snow had spread a foot deep over the woods, she seldom came at all.

Roxanna did work with her once, on the seventh of December, on the morning of the buffalo hunt. It was a damp, cloudy, frigid day, the temperature one degree below zero, the snow two feet high, when one of the Mandan chiefs stormed loudly into the fort at dawn on his black horse. He shouted out at the top of his lungs, as if he had come to report the end of the world: "Buffalo!" he cried. "Buffalo! Buffalo near!"

At the first sound of his cry, the cabins opened up and men poured forth, guns ready. Captain Lewis quickly pulled together fifteen of his best marksmen, they pooled together and rushed out to join the Indians waiting near the herd. Sacajawea, big with child but still looking as innocent as a maiden, stole quietly across the bare ground and stood next to Roxanna, as the men charged out of the fort, whooping and hollering, plunging into the deep snow in pursuit of the buffalo.

That afternoon the men returned triumphantly dragging the heavy carcasses behind the three horses in the snow and carrying the rest of the bodies in parts on their shoulders. The two women offered to help John Thompson, the cook, by butchering the buffaloes out in the open air, near the storehouse. Roxanna found the work disagreeable at first, but Sacajawea made it easier for her. She showed her how to slice the meat rapidly, with simple, neat strokes of the knife, and how to keep her hands flexible in the cold air by warming them in the buffalo's entrails. When the snow came and they hurried to finish, she explained how Indians managed to get their food in the cold months.

"The snow is too deep for Mandans to find buffalo," she explained as they stacked the last of the bloody red meat on Thompson's cart. They had dressed and cut five buffaloes in three hours.

"So they have to wait until the herds come near the village—like today?" Roxanna guessed.

Sacajawea nodded. "Yes. But they *make* them come near."

"Now how in the world would they make them do that?" Roxanna wondered.

Sacajawea knelt down and scooped up a handful of snow and washed the blood off her hands. "Buffalo dance," she answered. "Three nights of buffalo dance."

It wasn't until an hour later that she explained. They were in Roxanna's cabin, in front of a cozy fire. Sacajawea sat making a necklace, while the orange glow of the flames flickered a golden color on her smooth face. "Buffalo dance is important to Mandans," she began, at Roxanna's request. "First day, the oldest men in the village gather in big lodge and sit in a circle. Then in front of each old man a young brave comes and begs for the old man to take his wife and sleep with her."

"Are the wives there at the time?" Roxanna asked, wondering how the women could put up with such treatment.

"Yes, they are there," Sacajawea answered seriously. "They wear only a robe."

Roxanna shivered. "Sounds uncomfortable," she observed.

Sacajawea smiled knowingly. "Yes, very uncomfortable."

It occurred to Roxanna that perhaps Sacajawea had been presented to an old man once, but she didn't bring it up. She asked her, "Do the old men actually take the young wives, Sacajawea? Or is it just a ritual?"

"Oh no," Sacajawea looked up from her necklace, surprised. "They take them. The old men move to other lodges."

"Oh." Roxanna thought a minute, watching the

Indian girl try to find a certain bead in her bowl. "Do all of them do it?" she wondered. "All of the old men?"

"All that can walk do it," Sacajawea declared in a matter-of-fact voice.

Roxanna laughed. "Yes," she smirked, "I guess they would. I suppose they'd do it even if they couldn't walk. But tell me, what happens the other two days?"

Sacajawea shrugged her shoulders and let a bead slide down a leather strip. "The same thing happens other two days," she replied simply.

"And all that 'sleeping' is supposed to make the buffalo come near the village?" Roxanna queried skeptically.

"Something makes them come near," she replied innocently. "Could be the old men."

Chapter 12

As much as she delighted in Sacajawea's company, Roxanna didn't see her for three weeks after that. While the Indian girl attended to Charbonneau and Otter Woman, Roxanna stayed in her cabin trying to keep warm, as the temperature dropped lower and lower each day. During the daylight hours, the mercury would reach above freezing, but at night it would dip down to thirty below.

Never having experienced such cold in New Orleans, Roxanna was astounded at how easily the Indians could manage to move around outside in light clothing. Sacajawea, for instance, sometimes accompanied Charbonneau as he walked up to the fort to talk to Lewis and Clark, or Laroque, the North West Company man, or Anderson of Hudson's Bay, when they were visiting. She usually stayed outside in the sleet, rain or snow in her deerskin and buffalo robe, and waited for hours for him. Roxanna, on the other hand, hated to leave her hut, even to bring in wood for the fire.

For Roxanna the private cabin was both a privilege of position and an obligation to remain private. Lewis and Clark had ordered it built for her so that she might have some privacy from the men and, in good weather, she enjoyed the freedom that this lodging afforded her. But with the advent of snow and freezing temperatures, she found that she almost felt like a captive. Most of the men kept a respectful distance—or made only brief calls to see if she wanted anything—and as Sacajawea's visits became less frequent, Roxanna began to feel isolated.

But there was one comfort she enjoyed during that long, cold winter at Fort Mandan. Back in the fall, she had pleaded with John Collins to build a watertight, wooden tub for her—pleaded so much that he finally acceded to her whim. Now, once a week, she would fill it up with hot water and treat herself to a delicious bath.

It was a great deal of trouble for her. She had to cart in cakes of ice from the river days in advance, in order to let them melt next to the fire. Then she had to boil the water and add it to the tub to warm the other water. But all the effort was worth it, she decided. Bathing in a tub was about her only link to civilization out there in the frozen wilderness.

One night in late December, she had finished building up the fire to heat the room sufficiently, and she had poured the boiling water into the tub and tested the temperature with her hand. Deciding it was ready, she shucked her doeskin dress and slipped into the tub. She rested the back of her neck against the rim and let the silky hot water caress and warm her naked body.

After sitting there for a few minutes, she became drowsy, her thoughts ran idly to Sacajawea. As she had before, she wondered now why the rough, bearded men of Fort Mandan reacted to Sacajawea as if she were a delicate piece of porcelain, while, polite as they were to Roxanna Fairchild, all she ever seemed to be able to produce in their eyes was lust. It was puzzling.

As she drew a rough, wet wash cloth over her smooth, full breasts, she thought of Tom Wentworth. They hadn't seen each other much in the past month, she had tried hard not to think about him. But every time she sank down warm and comfortable in the tub, she found herself longing for him to be there, with her, reaching down into the water, touching her—

Suddenly her thoughts were interrupted by an abrupt, bumping sound against the wall of the cabin. She immediately sat up in the tub, felt the cold air of the room chill her wet breasts. Listening closely, she thought she recognized another sound, this one near the closed shutters on the window.

Quickly she jumped out of the tub, threw a buffalo robe over her body and ran to the window. She flung open the shutters with a loud clack. But she could see nothing outside except the white cover of snow laid out evenly beneath the dim moon. She listened and looked again but could detect no movement at all.

The air leaking through the cracks in the window facing made her damp body shake. She closed the shutters, walked over to the fire and opened her robe to let the heat warm her exposed skin. Then she heard another bumping sound outside. She instantly pulled her robe together, wrapped her arms around her chest and held her breath. Her heart was pounding wildly.

An oppressive feeling of dread seemed to consume her. Never had she felt so vulnerable. The cold winter had made everyone so isolated that a man—an Indian, a trapper, anyone—could break into her cabin and no matter how desperately she called out for help, no one would hear her. An intruder could do what he wanted to with her. And here she was, standing around without any clothes on, waiting for it to happen.

Her skin seemed to shrivel up on her frame when she heard the noise at the door. "Oh, God," she whispered to herself.

She took a step toward the door, but then

stopped, afraid to move. A minute later she convinced herself that she had imagined the noise. But then there it was again—a low, deadened sound against the wooden door!

Finally, after what seemed an eternity, a firm, strong voice behind the door called out her name. She waited to hear it again, to make sure; when she heard it, she rushed to the door and whipped it open.

There was Tom Wentworth, standing straight and tall, his hands buried in his pockets. The air was filled with huge flakes of snow that were floating down onto his long wool coat and wide-brimmed hat. After a few seconds of patient waiting, he lifted his scarf from his face. "May I come in?" he asked. "It's damned cold out here."

"Oh," she caught herself. "Yes. Please, come in."

"Thank you." He entered the cabin and shook the snow from his coat. He immediately crossed over to the fire and began rubbing his hands briskly in front of the flames. "I don't think I've ever been so cold," he complained.

Roxanna stood with her arms crossed, looking at him. "You certainly make a lot of noise about it."

"What?" he asked, knocking the snow off his hat over the fire.

"Never mind," she told him. "You just scared me out there."

He turned his back to the fire, pretending to notice the tub for the first time. "I didn't mean to interrupt your bath," he apologized and blew into his hands.

"You didn't interrupt me," she comforted him. "I was through."

He looked at her silently for a minute, then unbuttoned his coat. "Roxanna," he announced, "I've been trying for weeks to work up enough courage to apologize to you."

"You don't have to apologize," she stated coolly.

"Yes I do, so don't stop me. I lost control of myself in the storehouse, all right? I didn't mean anything by it, I just lost control. I'm sorry. I realized as soon as you ran out the door I'd been a fool. The only reason I can think of to explain what I did," he said longingly, "is that I love you."

"Tom, damn it!"

"Well, it's true. I can't help it. How could I? Look at you—you're so beautiful in that robe. . . ."

"I'm freezing in this robe," she declared. "I was just going to ask you to turn your back so that I could put on some clothes."

Tom obliged, turned to face the fire again. "Are you accepting my apology?" he asked.

"Yes, Tom," she answered. She pulled on her deerskin trousers and tied the leather strap together in front of her waist. "You didn't act much like the Philadelphia gentleman I thought you were, but I accept your apology."

"No harm done then?"

"No. No harm done."

"I won't do it again, Roxanna. I promise."

She slid the tight buckskin shirt down over her breasts. "You're like a little boy that's been caught with his hand in the pie, you know it?" she snickered.

He turned around and looked at her steadily. "Still, the touch of you was a fine thing."

She looked at him a minute, wondering almost abstractly whether to be offended or pleased by his frank words. The snow on his golden beard was beginning to melt and glisten in the firelight. He was an extremely attractive man; she could easily allow him to stroke her skin as she lay naked in the tub, just as she had imagined it so many times—but no! She shook her head, blushing. Stop imagining such things, she chided herself. "Tell me something," she said aloud, affecting a stern tone. "Did you get out in this cold just to apologize to me?"

"What makes you ask that?"

"I don't know, you looked awfully businesslike when you first came in."

"Well, yes," he conceded, "there is one other thing. It's not business, but it is important, I guess. Captain Lewis asked me to come over and tell you about it. Just now I was hoping I wouldn't have to tell you, but I suppose I may as well. You'll hear about it eventually—"

"Hear about what?"

Tom took off his scarf and coat and placed them carefully on the table near the fireplace, next to his hat. "It's about your husband," he began.

"Oh God, no. Is he dead?"

"No, no," he assured her quickly. "He's not dead. At least nobody has said he is."

"Then what is it? Tell me!"

"It's not proof, Roxanna, but they think it was Fairchild—"

"Tom—" she interrupted.

"All right, this is all we know. A couple of hours ago, one of Régis Loisel's men, Hugh Heney, was telling Captain Lewis about his friend Charles Chaboillez, who runs the North West trading post on the Assinboine up in Canada. Heney and Chaboillez were down in the Louisiana Territory last fall, exploring. Heney claims they ran across your husband at a post on the Souris River."

"Where is that? Is it near here?"

"It's up north a ways. It crosses the border from Canada."

She looked at him curiously. "I don't understand," she mused. "What was he doing up there? Are they sure it was Douglas they saw?"

"Heney seemed sure, Roxanna. He was English, he had red hair—and one of his Indian companions called him 'Douglas.'"

She sat down on a stool, dejected. "Canada," she intoned. A few seconds later she looked up at Tom. "He wasn't a captive or anything?"

"No, he wasn't anything like that. He was buying whiskey at a Grand Pacific Fur trading post on the Souris, getting ready for a trip west."

"West, where?"

"Heney said he mentioned the Chinooks once. They're a tribe of Indians out near the Pacific Ocean."

"Tom," she asked worriedly, "why is he doing this? What's he doing up there? And who are these 'companions?' I can't believe we're talking about the same person I knew in New Orleans. Douglas is such a gentleman. It must be someone else."

"I don't think so, Roxanna."

"It has to be."

"What do you know about him, Roxanna?" he asked her. "Did you know him long?"

She paused, considering whether to tell him about Douglas Fairchild. She was silent as she watched Tom throw another log on the fire and stoke the flames, his thoughtful way of giving her time to measure her answer. "I knew him a grand total of a week," she blurted out. "It sounds silly now, but then I really thought it was enough. He was absolutely charming. He was kind, attentive, educated, wealthy—" she stopped, pressed her lips together and closed her eyes.

"Go on," he prompted her.

"That's all," she evaded him. "He was kind, attentive and educated."

"And wealthy," Tom completed the thought for her.

She stirred a little. "I thought he was. Everybody in New Orleans thought he was, too. But I've wondered about it ever since I woke up and found him gone. I guess what you're saying now, about his not being captive, confirms what I was trying hard not to believe."

"Roxanna, I'm not following you."

"What I'm saying is, as long as I believed what I was told, that Douglas had been captured by Jean

Lafitte or his pirates, I didn't have to believe he did what he did to me."

"But what did he do?"

"He made me sign a draft," she turned away. But there was no stopping now. The confession sprang from her lips, mingled with self-reproach: "It was so stupid of me! We were together in our hotel room . . . in bed." She waited a few seconds, then went on. "He was teasing me, playing with me, claiming I really didn't love him. I swore to him that everything I had was his and he said, 'Prove it.' He had me sign a draft making his money and mine one. I thought he was wealthy, Tom, so I assumed it was just a joke—something we'd laugh about in the morning."

"But in the morning he drew out your money and ran."

"Yes. But I didn't know he *stole* it. I thought he was captured by those pirates that hang around New Orleans."

"You just didn't want to believe he'd robbed you. How much did he take?"

"He took all I had, over three thousand dollars. Every penny of my inheritance."

He shook his head. "I can understand why you've been chasing this scoundrel for eight months."

Roxanna felt ashamed. It was the first time she had admitted, even to herself, that Douglas had actually stolen the money. "I loved him, Tom," she insisted, trying desperately to buoy herself up. "And he loved me. I'm sure he did. There has to be some reason for what he did. There just has to be."

"There was," he concluded, plopping down on the log bench in front of the fireplace. "Over three thousand of them."

"Thank you for your reassurance."

"I can see why you've been so sensitive about my coming out here to make money. Considering what that no-good rascal did to you, it's enough to make you wary."

"Do you think we could forget Douglas for a while, Tom?" she asked.

"Sure. I'd be happy if we could forget him forever." He emphasized the word "we." "Why don't we just end your search right here and now? We can go back down the river in the spring, when Captain Lewis sends the specimens pirogue to Mr. Jefferson."

She shook her head. "No, we can't."

"Now listen to me, Roxanna. We can. We can just turn ourselves around right here and go back together and start a new life."

"What kind of life would that be, living on Royal Street like some New Orleans gentleman and his quadroon mistress? No thank you. We'd be outcasts in my own home, Tom."

"We wouldn't be if you wanted it badly enough. No one would have to know Douglas Fairchild is still alive."

"*I* would know, Tom. And so would you."

He went over and knelt down in front of her and took her hands in his. "But damn it, Roxanna, I love you. And you love me. I know you do. Admit it. You love me!"

She looked at him and smiled sadly. "It's pointless, Tom. Since I'm a married woman, whatever I feel for a man who isn't my husband doesn't matter."

He got to his feet, irritated with her. "So you're just going to keep tracking him down all your life?"

"I'm going to keep tracking him till I find him. Then I'll know, one way or the other, what to do."

"He doesn't love you, Roxanna. He was nothing but a thief. All he wanted was your money."

"Maybe he doesn't love me," she acknowledged. "But I have to know for sure. I have to see for myself."

He stood up. "God," he declared, "you must be the most stubborn woman who ever lived. You trail one man through a wilderness for over two thousand miles without so much as a whimper. Then when another man—a man who loves you—so much as touches you, you bolt like a young heifer!"

"Just what is it you expect me to do, Tom?" she demanded angrily. "Shall I forget everything, erase the past—deny who I am and what I've done just to please you? Is that what you want?"

"No! I just want you to love me. That's all I ask. Not even that—just *say* you love me. That would be enough."

"Oh, God," she cried. "You're as stubborn as I am, aren't you?"

"Yes, I am. Say it!"

"No," she told him. "I can't."

He sighed. "All right," he reached for his hat and coat. "You'll come around to it eventually. I've been waiting a long time now, I guess I can wait a little longer. We have a lot of time—it's going to be a long, cold winter."

She desperately wanted to fold her arms around him and kiss him, but she kept still. "Thank you for coming," she told him as he reached the door. "I'm glad to finally hear something about Douglas, good or bad."

"Could I come back, Roxanna?" he asked her.

"Yes, you could do that," she brightened. "But," she teased him, "next time, try not to be so noisy about it."

He looked at her seriously. "What do you mean? All I did was knock on the door a couple of times. I wasn't noisy."

"You didn't walk around the cabin before you got to the door?"

"No, I didn't," he protested. "I came straight from the captain's cabin to yours. What are you talking about?"

"Well, somebody, or some thing was out there," she muttered. "I heard two or three sounds coming from outside the walls. I naturally assumed it was you."

Tom frowned. "It wasn't me. Get me a lantern," he told her, buttoning his coat. When she had returned with it, they stepped out into the cold air. A few minutes later they were standing near the back side of the cabin. Tom held the light close over the ground, peered down at a series of half-filled footprints in the snow.

"What is it?" Roxanna asked. She held her robe together tightly.

Tom squatted down, dug a handful of snow out of one of the prints. "Somebody's been prowling around here all right. The tracks go all the way around the hut." He got up and followed them slowly for five or six feet. "Looks like he stopped here," he pointed. "These prints are deeper than the others. He must have stayed here awhile."

She stared at the ruts in the snow. "Can you tell who made them? Was it an Indian?"

He shook his head. "There's no way to tell, Roxanna. They're half-full of snow. I couldn't even say whether his feet were in moccasins or boots. Damn! If I had just noticed them when I got here. . . ."

"You didn't know, Tom," she consoled him. "I should've said something when you came in."

He panned the lantern beam over the footprints. "I'd guess from the depth of these tracks, he left about the time I got here. I probably scared him off."

Roxanna thought about that for a second and shuddered. "I wonder what he was doing out here at this time of night."

"I think I can guess what he was doing," Tom answered, moving the lantern closer to the cabin. The instant the light beam lit up a certain section of wall, his guess was confirmed. Between two of the logs that made up the wall, at a distance of four feet from the ground, was a small, round, open space. He examined it more closely, rubbed his finger over the place where the clay had been chipped out with a knife. He brought his eye close to the crack and peeped through it into the cabin. "Just what I thought," he fumed. "The son of a bitch!"

"What's wrong?" Roxanna asked.

He backed away. "You'd better see for yourself," he told her.

She looked at him quizzically, then stepped up and moved her face close to the crack. Holding her breath, she peered in. Through the peephole, she could look straight into the one room of the cabin. What she saw was a clear and unobstructed view of the wooden tub sitting near the fire. A wave of nausea poured over her. "Oh, Tom," she exclaimed.

"He was standing out here watching you take a bath," Tom replied. His face, dimly lit by the glow from the lantern, was rigid, pressed with anger.

"But *who* was watching? Who was out here?"

"I don't know. One of the men, a Mandan, a Teton Sioux following us up river—who knows? But I'll tell you one thing—I'm going to find out."

She clutched her arms over her chest. "I'm scared, Tom," she whispered shakily. "I knew something was wrong. I could feel someone watching me."

"I wonder if this could have been Buck Brussard," he fumed. "I've always hated the way he leered at you—"

"We haven't seen Buck Brussard for months, Tom."

"I know we haven't, but that doesn't mean he's not around. Chief Shalaka told me the other day one of his braves saw him in the Minnetaree village."

She shook her head. "He saved our lives, Tom," she reminded. him. "I can't believe he's the kind of man who'd sneak around and peek through cracks in a wall. I won't believe it."

"Well, maybe he's not, but these prints weren't made by the wind—somebody had to be out here looking at you." He traced the tracks around the cabin, back to the front door.

Saying nothing, he led Roxanna into the cabin

where they knocked the snow off their clothes and began warming themselves in front of the fire. Tom added more wood to the flaming stack of cottonwood logs, jostled the embers underneath with a poker.

There was a heavy silence over the room for a while, then Tom broke it. "Whoever it was," he tried to comfort her, "he won't be coming back tonight. I'm sure of that."

"Well, I'm not sure of it," she protested.

"Are you scared?" he asked with quick concern.

"Yes, I'm scared," she admitted. "I've known it for months, Tom. I just didn't want to admit it. Somebody has been watching me, everywhere I go. Now, even here in my own cabin. Every time I think about sitting there naked in the tub and him staring at me. . . ."

"Would you like for me to stay here tonight?" he asked in a hushed voice.

"I thought you were going back to Captain Lewis."

"The captains are up drinking with Heney; they won't miss me."

"I'd feel awfully guilty asking you to do that," she confessed. "After what I accused you of."

"You don't have to feel guilty," he assured her. "It's a reasonable thing to do. I ought to be here—whoever was out there could crash in through that door at any minute." He waited for a response, but got none. "Look, I'll get under this robe in front of the fire, and you'll never know I'm here. In the morning we can fix that crack and I'll make you a better latch for the door. Does that sound all right to you?"

"You're being more thoughtful than I deserve, Tom," she admitted. "I did accuse you of rape, you know."

"I know; forget about that. You go on to bed, I'll be fine. If anybody does show up, I'll drown him in that tub of yours."

She smiled. "Just like always—Tom Wentworth, my protector."

"I'm not 'protecting' you," he insisted, a bit provoked at her. "All I'm doing is sleeping here on the floor in case the bastard who was peeping through that crack in the wall tries to break in."

"Well, I thank you for doing it, Tom. I appreciate it more than I can say. I really mean that."

"Just go to bed, Roxanna," he muttered, a little embarrassed.

"Are you sure you'll be all right on the floor?" she asked doubtfully.

"No, as a matter of fact, I'll be cold on the floor. But—if that's the way it has to be, that's the way I'll do it."

Later, under a heavy stack of hide robes and Indian blankets, Roxanna couldn't fall asleep. Each time she began to doze off, something outside jerked her awake—the howl of the wind, a screech of an owl, the laughter of men playing cards somewhere in the fort. Every few minutes she'd flip over on her stomach, then her side, then her back again.

As the night wore on, the fire smoldered and the damp air in the room took on a piercing chill. She was luxurious and snug under her covers, but she could see in the fading glow from the embers that Tom was shivering beneath his robe. Once, in the early morning, she managed to sleep for a while, then awoke to find the room almost completely dark. The fire was gone, it was nothing but dead ashes; she couldn't even make out the shape lying in front of it.

"Tom?" she called out softly. When he didn't answer, she raised up and leaned on her elbow and squinted her eyes to try to see him. "Tom?"

"What is it, Roxanna?" he asked sounding wide awake.

"I'm sorry—did I wake you up?"

"No. What do you want?"

"Are you cold?" she asked him.

"Now what on earth would make you think that?" he growled.

She eased back down in the bed, laying on her back. After a minute, she asked him, "Are you sure you're all right down there?"

"No, it's wonderful," he grunted sarcastically. "It beats the Essex Inn in Boston."

She took a long, halting breath. She had fought the idea long enough. She had to do something or she would never get to sleep. She decided it was ridiculous for the man who was protecting her to be lying on the floor quaking with a chill while she was resting comfortably in bed. "Tom?" she repeated.

"Why don't you go to sleep, Roxanna?"

"I can't sleep," she answered, her voice quiet but insistent.

"That's because you keep talking."

"I always talk when I'm nervous," she explained.

"Just try to put him out of your mind, Roxanna. If he hasn't come back by now, he probably isn't coming back."

"That's not what I'm nervous about."

He sat up to look at her but all he could see was the vague outline of her bed in the darkness. "Roxanna, if you don't mind, I'm tired, I'm sleepy and I'm damned cold. I don't really want to sit here in the dark and talk all night."

"There's plenty of room for you in here," she announced, surprised at how easily the words had come out.

He let the invitation hang in the cold room for a while. "Do you mean," he spoke finally, "in bed?"

"Yes. I'll be quiet if you'll come to bed. I promise I won't disturb you."

"Roxanna, are you teasing me?"

"No, I'm not teasing you. I'm simply offering you one-half of my bed." Then she added, "Just one-half. That's all."

"Well a half is enough," he declared. He whisked

off the robe, got to his feet, and fumbled his way across the room toward the bed. When his toe slammed into a bed post he stumbled and reached out to balance himself. His hand landed on something soft.

"That's my leg, Tom," a warm voice in the blackness said.

"Oh, sorry," he mumbled. He felt for the empty side of the mattress, found it, lifted up the covers gently and climbed in as carefully and easily as he could. Then, turning his back to Roxanna, he drew up his knees and brought his arms in next to his body to try to bring some life and mobility back into them. But the gelid feeling in his bones lingered; he couldn't stop shuddering.

After a while, Roxanna asked him in a low voice, "Are you still cold?"

"I'm still cold," he answered. "I may never stop shaking."

"Oh, well, come over here then," she invited. "Turn around." He remained still, so she prompted him again. "Turn around, Tom."

It was then, at the instant he rolled over toward her, that he felt her soft, tender arms wrap around him, then her full, round breasts press against his chest through their deerskin clothes, and finally, her firm legs push solidly against his thighs.

Her warm, sensual body immediately eased his pain. It seemed to reach in and suck the cold out of his limbs. Minutes later in her comforting arms he felt his blood begin to flow easily in his veins. He closed his eyes and held on as tightly as he could without hurting her.

When Roxanna opened her eyes the next morning, she saw Tom Wentworth standing four feet away, with his back to a hot, blazing fire. He was sliding his arms into his coat and throwing it over his shoulders.

"Where are you going?" she asked him, rising up on her elbow.

"Well, good morning," he greeted her, buttoning his coat. "How did you sleep?"

"I slept very well, thank you. Did you?"

"As a matter of fact, Roxanna, I didn't sleep at all last night. I was warm enough, nestled against you, but, I don't know, something was missing."

She sat up in the bed. "Tom, I told you before you got in "

"I know what you told me," he smiled, holding up his hands. "Making love to the married woman is not allowed. Fine—I went along with it, didn't I? I just wanted to tell you it wasn't easy, lying there all night like a warm . . . monk, or something."

She tried to hide her amusement as she got up, covered herself with the buffalo robe and came over to the fire. "Where are you going so early? I thought we'd have breakfast together."

"Can't do it," he replied. "I'm going with Captain Lewis and Mr. Jessaume up to the Minnetaree village this morning. Captain Lewis is trying to find out from them if there really is a northern tributary of the Missouri. They keep talking about the River That Scolds All the Others, but he doesn't think that's the one we're looking for."

" 'We're' looking for? Does that mean you're not looking for money any more?"

He buttoned the top button of his coat. "I told you I'm not interested in that any more, Roxanna. Captain Lewis says if we can find a northern tributary of the Missouri that extends beyond the forty-nine-degree line, we may be able to extend the Louisiana Territory border into Canada."

"I don't understand. What good would that do? The Louisiana Purchase made the country twice as large as it was—isn't that enough?"

"It's not a question of 'enough,' Roxanna," he explained. "You see, that's established fur country up there. If there is such a tributary, then maybe it connects with the Columbia River. If we can reach and claim it, then the United States will have an unbroken flow of commerce from Canada down through the Missouri to the Mississippi, and from Canada down through the Columbia to the Pacific. That would connect our China-Pacific trade with the rest of the country and it would give us a continuous route for the fur trade in the Territory and Canada."

"Is that where we're going in the spring? Canada?" Roxanna recalled that Douglas Fairchild had been seen there recently.

"We're going to keep following the Missouri, but we'll probably be traveling over land a lot of the way. Sacajawea says the Shoshones, the Snake Indians, she calls them, can guide us through the mountains. They also have enough horses to outfit the whole expedition. We'll be trying to contact them next summer."

She smiled. "You're really caught up in this, aren't you?"

"Caught up in what?"

"In this expedition."

"I'm a part of it, yes," he admitted. He was a bit embarrassed that his enthusiasm was so obvious. "I just didn't realize when I came out here how important it would be." He looked at her stiffly. "What are you smiling at?"

"Nothing. Here's your hat."

He took it from her and put it on his head. A minute later, he asked seriously, "Do you think you'll be all right here?"

"Yes, I'll be fine," she replied. "Till it gets dark anyway."

"Here." Tom drew out his pistol. "I want you to have this, Roxanna. It's my father's flintlock." Tom held the weapon respectfully. Compared to the modern pistols, it seemed ungainly, with its long bore and heavy hammer. But it was a fine weapon and the expert craftsmanship showed in the inlay of the stock and barrel. Tom poured a small amount of powder into the pan and pulled back the sharpened piece of flint that was held in place by the hammer bolt.

"Keep the powder dry and don't draw the hammer until you're ready to fire," Tom instructed. "Then aim and pull the trigger." He sighted down the barrel toward a mark on the wall. Roxanna held up her hand to protest but Tom smiled and quickly lowered the pistol. "That's all." Gently, he lowered the hammer from the cocked position, then handed the flintlock to Roxanna, butt first.

She took the gun, looked at it. It seemed gigantic in her small hands. "Do you think he'll be coming back, Tom?" she asked.

"I don't know. What I do know is that you'd better keep that thing handy just in case. If someone breaks in, aim at his stomach. It shoots high, so you'll probably hit his heart."

"My God," she recoiled from the idea.

"Just keep it handy," he walked away from the fire. "You probably won't have to use it." He reached the door, laid his hand on the latch. "I'll be back this evening to look in on you," he promised her.

"Thank you."

He opened the door. "In case I haven't said it already, Roxanna," he said warmly, "you're a damned fine woman." He started to go, then turned around. "And you know what?" he added. "Asking me to sleep with you and then not breaking your marriage vows proved something to me."

"Did it?"

He smiled. "Yes, it did. It proved you loved me, Roxanna, I don't care if you admit it or not. And it proved that someday you'll be that faithful to me, and nobody else."

And with that proclamation, Tom closed the rough wooden door behind him and marched off into the falling snow.

Chapter 13

As the cold winter days came and went, Roxanna became more and more apprehensive about the invisible man who seemed to stalk her wherever she went. There were other incidents, other indications that someone was watching her constantly. Whenever she went out for a brief turn in the woods, she felt a presence near her, behind the trees somewhere. When she walked with Tom on the iced-over river, she thought she caught a glimpse of a man lurking along the bank—watching them.

Sometimes at night, she heard disturbing sounds outside her cabin. One morning just before dawn, she even detected the latch on her door moving slightly. She grabbed Tom's pistol and cocked it and waited for the intruder to force his way in, but nothing happened. "It must have been the wind," Tom told her the next day. "Or maybe you were imagining it."

But if she were imagining some things, other things were very real. She found real tracks outside her cabin again. A lace handkerchief she had brought from New Orleans was stolen from the hut. And once she returned from Sacajawea's lodge and found the latch broken, the door wide open, and the whole room littered with overturned furniture and melting snow.

During this time her social intercourse with the men naturally became strained. Besides the captains and Tom, she could trust nobody. On December 25, 1804, Captain Clark closed the fort gates to the Indians and everyone celebrated Christmas Day with shooting, drinking, eating and dancing. Roxanna felt uncomfortable every time a man got close enough to ask her to dance. She would stare into his face and wonder if he were the one who stalked her, day and night.

At eight-thirty on that evening, just before one of the swivel guns blasted the end of the festivities, Private Ned Craddock, drunk and boisterous, accosted her at the party in the captains' cabin.

"Well, well, if it isn't Lady Garcia," he bellowed derisively. "Had anybody flogged lately, Garcia?"

"Mr. Craddock. . . ," she tried to put him off.

But he stood his ground, glowered at her. "You're a superior bitch, aren't you?" he grunted in a low voice. "Don't you think so?"

"No," she replied calmly. "I don't think so."

"Well *I* think you think so." He laid his hand heavily on her shoulder. "And my friend Clive Barton thought you thought so—" he slurred his words.

"You're drunk, Mr. Craddock," she interrupted, wriggling her shoulder out from under his hand.

"Yeah, sure, I'm drunk, what about it? So was old Clive, but that didn't bother you any, did it? You had your boyfriend cut him up anyway, didn't you? Well, let me tell you something, you damn woman. I want to tell you I'll be fried in hell before I'll let you run over me again."

She looked at him, distressed at what she was hearing. "I don't have any idea what you're talking about," she told him. "I don't want to 'run over' you."

He stood close to her—too close—and breathed his rum-soaked breath into her face. "All I've got to say to you is, you'd better keep your door locked at night, lady. And you'd better keep those pretty legs of yours crossed."

"My legs are always crossed to people like you, Mr. Craddock."

He held up a finger and shook it in her face. "We'll see," he warned. "We'll just see about that, won't we?"

"Ned—" John Collins stepped up, grabbed his arm. "Come on, you're bothering the lady."

Craddock continued to stare at her. "Not yet I'm not. I haven't even begun yet."

"Come on, now, you've celebrated too much," Collins told him. "Hugh!" he called out across the room. "Give me a hand here."

"Leave me alone, John," Craddock grunted.

"I'm sorry, Mrs. Fairchild," Collins apologized. "He just gets rowdy when he gets drunk."

"That's all right."

"Merry Christmas, Mrs. Fairchild," Collins said.

"Merry Christmas."

A minute later, Tom joined her. "What was all that about?" he asked. They were watching Hall and Collins pull Craddock through the door.

"It wasn't about anything," she replied. "He was just drunk."

Tom put his hand on his sword. "Do you think he's the one, Roxanna?" he asked. "Do you want me to go see what I can find out?"

"No," she shook her head. "Don't do that. Just let him be. He was drunk, I don't think he meant a word he was saying."

The new year, 1805, brought more snow to the fort, more apprehensions to Roxanna. But Sacajawea came to her aid again by taking her mind temporarily off her fears. Ever since the Indian girl had gotten sick, she had been the center of the men's attention. As her belly swelled, she got weaker, but her face somehow kept its beauty and radiance. Every man in the fort seemed to think of her as his own daughter. They brought presents to her, made sure she had enough food and blankets.

She was very weak a good deal of the time, and since Charbonneau and Otter Woman were unconcerned about her, Roxanna took on the job of nursing her. Sacajawea bore her physical pain without complaining. And she was grateful to Roxanna. Each time Roxanna was about to leave her blankets, Sacajawea would kiss her cheek and thank her for caring for her.

Despite her good spirits, though, she did worry. One of her fears was that the unborn baby had been hurt when the Mandan threw her against the lodge.

"Put your hands here," she told Roxanna one day. She took her hands and drew them under her dress, placed them gently on her naked stomach. "Is the baby still alive?" she asked.

Roxanna felt Sacajawea's stomach move under her fingers. "Of course it's still alive," she assured her. "Can't you tell?"

"If he is still alive, then he is twisted," she replied.

"What kind of talk is that?"

"When I was little, Cameahwait told me about the twisted babies that were thrown away, down the mountains—"

Roxanna took her hand away. "Now don't you go telling me Chief Cameahwait stories," she admonished her. "You know I don't believe half of them."

"It's a true story," she claimed. "The mothers were kicked by Snake horses. Their babies were born twisted. They had to throw them away, into the gulch."

"Well, your baby won't be born twisted, Sacajawea, I promise you. You're a young woman; he'll be big and strong."

"Will you take him out for me?" she asked. "I am too young to do it alone. If I die, you take him."

"Hush, now. I don't want to hear that kind of

talk. Nobody is going to die. Anyway, don't you want one of your people to help you?"

She shook her head. "No. My people are Snake, not Big Belly." She looked at Roxanna plaintively. "Will you do it, Roxanna? Please?"

Roxanna was a bit afraid of the idea. "But I've never done it, Sacajawea," she protested. "I'm a city girl. I've never seen babies until they're sitting up in their cribs all plump and pink and saying 'ma-ma,' to everything that moves."

"You will see this one before I will see him," she predicted.

"Look, Sacajawea, you will have an easy time of it, you hear me? Indian women always have easy births."

She gripped Roxanna's wrist. "Please," she begged. "It will not be easy birth. Great Elk read it on the Medicine Stone. You must help me. *Please!*"

"All right," she gave in, "I'll help you. But you have to help me, too. Will you at least try to believe it's going to be easy? For my sake? I don't know a whit about this sort of thing."

Sacajawea smiled engagingly. "You are a strong lady, Roxanna."

"I guess I'll have to be," Roxanna answered grimly.

"Otter Woman will tell you how," Sacajawea nodded toward the squaw who sat in the corner of the lodge sewing deerskins.

Roxanna drew close to the Indian girl. "Well, if Otter Woman knows all about it, why doesn't *she* do it?"

Sacajawea's expression was calm, sweet. "Because I want you to do it," she answered. "You are a white woman, but you are a great woman. You are the strongest woman of all."

Tears came to Roxanna's eyes. "Sacajawea—" she began.

"Hush," she murmured, using a new word. "You will do it. I trust you."

On February 11, the day of Sacajawea's delivery, Roxanna was in the last stages of a severe case of pleurisy. The disease struck her down half-way through a hunting trip into the woods with Captain Lewis's party. Feverish, her side wrenched with pain, she was loaded up on an Indian travois, a sleigh made of two long poles lashed together with buffalo tendon. The travois was tied to a Mandan pony and Roxanna was dragged fifteen miles back to the fort.

The sickness took complete control of her body for a while. Captain Clark tried every cure he knew to ease the pain. He tried to sweat out the fever by applying hot stones rolled in blankets to her chest, and he drained a trickle of blood from her wrist for a short time every day, hoping that impurities in her body would pass out with the blood. But none of his efforts amounted to anything but discomfort for her. Roxanna grew steadily weaker for days, which lengthened into a week, then two.

Tom Wentworth spent every hour of those two weeks in her cabin. He slept on the cold floor, talked to her when she was rational, comforted her when she was in the violent throes of a fever. Finally, just when he was about to lose hope for her, she began to rally. On the sixteenth day of the pleurisy, she rested peacefully; on the seventeenth day she sat up in bed for the first time. That night, while she slept, Tom quietly celebrated her return to the living by quaffing down half a bottle of rum.

The next morning, though, he had to leave her. Before dawn, he awakened her with a gentle kiss on the forehead. "Roxanna," he said quietly, "I've got to go with Captain Lewis, but I'm leaving York here with you. I expect to return by nightfall, and I'll come see you when I return. If you need anything in the meantime, just tell York. He'll be right outside the door."

She sat up. "I don't need anything, Tom. I'm feeling much better."

"You do seem to have your color back," he smiled. "But I want him here anyway, while I'm gone."

"What's happening out there?" she asked, curious.

"Oh, the Sioux are up here stealing horses. They've killed two Mandans already. We're going to go out and look for them."

"I wish I could go," she complained. "I have a feeling I'm going to be awfully bored staying inside all day."

"I don't think you'd want to go, Roxanna," he told her. "It's a terrible day outside. Besides, you're still weak. I want you to do nothing but stay in bed till I get back. Will you do that?"

"Yes sir," she teased. "I will not move a muscle."

"I guess you can get up," he conceded, "but for God's sake, don't go outside. Captain Clark says another chill would probably kill you."

She touched his cheek. "I wouldn't worry about that. I certainly don't plan on getting another chill just yet. Anyway, where would I go to get one?"

"Just be reasonable, that's all I ask," he kissed her forehead. "I'll be back tonight. Please—take care of yourself, all right?"

"I will," she promised him.

An hour later, around eight o'clock, Otter Woman trudged up the hill through the snow path from Charbonneau's lodge and stopped in front of Roxanna's cabin. She was about to open the door, when Captain Clark's servant, York, came around the corner of the house. As soon as he saw her, he lunged toward her and seized her wrist. "Unh-unh, ma'am," he told her. "Can't go in there."

The Indian woman sneered at him, struggled to free herself from his grip. She swore at him in her own language until he released her. Then she looked at him indignantly as she straightened the shawl on her shoulders.

"Miz' Roxanna's sick," he told her. "She ain't going nowhere."

Otter Woman uttered a few more words, then tried to communicate in sign language, but York didn't understand any of it. He stood with his arms crossed, blocking the doorway, until she finally shrugged her shoulders at him and left.

Shortly after noon, Touissant Charbonneau showed up at Roxanna's hut. He was wearing trousers tucked into his boots, a beaver coat and hat, and a scraggly muskrat scarf draped around his neck. "I am Charbonneau," he announced in a French accent. "I have come to see Madame Fairchild."

York pursed his lips and shook his head. "She's sick," he explained to him.

Charbonneau wiped some snow off his brow and rubbed his chest with his fingers. "I am not going to hurt her, *singe*," he spat. "I just want to talk to her. You can come in and watch me."

He pushed himself past York, entered the cabin, and stalked over to Roxanna, who was placing a small log on the fire.

"Madame," he greeted curtly.

"Well," she turned around, "Monsieur Charbonneau. What can I do for you?"

He looked around the cabin, then at her. "There is nothing you can do for me," he answered. "But you can help my wife, Sacajawea. She is giving birth."

Roxanna was shocked. "Oh, no!" she gasped. "Is she all right?"

"I don't know," he admitted, stepping up to warm his hands by the fire. "She won't even speak to Otter Woman. All she does is ask for you."

Roxanna snapped up her robe, threw it on. "Well, talking about it won't do any good," she declared. "Let's go."

"Miz' Roxanna," York interceded. "You can't go out there. It's snowing."

"It's always snowing, Ben," she pointed out.

"Mr. Tom said for you not to go out."

"I don't care what he said. If Sacajawea is having a baby, I have to go to her. I promised her, just like you promised Tom, Ben. Only I promised first."

"Yes ma'am. But it's bad out there."

"I feel fine, York, really. I'm well!"

"No ma'am."

Charbonneau took a step forward. "Look, *singe,*" he rubbed his chest with two fingers, "I need for the squaw to live, no? Listen to me. I will pay the white woman here good money—"

"*Pay* me!" Roxanna exclaimed. "No you won't, either. I'm not taking a cent of your money."

"Then I will pay the black, instead," he suggested, gesturing toward York. "It's all the same to me. Will he let you go for five dollars?" he asked her. "She is worth ten times that to me."

Roxanna was appalled and disgusted. "Your wife is trying to deliver your baby and you talk about how much she's worth? What kind of man are you?"

"I am a practical man," he stated proudly.

"Oooh!" she threw up her hands, unable to express her anger in words.

Charbonneau was calm, businesslike. "My wife Sacajawea knows the Shoshones, the Nez Perces and the Paiutes. She is worth money as an interpreter."

Charbonneau's words incensed her, but she knew she couldn't waste time talking to him. She rushed toward the door, vaguely hoping he would stay there, but then she bumped right into York's big barrel chest. "Oh, get out of the way, York," she ordered, irritated with him.

"You are too sick, Miz' Roxanna," he cautioned.

"Will you leave me alone? I'm not sick, damn it! Now get out of the way!"

He shook his massive head. "Not till Mr. Tom comes back."

"York—"

"He told me, 'under no circumstances.' "

"I don't care what he told you. What he says doesn't matter right now. Whatever he thinks, Tom Wentworth is not my keeper. And you're not, either. I'm going out and there is no way on earth you can stop me."

"Miz' Roxanna—"

"Oh, hush, I'm tired of arguing with you, York. Move out of the way!"

York frowned at her, wrinkled his brow, then reluctantly stepped aside. Roxanna said, "Thank you" and whipped open the door and plunged headlong into the blowing snow.

But only a few minutes later she felt almost too tired to move. Her feet suddenly felt tied down, the six inches of snow on the path felt like sixty; the cold wind whirled around her, threatened to sweep her into the slush. Then her toes and fingers began to ache. She recalled Captain Lewis having to lop off the bluish, dead-looking toes of a Mandan boy with frostbite and she wondered if she were going to lose hers the same way. . . .

Charbonneau had passed her, was now far ahead, moving easily and swiftly through the high snow. Soon he disappeared in the distance. Breathless, Roxanna stopped, thought about lying down in the snow for a moment, to rest her aching body. She was about to ease herself down, to give in to her weakness, when she recalled Sacajawea's words to her, "You are the strongest woman of all." She took a deep breath. "Yes," she determined aloud. "I am, damn it. I must be!"

By the time she managed to reach Charbonneau's lodge, she was exhausted, her chest and side were racked with a sharp, digging pain. When she took off her robe in the big room, she began to shiver uncontrollably.

She got hold of herself, though, when she saw Captain Clark and Mr. Jessaume sitting with Sacajawea.

"Mrs. Fairchild!" Captain Clark exclaimed when

he noticed she had come. "What are you doing here? You shouldn't be out in this kind of weather."

"No, I shouldn't," she dismissed his concern. "How long has she been in labor?" she asked him, looking down at the Indian girl.

"Charbonneau says seven hours," Clark told her.

"Seven hours! Dear God. And I've been sitting around doing nothing all that time? Why didn't somebody tell me?" She looked at the Mandan interpreter. "Mr. Jessaume, could you get some more wood and build up the fire? It's too cold in here."

"Yes ma'am."

"Thank you."

She bent down to the Indian girl, put her hand on her forehead. "Sacajawea? Can you hear me?"

"I heard a waterfall, Roxanna," she opened her eyes. "Was it *Kookooskee?*"

"There's no waterfall, Sacajawea," she answered. "You're at Fort Mandan. We have nothing here but snow."

"It was a dream," she sighed with relief. "No one is drowning Baptiste in *Kookooskee.*"

"That's right, no one is drowning anything. You just try to relax."

Captain Clark looked at her with concern. "Roxanna, you look pale."

"Captain Clark, could we just concentrate on Sacajawea, please? She needs your attention a lot more than I do."

Three hours later Roxanna sat crouched near the blazing fire in the center of the lodge, waiting. Her hands and feet were cold, her body was weak and aching, but worse to her than her weariness was her frustration. Since she had arrived at the lodge, Sacajawea had been suffering through violent spasms of pain and Roxanna had been able to do nothing to help her. She had tried to comfort her with words, but sometimes the Indian girl's mind wandered and she was completely oblivious to what Roxanna was saying.

Now, she was writhing under her blankets, sweating, groaning, grasping desperately at her swollen stomach every few minutes.

Jessaume offered his help to Roxanna. Since he had witnessed a handful of births while he was an agent for Hudson's Bay Company, he knew that Sacajawea was going to have a difficult time of it. "I'm afraid the girl's too slight," he shook his head. "And her hips are too narrow. It'll be a hard delivery, I wager."

"It has already been hard, Mr. Jessaume," Roxanna reminded him. She looked over at Sacajawea. "The poor thing's been lying there in agony all day."

"Yes, I know she has, but what I'm saying is, it could get much worse," he cautioned her. "I've seen many an Indian girl Sacajawea's size have to give up the ghost, trying to birth a large baby. And you can see Charbonneau there is a pretty good-sized man."

"Mr. Jessaume," she chastised him. "If you don't mind, I would rather not hear that kind of talk right now. I'm scared enough as it is."

"I was only trying to help. Here," he drew out a vial from his pocket. "Give this to her. It'll help her, I'm sure. It never fails."

Roxanna looked at him curiously, took the vial, opened it and sniffed. She could detect no smell whatever. "What is this?"

"It's Mandan medicine," he explained. "A couple of crushed snake-rattles mixed with a little water."

"What's it for?"

"For pregnant women. Otter Woman knows about it."

Roxanna looked at Charbonneau's other wife, who was impassive, then at Captain Clark.

He nodded his head. "It's a harmless mixture, Mrs. Fairchild," he told her. "Let her have it."

Roxanna reluctantly gave the girl the medicine and Sacajawea quickly fell asleep. Twenty minutes later she awoke with a jolt. "Roxanna!" she cried. "Roxanna! Help me!"

Roxanna put her hand on her brow. "I'm here, Sacajawea," she comforted her. "I'm not going anywhere. Calm down. There's nothing to worry about."

"Roxanna—" she shrieked, her voice panicky.

"It's all right, Sacajawea; just try to relax. I'm going to do all I can to help you. You'll be fine."

"Roxanna—I can feel him coming. Please don't leave me."

"I'm not going to leave you," she assured her.

"Roxanna—" Sacajawea breathed rapidly, "it is now." She clamped her fingers onto the other woman's wrist and squeezed with all her might.

"Well, there you are," Jessaume proclaimed proudly. "That medicine will bring it out every time."

"Excuse me." Roxanna was irritated by his manner. She moved closer to Sacajawea. Then, shielding the girl from Jessaume and Clark with her back, Roxanna folded up the blankets and lifted Sacajawea's skirt. Her first glance at the lower part of the Indian girl's body startled her. The opening between her legs was greatly expanded, three or four times normal size. Her copper-colored skin was dripping wet and the blankets underneath the girl's buttocks had been doused by a great expulsion of liquid.

Then Roxanna saw something that nearly paralyzed her. Visible near the opening was the baby's reddish white skin! Seeing the flesh of the child sent a thrill through Roxanna's body. She felt excited, exhilarated. Just as Sacajawea had predicted, Roxanna was the first human being to see her baby.

Roxanna hastily replaced the covers. "Captain Clark, Mr. Jessaume," she announced firmly. "You'll both have to leave now."

Clark stood up. "Is she having the baby?" he demanded. "The men outside will want to know."

"Yes," Roxanna answered him. "Tell them she's

having it now. Now go, both of you. You too, Monsieur Charbonneau."

But the Frenchman stood fast. "She is my wife, madame," he protested. "I should stay."

"Roxanna!" Sacajawea shrieked in pain.

"Monsieur Charbonneau," Roxanna hastened him. "I've got work to do here. Please go."

"*Eh bien*," he agreed, looking over at his wife. "I will go. I hate to see a woman cry."

When the men had left the lodge, Roxanna got down on her knees between Sacajawea's outspread legs, raised the covers again. "Well, Otter Woman," she addressed the squaw looking down at her, "you should be glad. The time of birth is near."

The woman nodded. Her face was rigid, impassive, emotionless.

"Roxanna," Sacajawea entreated in a soft voice. "Is he dead? Is Baptiste dead?"

"No, damn it," Roxanna snapped. "He's not dead. Stop thinking that. I want you to think about breathing easily and steadily. And pushing. If you'll just do that," she tried to sound confident, "everything will be fine. Can you do that?"

Sacajawea nodded slowly. She smiled weakly as her friend bent over her, mopping her brow with a corner of the blanket.

Roxanna waited, nervously rubbing her knees with her damp palms. She reproached herself for being so ignorant of these things. Suddenly it made no sense to her to be able to play a Hewitt piano sonata by heart or to be able to quote a Wordsworth poem or dance a New Orleans cotillion—and yet not to know even which end of a baby came out of the womb first.

She had absorbed what instruction she could from Jessaume and Otter Woman, but now that it was happening, now that an actual human being was going to be coming to life in *her* hands, she realized they had told her practically nothing.

"Sacajawea," she tried to remain calm. "You're

going to have to push steadily. Think about what you're doing."

"Yes," the girl responded. "I am pushing. I am trying."

She took a deep breath. "Good," she encouraged. "Remember, I'm helping you. But you have to do your part. Steadily, easily. Do you understand?"

"Yes," she panted.

Roxanna smiled warmly and tried to console her with a few affectionate pats, but Sacajawea was hurting. Her face was distorted with pain. Even so, she wasn't about to complain, even when the convulsions wrenched her body and made her arch her back and thrust herself upward. She endured it all in silence.

Half an hour later, Roxanna could make out the position of the baby, it was emerging all right, head first. She massaged Sacajawea's thighs, spoke to her in a calm, assured voice, as the girl strained to expel the baby.

In spite of her exhausting effort, nothing happened in the next half hour. Finally Otter Woman leaned over and touched Roxanna's shoulders. She held her closed fist in front of the white woman's eyes and turned it from side to side, indicating a turning motion.

Roxanna perceived instantly what the sign meant. The baby's head was turned to the right. There wasn't enough room for it to come out. It had to be eased back toward the opening somehow. "Oh Lord," she sighed. She looked up at Otter Woman with pleading eyes. "Can you do it?" she asked pitifully.

Otter Woman was firm. She crossed her arms, shook her head resolutely. "You," she nodded.

"Yes, I know, I have to do it," Roxanna sighed resignedly. She felt her body calling out to her to stop and rest, but she resisted. "Sacajawea," she soothed the girl, "I want you to stay calm, now. It's nothing to worry about, but Baptiste has moved around a little too much in your stomach. I'm going to have to turn him. Do you understand?"

"Yes," she answered. "I understand."

Roxanna attempted a joke. "All I'm going to do is set him straight, the way we do all other men. Right?"

Sacajawea tried to reply, but a wave of pain grabbed her, making her grimace.

"We can do it, Sacajawea," Roxanna encouraged her. "You just take a rest. Try to relax." She warmed her fingers in her armpits a few minutes, then reached down between Sacajawea's legs. She wondered if both the mother and child would die if she didn't turn the baby's head. She wondered too how much time she had before that happened. And she wondered if touching the baby with her hands would damage it somehow. Her ignorance made her angry. Why had she spent so much time perfecting her social manners when there was so much to know about life and death?

With trembling fingers Roxanna massaged Sacajawea's legs, trying to relax her body as she manipulated her muscles and probed carefully with her fingers to turn the baby. Each time Roxanna's hands moved, she felt the girl flinch beneath them, but she said nothing.

Finally Roxanna managed to tilt the head back to the left so that the head was facing up. Now, with Sacajawea pushing downward, the tiny shape slowly, gradually, miraculously began to emerge. First the head, lined with strands of sticky black hair, then the round, pink shoulders. As the stomach and legs came out into the light, Roxanna gathered the warm little body into her waiting hands, then lifted it up out of the way as a gush of liquid washed out of the mother onto the blankets.

Otter Woman leaned over and cut the umbilical cord with a knife. Placing the baby in a fresh blanket, she picked up the squawling bundle in her arms. Roxanna placed another fur robe over the mother to keep her warm and watched Otter Woman dry the baby in the blanket. Suddenly it let out a loud, piercing wail that seemed to shake the roof and walls of the lodge. Roxanna smiled. The strange sound was as musical to her ears as a baroque trumpet.

"Roxanna?" Sacajawea cried out. "Is it male?"

"Yes, it's male, Sacajawea," she reported. "A beautiful, dark-haired boy. He's gorgeous."

"Is he twisted?" she asked anxiously.

"No, Sacajawea, he's not twisted. I told you not to worry about that. He's perfect."

As she reached over and touched the new mother's face with her fingertips, Roxanna all of a sudden felt very weary. She looked at her a moment, then at Otter Woman, who was methodically checking the various parts of the baby's body to see if they were all functioning properly. Gradually a veil seemed to drop down over what she was seeing, and everything began to take on the obscureness of a dream. Then the room became extremely cold.

"Roxanna," Sacajawea called to her. She sounded vague and distant. "Rox . . ." But her voice trailed off and Roxanna couldn't even hear the baby crying any more. She closed her eyes, felt her body go limp, and then she crashed down to the dirt floor of the lodge.

Everything went black.

Chapter 14

When the clamor of people milling about in the lodge awakened her an hour later, she discovered that she had been sleeping beneath a neat stack of hide robes near the corn bowls. She pulled herself up and looked around. The room was crowded with men gathering around to see Sacajawea's baby. Roxanna was surprised to see that these powerful young bearded hunters, carpenters and blacksmiths had actually brought small, infant-sized presents for Jean Baptiste—tiny moccasins, headbands and necklaces. John Coulter even gave him a miniature hunting knife he claimed had been made two generations ago by a Crow Indian chieftain.

Roxanna looked over at Sacajawea who lay propped up against a bundle of blankets with the baby in her arms. She thought she had never seen anyone so magnificent as the new Indian mother, or anyone so reverent and attentive as the adoring men who had packed themselves into the lodge to pay her tribute.

"What are you going to call him, Sacajawea?" Hugh Hall asked her.

"Don't make it anything French," Collins cautioned her playfully, "or Hugh'll never be able to say it."

The men burst into cheerful laughter, Collins slapped Hall good-naturedly on the back. Hugh joined in the laughter.

Sacajawea smiled sweetly at Hall. "His name is Jean Baptiste Charbonneau," she answered his question. "But we will call him Pomp: 'first born.'"

"Pomp's a good name," Collins offered. "I think Hugh can handle that."

The men laughed again, but Sacajawea ignored them and held the baby out. "You take him, Hugh Hall," she said in a soft voice. "You tell him he is Pomp."

Hall hesitated a moment, but then responded by cradling the baby awkwardly but carefully in his arms while the other men suddenly fell silent and closed ranks to get a better look at him.

Watching the scene with interest, Roxanna became aware of someone standing near her. "Oh, Captain Clark," she looked up. "I didn't see you there."

"Are you feeling any better, Mrs. Fairchild?" he asked with concern.

"To tell you the truth, captain," she admitted, "I feel very, very tired." She grasped his extended hand and pulled herself up and straightened her shirt. "I guess I'm not over the pleurisy after all."

"I didn't think you were, but then women never have listened to me very much. But sick or not, you did a fine job with Sacajawea's baby," he complimented her. "The men certainly approve of him. It's been a long winter; they've been looking forward to this."

"Since they all seem to have adopted her," Roxanna observed, "I suppose they'll adopt the baby, too."

Clark flushed. "I'm guilty of doing that myself, I guess, Mrs. Fairchild. I just told Charbonneau I'd be glad to pay for the boy's education. . . ."

Roxanna decided quickly to change the subject. "Where is Monsieur Charbonnaeu, by the way? You'd think he'd be here."

"He was here until a few minutes ago," Clark answered. "He went to the Minnetaree village to get a medicine man for Sacajawea." He looked into her eyes. "You really do need some rest, Mrs. Fairchild," he suggested.

"I'll be all right, captain," she insisted stubbornly.

"You will if you get about twelve hours of uninterrupted sleep. Come on, I'll walk with you back to your cabin."

By the time they reached her place, the sun was down. Clark went in with her, lit the lantern on the table beside the bed and built a hot fire with cottonwood logs.

"Captain Clark?" she called when he had finished with the fire, "I guess you know the men aren't going to let you leave Sacajawea and little Pomp behind when we leave next spring. She's such a lovely little thing everybody has gotten attached to her."

"I know. Meriwether and I have already agreed we should take her along, if she wants to stay with Charbonneau. She was born a Shoshone and she knows how they trade in horses. If we're going to cross the mountains, we'll need every spare horse we can find. Besides," he added thoughtfully, "if we have an Indian girl and papoose with us, the western Indians may be a little less likely to think we're a war party."

"I hope Baptiste will be strong enough," Roxanna sighed, her body aching with fatigue.

"Oh, he'll be strong enough," Clark responded confidently. "It's you I'm worried about. I want you to stop all this worrying about Sacajawea and take care of yourself. Get some rest."

Roxanna fell asleep minutes after Clark left her alone in the cabin. For hours she lay undisturbed in her bed as the hot fire cooled to red embers, then to black, and the lantern grew dimmer and dimmer until it finally flickered out. At about three o'clock in the morning she awoke with a start. The room was utterly dark. Where was Tom? she wondered suddenly. He had promised to return by nightfall. What had happened? The fire and lantern were dead, the shutters closed. It was eerie: there was not a gleam of light anywhere in the secluded cabin. Roxanna sat up in bed and listened. She could detect nothing, only silence. But for some reason the silence and the darkness frightened her tonight.

As she turned over on her stomach, Roxanna had the strange feeling that someone else was in the room with her, lurking in the darkness. She had denied the feeling in recent days. But now the impression overwhelmed her. Chills shot through her body. She lay very still, held her breath and listened.

Just when she was sure she was imagining things, she heard the frightening sound of deep, labored breathing, coming from somewhere near the door. It was real this time: someone was in her cabin! Her heart began to pound wildly in her breast as she turned over, trying to make out a human shape in the darkness. Could it be Tom, she wondered, back from the skirmishes with the Tetons? Or was it the man who had been watching her, stalking her for weeks?

"Tom?" she blurted out. Her voice sounded small and forlorn in the cool, dark room. "Tom! Is that you?" she asked shakily. She waited, got no answer. "Who's there? Tom, damn it, answer me!"

While she was waiting tensely for a response, the silence was suddenly shattered by the sound of something striking the water bucket with a thud. The bucket rolled across the floor with a terrible clacking noise until it rammed against the wall. The racket electrified Roxanna. She instinctively reached blindly over toward the lantern, but her hand accidentally knocked it over. One of the glass panes shattered as it hit the floor.

The room was inconceivably dark! She couldn't even make out her own hand in front of her. In that bleak darkness now she heard the falling of one foot-step, then another. Whoever was in the room with her was beginning to move—toward her.

Her hand quickly found its way across the bed to the pillow and under it to the flintlock Tom had given her. The warm metal barrel and wooden handle were comforting to the touch, but the weapon seemed unbe-lievably large and unwieldy as she drew it out and held it out in front of her.

"I have a gun here," she warned the person moving toward her.

The footsteps stopped.

"I'll use it," she threatened. "Don't come any closer." She fumbled for the hammer on the pistol, tried to cock it the way Tom had showed her, but it was too tight, she was too weak. She couldn't pull it back far enough to click it into place.

Suddenly, a hard, icy hand came out of nowhere and grabbed her arm and thick, powerful fingers gouged into her flesh. She struggled with the flintlock, trying to cock it, but then his other hand fastened itself to her wrist and with a jerk the gun flew out of her grip and landed somewhere in the dark.

As close as he was to her now, she couldn't see well enough to make out who the man was—not even as he pinned her arms behind her and brutally hurled her down to the bed. She knew that he was big and strong, but she could tell no more about him than that.

She was too infirm to run, too weary to resist his stout hands as they hooked onto the neckline of her shirt, yanked it down, ripping it open. Deciding that all she could do now was attract someone from the fort, she tried to scream out, but the man broke it off as his forceful fingers clasped her throat and his fingernails sank into her windpipe.

"Unh-unh," he warned her.

The sides of her throat felt as if they were being mashed together. She tried to speak, but the sounds wouldn't come out. She nodded her head to make him understand that she was going to cooperate with him. Instantly he loosened his grip.

"Please, let me go," she begged him. "I don't—" her voice was cut off as fingers clutched at her throat again.

She recoiled as she felt his big, cold hand clumsily paw over her naked breasts and his fingernails maliciously picking at her ribs and pinching the skin on her stomach. She managed somehow to spring her left hand free, and she lashed out at him with all her strength. But he only laughed and pressed his body against hers while her feeble blows bounced harmlessly off his broad back.

When he abruptly and violently jerked at the waistline of her pants, she began to kick and squirm, but her illness had left her debilitated. He had no trouble holding her down, even as he tugged her trousers down below her knees and exposed her lower body to the cool air.

She lay still for a minute, too dispirited to move, thinking if only she could put all her energy into one burst, perhaps she could shake herself free and break out of the cabin. Then someone in the fort would hear her and save her. As she made herself ready, he pressed his heavy chest against her heaving breasts and scraped his hand across her thigh, moving it slowly toward the area between her legs.

Now was the time! With all the effort she could manage, she shoved back at his massive body. But to her horror, she didn't even budge him! He was like a mountain on her chest. She was absolutely powerless to move him.

He was positioning himself over her now, bearing down hard on her throat with one hand, attempting to pry her legs apart with the other. In a few seconds, she thought, he would have her. Like all those poor, wretched frontier women Mrs. Daniel Boone had told her about, she was now going to become scarred for life, a victim of rape.

With a grunt he disengaged his thick outspread fingers from her throbbing throat and dragged them over her breasts. He raised himself up to loosen his pants. It was then that she summoned up enough strength to bring her leg up toward his groin.

The instant her knee popped into loose flesh, he wailed out a long, painful cry and rolled over to the edge of the bed. Roxanna took the chance to scramble off the mattress, but as soon as her bare feet touched the floor, her knees buckled under her and she collapsed.

Panting, terrified, she tried to get her bearings. The door, she decided, was only ten feet away from her. If she could only make it outside, she could scream and someone would hear her. But just as she pushed herself up to her feet, an invisible body grabbed her and enveloped her like a monstrous animal. A damp, slimy arm with the mass of an enormous snake wrapped itself tightly around her neck and began to squeeze out her air. She gagged, fighting desperately to get her wind, but all of a sudden the common act of breathing became the hardest thing she had ever had to do.

She could feel the black room filling up with his silent anger. He became more violent now. He whipped her neck around, flipped her over on her back, yanked off the rest of her clothes, leaving her completely naked.

Her heart thumped heavily as his clammy hands again groped like a snail over her nude body. Mrs. Boone's warning had been a real one: she was going to be raped.

As his bony knee pushed against the inside of her thigh, he pinned her arms to the floor. She was so tired, so worn down by pain, she decided she might just as well let him have his way. But she knew she could never tell anyone about it. She remembered what Mrs. Boone had told her. You will be raped, but don't tell the men about it: "They don't want to hear such things."

Since she wasn't resisting him now, he let go of her arms. He wanted them outstretched, though, so she docilely left them that way. She imagined how she looked now, naked, arms extended, legs spread-eagled, her body open to some vile, unknown rapist when she had allowed only one other man access there before. It made her sick to think of it.

She flinched when his big clumsy hand touched her below her stomach, but she was so drowsy, so utterly exhausted, she couldn't move her pelvis out of the way. If the thing was fated to happen, let it, she thought. Why shouldn't she be raped, just like all the other women on the frontier? Why shouldn't she be like all those Indian women who lived only to serve men?

But then her fingers felt the cool touch of metal on the floor. Was it what she thought it was? She strained to reach farther out into the darkness as his face came down against her neck. She felt the barrel first, then the wooden handle, then the trigger. It was Tom's flintlock. Somehow she was able to slide the long barrel into her palm and grip it tightly.

She felt him against her, pushing at her. At the instant he penetrated, she screamed and swung the heavy gun up into the air and slammed it into his skull. He groaned, eased back from her. Free from him, she blindly crashed the pistol into his head again.

This time his body fell forward, like a huge rock, upon her. She was able to move herself out from under him, but she didn't have enough strength left to get up. Naked, shuddering with the cold, she concentrated the power she had left into trying to cock the pistol before he came to his senses.

To move the hammer back far enough for it to lock seemed an impossible task, but she had to keep trying. She heard him begin to straighten up. "Oh, God, please," she prayed. "Please make it work!" She heard his hard breathing. Now he will kill me, she thought. Unless I kill him first.

He moved toward her again but held up when a loud click sounded in the room.

"It's cocked!" she shrieked excitedly. "I've cocked it. Now don't you come near me, do you hear me? I'll shoot you, so help me!" She aimed the pistol where she thought he was. At the first sign of movement, she cried out, "Stop! If you touch me again, I'll kill you! I swear to God, I'll kill you!"

She waited breathlessly. Suddenly she heard a scuttling sound on the floor as the door of the cabin burst open and a dark shape sped out through the doorway into the night.

She sighed loudly, allowed her fingers to let go of the heavy gun. The pistol dropped silently through the air, struck the floor, and exploded in a bright burst of light and smoke.

But Roxanna wasn't even startled by the shot. She was too tired. All she could do was sleep. She closed her eyes and fell prostrate on the cabin floor. A strange, almost comforting sensation began to overcome her as the snow swept into the room and showered her unprotected body. She recalled dreamily that Captain Clark had told Jessaume in Charbonneau's lodge that it was forty degrees below zero outside. She calculated dreamily that with her body exposed, it would take less than an hour for her to freeze to death.

But there was nothing she could do about it. Her energy was gone, completely spent. There was nothing left to draw on. To get up and close the door and go to bed—a simple, everyday act—was just too hard to manage. She simply couldn't do it. If only Tom would come to save her! But he was gone. She was deserted, utterly alone, unable to stir even to save her own life.

When Roxanna opened her eyes again, she saw handsome, bearded Tom Wentworth looking down at her seriously, with raised eyebrows. She smiled up at him and brushed a lock of hair from her face. "Hello," she managed.

"Good afternoon," he greeted, not changing his expression. "How do you feel?"

"I feel fine," she answered, looking around the room. She was in her cabin, in her bed. "I'm warm anyway. How long have I been out?"

"Almost four days," he replied.

"Good Lord. No wonder I feel so rested."

He shifted his weight nervously. "Roxanna," he went on in a firm, impassive voice, "if you don't mind, I would like for you to explain what happened to you." She found his condescending concern irritating. "Where were you? Why didn't you come?"

He ignored her question. "Roxanna," he persisted, "if someone . . . *did* something to you, I want to know about it. I've been wondering, ever since I found you. . . ."

"I called out to you," Roxanna responded in a low voice. "You said you would be back by nightfall. "I called out . . . oh, Tom. . . ." She turned her face away from him, unable to go on.

"Please, Roxanna, I had no way of knowing," he pleaded. She did not reply. "We didn't return until the next morning. Captain Lewis had us scout farther than we intended. I came to your cabin at once. I found your door wide open, my father's flintlock on the floor. The snow was blowing in on you. Please . . . can you tell me?"

"No!" she shot back. "You weren't there. It's no concern of yours."

"If I could have come any sooner. . . ."

"You couldn't. I understand that. And I'm grateful to you for saving my life."

"Roxanna. . . ."

"No!" And now she stared straight at him, her eyes burning. Like a doctor slowly registering the condition of his patient, Tom took in the sight of her flushed face, her wide eyes, alive with anger. Then, slowly, he stood up. He strode to the table and picked up her shirt as if it were an exhibit in a court room.

"I found this. It was torn apart."

"Must you persist?" she pleaded.

"Damn it, Roxanna, you're exasperating!" he growled, flinging down the shirt. He turned his back to her and went to the fire, where an aromatic pot of buffalo broth was simmering over the flames.

Roxanna pulled herself up a bit, fought a wave of dizziness for a few moments. As she tried to change positions in the hard bed, her hand lit upon a thin, circular metal object under the covers. Her fingers involuntarily clasped it into her palm. Stealing a quick look at it beneath the blanket, she saw that it was a gold watch, probably left by the rapist. She gasped—she believed she knew who it belonged to!

"The flintlock has been fired, Roxanna," Wentworth insisted. "How do you account for that?"

"I'm not accounting for anything, Tom," she answered, striking her pillow to fluff it up. Her voice hardened as she gained confidence. That single clue stiffened her resolve to keep her secret. "And let me tell you, I'm not going to be interrogated like some criminal, so you might as well stop asking all these questions. I haven't done anything wrong, and you have no right to assume I have. If I want to tell you what happened, I will. But you can be very sure it won't be because you or any other man forced me to."

He paused a minute. "I'm just trying to look after you, Roxanna," he said defensively.

She softened a bit. "Oh, Tom, I know that. And I appreciate it. I really do. But you're just going to have to stop assuming I'm an Indian squaw or a Philadelphia wife. I'm not even a New Orleans lady any more. I don't know what I am, but I do know I don't need looking after, any more than the men on this expedition need it."

"So you're just going to let all this remain a mystery?"

"Until I want to tell you about it, yes."

He looked at her, shook his head dejectedly, walked silently over to the fire, picked up the wooden spoon out of the bowl, and began stirring the broth.

Roxanna took the opportunity to sneak another look at the watch. It was an English timepiece, ornately engraved, just like another one she had seen once. It couldn't be the same one, she thought. That would be impossible!

She glanced at Tom, who was sipping the broth, then, keeping the watch hidden under the blanket, she flipped open the lid. She saw exactly what she expected to see, but seeing it still horrified her. On the inside of the watch cover was a miniature painting, slightly faded, but easy to make out. It was a picture of a naked woman.

Chills raced down her spine. She had seen the watch before, in New Orleans, lying on top of a silk brocade waistcoat. She remembered being shocked by it then and wondering how such a thing could be owned by such a man as—Sir Douglas Fairchild.

It was a staggering thought: the man who tried to rape her had been *her husband!*

"Don't you want to try some of this?" Tom asked, bringing her a bowl of broth. "It's two days old, but Captain Clark said to give it to you as soon as you woke up."

"I don't want any." She hid the watch behind her back.

"You haven't eaten for days, Roxanna," he reminded her.

"I know I haven't," she retorted. "I don't want it; take it away."

He put it down on the table, looked over at her. "All right, what's wrong?" he asked. "You're as white as the snow outside."

"What?"

"You looked scared, Roxanna."

"Oh, God, Tom," she sighed. She didn't know

what to say to him. She could never tell him that her own husband had tried to rape her. She found that impossible to believe herself. And yet there was the watch. She had to confront Douglas herself and find out why he would do such a thing.

Tom was trying hard to be patient. "Roxanna, it kills me to see you so sad. Please tell me what's going on."

"I *can't* tell you."

"You mean you won't."

"Just leave it alone, Tom. It's my business, all right?"

He came close to her, took her hand in his. "Roxanna," he whispered, "I love you. Everything that happens to you, happens to me. If you're hurt, I'm hurt. Can't you understand that?"

She touched his cheek. "Yes, I understand it," she told him. "And it's a wonderful thought, Tom. But I just can't tell you anything right now."

"Can you at least tell me why you can't?"

"No. You'll just have to trust me."

"Roxanna—if I had come an hour later last Tuesday morning, I would've found a corpse here."

"I know. I know why you're so concerned. But this is something I have to deal with alone."

"God, you're stubborn," he shook his head, almost laughing. "And tough."

"Tom," she confided, "I'll tell you a secret. However tough you think I am, I've got to tell you, right now I'm scared to death. I have reason to doubt everything I've ever been taught to believe in."

He started to ask her what she meant, but thought better of it. She had made her point. "Well, whenever you want to talk about it, let me know. I'm willing to listen."

She smiled. "Come here," she beckoned.

As he leaned over, she kissed him, warmly, passionately. Then she felt his arms around her, squeezing her tightly.

"God, I love you," he moaned.

She wanted desperately to respond to him, to admit her love for him, but how could she? She still wasn't free to love him. She was still married—and, she wondered, what kind of man was she married to?

A week later, Tom Wentworth was in one of the cabins in the fort playing poker with four other men, but his mind wasn't on the game. He kept thinking of Roxanna and losing track of the cards.

"Come on, put up or shut up, Wentworth," Ned Craddock goaded him. "Get your head out of the clouds. You in or out?"

"I'm out of money," he responded distractedly. "I guess I'll fold."

"You can bet that fancy cutlass your daddy gave you," Craddock suggested. "I'll give you good money for it."

Tom didn't hear him. "Count me out." He rose and threw his cards down. "I've had enough for one night. I can't concentrate on the game."

"The Fairchild chippie's raking you over the coals, isn't she, Wentworth?" Craddock dragged in the pot with both hands.

"Better leave him alone, Ned," Hugh Hall warned him.

But Ned kept it up. "What's the matter, Wentworth," he taunted him. "Wouldn't the little heifer let you play with her?"

Tom glared at him. "One more time, Craddock," he warned. "If you call her a name one more time, I'm going to cut your tongue out and make you eat it."

"Hey, take it easy, man," Craddock backed off. "I didn't mean anything. It was just poker talk."

"Well, keep your poker talk to yourself."

Collins broke in. "Never mind Ned," he told Tom. "He's always got an eye out for the ladies. He can't resist them. He even carries one with him. Show him your watch, Ned."

"Mind your own business, Collins."

Hall laughed. "Ned's got a watch with a naked woman in it, Tom," he announced. "Absolutely naked. Hair and all."

"Show him," Collins prompted Craddock.

"Shut up, Collins," Ned told him.

"Never mind," Tom cut in. "I don't want to see it I've got to go."

Ned scooped up the cards scattered about on the table and began to shuffle them. "I suggest you tie a bell on that heifer, Wentworth, so we can hear how you're doing with her."

Tom instantly reacted to his words; he lunged across the table, snatched Craddock by the collar. "I told you, Ned," he threatened, yanking him up from his seat "Don't even say her name."

The others quickly got to their feet, backed up to give them room.

"Let me go, damn it," Craddock gulped.

"You don't listen, do you?" Tom commanded.

"Come on, man, stop it. You're choking me!"

"I'm going to do more than choke you—"

Just then the door opened and Sergeant Ordway stepped in, his heavy coat splattered with snow. He kicked the door closed behind him. "All right, break it up," he yelled out. "Let him go, Wentworth."

Tom gritted his teeth and released Craddock's collar, pushing him back down to his stool. "You're damned lucky he stopped me," he told him. "But let me tell you something; if I ever hear you say anything about Mrs. Fairchild again—"

"*Mrs.* Fairchild? Ha! Chippies like Garcia don't get married, Wentworth—"

"Damn you—"

"Wentworth!" Ordway shouted. "Straighten up. The captains want to see you. Right now."

Tom continued to scowl at Craddock.

"I said *now,* Wentworth," Ordway ordered.

"All right," he acquiesced. "I'm coming."

Half an hour later, in the captains' cabin, Meriwether Lewis and William Clark sat behind a table strewn with a compass, a quill and ink, three wax candles and a disorderly stack of miscellaneous maps, charts, and descriptive journals. They watched Tom pace restlessly back and forth in front of them as he read the manuscript.

Captain Lewis leaned forward, pulled his pipe out from under a pile of maps and began to fill it with tobacco. "I'm sending that report to President Jefferson on the specimens boat," he began.

"It's a good report," Tom replied coolly, almost indifferently. He handed it back to Lewis. "But you didn't really send for me so that I could read this, did you?" he asked suspiciously.

"No," Lewis admitted, "we didn't. And if you'll stop pacing, we'll tell you why we did send for you."

Tom forced himself to stop. "I'm sorry, Captain Lewis," he apologized. "I'm a little agitated."

"We're all agitated. It has been a long winter. We'd all like to leave tomorrow."

"I know I would," Tom confessed absently. "I'm tired of Fort Mandan."

"Tom," Lewis commanded. "I want you to forget about Roxanna for a minute and think about our mission here. Monsieur Laroque just told us some news that makes it more important than ever for us to make this expedition a success."

"What kind of news?"

"He says the North West Trading Company has merged with Alexander Mackenzie's XY Company, which means Mackenzie is going all-out to set up a business on the Columbia River before we do."

"It also means," Captain Clark added, "a big chance for us. This merger proves what we've believed all along—Mackenzie wants to dominate the fur trade on the continent. Now that he's strong enough, he'll be taking on the other big British companies, Hudson's Bay and Great Pacific Fur."

Tom understood. "And while they're at each other's throats, we have a shot at establishing the American trade."

Clark nodded. "*If* we can cross the mountains and reach the Columbia in time."

"We can do that, can't we?"

"Yes we can. If someone doesn't destroy the expedition first "

Tom wrinkled his brow, puzzled at Clark's comment. "I don't understand. What do you mean, 'destroy' it?"

Lewis decided that it was time to explain. He lay down his pipe, unsmoked. "Tom, we've kept this quiet, but all winter long we've been plagued with robberies in the fort: first tools and instruments, then meat, corn, horses, even medicines."

"Indians?" Tom speculated.

Lewis shook his head thoughtfully. "I don't think so. This is too organized. And it's more than robbery. When we were breaking the keelboat out of the ice, we discovered a crack in the hull. If we hadn't repaired it, the keelboat would have sunk on the way back to St. Louis. The specimens, my report, everything that Mr. Jefferson needs to keep the government convinced that this expedition is necessary, would have been lost."

"And you don't think that crack in the hull was an accident."

"No," Lewis determined. "It wasn't an accident."

Tom clucked his tongue. "So Daniel Boone could have been right, after all. He warned us we might have a spy in our midst. Do you have any idea who's doing these things?"

Captain Clark stood up, went over to the fire to warm his hands. "We've come up with three possibilities," he declared. "It could be the Teton Sioux Partisan and his secret police trying to get their revenge on us for shaming them. It could be somebody on the inside: a spy, as Mr. Boone said. Or, it could be Buck Brussard."

"Brussard! Why would you think of him?"

"It's just a possibility. I keep thinking of that Hudson's Bay man we saw on Mr. Boone's place. We don't know of anyone else who would have the stomach to skin a man alive."

"Tom," Lewis broke in, "all of this could be related to what happened to Roxanna."

"How?" he asked, surprised.

"It would be an easy way to discredit the expedition," he replied. "We're on thin ice with Roxanna on board anyway. If Congress, or any of Mr. Jefferson's political enemies ever knew we were carrying a woman along, it would go very hard for the President. But think how it would be if we allowed the woman to get raped—"

"She wasn't raped," Tom pointed out quickly.

"I didn't say she was, Tom. But we do have to consider it a real possibility."

Tom nodded, agreeing. He looked at Lewis, then Clark. He had gotten to know each man: Lewis, brilliant and enterprising, but always slightly distant; Clark, clever, dependable, familiar. But every time he was in the presence of them together he realized all over again that these were very special men. Great men. He knew somehow that no matter what happened to come their way, they were equal to it.

"Captain Lewis," he asked, "why are you telling me this?"

"We're telling you this because we trust you. And because you're ideally suited for this kind of work. You're intelligent, resourceful, courageous—"

"Sir?" Tom interrupted him. "Just what kind of work did you have in mind?"

Clark cleared his throat. "Detective work, Tom. Until we reach the Pacific, your primary function will be to catch whoever is trying to wreck this expedition."

Before he could react, Lewis spoke. "You're close to Roxanna," he told him. "Start with her. Find out what happened to her after Sacajawea's baby was born."

"I've tried that already. She won't cooperate," he reported. "Roxanna has a mind of her own."

"Then don't tell her what you're doing. In fact, don't tell anyone. That is mandatory, Tom. The future of this country depends on our reaching the Columbia and the Pacific. We're counting on you to stop whoever it is that's so bound and determined to prevent us from doing that."

"Yes sir. I understand."

"Good."

"But there isn't anyone else I can tell?"

"No one. You're it."

"Yes sir," he nodded. "I'll find him myself."

"We have faith in you, Tom," Lewis declared. He took up his pipe again. "Now we need to make a few plans, gentlemen. After all, next month we'll be heading west."

PART FOUR
THE PLAINS

Chapter 15

On March 25, 1805, the weather warmed, the snow melted and the ice on the Missouri began to crack and break up into large white chunks on the yellow water. Five days later, Tom Wentworth helped Lewis and Clark load the keelboat for the return trip to St. Louis. The air was soft and fresh, the sun bright. On the Missouri six half-naked Indians were leaping about from one cake of ice to another, chasing the buffalo which were trapped on the little frozen islands that were floating rapidly down the river.

Tom inventoried the keelboat. It was packed with the skeletons of antelope, wolf and white rabbit; the horns of elk, deer and mountain ram; the skins of red fox, antelope, badger and prairie dog. Crowded together up and down the deck were crates of insects, mice, wooden cages containing live badgers, magpies and prairie dogs, and huge trunks of painted Indian robes and blankets depicting in bright colors the battle of the Mandans and the Teton Sioux.

On April 7, they launched the keelboat and its crew down the river. From St. Louis the cargo would be transported overland to Washington City, where President Jefferson waited anxiously for it to arrive. A few hours later the expedition, fifty-one men, two women and a seven-month-old baby moved westward in two pirogues and six cottonwood canoes out of Fort Mandan.

From his position as back oarsman in the rear canoe, Tom had to strain during the day to catch glimpses of Roxanna, who was riding with Sacajawea in the white pirogue at the head of the caravan. At night, he lingered close to Roxanna's tent, but she was usually busy with Sacajawea and Pomp in the captains' tent, so they seldom made contact.

And yet he thought of Roxanna Fairchild constantly. Whenever he did manage to see her, his passion for the woman surged up so powerfully within him he had to turn away from her in order to control his desires. He had to wait for her. If he understood anything at all about Roxanna from the past year, it was that she was a strong-willed woman who wasn't about to be forced into accepting any man as her lover. She could be overpowered and raped by a man, but she would never be seduced by one. And that included him. So he bided his time.

In May, the weather remained cool enough to snow lightly at times, even though the land they were passing through had turned green with spring. The great, lush expanses of prairie beyond the wooded river were like emerald oceans teeming with the now-familiar herds of elk, deer and buffalo.

Not so familiar to Captain Lewis and the party of six men that hunted on the banks of the Missouri was the man-eating monster the Indians feared more than any other animal—the killer bear.

On a crisp afternoon in early May, in the dim copper-tinted light of a dying sunset, Captain Lewis and Tom Wentworth knelt down in the black mud at the bottom of a steep bank of the river and examined a run of large, deep tracks. Lewis trailed a finger along the edges of the indentation, measured its depth with the length of his thumb. "It's a bear," he confirmed. "It looks to me as if it came down to the river here and jumped in," he speculated. "I'd guess from the angle of the tracks and the distance between them, he was running when he went in."

"But these tracks are twenty feet apart," Tom argued.

Lewis nodded. "I know. Which means he was big and moving at an incredible speed."

"Captain!" Hugh Hall yelled out from the top of a twenty-five-foot bank, forty yards up the river. "We've found some more tracks up here."

Lewis and Wentworth climbed the bluff and looked at the prints in the mud. "That's the same bear," Lewis declared. "He was coming out of the river here."

Tom wrinkled his brow. "Do you think he jumped into the water after something down there, and came back out up here?"

"It looks like it," Lewis concurred. He measured the depth of the tracks. "And whatever he was after, he got. These tracks are deeper than the ones downstream. He was carrying something heavy when he climbed out. Maybe a couple of hundred pounds."

"He climbed a twenty-five-foot cliff holding two hundred pounds?" Tom wondered.

"He'd be up to it," Lewis figured. "The Mandans claim a killer bear can swim a current faster than any boat and push through a dense forest faster than a horse can run a race on the prairie."

"Yes, but the Mandans tend to exaggerate," Tom reminded him.

"Yes, they do, but one thing they never exaggerate is the strength of their enemies. And every Indian tribe in these parts calls the killer bear one of their greatest enemies. They hold rituals in his honor and they put on their war paint when they go out after him.

And even though they attack him in force, in packs of a dozen or more, they always lose somebody."

The men were silent as they followed the tracks back into the woods for a half hour, until they reached a hillside that looked as if it had been turned inside out. The grass and bushes had been scooped up, roots ripped out, dirt overturned. Gigantic holes and ruts gutted the whole side of the hill. Lewis rested his gun on the ground and stared at the sight. "Have you ever seen such a thing?" he marveled.

"What could have happened, captain?" Hugh Hall asked, shaking his head in disbelief. "It looks like a hundred people have been digging around, looking for something."

"Look at the tracks, Hugh," Lewis pointed. "Not a hundred people—one animal."

On the hillside a few feet away, Sergeant Ordway reached down and picked up a dirty, dripping object from the dirt and held it up for Lewis and the others in the hunting party to see. "Look at this, captain," he brought it down to Lewis. "I'd say it's a badger," he guessed. "What's left of one."

Lewis nodded his agreement. "This is his work," he replied confidently. "He tore up the hill looking for this badger."

Ordway looked at him askance. "Captain, what kind of animal would be single-minded enough to rip apart a whole hill for one little badger?"

Before Lewis could answer, Tom called out to the others to look at the tree he was standing next to. When Lewis and the others had joined him, Tom pointed up at the first limb on the tree. Next to it, twelve feet above the ground, were four deep gashes in the bark, a foot long and nearly an inch deep into the wood. "Those are claw marks," Tom told Lewis. "They couldn't be anything else."

The men drew closer, examined the marks on the tree. "They're deeper and higher than any I've seen,"

Ordway observed. "But you're right. They're bear marks."

"This fellow's too heavy to climb trees," Lewis noted. "He must have stood here and sharpened his claws before he dug up the hill for that badger."

"But Captain Lewis," Ordway looked incredulously at the marks. "Look at how high they are. He'd have to be nine or ten feet tall."

Lewis nodded. "At least."

Since it was almost dark they turned back for camp. Late that evening, Tom was startled out of his sleep by a low, deep, guttural roar echoing through the trees around him. The frightful sound emerging out of the darkness like a ghostly shadow looming in the fog, sent chills through his body. He spent the rest of the night sitting up, wrapped in a blanket, keeping watch on Roxanna's tent, in case the bear decided it was time to attack.

A few days later the hunting party discovered more prints near the muddy river bed. "That's him," Lewis announced. "I was afraid of this. He's moving ahead of us."

"He's not after us, is he, captain?" Hall asked hopefully.

"I'm afraid he is, Hugh," Lewis told him. "The Indians say he eats men as well as he eats badger. I'd say he has in mind picking off his meals, one by one."

"But if he's ahead of us—" Hall began.

"If he's ahead of us, then he's moving a good deal faster than we are. Which means he can attack us whenever he takes a notion. We'll just have to be on the alert, Hugh." He looked over at John Ordway. "Sergeant, when we get back to camp, tell Captain Clark I want to double the guard for the next few days. If that monster comes prowling around our fires, I want somebody to see him."

"Yes sir."

"Fields, I want you to make it your business to tell everybody on the expedition to be prepared. Do it quietly, though. I don't want people excited, just prepared."

"Yes sir," Fields answered.

The next three days were tense. After he had picked up no sign of the bear for a day or so, Tom decided to go out to the edge of the camp to watch Patrick Gass teach Roxanna how to shoot her flintlock. Tom was irritated at the prospect of Roxanna using the gun *he* had given her to practice shooting with another man, but he said nothing to her about it. And though he wanted to break up the practice sessions too, he hung back out of sight and did nothing. But at dusk, when Roxanna's dark hair glistened in the twilight, and her face seemed to radiate in the orange glow of the sunset, he imagined holding her naked in his arms, making love to her.

Each time Gass drew near her to show her how to hold the pistol, or position her feet for a shot, Tom felt his whole body ache for her. When he caught her smiling at Gass, or when he noticed the bounce of her breasts inside her deerskin shirt as she raised the pistol to aim, he had to restrain himself from bursting into the clearing to claim the woman for himself.

He couldn't know that Roxanna was acutely aware of his presence each time he lurked behind the trees to watch them. His being there always excited her, made her feel warm all over. She wanted Tom Wentworth, longed for him, wanted to spend the rest of her life with him, but she wouldn't tell him how she felt. If she admitted her feelings for him, there would be no controlling him—or herself.

One evening at dusk, a few miles beyond the junction of the Milk River with the Missouri, Tom was arriving back at camp from watching Roxanna and Gass, when he saw Hugh Hall burst out of the trees, his rounded, boyish face red with excitement. "Captain Lewis!" he was yelling. "Captain Lewis! Come quick!"

Lewis burst out of his tent, holding the air gun by

the stock. "What is it, Hall?" he asked. "What's happened?"

"Captain—"

"Just calm down, private. Take a breath; tell me what's going on."

"It's the bear, captain," he panted. "Ned Craddock and I just saw him on a sandbar. He was just sitting there, scratching himself. But Captain Lewis—he's the biggest beast God ever made. He's as big as a mountain!"

"Well, it looks like we finally get to see him," Lewis answered soberly. "All right, men, get your guns!" He looked around the camp. "Ordway!"

The sergeant rushed up out of the crowd. "Sir!"

Lewis looked straight at him. "John, round up four of your best marksmen and come with us. Captain Clark will stay here in case he doubles back."

"Yes sir."

"Tom and I will be up front. Wentworth! Come on, grab your gun. Let's go."

They dashed quickly through the woods behind Hugh until, in a clearing a short distance from the camp, they found the bear. The men quietly huddled together behind trees and gaped at him, overwhelmed. The massive animal was more than nine feet tall, half a ton of hard flesh covered with grizzled brown hair. He stood humped over, clawing madly into the earth, growling fiercely, slinging chunks of dirt and grass over his shoulders with his huge, powerful claws.

"Look at the size of him!" Joseph Fields exclaimed.

"What about that mouth?" Hall gasped. "He could take a man's head in it."

"Captain," Ordway said dubiously. "I'm not sure our guns can kill him. I've never seen anything that big."

Lewis nodded, but he was unperturbed. "The Indians tell me killing range is less than ten yards. Any farther, the balls may not even penetrate the skin."

"I'm not sure they'll penetrate it at that distance, captain," Ordway fretted.

"If they don't," Lewis responded simply, "we'll just move in closer. We're not going to walk away from him. He's going to attack us when he gets hungry, so we'd better kill him first, while we have this chance." Lewis put his hand on Wentworth's shoulder. "You and I will draw him out, Tom." He looked around at the others. "You men stay behind us, in the grass. If we can make him think Tom and I are the only ones after him, we may be able to catch him off guard."

Tom stepped boldly out into the clearing. While he had great faith in the marksmen behind him, he knew that what he was doing was perilous, for not even Captain Lewis knew just how mean, how ferocious or how powerful a killer bear could be. He wondered if he weren't methodically—and stupidly—marching himself straight into the jaws of death.

As they walked slowly through the grass, all the sensations of fear began to take hold of him. His mouth turned dry, his hands became moist. His breathing was heavy and lax. His heart seemed to have leaped up into his throat and was pounding harder and harder with each step he took. He wanted to stop and shoot now, before the bear even noticed them. But Captain Lewis paced forward relentlessly, his eyes fixed on the bear, his air gun extended straight out in front of him.

At twenty yards, the bear suddenly cocked his head and looked up at them. Immediately he drew himself up on his hind legs.

"Captain!" Tom cried, only now seeing the shape on the ground next to the bear's legs. "That's a *man* he has! He's going to bury a man!"

"Hold it, Tom," Lewis whispered, raising his hand. "I don't think he's going to run. We'd better stand our ground here."

With a loud growl, the bear hoisted himself higher, stretching his great length still further into the air. Above a quick flash of teeth, his small black eyes peered intently out of a hard, mask-like face.

"He's coming toward us, Captain Lewis," Tom mumbled, kneeling down in the grass. He cocked his rifle, pulling the butt of the stock firmly against his quivering shoulder. He could hear nervous movement in the grass behind him, but he was certain the men wouldn't leave him and Lewis to face this monster alone.

"Wait until he reaches that stump over there," Lewis cautioned him. "And remember to aim for the heart or the head. He won't even feel anything else."

As the bear turned to face the hunters, Tom heard the clicking of four rifle hammers behind him, almost in unison.

"We've got him in our sights, Captain Lewis," Ordway called out from behind. "Four shots ought to bring him down. Just tell us when."

"Let us fire first," Lewis told him. "Stand ready."

"Oh, God," Hall cried out. "Here he comes. Look at that stride!"

The bear started slowly toward them, paused, lumbered laterally across the clearing on all fours, his gaze fixed on the men. He stopped, drew up and growled again. Then, suddenly, with a tremendous burst of power, he rushed forward, snarling wildly—directly at Tom Wentworth.

Lewis calmly lifted the air gun to his shoulder, waited a second, then squeezed the trigger. But nothing happened. He squeezed again. The gun was jammed.

"Captain Lewis!" Tom yelled, looking over at him. "He's past the stump!"

"My gun won't fire, Tom. Shoot!"

Tom drew a bead on the hulking mass of furious muscle headed toward him. The bear was barreling in low, his chest protected; Tom would have to aim for the head.

But then abruptly, ten yards away, the bear drew to a halt. Tom could see now that the animal's attention was riveted to the men standing behind him with their rifles leveled. The bear's beady black eyes were glaring, his cavernous mouth cracked open, showing his awesome teeth. He rose up high again, bellowed a roar so deep and heavy that Tom could feel its vibrations in his own chest.

While Lewis was working feverishly on his gun. Tom took careful aim and ripped off a shot. The ball slammed into the bear's chest, but it did no more than explode the skin and fur and produce a trickle of blood. The bear didn't even seem to notice.

"Ordway! Fire!" Lewis commanded.

Tom heard the quick succession of four explosions of powder, saw four slugs splatter directly into the upper torso of the enormous beast. But the animal barely flinched. Tom felt paralyzed. No animal alive should be able to survive such a battery of gunfire.

Captain Lewis bellowed a warning. "Ordway! He's after you. Get out of here, all of you! Quick! Head for the river!"

The bear growled, scratched furiously at the holes in his chest, ripping hair and flesh away from bone with his mighty claws.

"We can't leave you—" Ordway protested.

"Go, damn it! That's an order. We'll be all right. He's not after us. He wants you. Go—now!"

While the men scurried back toward the woods, the bear stood on his back feet and silently watched them. He cocked his head and growled ferociously as he clawed violently at his bleeding chest.

By this time Tom had reloaded. He fired again and another shot hit the right shoulder. The bear looked directly at him, bared his terrible yellow teeth. Then with a horrifying, wailing spurt of motion, he lunged forward.

The monstrous shape darkened the sky as the mammoth creature swooped down upon Tom with incredible force. Tom saw the blur of the bear's ponderous forepaw reaching toward him, felt a devastating impact on his chest. Tom's body crumpled. He was propelled through the air as though hit by an explosion. Falling, his head rattled. Some part of his shoulder collapsed with an agonizing crunch and then he was lying on the ground, dazed. When he managed to struggle to his feet, he could see through his bleary eyes that the bear was moving away. The terror was over. He was alive! But the bear was seeking new prey—the other men in the woods.

"Tom!" Lewis yelled, coming toward him. "He's going after them. Are you all right?"

As Tom got to his feet, he had to hunch over. Some of his ribs were broken, he realized. Breathing was difficult. But as soon as he regained his balance, Tom understood that the battle was far from won. He heard the rustle of bushes and the cracking of limbs as the bear crashed madly through the trees.

Lewis joined him. "Can you make it to the river?" he asked quickly.

"I think so," Tom groaned, holding his ribs in tightly to ease the pain of breathing.

"They've got a good head start on him, Tom, but even if they make it to the river, he'll go in after them. It's up to us to stop him."

Tom nodded, grimacing in pain. "I'm all right," he mumbled. "Where's my gun?"

"Here," Lewis handed it to him. "Let's go. He has it in his mind to get Ordway and the others. You remember what he did to that hill—he'll tear up the whole territory to get them."

The way back through the woods seemed to Tom to take forever. With every step his cracked ribs dug like knives into his lungs and halted his breath. But he pushed ahead with Captain Lewis, following the path of destruction left by the charging bear.

At the Missouri River, they saw the monstrous bear crouched low on top of a high bank, looking down into the water, waiting. Fifty yards away, in the swirling currents of the river, the four hunters were floating swiftly downstream toward him. Lewis and Tom stopped. "He must have known they would be going to the river," Lewis said. "He cut beneath them so he could wait for them to pass by."

"They're helpless in those currents," Tom explained. "We can't let him go in after them."

Tom lifted his rifle, aimed it up toward the bank. Out of the corner of his eye, he could see the heads of the men bobbing in the water, drifting unwittingly toward the bear that waited, ready to pounce. Tom held his breath and squeezed off a shot.

The bear didn't even flinch as the shot dug into his shoulder. His eyes were fixed on the men floating downstream.

Down in the river, Hugh Hall caught sight of the bear and cried out. "Sergeant Ordway! There he is—on the bank!"

Ordway looked up. "Oh, Lord. Go back, men!" he screamed out. "We're floating down to him."

They turned around and tried to swim upstream, but the current was too strong for them. All they could do was maintain their places in the tow of the water.

Then, as if he had understood their words, the bear put one of his forepaws down on the ground, pushed and flung his body twenty feet off the cliff into the water. Without a pause, he began swimming rapidly up the river.

"Let's go up the bank for another shot," Lewis suggested.

"It won't do any good," Tom grunted, holding his ribs. "Nothing will stop him, captain."

"Tom!" Lewis looked directly at him. "Listen to me. We don't have time to think about that. We've got to save those men, somehow. Come on."

They scrambled up the bank and looked down into the water. The bear was swimming up the current faster than any of the men. The beast was only ten yards from his prey, each stroke bringing him closer to the men who flailed at the water, struggling to gain against the current.

"You have one shot, Tom," Lewis muttered, shaking his head.

Tom reloaded, looking down. The bear had closed the gap to five yards, four, then three. Now, he was only a few feet away from Private Hall.

"Do you want me to shoot?" Lewis asked.

"No. I'll do it," Tom raised the gun.

There was only one place to shoot now—the head. And Lewis was right, he would have only one shot. If Tom missed, Hugh Hall would be nothing but a mass of blood and flesh floating down the river. By the time Tom loaded the rifle again, the bear would have done his work on all the helpless swimmers.

With pain racking his chest, Tom quickly tried to estimate the distance, the velocity of the wind, the angle of descent, the sighting error of the rifle. He aimed the barrel two feet higher than the animal's head and almost one foot to the left. Just as he was about to pull the trigger, he saw the bear's great paw rise up out of the swirling water like a sea serpent.

Despite his pain, Tom's body was perfectly still the instant the rifle cracked.

The tiny mass of lead flew down from the bank. The sound of its impact against the bear's skull was lost amid the roar of the water. But Tom knew instantly he'd scored a direct hit. The head plunged beneath the water line and then bobbed up again.

The bear was dead.

"Great shot, Tom!" Hall yelled from the river. "Great shot!"

The other men shouted jubilantly. Lewis flung his arm around Tom's shoulder. "You just saved the lives of four good men." Then, uncharacteristically, Lewis embraced the younger man and yanked him next to his body. "A damned good shot, Wentworth," he congratulated him, patting him hard on the back.

"Captain—" Tom gasped in pain.

Lewis quickly remembered Tom's chest and backed off. "Oh, sorry," he muttered. "How bad is it?"

Tom listened to the joyous yelling and laughing down in the river. "Oh," he grinned, "it's not too bad. Not too bad."

Lewis laughed heartily, shook Tom's hand vigorously. "Good," he stepped to the edge of the bank. He looked down at the four men coasting noisily downstream. "Ordway!" he yelled out through cupped hands.

"Captain Lewis!" Ordway returned. "Did you see that shot?"

"I saw it," Lewis called back.

"Lord, what a shot, Captain Lewis!" Ordway hollered. "Make that boy a sergeant! If you have to fire me to do it!"

Lewis laughed. "We'll see about that."

"Incredible shot—best shot I've ever seen!"

"John—we're going back to the clearing for that body," he told him. "You men take care of the bear."

"Yes sir!" Ordway answered. "Gladly!"

The sun had dropped below the horizon by the time Lewis and Wentworth made it back to the clearing, but the moon lit up the countryside enough for them to find their way easily across the grass, to the dark shape lying curled up on the ground.

Tom clutched the left side of his ribcage tightly as Lewis squatted down and laid his hand on the man's brawny shoulder. "He's unconscious, but he's still alive," Lewis spoke after a few seconds.

"Is it anybody we know?" Tom asked.

Lewis slowly, carefully turned the man over on his back and looked at the familiar bearded face below him. "Yes. We know him. It's the mountainman, Buck Brussard."

Instantly Tom dropped down to his knees. "Buck Brussard!" he exclaimed, ignoring the pain stabbing through his lungs. "What's he doing out here?"

Lewis quietly pushed the hair out of Brussard's

face. "I don't know," he answered. "He's not hurt too badly, though. His chest is ripped open and it looks like his left arm is broken—"

Brussard stirred, groaned loudly, opened his eyes. "Well," he murmured, "look at this. What do you say, cap'n?"

Lewis shook his head, smiled. "I say you must not be much of a mountainman, Buck, getting yourself tangled up with a bear like that."

"He caught me by surprise, cap'n," he explained. "I had to play dead on 'im, but he was just about to have me for supper when you showed up."

"Well, you can forget about that, Buck," Lewis told him. "He's dead. Tom killed him."

"Ah, you're a good man, Wentworth," Brussard praised him. "Looks like I got you out of those rattlers for a good reason, after all."

"Looks like it," Tom agreed.

Lewis stood up. "We need to get you back to camp, Buck. Tom'll wait here while I go back for a sled."

Two hours later Brussard was stretched out on his back on a pile of Mandan blankets in the captains' Indian-style tent. Lewis and Clark were standing nearby, waiting for Sacajawea to finish sewing his parted skin back together.

Soon she broke off the thread and stood up. "You will need bear grease on the wounds," she lectured him.

He resisted the idea. "If it's all the same to you, ma'am, I'd rather not get that close to a bear again. I figure a little Missouri mud will do pretty much the same thing, don't you?"

She shrugged. "You have a Shawnee wife," she replied. "Let her take care of you. She will know what to do."

He nodded silently, choosing not to tell her his wife was dead.

Clark stepped toward the Indian girl. "You did a good job, Sacajawea," he thanked her. "I don't think he would have ever let me use that needle and thread on him like that."

She nodded. "Men never cry when women nurse them." She took another look at Brussard, then turned and left the tent.

Captain Lewis stared after her a few moments, then handed Brussard a cup of whiskey. "This ought to ease the pain, Buck."

"Yeah, it ought to," Brussard agreed. He took the cup and brought it to his lips.

Lewis watched him drink. "You stayed with the Minnetarees last winter, didn't you?" he asked.

"Yeah," Brussard grunted as he swigged more of the liquor. "I stayed with 'em for a while. When the snow melted, they ran me off."

"And now we meet you out here," Lewis pointed out. "Isn't that a bit strange, Buck? According to our maps, we're moving into country no white man has ever explored. And yet here you are—again."

"Well, no, it ain't really all that strange, cap'n," he assured him. "I've been kind of trailing along with you all spring."

Lewis studied him silently for a moment. "And why would you be doing that?"

"Nothing simpler, cap'n—you folks are going where I'm going. I figured I'd join up with you again, some time or other. Meanwhile I've been keeping a look out for you, ever since you left your fort back there."

Lewis pulled at his lip thoughtfully. "Have you come across anything interesting?" he asked, a little impatient with him.

"As a matter of fact, I have. You got a man on your crew that wants you dead, cap'n. I'd say that was interesting. He's been leaving a trail of blood every day, so that bear would follow you."

"Damn!" Lewis exclaimed, throwing his cup

against the tent wall. "We could have been killed. What's he thinking? He even tampered with my air gun."

"I reckon the man's desperate, cap'n," Brussard concluded.

"He must be."

Brussard sat up and watched Lewis turn his back and walk away a few steps. "Well, anyway," he changed the subject, "that's a fine little squaw you men have working for you here. What is she, Minnetaree?"

"She was born Shoshone," Clark answered. "Brought up Minnetaree."

"Well, whatever she is, she's a pretty little thing. She reminds me of my own daughter. She'd be about that age now, I reckon."

Lewis turned around. "I didn't know you had a family, Buck," he remarked.

Brussard swallowed the rest of the whiskey. "Oh yeah, I had a family—once. But a bunch of bloodthirsty renegades took care of that right quick. They killed my wife and threw her away in the bushes and made off with my little girl. I've been looking for the bastards ever since."

Lewis came closer. After a pause, he said, "You told us you were going where we're going. . . ."

"As long as you're going the way they are, cap'n. I've known for a long time the leader of these renegades is a white man. They're all misfits—Tetons, Crows, Blackfeet—any warrior that's been kicked out of his own tribe can join up with 'em. What I didn't know till this winter was why he'd want to burn *my* place. There was nothing there but my family and a few pelts."

"Why did he?" Clark asked.

" 'Cause it was a trading post, cap'n. These renegades are paid to burn down trading posts. Simple as that."

"Paid?" Clark repeated, surprised.

"That's right. By the Great Pacific Fur Trading

Company of Montreal. They're paid to burn trading posts and kill every living soul on the place, including cows, children and dogs. A couple of times they even had a man skinned alive, like the fella you said you found at Boone's place last year."

"So the man who killed your wife is the one who mutilated that body in La Charrette," Clark deduced.

"One and the same, cap'n. He's got a style you can't miss."

"I don't understand what kind of man would do such a thing."

"Well, I can tell you, cap'n," Brussard offered. "He ain't like other men."

"What *is* he like?" Lewis asked him.

"Well, he's mean, he's smart, he's slippery. And he's vicious."

"What makes him so different from other men?"

"One other thing, Cap'n Lewis. This one's crazy."

Chapter 16

A few weeks later, several hundred miles northwest of the Lewis and Clark expedition, Morton McKain, agent for the Great Pacific Fur Company, ordered his man Miflin to land the flatboat on the north bank of the South Saskatchewan River in Canada. They had been standing on deck watching the dark smoke curl into the air for almost an hour. Now they had finally reached the site. The Mackenzie trading post was only half a mile inland from that point.

"You'll have to stay here, Miflin," McKain commanded as he climbed up the bank. "I can't trust a single man on this crew."

"Well, you can't trust *him,* either," Miflin gestured with his head toward the smoke. "He's crazy."

"I can handle him, Miflin," McKain replied haughtily. "Use the right words and you can handle anybody."

"At least take a gun, Morton."

"I don't use guns, Miflin, because I don't need them. Idiots use guns, I have brains. Now stay with this crew till I come back."

McKain buttoned his black broadcloth coat around his round chest and fat belly and proceeded to the trading post. Instead of a building, he found only black ruins, a jumbled mass of charred, smoking rubble in the middle of a clearing. He wasn't shocked by what he saw, however; he expected to see just that.

"What do you want, McKain?" questioned a voice behind him.

The agent turned around, saw a dark young man with close-cropped black hair and a ruddy face. He was dressed in a white cotton shirt and buckskin trousers tucked into high English riding boots. McKain knew him to be half white, half Pawnee Indian. "Where is he, Harmer?" McKain demanded. "I've come a long way."

"Red Hair is with the prisoners," he answered formally.

"Come on, don't give me that 'Red Hair' business. When you're with a white man, speak like one, especially if he pays your salary."

Harmer looked at him coldly. "Red Hair is with the prisoners," he repeated defiantly. "He is killing them. He likes to do it himself."

McKain swallowed hard. "Good. That's what he's supposed to do. I don't care for that kind of thing myself, it makes me sick at the stomach. But that's what has to be done."

Harmer gritted his teeth. "Would you like to see him do it?" he asked.

"Hardly," he replied stiffly.

"Come, you can watch him," he grabbed McKain's arm.

"No—get your hands off me," he ordered.

But the other man ignored his words. He pushed McKain ahead of him, through part of the smoldering debris, onto the path leading into the woods. A few minutes later, he stopped in front of a clump of bushes, raised his finger and pointed at it. "Look through there," he commanded him.

"I certainly will not," McKain protested.

"Look!" he insisted, jerking him forward as he pulled back part of the bush.

What McKain saw past the bush next to the tree made him gag. He had to turn his head away. "My God, man!" he exclaimed, holding his throat.

"Do you still say 'Good,' McKain?" Harmer asked behind his cool, penetrating eyes.

"Look, Harmer, I don't force the man to commit these . . . atrocities. I don't approve of this kind of thing any more than you do."

"He enjoys it," Harmer muttered sadly. "He hangs the man up like a deer—"

"All right, I saw it! I'm sorry, but there's nothing I can do about it." He turned and hurried back to the remains of the trading post. Finding a stump nearby, he sat down, took a deep breath and crossed his arms. "I'm going to wait here until he's finished," he announced in a shaky voice.

Harmer came up to him through the ashes. "You people in Montreal are no better than he is, McKain."

"I'd advise you to guard your Indian tongue, Harmer. You're the last person to feel superior to anybody. You stay with him, don't you? You and these no-account Indian friends of yours. You make it possble for him to do *that* to people, don't you?"

"I stay with him because he saved my life," Harmer defended himself. "No other reason."

McKain laughed derisively. "That's an admirable loyalty you have there, Harmer. You're faithful to the man who murdered your only brother."

"Half-brother," he corrected him. "He was white. He hated me. He tried to kill me."

"Spare me the story, if you don't mind," McKain growled impatiently. He pulled out his watch and looked at it. "It doesn't exactly make a man cry, you know."

Harmer looked at McKain with pleading eyes. "*You* could stop him. You have the power to do it."

"He works for Great Pacific, Harmer. I don't want to stop him."

"He is evil."

"You're boring me. Why don't you make yourself useful to the company and go get your boss for me. I have a business matter to discuss with him."

"You will have to see him in camp," Harmer told him.

"Look, Harmer, I don't care where I see him, as long as I see him. But I only have an hour."

"Come with me," he ordered.

Without another word, he led McKain away from the ruins of the Mackenzie trading post to the renegades' camp nearly three miles away. By the time they reached it, the agent was tired, winded and flushed. Obviously disgruntled, he sat down on the ground, loosened his tie and puffed.

Harmer stood nearby, at ease, completely unaffected by the long walk. "He will be here soon," he said. "He was almost finished when we saw him."

McKain drew his watch out of his waistcoat, looked at it, and held it up to his ear to see if it was still ticking. "I don't really care for this sort of thing," he complained. "This . . . hanging around." To orient himself, he gazed around the area. Lounging about on the ground were ten or eleven slovenly Indian warriors in various stages of dress. They were laughing, joking with each other, while four Indian women stood gloomily attending huge pots balanced over the smoky fires. He detected the sickening smell of rancid meat cooking, but no one seemed to be noticing it but him.

"You know, this isn't exactly what I expected," he felt compelled to observe.

"What did you expect?" Harmer responded. "Militia men in uniform?"

"No, not that, but I did expect something a little more organized than this . . . melange. Their leader is British, after all." He got to his feet, brushed the dust off the seat of his pants. Restless and impatient, he allowed his eyes to continue to wander over the camp, until they lit upon a young woman stooping down by a fire.

Dressed in a threadbare cotton dress, she seemed to be white, no more than sixteen years old. She was four or five months pregnant, he guessed, and very sickly. He decided that she had been pretty once, with brown eyes, dark hair, and regular features, but now she was homely, pale and unsteady on her feet.

He turned away from her when he heard the sound of approaching horses. The alarm brought the Indians in the camp to life. They stood up straight as rods. Even Harmer made himself more rigid as he waited for the other men to arrive. McKain instinctively straightened his cravat as the lead horse thundered into camp.

The leader of the returning renegades, Sir Douglas Fairchild, jerked back on the reins, pulled his horse to a halt, and stepped down with a flourish. He was a tall, attractive man with a thick red moustache, arched eyebrows, and a full crop of bushy red hair. He wore black boots, grey pin-striped trousers, and a long wool coat.

"What are you doing here, McKain, spying on us?" he groused. He yanked off his bloody leather gloves and flung them back at one of the Indians behind him.

McKain was unable to speak for a moment. Fairchild's large gray eyes always caught him off-balance, made him extremely nervous. He remembered them now. Fairchild always seemed to be looking past you, always thinking of something else, as if you were not the person he was actually speaking to.

McKain cleared his throat. "We have to talk about the Lewis and Clark expedition."

Fairchild didn't seem to hear him. He gave the reins of his horse to a Crow warrior and strode over to the white girl, who was stirring a pot of stew with a soup ladle. He snatched the ladle out of her hand, dipped out some of the stew and tasted it. "You let it boil," he spat it onto the fire.

"No, I didn't," she protested in a low, weak voice. "I swear I didn't."

He angrily snapped the pot of stew off the fire and heaved it across the yard. It banged against the ground, the contents spewed out, and a handful of warriors had to scurry to avoid being burned by the splashing liquid. "Do it again," he ordered her.

"But I didn't boil it," she cried. "It was only simmering."

He looked at her silently for a second, then raised his hand up and slapped the left side of her face. As she touched her stinging cheek, he said to her, "Move your hand." When she dropped it, he hit her again, in the same place. "Now," he ordered, "do it again."

"I'm sorry," she apologized tearfully.

He left her shaking his head. "The incompetent girl can't even cook," he told McKain. "I've never seen a woman who couldn't cook."

Standing close by, Harmer gnashed his teeth angrily. "She does the best she can," he interjected.

"Well then, her best obviously isn't good enough," Fairchild informed him. As he looked at Harmer's concerned face, an idea came to him. He turned back to the agent. "How would you like to have this girl, McKain?" he asked with a gleam in his eye. "It's true she can't cook, but she can still do other things."

McKain treated the suggestion as a joke. "What would I do with a pregnant woman?"

But Fairchild's voice was deadly serious. "She won't be pregnant when I send her to you. I don't expect to allow a bastard Fairchild to run around out here in the wilds."

"But she's a white girl," McKain pointed out. "You could marry her."

Fairchild laughed condescendingly. "She's not white, McKain," he corrected him. "She's the daughter of a Shawnee squaw and a destitute mountainman named Brussard. Surely you don't expect me to let my blood flow through sewerage like that, do you?"

"I don't see you have much choice about it, Douglas," he declared uncomfortably. "I mean if she is carrying your baby."

Fairchild's eyes glazed over for a few seconds. "I will send her to you after she's foaled." Then he stared directly at McKain. "There won't be any quarter-breed Fairchild hanging onto her hems, either," he added.

"No, really—"

"I insist on it, McKain," Fairchild glanced over at Harmer. "My gift to you."

"No, I couldn't take her. I wouldn't know what to do with her. I'm an old bachelor."

"McKain, don't argue with me. If you say 'no' one more time, I will send both of them to you, mother and child, all chopped up in little pieces."

McKain almost responded, but caught himself.

"That's better," Fairchild nodded. "I'll confess to you, I've always had a passion for that girl. I shall hate to see her go. At one time she was rather good in bed." He grinned as he watched his words dig painfully into Harmer. He laughed at him. "What's the matter, Big Tree?" he chided him. "Does that kind of talk stir you up?"

"She has been good to you," he stated. "You have no cause to hurt her."

"There, you see, half-breeds do have normal feelings after all, McKain," he sneered. "Big Tree Harmer may be human after all."

Harmer almost spoke, but then turned and walked away.

Fairchild laughed. "The poor bastard actually loves that Brussard girl. He always has."

"Then why don't you give her to *him?*" McKain suggested, pleased with the cleverness of the idea. But then his blood turned to ice when Fairchild glowered at him with his cold, distant eyes.

"You know what you just did, McKain?" he

asked. "You just uttered a 'no.' You can expect the girl's remains in Montreal sometime in November. In a box about yay size," he held his hands a foot apart.

"Now just a minute, Fairchild, you can't just kill an innocent girl—"

"Remember where you are, McKain," Fairchild reminded him. "You are not in Montreal. The only reason you're sitting here now with your head still on your shoulders is that we are in business together. But don't presume, sir." He reached over and grabbed McKain's collar and squeezed it. "And let me tell you something else," his eyes burned with hate. "Don't you *ever* tell me what to do with my life. Not ever. Do you understand that?"

"Yes," McKain responded shakily. "I'm sorry."

"People tried to run my life back in England. I won't have it any more. *I'm* running my life."

"I understand. That's fine."

"Good," he released McKain's collar. "We agree. Now why don't you just state your business."

McKain loosened his tie, scratched his neck nervously. "It's about the Lewis and Clark expedition."

"What about it?"

McKain took a deep breath to try to rid himself of his fear of Fairchild. "It has to be destroyed. Every last vestige of it. Men, boats, supplies, journals, everything."

"You sound desperate, McKain," Fairchild raised his eyebrows.

"It's a desperate situation," he replied anxiously. "Until now I've been able to keep our heads above water with our British backers by convincing them the Indians out here have been raiding our competitors' trading posts. But if that expedition reaches the Pacific, the rush of American trading companies will be too much for us to handle. They'll back out and we'll go under."

"What about your man Craddock, McKain? Wasn't he supposed to sabotage that operation?"

"He's been trying to. But these Americans are too clever—"

"It's not the Americans, McKain. It's Ned Craddock. I know the man. He's incompetent. You were stupid to hire him in the first place."

"All right, I agree, it was a bad move. I thought he could handle it with a minimum of violence. I was wrong. He can't handle it at all. That's why I came to see you. Montreal wants you to do it."

Fairchild smiled. "Do they indeed."

"They didn't specify how, either," McKain added. "So do it any way you like, as long as there's no trace of them left."

Fairchild brightened, smiled thoughtfully. "Now I would enjoy taking care of Ned Craddock for money," he mused. "I was going to do that anyway. He stole a watch from me in St. Louis—"

"I don't care anything about that, Douglas. All I want, and all Great Pacific Fur wants, is for you and your men to stop Lewis and Clark."

"Good. Consider it done. The whole crew, dead and gone."

Just then an Indian boy on a spotted pony appeared at the edge of camp, leading another horse with a body slung over the saddle. The boy, a Blackfoot, got down from his pony, grabbed the belt of the man on the other horse, and tugged him down. The white man rolled off the saddle and hit the ground with a thud.

"Mackenzie man," the Blackfoot addressed Fairchild as he walked up.

Fairchild nodded. "Good work," he praised him. "Take him out behind a tree and kill him."

"No, wait!" the Brussard girl cried out. She dropped the meat she was slicing into the dirt and rushed to the side of the man on the ground. "Mr. Thompson!" she cried.

"What are you doing, girl?" Fairchild looked around to see who was watching. "Get up from there."

"I know him!" she exclaimed. "He knows my father."

"I don't care. Get up!"

She ignored his command, tried to bring the man to consciousness. "Tell me! Where is he!" she pleaded. "Is he alive?"

"Miss Brussard?" the man mumbled groggily. "Is that you?"

"Yes—are you all right?"

"Praise the Lord. What are you doing here?"

Fairchild had heard enough; he unbuttoned his long coat, flipped out a long knife from a sheath under his arm.

"Douglas, wait—" McKain began.

"Keep your tongue in your head where it's safe, McKain," he warned him. "This isn't your business."

"Where is he, please tell me!" the girl pressed.

"I don't know, Miss Brussard," he replied weakly.

Fairchild lost his patience. With a loud grunt, he slammed his boot into the girl's back, knocking her into the Mackenzie man's arms. Then he reached down, grabbed her hair and pulled her up. "Get back to your cooking," he ordered her.

"No!" she defied him. "I won't. I won't!"

Fairchild was boiling over with rage at her. He crooked his knee and rammed it into her stomach. She shrieked in pain as she doubled over.

Immediately the man on the ground sprung to life. He leaped up, shouted "Damn you!" and pounced on Fairchild, his big hands open and groping for the throat. But the instant he crashed into the other man's body, he stopped. With an expression of shock and dismay, he looked slowly down at his chest. Then he backed up, watched the long bloody knife in Fairchild's hand slip out of his chest as he fell backwards to the ground.

Fairchild shook his head in disgust and without bothering to wipe the dripping blade, crammed it back into its sheath. Then he reached down and helped the girl up. "I hope I didn't hurt you, ma'am," he mocked her.

"You didn't hurt me," she gasped.

"Good. Then you won't mind going back to the fire, where you belong."

"No," she murmured submissively. "I won't mind."

"While you're doing that," he said to her as she walked away, "think about what you just caused to happen. You just had a man killed."

Morton McKain stared incredulously at the dead man lying with a pool of blood on his chest. The sight of blood oozing from the wound made him slightly sick. "It's a shame he's dead. He could have given us some valuable information: plans for new trading posts, new shipping routes. . . ."

"Yes, it's a shame," Fairchild agreed, "but this girl is exactly the same as every other female in the world. They all turn men against each other. They should be stripped naked and tied to bedposts until it's time for them to foal."

"For God's sake, Fairchild, she *knew* the man!" McKain exclaimed. "Surely you don't blame her!"

"Why can't I blame her, I own her."

"All right, you own the poor girl. But why do you abuse her? You may have killed your own child, kicking her that way."

"Well, that would hardly have been a loss, McKain. When I get a child, it will be legitimate, not like that quarter-breed festering in her belly. It will be a real Fairchild, nurtured in my wife's womb."

"Your wife," McKain shook his head. "Somehow that's hard to believe."

"Is it? As it happens, McKain, I have a wife. In New Orleans."

McKain was too surprised to speak.

"As a matter of fact," Fairchild went on, "except for being a bit rash, she's a rather excellent wife. She has poise, charm, and—for an American—she comes from a good family. She's home now, waiting for me."

"If she's like other women," the agent offered boldly, "she may not be."

Fairchild's eyes grew large and round and frightening. "She isn't like other women. If I ever discovered. . . . Well, let's say she had better be back in New Orleans where she belongs, waiting for me."

"I'm sure she is," McKain tried to assure him.

"If my wife ever allowed another man to touch her—No," he caught himself. "That kind of thinking turns my stomach. There is no need to imagine such a detestable thing."

"No," McKain agreed. "Of course not."

Fairchild looked off in the distance. "Not her," he muttered absently. "Not Roxanna."

Chapter 17

When the hunting party moving down one of the banks of the Missouri River first heard the low, steady rumble of falling water, they stopped to listen. Poised on a bluff at the end of a range of hills, they were overlooking a plain that stretched out for forty or fifty miles. It resembled a calm sea, dotted with dark islands which were great herds of grazing buffalo.

"There's the spray of water over the plain," Lewis told Tom. "That's it, exactly where it's supposed to be."

"Are you sure, Captain Lewis?" Tom asked doubtfully. "It looks like smoke to me."

"No, it's water," he declared confidently. "That's the Great Falls of the Missouri. We're not far away."

Later, at noon on June 13, 1805, Tom Wentworth got his first glimpse of the great spectacle. All he could do was stand in awe of the sight. He felt consumed by the powerful, deafening roar of the rushing water. He watched it pour out over the ledge and cascade nearly a hundred feet below onto massive rocks, shooting great sheets of foam and spray two hundred yards into the river. The white water gushed off the rocks, burst into strange, fleeting shapes and made brilliantly colored rainbows in the sunlight. The beauty of the scene mesmerized him; for a long time he couldn't pull himself away from it.

Three days after that, a few miles downstream, he was pausing to look up admiringly at another of the five falls in the ten-mile strip of the Missouri. He stood precariously on top of a boulder at the edge of a bottom of cottonwood trees, feeling in his own body the power of the water crashing down from the precipice onto a maze of rocks and then breaking out into white-water rapids.

Suddenly a sound from behind him shook him out of his daze. "It's a beautiful sight, isn't it?" a voice called out.

He wheeled around and looked down. "Roxanna!" he exclaimed. "What are you doing here?"

She shielded her eyes from the sun as she looked up at him. "To tell you the truth," she admitted, "I was looking for you."

Tom jumped eagerly down to the ground, led her away into the shade, away from the overwhelming roar of the falls. "I thought you were back taking care of Sacajawea."

"She's well enough, Tom. Captain Clark was too concerned about her. I told him it was nothing but a woman's problem, but he insisted on worrying."

"I can understand that," Tom reflected. "I know Sacajawea's strong, but she looks so delicate, you feel obliged to worry about her when she's sick. Besides, Captain Clark knows our lives may depend on her. When we get past these falls, we'll be in the mountains. If Sacajawea doesn't get us some horses from the Shoshones, we'll never get out of them."

"Sacajawea will be fine, Tom. Really. You don't have to worry about her. But what about you?" she asked him. "How is your chest?"

"Oh, my ribs still ache, but I'm used to it by now."

"Good," she nodded. She thought about telling him why she had come, but decided it wasn't time yet. Instead, she gazed around the small stand of trees that shaded them. "What are you doing down here, anyway?"

"I'm looking for hardwood," he explained. "Captain Lewis wants to make a couple of carts to transport our gear overland for the next twenty miles or so, till we get beyond the falls. The cottonwood is too soft to make good wheels, so he went me down here to find something better. Brussard says there may be some willows on the banks farther down, but I haven't seen any so far."

"There isn't much wood of any kind around here," she remarked.

"No, there isn't. Just grass. And cactus."

There was a tense, awkward silence for a minute, then Roxanna said to him, "You've really been avoiding me, haven't you?"

"I wouldn't say I've been 'avoiding' you, Roxanna," he replied quickly. "I've been busy, that's all."

"We've all been busy, Tom."

"Yes, I know that. I mean besides the usual work."

"You mean your assignment to find out who is trying to sabotage the expedition. Captain Lewis told me about that."

"He might as well tell everybody about it," Tom sulked. "All I've done so far is guess. Whoever is doing this, Roxanna, he's always a step ahead of us. He stole supplies during the winter when the Tetons were around to take the blame, he got to the specimen boat before we did, and he left a trail for that bear to follow before we even knew there was a bear. And do you remember the accident with the white pirogue last May? That was his work; he weakened the mast weeks before so that it would eventually break. That boat contained not only all our instruments, but the captains' journals, too. The whole operation would have gone down with it. I should've anticipated it, but I didn't."

"Then you have no idea who's doing these things?"

"Oh, I have an idea, but I can't say yet. Not till I have proof."

She nodded, and they were silent again. He watched her walk slowly over to a tree and rub her hand lightly, nervously over the bark. After looking around for a while, she turned to face him. She was beautiful, standing in the shade near streams of sunlight pouring down through the leaves above her. His desire for her was stronger, harder now than it had ever been.

"Tom," she said finally, coming out of the shade, "I'm sorry about the way I acted after that business last winter. God knows, I didn't mean to run you off."

He looked at her closely. "You didn't run me off. It's just that you didn't trust me. I saved your life and you wouldn't even trust me enough to tell me what happened to you."

"I'm still not going to tell you," she answered. "It's not your concern."

"Damn it, Roxanna—"

"Well, it isn't," she insisted. "But even if I won't tell you what I did while you were off hunting somewhere, you don't have to look the other way when I walk by, or act so formal when we're in company."

"Have I been doing that?" he asked her.

"Yes. You have."

"I'm sorry," he apologized. "I'll be more civil."

" 'Civil?' Is that how you're going to be: civil?"

"What do you want me to say, Roxanna?" he asked her with irritation. "I'll be any damned way you want me to be, all you have to do is tell me." He took a few steps toward her. "You have to know by now that ever since I first saw you in St. Louis, you've been my whole life—"

"Tom—"

"No, let me say it. Roxanna, I'm going on with my life just like everyone else, but it doesn't mean a thing without you. You're the only thing that matters to me. All right—I joined this expedition to make a fortune so that I could go back East, marry Isabel and spend the rest of my life in the practice of law. I had my whole life planned out. But when I met you, it all paled. It all seemed stupid and pointless. You mean more than anything else in my life."

She looked at him longingly. But her smoldering desire for him, the very thing that had pushed her out to find him, was making her uneasy. She decided to change the subject. "Is that an old Indian lodge?" she nodded at a conical structure a few yards into the woods.

"Yes," he replied, a bit exasperated. "There was a village here once. There are a lot of those around."

Roxanna walked over to it, her heart throbbing with excitement, as she felt him following her. She peered inside the opening, turned around, and there was Tom, blocking her way. He was inches away from the tips of her breasts. She looked into his eyes. "You don't give a lady much room, do you?"

"I've given you room for a year, Roxanna," he told her. "For a year my body has been like a volcano, ready to explode. If you only knew how it feels to want someone so badly—"

"Oh, I know how it feels, Tom," she sympathized. "Don't think I don't."

"You mean your husband. . . ."

"No! I don't mean my husband. You know perfectly well what I mean."

Tom was terrified that he might be misunderstanding what she was saying. Could she possibly mean *him*? "You don't have to explain it," he told her, trying to remain a gentleman.

"I've been not explaining it too long as it is," she said, taking his hand. "I've been on fire, too, Tom. I've had a hot, burning ache, too." She touched the flat of her stomach and began to breathe harder. "Don't ever think it's just men that have such feelings. Every time you come near me, my knees get wobbly."

"Don't tease me, Roxanna."

"Oh, God, I'm not teasing," she squeezed his hand. "You think you've been suffering this past year—well so have I. I've lain awake a hundred nights hoping you'd forget everything I ever said to you and come to my tent and touch me—"

He couldn't hold back any longer. He reached out, took her into his arms, kissed her. "Oh, Roxanna," he cried excitedly between kisses. "I love you so much!"

She held him close. "Oh, Lord," she murmured anticipating.

"I've wanted you for so long, Roxanna. I love you."

She buried her face in his shoulder. She had to tell him, now. "Oh, Tom," she cried, "I love you too. I've always loved you."

Her words, her declaration of love, inflamed him to a fever pitch. He slipped his hands inside her shirt, touched the searing flesh of her breasts with his finger tips. He squeezed her gently as they kissed each other deeply and passionately.

Inside the old Indian lodge they hurriedly undressed and fell into each other's arms. Roxanna had never known such maddening excitement and then such ecstatic pleasure as she experienced in the next few hours. Douglas had been rough with her, she had thought all men would be. But Tom Wentworth was a gentle, thoughtful lover whose soft caresses lifted her again and again into waves and peaks of excitement and release. She found his loving touches unbearably arousing; they made her quiver with desire, over and over. . . .

By afternoon the air in the tent had gotten heavy and warm. Their tired bodies were flushed and slick with the sweat of lovemaking. Tom held Roxanna's voluptuous nude body next to his chest and ran locks of her long dark hair through his fingers. After half an hour of lying silently together, he asked her, "How would you like to go for a swim?"

"In the rapids? No, thank you. If I'm going to die, I'd rather do it here."

"I don't mean the rapids, Roxanna. There's a basin a few yards downstream that's as calm as a pool."

"I'd rather stay here," she snuggled up against him.

"Come on," he urged, "I want to see you swim. There's nobody around for miles, Roxanna. It'll be just you and me."

She rose up and looked at him. "Are you sure?"

"I'm sure."

"Then let's do it," she decided.

They threw on their clothes, left the tent and walked hand in hand downstream about fifty yards, stopping on a low bank overlooking a clear basin in the river. "What do you think?" he asked her, looking out over the water.

She glanced around the river for a minute, then pulled her shirt over her head. "I think we should do it," she smirked.

He stood still as she stepped out of her buckskins and dove into the water. Her graceful white body slid through the currents so smoothly and rhythmically he could have looked at her for hours.

But after a while she called for him to come in, so he shucked his clothes and plunged in.

Ten feet above the basin, on the very bank they had jumped from, Ned Craddock walked up, knelt very deliberately and watched them swim naked in the basin. He had followed Roxanna from camp, so he had seen them go into the abandoned tent hours before. He had sat near the precipice of the falls, fuming with anger and frustration while they had made love in it.

He hated Roxanna Fairchild for getting him flogged and for repelling him that night last winter in her cabin. And he despised Tom Wentworth for being her lover. He looked down at them frolicking obliviously in the river. They were splashing about in the waves, laughing, teasing each other.

"Ducks in a pond," he muttered aloud.

He raised his rifle. First he would shoot Wentworth, then the woman. It would be two very simple head shots; at such close range, he could do it blindfolded. Then he could slip away and no one would ever know who had done it. They would probably suspect Indians, he figured.

He drew a bead, let the end of the long barrel follow Tom as he cut through the water toward Roxanna. Even if he missed, he thought, they wouldn't have time to get away. He could shoot at them until he hit them.

He held the barrel still as Wentworth glided into Roxanna's arms and they embraced and kissed. Then slowly, easily, he cocked the hammer back, took a deep breath, and curled his finger carefully around the trigger.

All of the sounds seemed to happen at once, the crack of the rifle, the whiz of the ball over their heads, and the splash of the water three feet away. Tom and Roxanna broke apart, treaded water as they looked around them for the gun. Tom quickly noticed the dark figure on the bank, but the setting sun behind the man's back blinded his view. As the man stood up, with the sun seeming to rest over his shoulder, he leveled his rifle again.

"Roxanna—get down!" Tom shouted, dragging her with him beneath the surface of the water just as the second shot burst between them.

Underneath the cool water the undertow of the river began to whisk them rapidly downstream. A minute later they each emerged to the surface, looked around them. The shadowy figure galloping along the bank with the sun at his back stopped when he saw his targets again; he raised the rifle to his shoulder.

"There he is again," Tom cried. He grabbed Roxanna's wrist and they plunged under again, but in the confusion Roxanna's hand slipped out of his grip. He came up to look for her, but he couldn't see her anywhere. An instant later, the rifle on the bank exploded and a lead slug ripped through the air and sliced a neat gash into his forehead.

The cut was only a graze, but it made him suddenly sick. The river bank, the man with the rifle, the orange sky behind him, all began to swirl madly around him. When he finally got his bearings again a few minutes later, he thought first of Roxanna. "Damn it," he muttered to himself, "where is she?"

As he was frantically looking about for her, freezing swash abruptly seized his body and thrust it downstream. He was too dazed from the head wound to fight it, all he could do was keep his head up as it washed him away.

Then he hit the rapids.

All he could do now was to keep water out of his nose and mouth and try to hold himself upright as the relentless current swished his body about in eddies and swirls and slapped it mercilessly against slick jagged rocks.

A few minutes into the churning water, he managed to reach out and latch onto the edge of a sharp stone sticking out of the river. The blood streaming from his wound obscured his vision, but he could still make out the solitary figure running smoothly along the bank like a fast-moving cloud wafting in front of the sun, blocking rays of light at intervals as it moved across the horizon.

He called out Roxanna's name, but his eyes were blurry; he couldn't see anything but rushing water. He was afraid she had been hit. Hanging onto the rock, he tried to count the shots and remember where they had struck, but he couldn't make his mind do the calculations.

He strained to look up at the approaching figure on the west bank. He was getting closer now, Tom could see the long rifle jerking up and down as he ran. He decided he had no choice now but to keep drifting, to get himself beyond his range. He let his hands slide off the rock and allowed the current to sweep him up and rush him downstream again. The water, harder than he ever could have imagined it being, slapped at his bloody face while the hard protrusions he bumped into dug into his body like pickaxes. His ribcage felt as if it had caved in upon his heart and lungs.

Then he heard Roxanna calling him above the noise of the rapids.

She was ten yards down from him, treading water against the current. He pushed forward, tried to swim across the surging flow toward her, but he couldn't make it. He wrapped his arms around another rock and held on.

Roxanna somehow swam the twenty-five feet upstream to reach him. "Dear God, Tom!" she cried, looking at his bloody face.

"I thought I'd lost you," he grunted wearily.

"Your head—"

"It's all right," he assured her.

She held onto him. "Can you hear the roar?"

"Hear the what?"

"The roar—listen."

His head ached; he could hear only the swirling rapids around him. "I don't hear it," he answered. "What is it?"

"It's another waterfall, Tom," she warned.

He held his breath and listened again. Above the rush of the choppy rapids he could hear it now—the distinctive rumble of another one of the Great Falls of the Missouri. He held onto the rock with one hand, wiped the blood out of his eyes with the other, then looked at her. "Don't think about it," he told her. "It's a long way off."

"But it isn't a long way off, Tom. Can't you hear how close it is?"

"We've got to get away from that rifle, Roxanna." He took her hand. "Stay with me. We're going to go with the current."

"Tom, if we get close to those falls —"

"We won't get close to them. Come on!"

She resisted another few seconds, then gave in to him. They kicked away from the rock, let the formidable undertow sweep them up again. The force of the water pried their hands loose from each other, but they managed to stay close as they were flung about like dried twigs in the torrent.

Tom felt his strength oozing from his body. Every breath was a struggle now; at every heave of his chest a sharp pain vibrated through his entire frame. He raised his hand out of the water and pointed at another rock. "We have to stop. Over there!"

She nodded, pushed herself through the water and landed at the spot. But suddenly it looked to her as if Tom were going to miss it. She secured her hold and as he drifted by, she reached out and clamped down on his hand. The force dragging on him was tremendous. Her shoulder felt as if someone were wrenching it painfully out of its socket.

"Let go, Roxanna," he cried out to her.

"No!"

"You can't do it. Just let go!"

She tugged with all her might but the current was crushing her against the rock, forcing Tom's hand out of her grasp. She felt him try to wriggle his hand out of hers. "Tom!" she cried to him, "don't fight me, for God's sake. Help me!"

"You can't do it, Roxanna," he told her.

She heard him but the words meant nothing. She would hang onto him as long as she had a breath left.

"You're wasting your strength, Roxanna," he panted. "Let go!"

"No. I won't," she shouted stubbornly. "I won't let go." The right side of her body was paralyzed with pain, but she wouldn't loosen her fingers.

Just then the rifle went off and a ball smashed against the rock a few inches above her extended arm.

"Roxanna," Tom yelled. "There's a bend in the river up ahead. Maybe we can lose him there."

"The falls are around the bend, Tom!"

"We don't have any choice, Roxanna."

She thought a second. The rifle could be pointing at her head right now. Or his. In another minute he could be dead.

She released his hand, eased herself farther into the water and let the river take her through the rocks, on the way to the falls.

But as they turned around the bend, the rapids dissipated, the white water turned yellowish brown and evened out. In the smoother water Tom could hear the waterfall; it was close.

All he could do now was rally his strength into one long swim across the tow to the bank. He felt he had one big push left. His cracked ribs and his wounded head wouldn't allow him any more than that. If he could reach the bank, he might have time to escape the gunman. If he couldn't reach it, he would be dashed helplessly over the cataract to his death a hundred feet below.

Roxanna was a few yards away, struggling to reach the bank, too. With as strong a stroke as he could manage, he caught up with her.

"Keep going!" he encouraged her.

"I can't, Tom," she gasped. "I can't make it."

"Yes you can. It's just a few more yards."

"Tom," she cried fearfully, "I'm losing ground."

"No you're not. Swim! Come on, damn it, swim!"

Three feet apart, they moved across the current, toward the bank. Each time Tom pulled his right arm through the water down past his side, he listened to the surface sounds. In his left ear he expected to hear at any minute the crack of a rifle. In his right, he could hear the noise of the constant rumble of the waterfall.

He closed his eyes and swam until he was choking for breath and his lungs were throbbing with pain—until the bank was only a few feet away.

"Tom!" Roxanna yelled to him. "I can't do it!"

"Just a little farther, Roxanna. Don't give up!"

"I . . . can't," she gulped.

She made another desperate kick, but then she had no more strength to draw on. Her arms and legs went limp, and she began to drift away from him.

Tom tried to stand up in the shallow water, to call out to her again, but his knees buckled under him and he crumbled down into the water with a splash. Twenty yards away the gap between him and Roxanna was widening by the second.

He didn't have any choice, he had to try to save her. Stretching his weary, aching arms out in front of him, he pushed off after her. He caught up to her downstream in a few minutes, then, without saying a word, he slid his arm under her breasts and pulled her close.

He knew to get across the two was going to require every ounce of strength he had left, yet he had to do it. But as soon as he extended his arm out into the water, he felt Roxanna go heavy under the other. He pulled and kicked through the water with all the force he could muster, but he could do no more than hold their ground against the fierce power of the current.

Finally, he couldn't fight it any longer. He wrapped both his arms around Roxanna and gave in to the river. Dazed and exhausted, he still managed to keep their heads out of water as they sped down the river. Then, just ahead of them, he witnessed a sight that made his blood turn to ice.

The river current ahead of him was narrowing into a great surge of water that gushed out over a precipice.

The undertow was incredibly strong now, near the edge of the waterfall. He was barely managing to keep them afloat.

Then he saw up ahead, no more than fifteen yards from the overhang, a fallen cottonwood tree still rooted to the bank, extending out into the river.

"Roxanna!" he shook her. "Roxanna—listen! We've got to make it to that tree."

"What?" she mumbled groggily.

"The tree—there!"

She nodded, gasped, "I can't make it."

"Yes, you can."

"Tom—" she clung tightly to him.

"All right," he instructed, "just hang on. We'll both make it."

Somehow he dug down far enough inside himself to find enough strength to swerve their bodies against the flow toward the tree. They rammed hard against the wood, but reached out and clutched limbs and held on.

"Slide down the tree to the bank," Tom yelled at Roxanna.

She clung to her limb and didn't answer.

"Roxanna—do you hear me? Slide down the tree."

She looked at him, nodded, closed her eyes to the falls ahead and began blindly moving herself along the trunk of the tree toward the shore. Tom stayed a foot away, ready to catch her if she should slip.

The slow progress over the rough bark of the tree, across the broken limbs hidden by the water, seemed to take hours. Finally they reached the base of the tree, and with one last supreme effort of will, they dragged themselves out of the water and dropped to the ground. Then for both of them, everything went black.

The next thing Tom was aware of was that he was lying face down on a sandbar somewhere near the noisy falls. Then later he woke up in darkness. On the sand, close to his face, was a long shadow of a man. When it moved, he could tell the shadow was being cast on the ground by a swinging lantern. All of a sudden he knew what was happening. Someone was standing over them!

He lay still for a moment, involuntarily cringing as he waited for the rifle shot in his back. He considered for a moment springing up to attack the gunman, but he knew that was impossible. Just to turn over and face his killer would take all his strength. But at least he would do that. After all his efforts to stay alive, he had to see who was going to kill him with such ease.

He turned slowly on his back, looked up through misty eyes at the glow of the lantern. He saw nothing recognizable at first, then the lantern moved and he caught the familiar cast to the man's rugged face. He knew him.

It was Captain Lewis.

PART FIVE

THE MOUNTAINS

Chapter 18

It took three weeks to move fifty men and two women and thousands of pounds of equipment over eighteen miles of hard ground and cactus around the Great Falls. By July the eight small boats of the expedition were on the Missouri course again, proceeding southeast between mountain ranges. Sacajawea, with little Pomp in the papoose cradle on her back, stayed in the head boat with Captain Clark. Being familiar with the path of the river, she pointed out to him the places she had known as a child, before the Minnetarees took her captive. Roxanna was in the second boat with Captain Lewis.

The river finally came to a head at Three Forks, and they took the Jefferson tributary farther south. As the weeks passed, the captains became worried. There were no more buffalo. Food had become scarce. They were deep into the mountains and they hadn't yet seen the first sign of the Shoshone Indians.

On the eleventh of August, a hunting party went out to find them. Captain Lewis, Tom and Hugh MacNeal walked together, George Drewyer and John

Shields formed the flanks, and Buck Brussard scouted ahead.

Lewis had been distant with Tom ever since he had found him and Roxanna on the bank. Alone with Lewis for the first time in weeks, Tom was trying to explain his position to him.

"Captain Lewis," he was saying as they walked, "I really don't think what we did was wrong."

Lewis continued to look straight ahead. "It wasn't wrong for you, Tom. And maybe it wasn't wrong for Roxanna, either. But it was wrong for this expedition. And right now, this expedition is all I'm concerned about. My personal feelings have no bearing on the situation, I assure you. I'm not judging either one of you."

Tom spoke softly to keep MacNeal from hearing. "We haven't done it again, captain."

"I know you haven't. Roxanna told me. I appreciate that. But both of you have to understand how this kind of thing is going to look back in Washington City. We're on a government mission, Tom. A great mission. This single expedition can change the whole course of American history. Everything we do here Captain Clark and I, and four or five of the other men, record in our journals. And those journals will be published, Tom. The story of this expedition will be told over and over, maybe for another hundred years."

"I wasn't thinking of that," he admitted.

Lewis looked at him. "That's why I wanted you alone to find the saboteur," he explained. "I wanted to keep it under cover. It's very possible that all of this could explode on us like a ship load of gunpowder. The attempted murders, the sabotage, the presence of a woman on the trip, your affection for each other—don't you see what could happen? Mr. Jefferson's hopes for the Louisiana Territory, his dream of establishing American trade out here and tying the country together—all that could suddenly erupt into nothing more than a presidential scandal."

"Captain Lewis, the man who shot at us has to be the same man who's trying to destroy the expedition. He must know I suspect him; that has to be why he would try to kill me. If I could catch him—"

"Yes, catch him, Tom. But don't play into his hands again. If he's clever he may be planning right now to use you and Roxanna to ruin our credibility back East. I just hope he's not. Maybe if you catch him soon, we can keep it all quiet."

Tom nodded but decided he couldn't tell Lewis who he suspected. He would catch this man in the act and turn him in somehow, and redeem himself in the captains' eyes. He also wouldn't tell Lewis that his regard for Roxanna wasn't just affection. He loved her now more than ever. He didn't know if even a man as brilliant as Meriwether Lewis could understand that his keeping his hands off her was the hardest thing he had ever had to do.

A while later Buck Brussard returned to the party. Whipping his buffalo robe off his shoulders and spitting on the ground at the same time, he warned, "Indian up ahead a couple of miles, cap'n. By hisself."

"Is he Shoshone?" Lewis asked anxiously.

"Yeah, I reckon he is," Brussard eased the butt of his rifle to the ground. "He was riding bareback, carrying a sack of arrows."

Lewis looked relieved. "I was beginning to wonder if they existed. Let's see if we can talk to him."

When the party finally did encounter the Indian two hours later, Captain Lewis stepped forward, ahead of the other men. The Indian sat quietly on his horse and looked apprehensively at the white men.

"You two stay back," Lewis ordered Brussard and Wentworth. "We don't want him to start using that bow."

"I don't figure he's hostile, cap'n," Brussard explained. "Looks to me like he's just suspicious."

"Well, that's what I'm counting on," Lewis pulled a blanket out of his pack. He held it at two corners and flung it ceremoniously up into the air, letting it spread out on the ground. The Indian didn't move.

Drewyer, ten yards away, called out, "He doesn't know the friendship signal, Captain Lewis."

Lewis left the blanket on the grass and drew out a few trinkets and held them up for the Indian to see. *"Tab-ba-bone!"* he intoned.

The Indian sat still.

"Tabbabone!" Lewis repeated, pulling open his shirt to show the Indian the color of his skin. "White man—*tabbabone!"*

The Indian looked at him intently, showed no recognition in his stone-like face. After a moment of glancing around at the others, he dug his heels into the flanks of his horse and sped away.

Lewis picked up his blanket disgustedly. "Damn!" he exclaimed, discouraged. "We have to make contact with these people soon, Buck. The river is down to nothing but a stream now. We've got to have horses to get out of here."

"I say we follow 'im, cap'n," Brussard spat, leaning on his rifle. "Where there's one Indian, there's usually a lot more."

"He could be miles away from his village," Tom pointed out.

"A lot of miles," Buck acknowledged. "But there ain't much else we can do, is there?"

"No," Lewis agreed, "there isn't much else we can do. All right, Buck, you go on ahead. The rest of you spread out. Let's see if we can pick up his tracks."

They found his trail, which led to an Indian road, which they followed for more than twenty miles, over steep hills and deep valleys, through a narrow pass between two ranges of snow-capped mountain.

On the second day of pursuit, Lewis and the others traced Brussard's signs into a lush green valley. Lewis first saw the three Indian women digging roots from the ground, then he noticed the mountainman emerging from his hiding place in a ravine.

"They've been digging here for hours, cap'n," he reported.

"Have they seen you?" Lewis asked him.

"Unh-unh, I've just been sitting here minding my own business."

Lewis lay down his gun, walked ahead a few yards with his hands up and out. When the women saw him, they instantly fell to their knees, lowered their heads and covered them with their hands. He approached an old woman and pulled her up gently. *"Tabbabone,"* he spoke softly and showed his chest.

When the women saw the whiteness of his skin, they sprang into life. They jumped up, gathered around him, entreated him in their language to give them beads and necklaces. They became even more exuberant when Drewyer asked them in sign language if they would lead the party to the rest of the tribe. They quickly responded and led the white men down the river road.

Two miles later, sixty armed Shoshone warriors came riding up on powerful horses. Lewis quickly called the men to stand ready at arms, but the order was unnecessary. The Shoshone warriors, grinning and laughing, jumped down from their horses and rushed across the grass to greet the leader of the white men. *"Ah-hie-e!"* one of them cried as he embraced Lewis, pulled him close and pressed their cheeks together.

Then the other warriors ran up to him and smeared ceremonious bits of grease and paint on Captain Lewis's face and shouted to the others, *"Ah-hie-e! Ah-hie-e!"*

Later, when the Indian braves led them into their camp four miles away, Tom observed how bony and thin their short bodies were. Even their chief, Cameahwait, taller than the others and more erect, seemed undernourished. And when the scouting party was joyously greeted by the inhabitants of the Shoshone camp, he noted that the women and children appeared to be even weaker and more emaciated than the men.

Inside the camp, Lewis posted Tom and Brussard outside a lodge while he and Drewyer and Shields went in to smoke and talk with Cameahwait. After half an hour or so, Buck Brussard came back from a long talk with a handful of Shoshone braves standing nearby.

"Do they have enough horses for us?" Tom asked him as he walked up.

"Oh yeah," he nodded. "They've got enough. Three, four hundred, maybe. But they ain't going to deal for 'em. Not yet, anyway."

"Why not?" Tom wondered. "I thought the Shoshones were friendly to white men."

"They're friendly all right. The problem is, they're also hungry. They want food, and they want it fast. Cap'n Lewis'll have to be mighty clever to get 'em back up to the Forks to meet the others."

"He'll do it," Tom assured him. "He handles Indians very well."

"Yeah, I reckon he does. I always said he knew what he was doing."

Tom thought the mountainman seemed distracted. His eyes had looked vague and distant ever since he came back from talking to the Shoshone warriors. "What else did you find out from them?" he asked, trying to draw him out.

Brussard looked directly at him. "Matter of fact, I found out Red Hair was here, last fall. Which means only one thing: I got to go after 'im."

"You mean the renegade you've been looking for?"

"One and the same," he acknowledged. "These folks say he had a girl with 'im when he was here. Half-breed girl. Could be my daughter."

"Did they know where he went from here?"

"They tell me he went straight up north, into Canada. Since he ain't likely to be going out to the Pacific with us, I reckon I got to go where he is." He threw his rifle over his shoulder.

"You don't mean right now, do you?" Tom asked. "This second?"

"I reckon one time's as good as another."

"But you're not going through these mountains by yourself, are you?"

Brussard laughed. "Going by myself's a lot easier than going with other folks. You tell Cap'n Lewis I'll see 'im on the way back to St. Louis next year. I'll be sporting a red scalp by then."

"You can't walk through these mountains, Buck."

"Don't plan to walk. There's stray horses all over these parts. Well, you keep yourself away from those rattlesnakes, son. And kiss that good-looking woman for me—something I always wanted to do myself." He spat on the ground, straightened his robe, turned his back to Tom, and walked away. Tom had a strange feeling that it was the last time he would ever see him.

A few minutes later Lewis emerged from the tent with Drewyer and Shields. "Cameahwait's damned stubborn," he complained to Wentworth. "He agreed to go with us to the Forks, but he thinks I'm lying about Clark and the others."

Drewyer nodded. "He thinks this is a Blackfoot trick."

"William had better make it to the Forks by the time we do," Lewis said. "These people are too hungry to sit around and wait. Cameahwait doesn't even believe we have a Shoshone woman with us."

"Is he going to sell us the horses?" Tom asked. "Buck said they have four hundred or so."

"He won't tell us whether he is or not," Lewis answered, exasperated. "He's waiting to see how much food we can offer him. Where is Brussard, anyway?" he asked, looking around.

"He's gone, captain," Tom replied.

"What do you mean, 'gone'? He was supposed to stay in camp."

"I mean gone away, captain. He left a few

minutes ago, for Canada. He's on the trail of that man he calls Red Hair."

"Damn! He could've stayed with us till we reached the Columbia, anyway. I was counting on him."

"I guess he just goes when he has to, captain. He said he'd see you on the return trip."

"Well, I hope he finds who he's looking for, but damn it, he could've picked a better time to leave us. I don't like this, standing in the midst of a tribe of starving Indians."

On the way back to the rendezvous point at Three Forks, where the Jefferson, the Madison and the Gallatin Rivers met to form the Missouri, Tom rode bareback on a rough horse, in the middle of the procession. Like Captain Lewis, he too felt uneasy in the presence of the Shoshones.

The Mandans had told them the Snakes, as they called them, were hungry people, always on edge. Since they weren't interested in agriculture, they ate game and berries, and when there were no game or berries, they starved. But Tom's uneasiness turned to disgust, when he witnessed something they did on the trail.

One morning an excited, piercing series of yells from one of the Shoshone warriors riding up the caravan abruptly stopped the horses. Before Captain Lewis could ask what was happening, the other Indians began screaming and yelling madly, then suddenly burst off on their horses across the plains. They whooped and hollered and shrieked like tortured animals as they raced directly toward the carcass of a deer George Drewyer had just killed.

They leaped from their horses before they had stopped, sprang upon the dead deer lying in the grass like a hundred hungry wolves. Some of them ripped away at the flesh and hair of the beast, others began ravenously eating the kidneys and heart and lungs Drewyer had cast off into the dirt.

When Lewis and Chief Cameahwait arrived at the scene, the warriors looked up guiltily from their feast, then grinned sheepishly as trickles of blood oozed from the corners of their mouths. One of them had looped ten feet of the deer's intestines around his neck and was chewing voraciously on the end of the gut. When he saw his chief, he carefully unwrapped it as if it were precious and presented it silently to Camcahwait.

Acting on Lewis's orders, Drewyer slaughtered the animal quickly and properly, while the Shoshones looked on hungrily, scrutinizing his every move. Drewyer cut off a quarter of the venison for the white men, backed away from the rest and let the Indians pounce gleefully on the skinned deer. They clawed into its muscles with hands and nails and devoured the entire carcass, leaving only the bones and parts of the hooves.

Tom watched the scene with horror. He was shocked at the state a human being could be reduced to by hunger. For the rest of the day he couldn't force himself to eat anything.

The next day, Roxanna Fairchild was standing with Sacajawea and Charbonneau and Captain Clark when they caught sight of the Shoshones and the Lewis party arriving on the river bank. Sacajawea's eyes brightened when she saw a friend among the Indians. She rushed quickly over to her, met her with open arms as she came down off a horse. Locked in an embrace, the two women laughed excitedly and began comparing each of the ornaments on their dresses. Then, while Sacajawea beamed proudly, the other Indian girl lifted Pomp out of his cradle and displayed him to the other Shoshone women.

Roxanna was watching the reunion of the two women when she noticed Tom ride up and slide down off the bare back of his horse to the ground. His presence immediately made her nervous. She continued to look at Sacajawea. "She's really beautiful, isn't she?"

Roxanna observed. "The other Shoshones are so hard and she's so delicate."

Tom glanced over at the Indian girl, then back at her. "Roxanna," he began, "I talked to Captain Lewis about us."

She shook her head. "I don't want to hear about it, Tom," she put him off. "Just don't tell me."

"We have to do something, Roxanna. At least I have to do something. You're all I can think about, every waking minute of the day. I find myself thinking about that afternoon at the falls all the time. I can't get it out of my mind."

"That afternoon was just a few hours, Tom," she reminded him. "We were both lonely. Can't you just leave it at that and forget it happened?"

"No," he barked. "I can't forget it. I'll always remember it."

"All right, remember it then. But we don't have to talk about it, do we? It just makes it worse, Tom, you know it does."

"That was the most wonderful day of my life, Roxanna," he pressed on. "You're even more lovely than I imagined you could be—"

"Tom," she implored, "don't do this. Please. Why do you keep talking about it? Do you want me to admit I still love you? Fine: I love you. I'll always love you. But it doesn't change anything. I'm not free to do anything about it, so let's just leave it at that."

"We can't, Roxanna," he argued.

"I don't see that we can do anything else."

He shook his head. "I'm sorry. I just won't accept that."

"I'm *married*, Tom, damn it! How many times do I have to say it?"

"You don't ever have to say it again, Roxanna. All you have to do is get up on this horse and come with me. Right now."

She felt her eyes moistening, about to burst into tears. She had to turn her back to him and concentrate on something else. Through bleary eyes she watched the Shoshone men walking with Lewis and Clark, the women hanging behind. "Every Indian tribe is the same," she tried to hold back the tears. "The women are nothing but slaves. And they don't want to be anything but slaves."

"Roxanna—"

"But look at Sacajawea," she went on. "She's so different. The men respect her because she respects herself. She's a real lady, Tom."

He wasn't listening to her. "Roxanna, will you come away with me? Do it. Right now. Just climb up on this horse and come with me. Please."

She looked up at him with tearful eyes. "Oh, Tom, we couldn't find our way out of these mountains. You know that."

"Then we'll go back down the Missouri."

"*No*, Tom. I won't do it. I'm sorry, I just won't. I would never have any respect for either one of us. I couldn't live like that."

He took her shoulders in his hands. "Damn respect! I can't stand not being with you. I'd rather die out there in the mountains than be this close to you and never touch you."

She almost melted into his arms, but somehow she forced herself to pry her body from his. "Stay away from me, Tom Wentworth. I mean it. Just stay away!" Clutching her mouth with her hand, she hurried off in the direction of Sacajawea and the other Indians.

A few minutes later Ned Craddock ambled over. "That Garcia's quite a piece of pie, isn't she?" he asked, watching Roxanna talking to Sacajawea and the other Shoshone women. "She's got a lot of sophistication, you know. And a lot of chest, too."

"Watch yourself, Craddock," he warned him. "I'm in no mood to listen to your slander. In fact, I'm in no mood to listen to you at all."

Craddock faced him. "Hey, don't take it out on me, friend. Take it out on one of those red savage gals.

They tell me those hungry bony ones will grind you up like an ear of hard corn."

Tom looked at him and gritted his teeth. "Look, Craddock. Just so we'll understand each other from now on, I want you to know I'm onto what you've been trying to do here ever since last winter. I don't know why, but I do know you're trying to destroy this expedition."

Craddock was silent for a few seconds, trying to collect himself. Then he retorted nervously, "What in the hell are you talking about?"

"You know very well what I'm talking about. *You* stole those supplies, *you* baited that bear, and *you* tried to sink the keelboat and the pirogue. And damn your soul, you tried to kill Roxanna."

"Some lawyer you are, Wentworth," he spat. "If I had done all that, your captain friends would've strung me up from a tree by now."

"Yes, you're right; they would have. If I'd told them. And make no mistake about it, Ned. I am going to tell them—just as soon as I have some proof."

"You must have me mixed up with someone else, Wentworth," Craddock tried to appear casual. "All I do around here is work, just like the other poor bastards that don't get to bed down with the captains."

Tom ignored his words. "And while I'm at it," he went on, "I'll tell you something else: I'll give you a warning. If I ever find out you've put your dirty fingers on Roxanna Fairchild, I'm going to rip open your chest and feed you to these starving Shoshones."

"Mighty big words for a Philadelphia lawyer," he replied limply.

"They're words you'd better remember, Craddock," he stalked away.

Craddock stood alone for a while, his face pale and drawn as he went over what Tom Wentworth had just told him. An ugly look came into his face and his hands clenched. He felt the same kind of blind, uncontrolled wrath that had made him plunge his knife into the deer carcass. The world turned grey. Objects faded. He didn't even notice Hugh Hall coming up to him. "Real rough-looking, ain't they!" Hall exclaimed.

"What?"

"Those Shoshones—they're real rough-looking."

"Oh, yeah," Craddock said indifferently, trying to still the blind rage that seethed under the surface. He was still watching Tom walk toward the captains. "I wonder why it is, Wentworth always gets to attend these powwows with the Indians. How does he come by such privileges? Does he have something on Lewis or what?"

"I don't know, Ned. What difference does it make? He's not bothering you."

"Everything he does bothers me," Craddock asserted. "I hate the bastard."

"Oh, Tom's all right. He was a little silky at first, I'll admit, but he's as good as the rest of us now."

"He's Lewis's puppy, is what he is."

"No, he's not," Hall disagreed.

"Which isn't as bad as what you and Collins and Werner have become," he growled. "You three are nothing but a bunch of frogs, ready to hop whenever he says jump."

"We just do our part," Hall stated. "Captain Lewis deserves it. The mountainman set us straight on that."

"Yeah, well, there's another one, that mountainman. You tell me what gives Buck Brussard special rank? Why do we bust our guts back here while Brussard gets to go off ahead with Lewis and hop on those red savage squaws back in the woods?"

"I don't see what Buck Brussard does would matter to anybody now, Ned. Shields just told me he's gone off again."

"Oh yeah?" Craddock brightened.

"That's what he said. He just up and left the Shoshone camp. Off to Canada."

"I'll be damned," Craddock smiled. "Buck Brussard gone. That's going to make things a lot easier around here."

"What 'things'?"

"Never mind what things." He put his arm around Hall's shoulder. "I'll tell you what, Hugh. Why don't we get us a couple of handfuls of salt meat and have ourselves a little trading session with these Shoshone warriors. Let's see if we can finagle a couple of red squaws for a few hours. What do you say?"

"Charbonneau says they're not that free with their women, Ned."

"Ah, what does a Frenchman know about it? Come on, I've already got my eyes on a few good prospects."

Chapter 19

With Sacajawea's help, the Lewis and Clark party was able to buy from the Shoshones twenty-nine pack horses for the trip up the mountains. Cameahwait and a number of warriors trailed along with them for a while, to guide the expedition and to eat as much deer and elk as the hunters would give them.

The Shoshone path up the long rugged canyon was rocky and treacherous. The narrow trails along the mountains were steep, slick and stony. At times they had to stray off the rock-covered path and clear their way through yards of thorny thickets to get back to the main trail.

The Indians dropped back on September 1, left a single guide to lead the party to the Nez Perce Indian trail that led out of the northern valley west across the mountains to the western plains where the buffalo lived. After days of painfully slow movement on the high ridges, it began to snow. Then the snow turned into cold rain. They could move through the freezing slush no more than a few miles a day.

Along the sheer, snowy, wind-swept cliffs of these

mountains, there was no game. They had to settle for cereal and berries. By the sixth of September, the flour supply was gone, the corn had to be severely rationed. The Shoshone guide, Toby, seemed never to be bothered by the cold or tempted to eat, but the others, even Sacajawea, grew despondent, weary of being tired, wet, cold and hungry.

Finally, three days later, they entered the large green valley and camped near a creek they named Travelers Rest. Captain Lewis immediately proclaimed a day of rest for everyone.

"From here we follow the Nez Perce trail southwest," Lewis explained to Tom as they strolled leisurely through the camp. The weather in the valley was warm and fair, the whole crew was up and about, talking, wading in the creek, playing cards.

"I hope it gets easier," Tom replied.

"It gets worse," Lewis told him. "The Nez Perces use it, but they're used to the cold and they don't have to travel with nearly fifty men and twenty pack horses at a time. The higher trails will be almost impossible to cross."

They walked past a group of men playing poker on the grass. One of them, Craddock, looked up from his cards and eyed Tom closely as he went by. Wentworth could almost feel the man's eyes burning into his back as he walked.

A few minutes later George Drewyer came toward them across the valley. He was holding a rifle in one hand, the broken shaft of an arrow in the other.

"Our man's not a Nez Perce, captain," he announced as he reached them. "He's not a Flathead, either. Look at this," he handed Lewis the arrow.

Lewis ran his finger over the feather on the end of the shaft. "Someone's been watching us from the top of the ridge," he explained to Tom. "George has been up there looking for him."

"That's strange," Tom muttered. "I haven't noticed anyone."

"Captain Clark saw him three days ago," Drewyer reported to Tom. Then to Lewis, "This arrow's all I could find, captain. He covers his tracks."

Lewis turned the wooden shaft over in his hands. "It looks new," he observed.

"It is new. Broken today, I would say. There's no doubt about it, Captain Lewis. It's his."

"This feather isn't Shoshone, either, is it?" Lewis asked.

"The feather is Pawnee, captain."

"Pawnee? Are you sure?"

"My father showed me one like that when I was a boy. It's Kitkehahki Pawnee."

"That doesn't make sense, George. The Pawnees live hundreds of miles from here."

"I know they do. So why is one here, and why is he interested in us?"

"I don't know," he tapped the arrow against his left hand. "But I'm going to find out. George, who could tell us more about the Pawnees? Labiche? Cruzat?"

"Yes sir, Labiche and Cruzat are half-Omaha," he acknowledged. "They might know something about them. I was thinking of Ned Craddock, though."

"Ned Craddock!" Tom exclaimed.

"How does Craddock know anything about the Pawnee?" Lewis asked.

"He used to live on the Platte River. He'd have to know something about them."

"All right, go get him."

By the time Drewyer had paced off ten or twelve yards, Wentworth couldn't hold his words any longer. "Captain Lewis, I don't think Ned Craddock would be a very reliable source."

Lewis detected the resentment in his voice. "Private Collins told me you and Ned had a fight. I take it you don't like the man."

Tom wanted to tell him his suspicion, but he couldn't, yet. He had nothing more than a feeling to base it on. He wouldn't prejudice Lewis against Craddock until he had proof. "No sir," he responded, "I don't like him." Then, realizing his statement sounded empty, he added, "He's a coward."

"Well, at times even a coward can give you the information you need, Tom."

"Yes sir."

"Then why don't we see what he has to say before we judge how reliable he is," Lewis decided.

A few minutes later Drewyer returned with Craddock, who looked as if he were being led to his own hanging. He glanced suspiciously at Wentworth, then Drewyer, then at Lewis. "Drewyer says you wanted to see me."

Lewis handed him the broken shaft. "I want you to tell me all you can about this."

Craddock looked at the object, recognized it instantly. "This is a Pawnee arrow," he proclaimed confidently. "Haven't seen one in a couple of years." Then on a second glance, he noticed something about it that made him cringe. Near the splintered end of the shaft he saw a spot of blue paint.

"Is that all you can tell us about it?" Lewis asked.

"That's all I know about it." Craddock tried to swallow, but his throat was too dry and constricted. The blue paint scared him. He had seen a blue-tipped Pawnee arrow once before—in the bow of Harmer, the half-breed bodyguard of the man the Indians called Red Hair.

"What's wrong, Craddock?" Drewyer asked him. "You look pale."

"Where'd you find this?" Craddock asked, trying to appear calm.

"It belongs to the Indian warrior who's been following us for the last two or three days. He's still up there on the ridge, probably watching us right now."

Ned involuntarily looked up at the mountains, then cleared his throat. "Did you see what he looks like?" he asked excitedly. "Was he Indian? White man? Both?"

"He was an Indian," Drewyer answered, puzzled at Craddock's excitement. He paused. "Although now that you mention it, he didn't look particularly Pawnee."

"Well, come on, man, what did he look like?"

"I was thinking of his hair. It was black, but cut close to the head. I thought for a minute he was bald."

Craddock's heart sank. The blue-tipped arrow, the close-cropped hair: there was no doubt about it; it was Harmer! And Harmer's presence meant the vicious Red Hair was the man McKain had hired to kill *him*.

"Do you know this man, Private Craddock?" Lewis asked.

"No, I don't know him," he lied. "All I know is," he handed Drewyer back the arrow, "this is a Pawnee weapon. Anything else I can do for you, captain?"

Lewis sighed. "No, thank you. We'll take it from here."

Craddock nodded, then turned and walked back across the valley. His eyes scanned the mountains apprehensively. Who, he wondered, was up there? Was it Harmer, reporting back to Red Hair? Was he going to be skinned alive, as McKain had promised?

How much longer did he have to live?

Just before dawn the next morning, September 10, 1805, as Lewis and Clark sat their pack horses on the Nez Perce buffalo trail and proceeded slowly southwest, Buck Brussard stood outside the renegades' camp on the western bank of the Columbia River in Canada and waited for the first light of day.

When the rim of the sun appeared over the treetops, he surveyed the grounds carefully. He guessed there were about thirty warriors, three or four squaws, and the infamous Red Hair, Douglas Fairchild. He decided that the largest of the nine tents had to be Fairchild's. And in that tent, he figured, would be his daughter.

Looking up at the sun, he knew it was time to move. He slipped out his knife, wiped the long blade on his buckskin pants and moved his huge body quickly and silently along the perimeter of the camp toward the Indians' horses. He cautiously approached the first horse, a stallion.

"Easy, boy," he whispered, touching and then searching the blaze on his forehead. "I'm not going to hurt you." The horse started to neigh, but Brussard clamped his fingers on his nose and stopped him. "Whoa, now. It's all right. I ain't going to hurt you."

He released the horse's nose, petted him, then rubbed his own body against his flanks. Then he handled and spoke softly to the other horses, making them used to him and his smell. If one of them spooked while he was out in the middle of the camp, he would find himself surrounded by renegade cutthroats within a heartbeat.

Fairchild's tent was in the center of the camp, fifteen yards away. To get to it he had to make his way through a maze of tents, around a couple of fires and past a single sentry dozing just outside the tent.

He walked as softly as he could, but just as his boot came down a few feet from the head of the sentry, the Indian grunted, rolled over, and looked up with sleepy eyes. Brussard immediately shoved the handle of his knife down into the warrior's forehead and he fell back unconscious. He quickly pressed the sentry's mouth shut to muffle the groan he made as he went under.

The sentry taken care of, Brussard paused outside the tent and held his breath and listened. The place was dead with sleeping Indians, but somewhere in camp he could hear over the rush of the river a low rumble of talking voices. He couldn't make them out, but he knew he had to hurry. If someone was talking, others would be rising soon.

He used the point of his knife to pull aside the doorway flap and lowered his head and stepped in. The tent smelled like wet coals and rancid meat. It was bare, except for a lump of beaver pelts against the back wall. After a few seconds in the dim light, he could see the stack of furs rising and falling with someone's breathing. If it was Fairchild, he vowed to himself, he would never wake up. He took two steps, then knelt down beside the pelts, holding his knife blade poised and ready to slice a neck open with a quick flick of the wrist.

He grabbed hold of a corner of the pile of furs and yanked them down. "Cathy!" he cried, instantly recognizing his daughter.

She looked up. "Poppa!" she sobbed. "Oh, God—Poppa! Is it really you?"

"It's me," he pulled her up to his arms. "Come here."

"Oh, Poppa," she burst into tears. "I can't believe it. I waited for so long! I thought you were dead or something—"

"I know," he patted her back. "Never mind, it's all over now."

"Poppa—it was so awful," she sobbed. "They killed Momma—"

"I know," he cut her off. "Don't talk about it. Just tell me where Red Hair is so I can get us out of here."

"What are you going to do?"

"Just tell me where he is, Cathy."

She squeezed him. "Please take me home, Poppa. Please?"

He felt the bigness of her stomach against his knees. He reached down and ran his big hand over her swollen belly. "Is that his?" he asked calmly.

"Poppa, there wasn't anything I could do—"

"Damn his black soul!" he cursed, rising to his feet.

She held onto him. "Don't go, Poppa," she

pleaded tearfully. "You don't know what he's like. He'll do terrible things to you."

"He won't do nothing to me, Cathy," he assured her. "You just tell me which tent he's in and wait here a minute for me."

"I know what you want to do, but you can't. You can't kill him. No one can. All the Indians say it. No one can kill him."

"Never mind what the Indians say," he told her. "I reckon I can kill 'im all right."

She stood up, threw her arms around his waist and buried her face in his chest. "Poppa, please, take me away from here. Please take me away. I just want to forget it ever happened. Can't we do that?"

"We can't do it yet, daughter," he disagreed, pushing her back. "I've got something I have to do first. Then we'll go home. Tell me which tent he's in."

"No!" she resisted. "I'm not going to tell you. He'll kill you!"

At that moment, Douglas Fairchild was in the tent closest to the river with Morton McKain, agent for the Great Pacific Fur Company. They were squatting down, looking at a map spread out on the Englishman's trunk, held apart by Fairchild's matched London dueling pistols on each end of the parchment.

McKain was shaking his head. "You can't navigate the Columbia River down to the Pacific. It can't be done. Certainly not by the caliber of men you have in this camp. They'd drown inside of a week."

Fairchild placed the point of his knife on the map. "We're not going down the Columbia, McKain," he corrected him. "We're going through the mountains—here." He moved the point across the map. "Then south, this way, to the coast."

The plan frightened McKain. "I told you I had no business coming with you. I don't know why you made me come. I'm not a mountainman, I don't know anything about this kind of travel. I can't make it over that kind of terrain, Douglas. I'll have to go back to the Saskatchewan."

Fairchild gritted his teeth. "You're not going anywhere, McKain, except where I tell you to."

"Look, Fairchild—"

"I don't argue with people, McKain," Fairchild stated coldly. "When I lived in England, my family told me what to do. They told me what to eat, what to wear, what to say. I had nothing to say about it. Well, I do now. Now *I* do the telling. And I'm telling you we're going through the mountains. Do you understand?"

"I understand."

"You don't have to be so terrified, you know," he added disdainfully. "We'll take care of Lewis and Clark. Your little job with Great Pacific Fur will be safe."

He looked at Fairchild. "I'm not so sure any of our jobs is safe anymore, Douglas. I don't know, maybe it's useless after all to try to stop the Americans. Maybe Lewis and Clark are just the beginning. I know this man Zebulon Pike is exploring the Mississippi now. When he finds Great Pacific Fur trading posts on American soil, he's going to claim all the fur trade on the Mississippi and the Red River for America. If Lewis and Clark make it to the Pacific, that could start a war."

Fairchild stuck his knife back in its scabbard under his coat. "Surely Great Pacific Fur has planted a man on Pike's expedition."

A worried look passed over McKain's face. "I don't think they have," he shook his head. "They're so upset over the success of this Pacific expedition so far, they're running scared. Because of Lewis and Clark, the American Indians are turning away from us. They're beginning to accept American dominance in the Louisiana Territory. It can only lead to a monopoly of trade that will squeeze us out."

"Then we will step up our pace, McKain," Fairchild decided. "We'll raid a few more posts, create a bit more havoc—"

"With what? Half-breeds, misfits and cast-offs? Uuh, unh. We have to have better men than these out here. More disciplined men—men who believe in Great Pacific Fur Company."

Fairchild laughed critically. "You're a fool, McKain, if you believe in anything but yourself." He got to his feet, walked over to the English saddle resting on the floor of the tent. He lifted it up carefully, drew out a bottle of Scotch whiskey and a metal cup from underneath the leather. He held up the bottle, examined it, opened it and poured himself half a cup. "Besides, when Mr. Jefferson sees what has been done to his beloved Captains Lewis and Clark, he'll be putting an end to all this exploring for a while. That's what you want, isn't it?"

"Yes," he replied. "That's what we want."

As Fairchild raised the cup to his lips, a massive, grizzled figure suddenly appeared at the doorway of the tent. When the Englishman saw him, he lowered his cup slowly. "What are you doing here?" he demanded in an authoritative voice. "What do you want?"

Brussard raised his long knife in front of his chest for the two men to see. "I want . . . your scalp, Red Hair," he growled. "You," he motioned to McKain, "stay put."

Fairchild quickly stole a look at the dueling pistols on the trunk. The pearl handle of one of them was only a few inches from McKain's fingers. He could snatch it up before the other man could move a foot. "Morton," he ordered in a low voice, keeping his eyes on Brussard, "I want you to pick up that gun and shoot this smelly creature between the eyes. Now, while he's not moving."

But McKain was frozen with fear. "I can't, Douglas," he quaked. "I've never even held a gun in my hand."

"Never mind that. Just pick the thing up and shoot him."

"I *can't*."

"That's enough, Fairchild," Brussard stepped into the tent. His daughter, pale and thin, except for the giant belly bulging under her doeskin dress, clung to his arm.

Fairchild looked her over, then nodded knowingly at Brussard. "Is it the girl?" he asked. "Is that what all this is about? Go ahead, take the little bitch. I'm through with her."

"The girl is my daughter, Fairchild," Brussard tried to control his hatred.

The Englishman was unruffled. "You must be very proud of her," he picked a piece of lint off his shoulder. "She's carrying a Fairchild, you know. Not many anemic little half-breeds can say that." With composure, Fairchild drank some of the Scotch, eyeing McKain hatefully over the rim of his cup.

"Poppa," Cathy pulled on his arm. "Let's go. Can we, please?"

Ignoring her, Brussard stared at Fairchild. Seeing the man so bold and defiant made Brussard loathe him even more. "You killed my wife, Fairchild. You raped her, killed her and threw her into a clump of bushes like a sack of rotten potatoes."

"Did I indeed?" Fairchild raised an eyebrow as he sipped more of the liquor.

Brussard glared. "You son of a bitch, you know you did."

"Now if I did do all that, it's nobody's fault but yours, Brussard. You should never leave a defenseless woman alone out here in this wild country."

"You cold-hearted bastard."

"Poppa—"

"Shut up, girl."

"Why don't you let her talk, Brussard," Fairchild commented, taking an easy step toward the trunk. "She knows more about me than you do. She knows, for instance, that no one has ever burst into my tent and insulted me and lived to tell about it. Ask her about that."

Cathy caught his stare, then looked pleadingly at her father. "Poppa, if we don't leave now, we won't ever leave. I swear you'll die, Poppa. Somehow it will happen. You will die and then where will I be?"

"I'm not going to die, daughter," he assured her confidently. "It's Red Hair that's going to die. I've waited a long time for this."

"Poppa—I've had to look at so much death. Please—"

"Perhaps you should listen to her, Brussard," Fairchild took another step toward the trunk. "She's a bright girl. She knows I lead a charmed life. Nobody can kill Red Hair."

"Be still, Fairchild!"

But the Englishman boldly inched himself closer to the trunk.

"Stop, damn you!" Brussard called out. But Fairchild had already made his move. He slung the cup of liquor at Brussard and in the same motion pounced on the trunk and scooped up one of the pistols in his hand. But before he could get it cocked, the mountainman lunged forward and grabbed his wrist.

"Hold it right there," Brussard grunted.

"Ah! You smell!" Fairchild growled disgustedly. "Get your vile body off me."

"Let it go, Fairchild; I'll break your arm."

Fairchild grimaced. "All I have to do is call out one order and you're a dead man, Brussard."

"Call it out, then. See how long you stay alive."

"McKain!"

The agent was sidling around the wall of the tent, on his way out. "You brought this upon yourself, Douglas. I can't help you."

"I'll remember that, McKain."

Brussard wrenched the Englishman's wrist enough to make him drop the pistol. Then he pinned his arms down to the floor with his knees and sat on his chest. "Now how about a little Shawnee haircut, Fairchild," he twirled a lock of his red hair around his fingers.

"Poppa!" the girl cried out in horror. "Don't!"

Brussard didn't hear her. He had Fairchild's scalp drawn back and tight, stretched and ready for his knife. He raised the long blade up, in front of the Englishman's eyes. "I'll do it slow, so you'll be able to remember my family for a long time. I want you to die with my family on your mind."

"Ah, your family is nothing but American trash, Brussard," he sneered. "And there isn't one American in this country that is worth an Englishman's spit. And that includes your dowdy little squaw wife."

Brussard laid the edge of the blade against Fairchild's hairline. But then Cathy fell to her knees beside them. "Poppa!" she cried, tugging desperately at his arm. "Poppa! Do you hear me?"

He didn't look at her. "Go away, Cathy," he ordered her. "I don't want you to see this."

"There's been so much death, Poppa. Do you have to kill him, too?"

"He killed your mother, girl."

"I know he did. God knows, I saw him do it! But does killing him make you any better than he is? Can't we just go home?"

"I'll go home when I'm through taking his scalp," he replied. "It's owed to me."

"Poppa, for God's sake. I don't want to remember you as a killer, too. I've seen so much of it. I couldn't stand it!"

He lifted the blade up, leaving a thin red line of blood on the forehead, and looked at her. "Is that how you'd think of me?" he asked her. "A killer?"

"Yes," she answered him. "If you do this, yes!"

He thought a minute, then sheathed his knife. "Get up."

Fairchild wiped the blood off his forehead with

one finger. "Well, someone in your little tribe has a bit of sense, anyway," he muttered.

"Get up, Fairchild, I'm not through with you."

Fairchild gnashed his teeth and started to rise, but suddenly felt Brussard's boot smash deep into his groin. Before he could even double over with the pain, a knee landed hard under his chin and cracked his head and body back to the ground. He scrambled up quickly, but ran straight into Brussard's arms. "Wait!" he cried, but his words sounded empty and ridiculous in the room. The mountainman's heavy fist plowed into his face once, twice, three times. A final solid blow to the chin knocked him down to his knees. As soon as he raised his hand to mop the blood from his mouth, Brussard hoisted him up by the collar, drew his face to within inches of his own.

"I ought to beat the life out of you, Fairchild," he threatened him.

Fairchild turned up his nose disdainfully. "Your breath is foul, mountainman."

"I reckon I'll just have to settle for *this*," Brussard rammed his knee into Fairchild's crotch.

The Englishman gasped quietly in pain then staggered back and dropped to his knees again, clenching his stomach with both hands.

Brussard had had enough. He spit on the floor, then snatched his daughter's hand. "Let's go, Cathy. I'm tired of wasting muscle on 'im. He may look like a gentleman, but he's worse than any savage I've ever seen. Can't figure how a woman like Roxanna could've ever married such a man."

Fairchild looked up, shocked to hear his wife's name. But he continued to hold tightly onto his aching stomach and said nothing.

"I didn't know he had a wife," McKain spoke from his place by the doorway. "I never heard him say he had one."

"Oh he's got one all right," Brussard told him. "She's on the Lewis and Clark expedition. Which," he turned to Cathy, "is where you and me are going, girl. We've got to tell 'em all about this flock o' buzzards."

"Do you mean to the Pacific?" she asked excitedly.

"Yeah, the Pacific Ocean. They'll be there by the time we reach it."

"Oh, Poppa. Can we go now?"

"Just one minute," the big mountainman said. He reached down and jerked Fairchild up again, looked him in the face. "I'd like to finish the job on you, Red Hair. But I reckon I owe my daughter something. You can thank her for saving your miserable life."

"Your daughter is a whore, Brussard," Fairchild retorted.

Brussard instinctively swung his fist again. The big knuckles hammered into Fairchild's temple, sending him crashing to the floor. The Englishman tried to get up, but rolled helplessly onto his back. Casting one last contemptuous look in Fairchild's direction, Brussard clasped Cathy's small hand in his enormous palm. "McKain, I'm leaving the rest of it to you."

The agent wrinkled his brow worriedly. "What do you mean, 'the rest of it'?"

"I mean if you don't kill this snake while he's squirming around on the ground, he's going to kill you when he gets up."

"Me?" McKain asked, surprised. "He wouldn't kill me."

Brussard reached over and picked up one of the dueling pistols off the trunk, handed it to the agent. "Take it," he poked him in the stomach with the pearl handle. "Just aim it at his head and pull the trigger. It'll do the rest."

McKain found his fingers clutching the unfamiliar object. It felt warm and heavy in his hand. "Wait, I don't know anything about guns," he confessed nervously. "I've never had to use them."

"Then learn," Brussard ordered.

"I can't believe he would do anything to me," McKain whined hopefully.

Fairchild groaned. "You'd better . . . . leave with them, McKain." He struggled to get up on his knees. "If you want to stay alive, you'd better go with them."

"Oh, God," McKain swallowed.

"Here," Brussard cocked the pistol for him. "Just aim and shoot. You'll be doing the world a favor."

McKain nodded. The pistol shook violently in his trembling hand as he held it out toward Fairchild.

"Come on, Cathy, let's go." With his daughter by his side, Brussard marched out of the tent, into the bright sunlight. He felt good, better than he had in years. He glanced appreciatively at the rising sun. "Looks like it's going to be a fine morning," he squinted. "May be one of the best I've had in a long time. I reckon I might take a bath today."

"Are we really going to the Pacific Ocean?" Cathy asked him.

"Yeah, we're going. Why not? There'll be a few folks there I want you to meet. One of 'em's an army cap'n, one's a young Philadelphia lawyer and one's a real fine lady from New Orleans."

"A lady, Poppa?"

"Can't an old trapper like me meet a lady once in a while if he's a mind to? Besides—"

He stopped when he heard the loud gunshot behind him, coming from the tent. They turned around and looked back. "I reckon that's the end of Red Hair. Good riddance."

"I'm glad," Cathy declared. "And I'm glad you didn't do it."

"Yeah," he sighed. "I'm glad I didn't do it, too, Cathy. I feel real good about it."

As Brussard was about to turn around, a horrifying sight suddenly appeared at the doorway of the tent. Douglas Fairchild, his bruised face twisted with anger and drenched with blood, stepped abruptly out onto the grass with the second dueling pistol in his hand.

Without a word, he raised the gun to eye-level, aimed, and squeezed the trigger.

The powder exploded with a white flash, the cracking sound reverberated against the trees around the camp, and the lead slug struck Brussard squarely between the eyes.

He was dead before his massive body could hit the ground.

"Poppa!" Cathy Brussard screamed when she saw him crumble in front of her. "Oh no, God, no!" she cried, prostrating her body on his chest. She held her breath but could feel no life pulsating under her. "Poppa!" she moaned. "Please don't die. Poppa!"

Fairchild watched the scene for a moment. Then he called out to one of the Indians in the camp.

Cathy looked back at him, her red, crying eyes filled with hatred. "You beast!" she shouted. "You horrible beast! You've killed my whole family!"

"Yes, I have," he acknowledged stiffly. "Sometimes I can be rather effective." He looked at the Blackfoot warrior who had hustled out of the gathering crowd of Indians. "White Eagle, take this odorous body and the one in the tent and string them on a tree. I'm not through with them yet."

The Indian nodded knowingly.

"And take this stupid girl to my tent and tie her up. As soon as I can make myself presentable," he blotted his face with a lace handkerchief, "I'm going to teach her a lesson—a very hard lesson."

"I will take her," the Indian agreed.

"After that," Fairchild told him, "we'll be breaking camp and heading for the Pacific Ocean. It seems my faithful, loving wife has been traveling around the country like a harlot, doing all she can to smear my family's name. I'm afraid I'm going to have to do something about that."

PART SIX
THE PACIFIC

Chapter 20

Roxanna Fairchild saw very little of Tom Wentworth the next few weeks as the expedition moved out of the high mountains onto what the Indians called the Kooskooskee River. It was obvious to her he was trying hard to stay out of her way. He never missed a chance to avoid her. When Captain Clark went ahead with a hunting party, Tom went, too. When Captain Lewis left the main group to explore, Tom volunteered to go with him.

"I don't suppose I blame him," Roxanna told Sacajawea one afternoon. The Indian girl was sitting on one of the pine dugout canoes, trying to get Baptiste to eat a sliver of dried salmon; Roxanna was idly mashing camas bulbs into flour. "He asked me to go away with him, and I wouldn't go," she continued. "Why should he pay any more attention to me?"

"Do you love Tom Wentworth?" Sacajawea asked.

"God, yes," she admitted passionately. "I never knew it was possible to love a man the way I love him."

Sacajawea nodded. "I knew it was so, a long time ago."

"Was it that obvious?" Roxanna asked, amused at herself.

Sacajawea smiled and nodded sweetly. "If you love Tom Wentworth, why don't you take him as your husband? You are strong woman."

"Well, not that strong," Roxanna answered. "It's not that easy. I can't marry Tom because I already have a husband."

"He is not your husband if he is not with you," she stated simply. "If Charbonneau is not with me, he is no longer my husband. It is not like family."

"That may be the Indian way, Sacajawea, but in New Orleans we have laws for that sort of thing. Written laws. One of them says I can't be Tom's wife as long as I'm Douglas's."

Sacajawea shrugged her shoulders, looked at her with interest. "But this is not . . . New Orleans."

"No, you're right, it isn't. I think I'm finally beginning to understand that, too, Sacajawea. There are some things that matter more than what other people will say about you."

"Things like Tom Wentworth."

"Yes, as a matter of fact, like Tom Wentworth," she acknowledged, determinedly crushing a camas bulb with a rock.

A while later Roxanna noticed Tom striding briskly across the tall grass toward the captains' tent. Immediately she lay down the rock and camas and caught up with him. She was surprised to see him in his Philadelphia clothes instead of buckskin, but she didn't say anything about it. "Good afternoon," she greeted cheerfully.

"Roxanna," he pretended indifference.

"Ah, well, you remember me," she teased. "I'm flattered."

"Excuse me, Roxanna. I'd like to talk to you, but

I have to go. Captain Lewis is waiting for me in his tent."

She grabbed his arm. "Are we going to keep doing this, Tom?" she asked. "Forever?"

"Doing what?"

"You know perfectly well 'what.' Keeping out of each other's way, pretending we don't love each other, acting as if we never slept together. . . ."

"No," he replied. "We don't have to do it forever. We'll be on the Columbia tomorrow. From there it's straight down the river to the Pacific Ocean. When we get to the coast, we can go our separate ways."

"I don't understand," she grumbled, puzzled. "Aren't you going back to St. Louis with the expedition next spring?"

"No, I'm not. I'm going to take a ship back to Pennsylvania, Roxanna. I'm going back to Philadelphia and I'm going to fall in love with a nice safe Quaker girl who isn't married."

She tried not to show her dismay. "And when did you decide all this?" she asked him. "Overnight?"

"No. I've been thinking about it for a long time. Ever since you turned me down back at the Forks."

"So after living out here for eighteen months you're going back to a stuffy old law office in Philadelphia. Is that really want you want, Tom?"

"Roxanna, I don't have to tell you what I want. I want you. But you've said it so many times, I think I finally understand it—you're not free to love me. So why don't we stop torturing ourselves and just avoid each other until we get to the Pacific. Then it'll all be over."

She squeezed his arm. "Tom, will you listen to me, just for a minute?"

"Captain Lewis is expecting me, Roxanna."

"Well, Captain Lewis can just wait. I want to say this."

"Roxanna—"

"Just stand there and listen, will you do that? In

the past year and a half I've learned something." She paused. "Something important. When I first came out here, I was embarrassed for all these poor Indian women acting like slaves, but now I realize they aren't concerned with how somebody from Royal Street in New Orleans looks at them. I don't say the way they are is right, but they do have their own dignity and self-respect, Tom. Sacajawea, for instance—"

"Roxanna—" he interrupted impatiently.

"It's the self-respect that matters, Tom," she went on, "not what other people think. If you have that, you can live with yourself." She waited a few seconds, then added, "Or, to be perfectly obvious about it, you can live with someone else."

He looked at her, touched her cheek with his fingertips. "Are you saying you could forget you're a married woman and go away and live with me?" he asked.

"Yes," she answered boldly. "That's what I'm saying. I couldn't have done it a year ago— I couldn't have done it a week ago. But I can do it now."

He shook his head. "No you can't," he disagreed. "You were right in the first place. We'd never forget, Roxanna."

"Not back home in New Orleans or Philadelphia," she conceded. "But out here, it wouldn't matter to anyone, Tom. And if it did, we just wouldn't care. We could do it!"

"No, we couldn't," he pulled away.

"Tom—"

"It's just not meant to be, Roxanna. I was wrong to ask you to go away with me. As long as you're married to Douglas Fairchild, we can't be together. I wish we hadn't ever slept together—"

"Don't say that."

"I'm sorry," he walked away from her. "I just don't see any future for us, Roxanna."

She stood in the tall grass, hoping he would turn around. But he didn't waver; he marched straight into the captains' tent and closed the door flap behind him.

Roxanna stared at the tent for a while, then reached down into her trousers pocket and drew out the watch. Clicking open the cover, she looked at the picture of the naked woman inside.

Douglas Fairchild, she thought: Sir Douglas Fairchild of Sheffield, England. What a strange twist of fate; everything that mattered to her now depended upon a man who had married her and robbed her more than two years before. And where was this man? she wondered. Would she find him before they reached the Pacific and Tom was lost to her forever?

She snapped the cover of the watch shut and gripped it tightly in her palm. Douglas's timepiece would be her last resort. If she hadn't won Tom back by the time they reached the ocean, she would show him the watch and tell him that her own husband had tried to rape her.

And then. . . . She didn't know.

The next two weeks on the Columbia River went smoothly, easily. The great river, so clear you could see huge salmon twenty feet below the surface, carried the expedition swiftly toward the mountains at an average of more than forty miles a day in the dugout canoes.

Along the banks of the river the party saw numerous Indian settlements. The tribes lived in large oblong huts made of rushes instead of in the small conical tents used on the plains. They wore much simpler clothes, leather sheets tied around the waist or chest, intead of elaborate dresses or shirts. The stout sedentary women seemed to Roxanna to do nothing but dry and pound fish on rocks all day, while the men fished or smoked and talked at their leisure.

The expedition took to the ground past the dangerous rapids Captain Clark called The Great Chute. As they headed into the mountains, the clear waters of the river turned into a powerful torrent and rushed noisily through a gorge cut between great rises of stone. From the river they could see Mt. Hood in the range to the south, and Mt. Adams and Mt. Rainier to the north.

Then came the rain—hard, pelting, relentless rain, day after day. The party was constantly soaked to the skin, the bedding was always wet and riddled with fleas. The wind blew down tents, made enormous rocking waves on the water, dashed canoes up against the rocks. The weather was too bad to hunt; most of the men grew weary, then sick of their diet of wapato roots, dog and fish bought from the Indians along the river.

Worse than all of this for Roxanna was the absence of Tom Wentworth. As usual, he had volunteered to go with Lewis's scouting party ahead, this time all the way to the coast. As each day passed the rain grew heavier and land travel seemed to her impossible. She became more and more concerned about him.

Finally she had to talk to someone about it. She went to the captains' tent. "Good evening, Captain Clark," she greeted, removing her hat and shaking the water off the brim.

Clark was the only person in the room. He was sitting near two candles on his trunk, cleaning his fusil with an oily cloth. He looked up at her and nodded. "Come in, Roxanna," he invited. "Have you ever seen weather like this? The wind and rain are malicious. They seem to be coming at us from all directions."

"Yes, they do," she attempted to appear at ease.

"We've had over a week of it without a pause," he reflected gloomily. "The river's up to its banks now, and the tide hasn't even come in yet. The cliffs are too steep for us to go up—if the river floods, we may be trapped here."

A crackle of thunder outside made Roxanna shudder and cross her arms. She had been wet for two weeks, every disturbance grated on her frayed nerves. "Captain Clark," she uncrossed her arms, "I—" she began but then another clap of thunder drowned out her words.

Clark looked up from his pistol. "We'll make it out, Roxanna," he assured her. "We haven't come half-way across the continent to be drowned like rats."

"Oh, no, I wasn't thinking about that. I have faith in you, Captain Clark. God knows, after all this time, I should."

"Then what's the matter, Roxanna?" he asked. "You look worried."

She took a deep breath. "I am worried," she admitted. "I'm worried about Captain Lewis . . . and Tom. I don't know what to think. Haven't they been gone an awfully long time? In all this rain, anything could have happened to them."

Clark lay his pistol on the trunk. As he was about to speak, Lewis entered the tent.

"Captain Lewis!" Roxanna exclaimed cheerfully, relieved to see him. "We were just talking about you. I didn't know you were back."

"It wasn't easy, getting back." He entered and took off his coat. He turned it inside out and shook it. "I wouldn't have believed there was this much water in the whole world."

"I wouldn't have, either. It hasn't stopped for days."

"William," he addressed the other man, "I didn't see the canoes out there."

"No, we laid them under water," he explained. "The waves were knocking them against the rocks and tearing them up, so we tied them down and sank them with stones. We can pull them out in the morning."

Lewis nodded. "Good. I was worried about them on the way back. I think we'll have to use more ballast than we have been using though. The river's a fury downstream."

"If we can get out tomorrow," Clark added. "Most of the men are sick, Meriwether. Some of them can barely move. We may have to ride out this storm for a while."

Lewis nodded, but didn't respond; he was looking at Roxanna, waiting for a chance to approach a certain subject with her. "Roxanna," he plunged in, then paused.

"Yes sir?" she replied congenially.

"Roxanna, there is something I have to tell you," he announced. "About Tom."

His tone of voice frightened her. "Oh God." Her voice was cold with fear. "He isn't hurt, is he?"

"No, he's not hurt," Lewis searched for the right words.

"What is it?" she demanded. "Is he dead? Tell me!"

"It's just that . . . he didn't come back with us."

"Then he is hurt. Or sick—"

"No, he's not sick, Roxanna. He's quite healthy. He feels fine. But when we reached the ocean, he came to me and asked to be relieved of his responsibilities. I tried to convince him to stay with us, but he insisted. He wanted to leave the expedition."

"Oh, no."

"I told him his father wouldn't approve of what he was doing, leaving us behind once we'd made it overland, but he'd made up his mind. He said he was signing aboard the next ship out. Even if it's headed for China."

"How could he even think of doing such a thing?" she whimpered, stunned. "Why didn't he tell me?"

Lewis drew out a lead gunpowder canister out of his coat pocket and opened it. "Maybe this letter will explain," he slid a rolled sheet of paper from the can.

The dry paper smelled of gunpowder when she unrolled it. She glanced at the formal signature, closed her eyes, took a deep breath, then opened them and read his words:

My dear Roxanna,

Forgive this abrupt means of saying goodbye, but I know that if I saw you again, if I ever touched your hand or looked into your eyes again, I would never be able to find the courage to leave. But I am leaving, my love. You have a husband you must return to; I have a life in Philadelphia I must return to—some day.

I hope you understand. This afternoon I stood on the white beaches of the mighty Pacific Ocean and looked across the darkening horizon at the sails of a great ship silhouetted against the sky. I was stirred by the sight; it seemed to pull at me somehow. Perhaps out there somewhere, on the sea, lies that 'fortune' you were always so disdainful of.

Please know always that I love you, and if we had only met before Sir Douglas Fairchild, I truly believe we would have happily passed the rest of our lives together. But that was just not to be, was it?

Goodbye, my love.

Tom Wentworth.

With tears in her eyes, Roxanna crumpled up the letter. "Damn him!" she cried. "How can he do this? How can he just . . . go! A woman would never do that."

Lewis threw his coat over on his cot. "He said he didn't see any other way, Roxanna."

She thought a minute. "How often do the ships come in, Captain Lewis?"

Lewis rubbed his chin. "Not very often," he replied. "There are no white settlements on this part of the coast."

"The kind of ship Tom would be looking for would come in once a month at best," Clark offered. "Probably not that often."

"Then we still have time. When are we leaving, Captain Clark?"

"We'll leave as soon as it's safe to get back on the river, Roxanna," he answered.

She picked up her hat. "I've got to see him one more time," she declared, opening the tent flap. "If he signs his life away on some God-forsaken voyage, he's signing mine away, too."

A few days later, on a cold morning in a mountain pass in western Canada, near the forty-ninth parallel, Harmer got off his horse and whistled the appropriate pass call to the Blackfoot sentry. When he heard the response, he led his horse in, gave the reins to the sentry and walked into the camp of Douglas Fairchild.

It was set up as usual: the farthest tent on the outer perimeter was used for Fairchild's council meetings; the seven renegade huts radiated from the tent in the center of the clearing. Harmer trod the rough ground painfully. He was tired, weary from hundreds of miles of travel and months of being alone. The other Indians in camp gradually began to ease out of the woods and move in closer toward him as he walked, but he ignored them and went straight to the leader.

Fairchild met him outside his tent. "Well, Harmer, what do you have to tell me after all these weeks? Is the expedition still intact?"

"It's still intact," Harmer acknowledged.

"Good. To tell you the truth, I'm relieved to hear it. I'm glad Craddock is so incompetent. I've been looking forward to doing my work; I would hate to be cheated out of it."

"Why don't we go inside, Douglas?" Harmer suggested.

Fairchild looked around at the Indians. Lifting up the tent flap he turned and went inside. When they were alone, Fairchild stared at Harmer intently. "What do you have on your mind, Harmer?" he glinted suspiciously. "I don't like the expression on your face."

"Where is McKain?" Harmer asked. "He'll want to hear this, too."

"Never mind McKain," Fairchild answered offhandedly. "The fool tired to shoot me. I had to kill him."

Harmer was shocked. "*McKain* tried to shoot you? He never held a gun in his life!"

"He held one—once," he retorted. "But let's forget McKain. I want to hear about Captains Lewis and Clark."

Harmer looked at him for a moment, removed his quiver of arrows and put them on the floor. "The expedition is on the Columbia River," he began. "I'm sure they will make it to the Pacific. Craddock won't be able to stop them."

"Then we shall put a period to Captains Lewis and Clark ourselves," he smiled. "Believe me, it'll be my pleasure."

Harmer gritted his teeth. "There's no longer any need to do that. Do you remember McKain's man, Miflin?"

"Yes, I remember him. I don't forget anybody. He was an insect. What about him? What does Miflin have to do with anything?"

"I met him at the Great Pacific Fur trading post on the sound a couple of weeks ago. Or what *was* the Great Pacific Fur trading post."

"What are you trying to say, Harmer?" he snorted impatiently. "I asked you about the expedition, not about Great Pacific Fur."

"What I'm trying to say is, the company is dead, Douglas, out of business. Miflin says the British backers have lost faith; they've drawn out their money. There is no more Great Pacific Fur Company."

Fairchild gripped the handle of his knife and twisted it in its sheath. "That's impossible," he contended. "Miflin is nothing but an underling—he doesn't know what he's talking about. McKain would have said something—"

"McKain didn't know, Douglas."

"No," Fairchild shook his head angrily. "This

can't be. I have a great deal of money invested in that company—all the money I have."

"Well, your money is gone, Douglas. Miflin is not working for Great Pacific; he was on his way to the Pacific to try to find work on the next ship."

Fairchild drew out his knife and slapped the flat side of the blade nervously against his palm. After a moment he accepted the fact. "What happened?" he asked.

"Miflin says the London backers have gotten reports of the Lewis and Clark expedition, and other expeditions—"

"So they're giving up?"

"The main thing is, they know about *us*, Douglas —our tactics. They've lost faith. The posts are closing—there's an end to it. The other British companies may as well fold, too. The Americans are going to control the Northwest fur trade."

"Damn Craddock!" Fairchild exclaimed, sticking the knife into the ground. "If he had taken care of Lewis and Clark when he was supposed to, when he was *hired* to, I wouldn't be hearing this. I wouldn't be losing every penny I managed to acquire in New Orleans."

"Maybe not. Now it doesn't matter."

Fairchild laughed derisively. "Oh, it matters, Harmer. It matters more now than ever." He picked up his knife and rubbed the blade on his fingers. "No company folds its tents that easily. When London hears there is nothing left of the Lewis and Clark expedition but a pile of smoking corpses, they'll find 'faith' again. The British are practical people; they will back us again when they see money in it."

Harmer looked at him incredulously. "You don't mean we're going ahead with this?"

Fairchild sheathed his knife. "Of course we're going ahead with it, Harmer," he told him. "I want Ned Craddock. I want to stare in his cowardly eyes and feel his last gasping breath puff against my face."

"Then kill him. But massacring a whole government expedition is madness. There are good men in that company. They even have two women traveling with them."

"Oh, I know all about the two women traveling with them, Harmer. One of the whores happens to be my loving wife."

"Your wife!"

"That's right. Roxanna Fairchild, my cheating harlot." He walked a few steps, turned around. "No, Harmer, I want them all dead. All of them. Every man, woman, horse, dog, flea and mosquito. I don't want there to be a trace of them left. I don't want my family's name on that expedition's journals—not as the husband of the company whore."

"You're talking about fifty people, Douglas."

"I'm talking about fifty dead people, Harmer, lost in a wilderness where there will be nothing but illiterate red men and crawling vermin to say they ever lived."

"But there's no *reason* to do this," Harmer protested.

"All right, Harmer," he snapped. "So the company is dead. I don't care about that. This is personal."

"You're going too far, Douglas," he warned him. "I've turned my head while you've slaughtered innocent people at trading posts, while you've peeled their skin off their bodies like dead rabbits. I've said nothing when you've seduced and abused helpless girls like Cathy Brussard. But fifty people! In the name of all that's decent, man, you can't do this!"

Fairchild smiled, reached out and patted Harmer's cheek. "I'm not in England any more, my good man. I can do whatever pleases me. And right now it pleases me to lead a surprise attack on the Lewis and Clark expedition. Now, Harmer, are you with me? Or have you forgotten that I killed for you? Have you forgotten I saved your miserable life?"

"I haven't forgotten."

"Good. Then you are with me," he stated confidently.

Harmer nodded. "Yes," he muttered, resigned. "I am always with you."

"I am very pleased to hear that," Fairchild smiled. "I think I'll go tell the men the good news. They're getting bored; this will cheer them up."

Harmer followed him from the tent, watched him call the Indians together around him. They listened eagerly and intently, recognizing only a few key English words like 'war' and 'battle' in his harangue. Each time they heard one they knew, they cheered wildly.

Disgusted, tired and hungry, Harmer flung the quiver sling over his shoulder and trudged across the campground to a cooking fire. As he was about to sit down to eat, he heard a muffled moaning emerging from Fairchild's tent. He recognized the voice and tried to ignore it, but when the moan became a wail, he jumped up and went to investigate.

Cathy Brussard was in the tent, lying curled up on a bed of elk skins, crying. He rushed in and dropped to his knees beside her. He could see the girl was nearly dead; her face and arms were covered with old and recent bruises and abrasions. Her left arm looked broken. One of her eyes was closed with puffy black tissue, the other was as red as blood.

He glanced up at the Pawnee woman standing nearby. In their language, he asked her what happened to the girl.

"Red Hair," she answered, shaking her head. "He beats her every day."

Harmer touched her stomach. "She has had the child?"

The woman nodded. "Born dead," she replied.

He took a deep breath. "Red Hair goes too far," he grimaced coldly. Then, looking at the girl, he whispered, taking her hand, "Cathy? Can you hear me?"

"Yes," she whimpered in a low voice.

"Good. Now listen to me. Your arm is broken.

I'm going to have to set it. Do you understand what I'm saying?"

She continued to cry in pain, her eyes closed.

"Cathy?"

"I understand," she answered, squeezing his hand with all her strength. "Please don't hurt me."

"I'm going to pull the bone back together." He instructed the Pawnee woman to press her weight against the girl's shoulders, to keep them flat against the ground while he pulled. Then he stood and braced himself and took a tight hold on her left wrist.

"What are you doing, Harmer?" a cold, hard voice bristled from behind.

He knew who it was but he didn't bother to look around. "Her arm's broken, Douglas," he answered. "I'm setting the bone."

"We don't have time to wait around while you play doctor, Big Tree," he growled contemptuously. "We're breaking camp."

"I'll catch up," he answered calmly.

"If you don't mind, Harmer," Fairchild observed, "it's a long way to the Pacific, and I'm in a bit of a hurry to get there."

Harmer ignored him and began pulling slowly on Cathy's arm. "This will only take a minute, Cathy," he explained as she began to squirm under the Pawnee woman's weight. "It'll hurt bad for a minute, then it'll be over."

Fairchild pursed his lips and scratched his chin thoughtfully. "Some day that defiant half-breed attitude of yours will cost you something very dear, Harmer," he hissed.

"My lack of defiance has already cost me more, Fairchild. My self-respect."

"I'll remember you said that," he told him. He started to go, then looked back. "While you're doctoring your girlfriend there, Harmer, you might tell her for me if she ever even mentions her lowly family again in my presence, she will wake up one morning with the other arm dangling from its socket."

"I'll tell her," he glared, looking directly at Fairchild.

"That goes for you, too, Harmer," Fairchild grunted and left the tent.

Chapter 21

When Roxanna reached the Pacific Ocean with Captain Clark's overland party, she stood on the sand and watched the surging, pounding surf beat upon the beaches, and she thought of Tom Wentworth. Later, while some of the other members of the party began to set up camp on the northern side of the Columbia, she and John Collins went out to look for him. A six-hour search of the beaches and mountains turned up nothing. She was saddened by the thought that he had already found a ship and was now sailing somewhere on the vast Pacific on his way to another part of the world.

But she was heartened a few days later by information from one of the Chinook Indians who congregated around the camp to sell dried sturgeon, wapato roots and the berries called *shelwell*. A minor chief named Chillarlarwil, of the Chinook stood in the captains' tent and answered Roxanna's questions with a serious expression on his impassive face.

"There has been no ship in one moon," he declared.

"But if Tom hasn't gone onboard a ship," Roxanna worried, "where is he?"

The Indian rubbed his long fingers against his beaded belt, looked over at Captain Clark, and shrugged his shoulders.

"Is there another ship due any time soon?" Roxanna asked him.

" 'Due'?" he repeated.

"Will another ship be coming here soon?" she asked patiently.

He nodded knowingly. "Haley comes in four moons. Mackey comes in three moons. Youin comes to trade *tiacomoshack* in two moons. One-Eyed Skellie in ship with four masts. . . ." He went on for another five minutes, listing French and English ships, brigs, schooners and sloops, with their captains, and their expected dates of arrival. But he didn't expect any of them soon.

"You have quite a memory," Clark offered, impressed.

Roxanna persisted. "Is it possible there will be a ship coming tomorrow? Or the next day?"

"Possible," he shrugged. "Bowman was here twelve moons ago. He could be here soon."

"But *when*?"

He shrugged his shoulders again.

At that moment Captain Lewis entered the tent, slapping his soggy hat against his leg. "I wonder if it will ever stop raining."

"Chillarlarwil just told us it never stops raining here," Clark told him. "He can't understand why we're so concerned about it."

"Well, Chillarlarwil is one very tolerant Indian. William, the Chinooks were right, there is game on the other side of the river; but the land is mostly saltwater swamp. We had better keep the camp on this side."

Clark wrinkled his brow slightly. "Don't you think we'd be better off back upriver, Meriwether?" he asked.

"No!" Roxanna exclaimed. "We can't leave the coast. If Tom is going to catch a ship, he'll have to catch it at the mouth of the river, won't he? If we go back up river, we'll miss him."

"We can't very well stay here to wait for Tom, Roxanna," Clark reprimanded.

"We do need the supplies a ship would bring," Lewis reminded him. "Our blankets are rotten, our clothes are worn, most of our powder is wet, and we need a great deal of medicine."

"I know we do, Meriwether," Clark relented a little. "But the men don't like the coast. They want to move back inland."

"We will move inland," Lewis replied. "After a ship arrives or when we decide it's too late to wait for one."

Captain Clark sighed and sat down on the edge of his clothes trunk. "We don't have time to wait," he stated firmly. "We have to start building winter quarters *now*, Meriwether. If the rain continues, it'll take us longer than it did at Fort Mandan."

"Please, Captain Clark," Roxanna pleaded. "Just a few days. When Tom hears we've set up camp, I'm sure he'll come by. That's all I want. Just to talk to him one more time."

"I understand how you feel, Roxanna," he sympathized. "But you know the men are either sick or restless. They're anxious to put up some shelter against this damned rain. It's driving us all crazy."

"We need those supplies, William," Lewis maintained resolutely.

The Chinook nodded ceremoniously. "Bowman will have supplies," he stated. "He will have sailor clothes and goat blankets."

Clark looked at the Indian, then at Lewis. "You're right," he agreed. "We do need those things badly."

"We need to get the quarters up by the first

of the year," Lewis pointed out. "If the rain doesn't let up, it will take us a month to finish the job."

"About that," Clark concurred.

"That gives us a week on the coast to wait for a ship."

Roxanna stirred. "A week isn't very much, Captain Lewis. We may not see Tom in that time."

"Roxanna," Lewis responded, "Tom *chose* to leave us; we can't afford to send a hunting party out to find him. And we can't stay on the coast and hope he'll change his mind when he finds out we're here."

"Then I'll stay here," she insisted.

"No, you won't stay here," he told her sternly.

"I can take care of myself, Captain Lewis," she said.

"It's hardly that, Roxanna," he assured her. "I know very well you can. The fact is, we need you. We have another hard winter coming. The men are weak, our food is bad, we need you to nurse them back to health."

"Sacajawea can do that."

"No, she can't do it. She's a wonderful woman, but she's not you. You have a real gift for it, Roxanna. You saved Tom's life, you saved Sacajawea—God knows how many others you've saved. We have lost only one man on this expedition, Roxanna; I'd hate to think how many we would've lost without you."

Roxanna tried not to let his words sway her. "You let Tom go, Captain Lewis," she reminded him. "Why not me?"

"I let Tom go," he replied quickly, "because as good a man as Tom Wentworth is, Roxanna, he's not as valuable to this expedition as you are. No man is."

"I'm flattered, captain—"

"I'm not trying to flatter you, Roxanna," he cut her off. "I'm trying to tell you, if this expedition is a success, we owe a great part of that success to you. You've kept us alive and you've kept us interested."

She was puzzled. "*I've* kept you interested?"

Captain Clark broke in. "Roxanna, from the first, I was against your going on this expedition. I thought a woman had no place on such a dangerous mission. Well I was wrong. You've proven that in courage and stamina you are the equal of any man I've ever known. No matter what the hardship has been, you've been superior to it. You've never complained, you've never wavered. Well, I can tell you it's no coincidence that the men didn't waver, either. They started out watching you, naturally, because you're a beautiful woman. But then they were admiring you. Now, frankly, they are looking up to you."

"Captain Clark, I appreciate what you're saying. Really. More than you can imagine. But I must find Tom."

"Roxanna," he continued. "We want very much for you to stay. We have twenty sick men and winter is coming."

Roxanna considered his words. The choice he was putting before her was simple, but difficult: she could stay with the Lewis and Clark expedition, where she was needed, or she could leave it and go after Tom Wentworth, who evidently didn't need her.

There was a heavy silence in the room until Chillarlarwil broke it. He dug into the otterskin pouch hanging from his belt and drew out a twisted black root. "For you," he handed it to her. "*Shannatahque*. Cook it in coals and eat. Let no man touch it."

"Thank you," she answered politely.

"It is Chillarlarwil that is honored," he declared. "Roxanna is President of White Women, no?"

Roxanna laughed. "No," she answered. "I most certainly am not."

"Ah—pity," the Indian replied.

For some reason she felt like kissing all of them, Lewis, Clark and the Chinook chief, but she resisted the impulse.

Just then Sergeant Ordway stuck his head into the

tent, cleared his throat, and stepped in. "Captain Lewis?"

"What is it, John?"

"Captain, there's an Indian brave out here, demanding to see the chief. He says it can't wait."

Before Lewis could respond, Chillarlarwil flipped his beaver robe over his shoulders with a flourish and bolted out of the tent into the storm. With the captains and Roxanna looking on curiously, he stood straight and tall, oblivious to the wind and rain as he waited for a young Indian wearing a thick blue and white beaded headband to approach.

The two men talked privately in Chinook for several minutes, all the time glancing around the camp and shaking their heads decisively. Finally, they arrived at a decision between them.

Chillarlarwil came over to Lewis with it. "We will be going now," he announced loudly, above the sound of the falling rain.

"Going?" Lewis expressed his surprise. "Where? I thought you were going to stay in camp," he shouted, pointing his finger at the ground.

"No," Chillarlarwil shook his head. "It is your camp. We will be going."

"What happened?" Lewis asked him. "What did your man say?"

The chief paused a minute, to choose the right words. "He said trouble," he finally answered. "We will be back when trouble is over."

"What are you talking about? What kind of trouble?"

Chillarlarwil turned to go. "We leave him to you. You two white chiefs. Chinooks are not warriors, like white men. We leave him to you."

Lewis called out to him as he walked away. "Chillarlarwil—leave *who* to us? Who are you talking about?"

The Indian turned and looked back through the rain with hard, unfeeling eyes. "I am talking about Red

Hair," he answered, then hurried off with the other Chinook.

An hour later, secluded in a pine thicket a mile north of the Lewis and Clark camp, Douglas Fairchild paced back and forth in a slow, drizzling rain while he listened to Harmer's report on the expedition.

"They are set up the same way they always do it," Harmer was saying. "The captains' tent in the center, four armed sentries, not much precaution."

"How many men do they have now?" Fairchild asked him.

"I would say there are at least forty-five—maybe more. They haven't lost anyone."

"I'm glad to hear it. That'll make this business a great deal more interesting." He reached up and patted Harmer's cheek. "Don't you think so?"

Harmer quickly grabbed Fairchild's wrist and pulled his hand down.

Fairchild stared at it until he let it go. "You know I've told you not to touch me, half-breed," he rebuked coldly. "I don't like for people to touch me."

Harmer looked him straight in the eye. "Look, Douglas. Those people have finished their mission. They've done it. They've reached the coast all the way from St. Louis. Why kill them now? It's all over."

"No, it's not 'all over,' Harmer. It's not over until I say it is. Until we sink every last one of their bodies in the swamp. And we should be doing exactly that shortly after eleven o'clock tonight."

"Tonight!"

"Why not tonight? My plan is so simple and quiet, it's elegant. Each man will be responsible for taking care of two sleeping men. Beginning with Ned Craddock. There won't be a single gunshot. Just fifty clean swipes and it'll be done with."

Harmer sighed deeply, looked up at the dark, smoky sky. "It would be easier if we waited for the rain to stop," he stalled for time.

"Never mind the rain," Fairchild told him. "It makes good cover."

"I doubt if we'll need cover," he argued. "They'll be so surprised they won't be able to see anyone anyway."

"Now you're beginning to see it," Fairchild told him. "Now tell me: did you see Roxanna this time? How did she look?"

"I saw her. She looked very beautiful."

"Who was with her?" he pressed. "That same boy?"

"She was in the captains' tent."

Fairchild nodded. "At least the whore has acquired enough decency to consort with leaders now," he sneered disgustedly. He turned toward his tent, then paused. "I'm going to go relax. I tend to get very excited before I go into things of this sort."

Harmer knew he was going to Cathy Brussard. He clenched his fist in anger at the repellent thought of Fairchild touching her again, but he remained calm. "The girl is hurt bad, Douglas," he reminded him. "Why don't you let her get well before you do that to her again?"

Fairchild smiled at him. "When the girl can't take any more of me, Harmer, then I'll slice her throat open and throw her away, the same way I threw away her dowdy mother. You may as well know, 'doctor.' By this time tomorrow night you won't have to worry about putting Cathy Brussard's little broken bones back together again. I'll have my own loving wife with me then."

Harmer felt a powerful disgust for Fairchild surging within him, building to a peak, to the point of rage. He unconsciously wrapped his fingers around the handle of his knife.

Fairchild's eye caught the move. "Does that gesture mean you're objecting, Harmer?" he taunted. "Or is it that you want the girl when I'm through with her?"

"I want you to leave her alone, Douglas."

Fairchild laughed. "And what if I don't leave her alone? Are you going to repay the man who saved your life by killing him? Is that the Pawnee way, Big Tree?"

"I may just do that," Harmer grunted boldly. "If you hurt her again."

Douglas laughed. "You can't kill me, Harmer. Nobody can kill me. You just stand watch out here a while like a good little half-breed soldier and let me go about my business. Wake me in about an hour, if I'm asleep. I want to see the layout of their camp before it turns dark."

Harmer stood flexing his fingers on the handle of his knife as he watched Fairchild stride back to his tent, chuckling to himself, shaking his head and unbuckling his belt.

At that moment on the shore at Tillamook Head, twenty miles below the mouth of the Columbia, Tom Wentworth stood patiently watching a two-man dinghy bobbing up and down in the waves, as it moved steadily toward him. Just behind the skiff he could see the outline of a four-masted ship anchored out on the ocean in the dark mist.

On the beach with him were four other men, each one waiting anxiously and silently for the dinghy. Two of them were bearded trappers from the north, one a blond boy of sixteen, the other an educated-looking man in business dress, with a heavy raincoat that reached down to his ankles.

This last man surprised Tom by ambling slowly across the sand to where he was standing. "How long have you been waiting?" he asked him, looking out with him at the approaching boat.

Tom glanced at him, then back to the skiff. "I've been waiting a long time," he admitted. "I didn't know this place was a pickup station for sailors until yesterday."

The man looked at him, cocked his head. "You're

on the Lewis and Clark expedition, aren't you?" he asked.

"I was on it," Tom corrected him. "I left it a while ago."

"They're camped on the Columbia, next to the ocean, you know. I saw them yesterday."

"I wouldn't know about that," Tom said absently, thinking of Roxanna.

The man extended his hand. "My name's Miflin. Morton McKain and I visited your camp last winter. I remember seeing you there."

Tom shook his hand. "Tom Wentworth," he identified himself. He tried to recall the two men, but could bring to mind only one of them. "Mr. McKain tried to threaten his way into the expedition, didn't he?" he asked rhetorically. "What's he up to now?"

"I don't have any idea," Miflin answered. "Since I left him in Canada last summer, I haven't heard a word from him."

"Well, I'm sure you'll hear from him eventually," Tom declared. "Of course, if we sign on with that ship out there, we won't be hearing from anybody for a long time."

"That's true, but I'm afraid signing on with that ship is all that's left for me," he remarked apathetically. "But what about you? I don't see why a young, cultured man like you would be going to sea. Surely you realize having been on the great Lewis and Clark expedition can make you a fortune. The rest of the men here are destitute, and I'm destitute, but you. . . ."

"I'm destitute, too, in a different way." After a pause, Tom added. "It's the usual story: a woman. In this case, a married woman."

"Ah, I see," Miflin nodded. "Where I come from, they say that's the _main_ reason for going to sea."

They were silent as they watched the hull of the skiff slap violently against the huge waves and then crunch up against the sandy beach. Quickly a young, clean-shaven man leaped out into the water and tugged the boat onto the beach by the tow line. When the hull was steady, a gray-haired old man with crooked teeth and dark, sunken eyes, clambered down onto the beach.

"All right, mates," he called out, straightening himself up and waving a sheet of foolscap. "That's His Majesty's Ship *Claiborne* out yonder, eighteen months and twelve days out of Liverpool, headed for the Sandwich Islands. If ye've a mind to, sign up; otherwise, be off with ye. Captain Hawkins will not be putting ashore here for any man."

The two trappers shuffled forward to make their marks, while the blond boy hung back, nervously twisting his hat in his hands.

"Those islands are almost three thousand miles away," Miflin observed to Tom. "Are you sure you want to leave that woman for that long?"

"No," he answered thoughtfully. "I'm not sure." Then, after another thought: "Well, yes, I am sure; I don't want to leave her at all. I just don't see anything else to do at the moment. I wish I did."

"Well, I was a seaman once," Miflin told him. "I guess it won't be such a bad life for a strong young man like you. For my part, I've seen enough of Great Pacific Fur Company to last a lifetime. I hated the kind of people McKain got to work for him. Most of them weren't worth much. You knew one of them: Ned Craddock."

"Ned Craddock!" Tom exclaimed. "Craddock worked for McKain! When? What kind of work?"

Miflin took a step toward the boat where the old man was sitting on the rim, questioning the trappers. "Well, since the whole affair is over, I guess there's no harm telling you about it. McKain hired Craddock to sabotage the Lewis and Clark expedition."

"Damn! I knew it was Craddock!"

"You knew about the sabotage?" Miflin inquired.

"I knew about it. I just didn't have any proof.

What I needed was something like the fact that Ned worked for a trading company."

Miflin looked at him quizzically. "Craddock *is* dead, isn't he?"

"No," Tom answered, raising his eyebrows. "He's not dead. Why should he be dead?"

"Never mind." Miflin knew he had said too much. He wanted to back quietly away from the subject.

But Tom wasn't about to let him off so easily. He grabbed his collar. "Why should Craddock be dead, Miflin?" he demanded. "Answer me!"

"Let go, Wentworth—"

"Tell me!"

"All right—I'll tell you. Why not? We're going to be thousands of miles away, anyway. It's simple logic: if the expedition made it to the coast, that means Craddock's sabotage attempt failed—which means he's been executed. I assumed it was a fact because McKain arranged it, and he always follows through."

Tom let him loose. "Executed! But he hasn't been."

"Then he will be," Miflin announced, straightening his collar. "Unless news of the company breaking up has made it that far north—"

"All right, mates," the old man growled at them. "What'll it be? Are ye fighting or sailing? Make up yer minds."

Tom ignored him. He looked at Miflin. "*Who* was supposed to 'execute' him, Miflin?" he asked. "Somebody on the expedition?"

"No, Great Pacific Fur didn't have anybody else on the expedition. It was hard enough to get Craddock on."

"Well, who then?"

"That Englishman, Fairchild. I left McKain with him last summer."

Tom stared at him in disbelief. The name stunned him. "*Fairchild!* Not Douglas Fairchild."

"Yes," Miflin nodded. "Douglas Fairchild. The Indians call him 'Red Hair.' "

"Roxanna's husband!" Tom swallowed hard. "My God. She has no idea what kind of man she married "

"All right there, mates," the old sailor grumbled impatiently, "what'll it be?"

"I'm signing on," Miflin answered him. "I've always wanted to see the Sandwich Islands."

"What's it going to be, son?" the old man asked Tom. "Are ye coming aboard, or no?"

Wentworth didn't hear him. "I can't believe what you're saying. Roxanna's husband is a hired killer — and he's going to execute Craddock?"

"What difference does it make, Wentworth?" Miflin wondered. "From what I've heard of Craddock, he's worth killing."

"You don't understand," Tom cried. "Roxanna is there. When he sees her with all those men, when he finds out what we've done—my God, I've got to go to her. If he finds out, he'll kill her!"

"Wentworth!" Miflin shouted as Tom dashed out across the sand and headed north up the coast. "Wentworth! Wait! You can't stop that man! He can't be killed!"

The old man spit into his left hand and rubbed it on his pants leg. "Sign here," he said, handing the page to Miflin. "I ain't got all day." As Miflin took up the quill, the old sailor watched Tom race up the coastline into the wind.

At first he ran at full-speed, spurred by the abhorrent image in his mind of Douglas Fairchild finding his wife, making her confess to adultery, and then . . . murdering her. But he forced himself to slow down. As much as he wanted to hurry, he had to pace himself or he would never reach the camp.

He guessed it would take four or five hours to reach her, if he had the strength and stamina to run most of the way. That would put him into camp late that night. As he ran, as the wet sand splattered regularly under his feet, he kept asking himself, *Will I be in time? Will I be in time?* Or, he wondered, would he find his beloved Roxanna dead at the hands of her enraged husband, Sir Douglas Fairchild?

Shortly before eleven o'clock that evening, Douglas Fairchild rose up from the ground and wiped a spot of mud from his trousers. He glanced at Harmer, then at the band of impatient Indians squatting, kneeling or pacing behind him. They had been waiting for hours and were anxious to begin the slaughter Red Hair had promised them.

Twenty yards in front of them was the Lewis and Clark camp, spread out among the pines next to the river. Fairchild slid his knife from its sheath. "Well, you got your wish, Harmer," he said in a low voice. "It did stop raining. We even have a full moon. You'll be able to see exactly what you're doing."

"Douglas," he whispered, "let's get out of here. They have four times as many sentries as usual. They must suspect something."

"I don't mind if they suspect something, Harmer. It might be more interesting that way. Besides, if we're clever, it won't make any difference." He took a step toward the camp.

"You're not going in alone, are you?" Harmer asked him.

"For the moment," he replied. "Thanks to you, I know where Craddock is, and I know where my wife is. When I've taken care of those two, I'll be back. Then we will start the general festivities."

"The men are restless, Douglas," he reminded him.

"Good. Keep them restless. It puts an edge on the appetite. If I'm not back in twenty minutes, give them their heads. Let them have their way with every man and woman in this camp."

The Indians began to rumble out their approval of

Fairchild and their delight at his words. He had to raise his hand to quiet them down.

Moments later he stole out of the cover of the pines at the edge of the camp, bent low as he burst quickly across the grounds to the lighted captains' tent in the center of the camp. He hung close to the back wall of the tent, in the shadows. He could hear one of the captains inside saying to the other, "Gass talked to him, Meriwether. He said he wouldn't tell him any more than he told us."

"Chillarlarwil is a confidence man, William," the other captain replied. "You never know if what he says is true. But he looked scared, damned scared."

Fairchild waited until a sentry had marched past the tent and turned his back, then he slid across the wet grass to where Harmer told him Craddock would be. With his knife out, he eased stealthily through a maze of sleeping bodies, sometimes stepping as close as a foot to a head or a pair of boots.

After only a few moments he recognized Craddock in the glow of the firelight. He squatted down to where he was sleeping, placed the sharp tip of his knife under his chin, and applied slight pressure to it. Craddock jerked awake immediately.

"Don't move, Craddock," he whispered. "Don't even breathe hard."

Craddock looked at Fairchild in horror. "Red Hair!" he gasped and started to move, but the pain of the point of the knife made him stop.

"You just come with me, Ned," Fairchild ordered. "We have some business to discuss."

Craddock nodded, carefully got up with him and let Fairchild push him into the darkness beyond the glow of the fire. "Look, Red Hair," he whined, terrified. "Don't hurt me, please. I'll do anything you want. Just don't hurt me."

"I'm not interested in hearing a man beg, Craddock."

"For God's sakes, man. Not like this! Not in cold

blood. Give me a chance. I *tried*. McKain can't say I didn't try. They were just too clever. Tom Wentworth was watching me, all the time. I couldn't make a move without Wentworth being there—"

"Who is this Wentworth?" Fairchild asked him.

"I don't know, some Philadelphia lawyer. Lewis's pet. The woman's boyfriend. I don't know."

"What woman?"

"The white woman, Roxanna, Garcia, whatever her name is."

"For your information, Craddock, that woman is my wife."

"Your wife!" he gulped. "Look, Red Hair," he almost choked on his saliva, "I tried to kill Wentworth, back at the falls. I shot at him, I even hit him. I would've killed him, too, if Lewis hadn't come along."

"Never mind citing your failures, Ned," Fairchild muttered.

"No, listen, man. I almost killed him. Both of them."

" 'Both of them,' Ned? Are you saying Wentworth and my wife were lovers?" he asked calmly. "I hope you're not saying that."

Craddock decided he had better change his approach quickly. "No, look," he told him, "I don't know anything about that. I don't know what they were. I was just trying to kill him. I hate Wentworth. I've always hated him. He killed a friend of mine back in St. Louis. That was why I was trying to shoot him. I don't think they were lovers."

Fairchild shoved the knifepoint into Craddock's throat a bit. "You're everything I detest in a man, Craddock. You're a coward—a lowly insect looking around for somebody's blood to suck. And the worst of it all is, you're incompetent. And I loathe incompetence. Unfortunately, it's a quality you Americans have in abundance."

"Look, Red Hair, it's not too late. We can still sabotage the expedition, together. Lewis and Clark haven't reported to Jefferson yet. We can get them before it becomes official. We can destroy the journals. We can do it tonight, if you want. I'll show you where everything is."

"As a matter of fact, Ned, I already know where everything is. I don't need you."

"No, wait. Don't."

Suddenly a voice rang out in the dark. "Ned?" someone called out. "Ned? Is that you?"

Fairchild quickly wrapped his forearm around Craddock's neck and dug the point of the knife between his shoulder blades. "Don't say a word," he whispered in his ear.

"Ned? Is that you out there? Answer me."

Fairchild pressed his face against Craddock's cheek. "Not a sound, Ned," he told him.

"Ned!" the voice called again.

Craddock knew the voice: it was John Collins. And he also knew if Collins didn't discover him now, he would have no chance later. He had to risk it. He gasped for breath in order to blurt out Collins' name, but he didn't even get to make a sound.

Without hesitation, Fairchild jerked Ned's neck back, crushing his windpipe, and pressed his lips against Craddock's ear. "Goodbye, Ned," he whispered, and thrust the knife into his back.

But the blade hit an obstruction, stopped at four inches. Craddock struggled, trying to cry out, but Fairchild's arm choked off the sound. Then he rammed the knife in, to the hilt. Craddock gasped silently and vomited up blood.

Then he was nothing but dead weight as Fairchild lowered himself into the shadows out of sight of the sentry.

A few minutes later Roxanna stopped stroking her long black hair, laid the hairbrush down next to her cracked and cloudy mirror, and listened again to the noise outside the tent. She could hear low, muffled voices, then the sound of people shuffling about outside, another exchange of words—then silence.

Her heart began to beat rapidly, her palms started to sweat. Since the rain had stopped, everything had seemed unnaturally still and quiet, as if nature were waiting for some terrible calamity. She felt strangely apprehensive, even afraid. Then came a swishing sound outside the tent.

Slowly, carefully, she reached over and picked up the heavy flintlock from the Mandan blanket and brought it to her lap. Her breathing quickened as she pulled back the hammer of the pistol and aimed the barrel toward the doorway.

Suddenly the ominous sounds of someone running through the wet leaves and pine straw, came toward her, closer and closer—until finally a man burst through the doorway into her tent.

"Tom!" she cried, surprised and relieved.

Wentworth rushed over and took her into his arms. "Roxanna!" he exclaimed excitedly. They embraced and kissed, then he pushed her back to look into her eyes. "You have to get out of here," he told her. "Now!"

"Why?" she asked. "What's wrong?"

"I don't have time to explain," he pulled her by the wrist. "Just come with me. We have to get out of this camp, right now."

She resisted him. "Now wait a minute, Tom. Why should we leave camp? What are you talking about? I can't just . . . go with you. Captain Lewis said I'm needed here."

"Roxanna," he said impatiently. "I'll tell you about it later. We have to go."

"If you want me to leave this place, Tom, you're going to have to tell me why. I'm not budging until you do."

"All right, Roxanna. I'll tell you: it's your husband."

"My husband!"

"That's right, Douglas Fairchild. The man the Indians call Red Hair. Captain Lewis just told me he is on his way here—now. He didn't know what that meant, but *I* do."

Roxanna looked at him with curiosity. "If Douglas is coming here, then I'm staying. That's what I came all this way for, Tom. He has a lot of explaining to do to me."

"Roxanna, please understand, if he finds you here, there's no telling what he may do. You can't stay; the man's a killer."

"Tom—"

"I mean it, damn it! He's a murderer! Don't you understand? You have to leave. Please. Trust me. All I want to do is get you out of here before he comes. So stop resisting!"

"Tom, I love you, but you can't keep *protecting* me like this."

"Well, I'm sorry, but this time, like it or not, I have to protect you," he said, jerking her toward the doorway.

Just as they reached the door, a tall, red-haired figure in a long dark coat stepped through the flap, holding a dripping, bloody knife in his hand. He smiled as Tom and Roxanna instinctively flinched from him. "This is cozy," he commented, looking around the tent. "What are your rates, Roxanna? A dollar for privates, two for officers?"

"What do you want, Fairchild?" Tom demanded.

He turned toward Tom, looked him over. "You must be Wentworth," he guessed. "They tell me you're my wife's favorite customer."

Tom's temper flared and he reached for his sword, but Roxanna reached out and stopped him.

She looked at Fairchild. "Why are you here, Douglas?" she asked him. "Why, after all this time. . . ."

"I'm here for you, dearest," he explained, keeping

his eye on Tom. "You're still my lawfully wedded wife, you know. I'm here to take you home with me."

"You say that to me, after what you tried to do at Fort Mandan?"

He looked at her, puzzled. "I've never even seen this Fort Mandan. What're you talking about?"

"I'm talking about this," she took the watch out of her pocket. "Your watch. You left it in my cabin, the night you tried to rape me!"

"Rape you!" he exclaimed, laughing. "That sounds like fun, Roxanna, but it wasn't me. That's not my watch."

"It *is* your watch," she insisted. "Look," she insisted, opening the cover. "What other watch would have a picture of a naked woman in it?"

Fairchild's expression turned hard. "That bastard —he stole it from me."

But Tom had already recognized the watch and he stared at it, open-mouthed. "That's Ned Craddock's!" he exclaimed. He turned to Roxanna. "Ned Craddock attacked you?"

"Forget it, Wentworth," Fairchild broke in. "Ned Craddock's dead. I just killed him." He held out a hand to Roxanna. "Let's go, love—"

"You're not going anywhere, Fairchild!" Tom whipped out his cutlass.

Fairchild shook his head condescendingly at Tom, and spoke to his wife, "Roxanna, before we go, it looks as if I'm going to have to cut your boyfriend into pieces. I hope you don't mind."

"Just try it," Tom defied him.

Fairchild held up his knife. "What you see on this blade is blood, Wentworth. Ned Craddock's blood. It'll be a great pleasure to mix yours with it. Of course you have the advantage, with that sword; but then, that's the American way, isn't it? Always put your opponent at a disadvantage before you fight him."

Tom gritted his teeth in anger, then flung the cutlass to the ground and drew his hunting knife. "Is that better? Now come on. Let's see what you can do with that knife."

"Tom—" Roxanna cried.

"You're a stupid man, Wentworth," Fairchild chided him. "Very, very stupid. You deserve to die."

"Douglas!" Roxanna entreated. "Why don't you just go away and leave us alone! He hasn't done anything to you!"

He laughed at her. "You're not a very understanding wife, are you?"

"For God's sake, Douglas!"

"Stand back, Roxanna," Tom commanded. He crouched slightly, holding his knife ready. Then Fairchild lunged. Tom tried to sidestep, but the Englishman lashed out with incredible quickness flicking a deep gash into Tom's left arm.

"You move like an old woman, Wentworth," Fairchild gloated.

Tom said nothing. He moved about the tent slowly, cautiously, waiting for an opening. Finally, he pounced. Fairchild countered and the blades of their knives scraped as the two men went into a clinch.

"You have no finesse, Wentworth," Fairchild sneered. "Your technique is crude. Very American."

Tom felt the Englishman's greater strength begin to force him back and felt the blade of the other knife moving down until it was only inches away from his chest. With a loud grunt he shot his knee up into Fairchild's stomach, hurling his attacker backwards.

Tom did not wait for the man to rise. He leaped again. But Fairchild was elusive. Tom had no experience with such agility. Just when he thought he had Fairchild in his clutches, the Englishman's knife whipped out and found a vulnerable spot on Tom's chest. The skin split open. Tom fought back violently, drawing blood, but his torn chest was scarlet and the pain agonizing.

Five minutes later Tom was lacerated and bleeding in six places; Fairchild was bruised and battered in the

ribs, stomach, and face—but hardly scratched. They
stood apart for a moment, getting their wind. Then
Fairchild bounded forward, ready for the kill. Sum-
moning all his energy, Tom steadied himself. Fairchild
came at him brandishing his wet knife. The blade
arched toward Tom's neck.

Somehow he was able to duck low enough to
throw his shoulder into Fairchild's waist and send him
crashing to the floor. The Englishman down, Tom had
the advantage. He quickly yanked Fairchild to his feet
and rammed his fist into the man's face. Blood spurted
from the man's nostrils. Tom pounded two blows into
the stomach and another into the face again, and Fairchild keeled over.

Catching his breath, Wentworth raised the battered
man by the collar to finish him off. Fairchild sprang
forward. Tom found himself enveloped in a crushing
bear hug that threw him off balance. The two men
spun around the tent, knocking over the lantern and
the cot. Suddenly Tom realized there was only one
hand around him; the other was holding the point of a
knife at his belly. At that instant, he seized Fairchild's
wrist, held it back. But Tom's strength was waning. He
could feel the point of the blade pushing at his skin.
With an explosion of pain, the blade penetrated.

"Douglas!" Roxanna shouted.

"I'm going to enjoy opening you up, Wentworth,"
Fairchild growled.

But the blade had only punctured the skin. Tom
wriggled free a hand. A swift, solid blow to the chin
sent Fairchild reeling back, out of the tent. Tom burst
through the doorway after his assailant. The Englishman lay prostrate on the ground. Tom stood back.
Fairchild curled up helplessly in the wet grass, like a
caterpillar protecting itself.

"Tom!" Roxanna approached him.

"I'm all right," he answered, watching the men in
the camp begin to gather around them.

But a moment later they all stopped and began

looking nervously around the rim of the camp. Only now did they realize they were surrounded by a band of Indians in warpaint, holding long rifles and muskets to their shoulders, poised and ready to fire.

"Tom!" Captain Lewis called out. He and Clark were standing outside their tent, holding their rifles diagonally across their chests.

"We'd better be still, captain," Tom suggested. "They have us."

Tom held his knife hand to the cut on his forearm to stop the bleeding and looked apprehensively around the camp. The men were well-trained, efficient, courageous, but he knew Red Hair's renegades were in control. All it would take was a command from their ruthless leader and the Lewis and Clark expedition would be nothing but a memory.

Fairchild began to stir on the ground. "Harmer!" he called out, getting to his knees.

"I'm here," Harmer returned from the edge of the camp.

"No prisoners, Harmer," he ordered angrily.

"Douglas—"

"I said, 'No prisoners.'" He stood up and glared at Tom. As he was wiping blood off his face, he noticed his knife on the ground, a few feet away, partially covered by wet leaves. He bent over and clutched his side, pretending to be in pain, then staggered to the knife. Then in a smooth, rapid movement, he scooped up the weapon, swept over and grabbed Wentworth and held the blade against his throat.

"Fairchild!" Captain Clark called out. "Drop the knife, or so help me. . . ."

"One more word, captain, and your friend Wentworth is dead. Do you understand me? Just one more!"

"Douglas!" Roxanna screamed. "No—don't! Don't hurt him! Please!"

"You'd better come with me, Roxanna," he warned. "If you choose to stay, you'll die with Wentworth and the rest of them."

"Then I'll die with them," she declared.

"It's your choice, lover," he replied, dragging Tom back toward Harmer.

"Douglas, you can't just kill us. Not *all* of us!"

"Oh, you don't know me, Roxanna," he smirked. "You don't know me at all."

"Fairchild!" Captain Lewis called. "Let me warn you—we're not about to lie down and die for you. If you hurt Wentworth, we'll fight. And we won't give in until the last man drops in his own blood!"

"Those are strong sentiments, captain," Fairchild replied flatly. "But the fact is, you're surrounded by my men." He backed up slowly, holding the edge of the knife against Tom's skin. "You won't even have time to get off a shot."

"Douglas!" Roxanna shouted, horrified at the sight of Tom being dragged backwards. She was expecting to see his neck sliced open at any moment.

"Harmer!" Fairchild turned his head slightly. "When I cut Wentworth's throat, open fire."

There was no answer.

"Harmer! Do you hear me!"

"I hear you."

"Then get ready."

"Not the woman, Douglas," he begged.

"Yes, the woman, half-breed. She made her own choice."

"Damn you, Fairchild," Tom gasped under the blade.

"Be still, lover," he told him. "Three more feet and it'll all be over for you."

"You can't do this, Douglas," Harmer told him calmly. "The woman's your wife. You have to have respect for something, man. You can't just kill her, too."

"I'll do it myself, Harmer," he growled, looking back. "Right after I take care of her boyfriend. You keep—" he stopped abruptly when he saw Harmer raising and aiming his musket at him. "Harmer—what in the hell are you doing!" he demanded incredulously. "Put that thing down!"

"Let him go, Douglas. We've gone too far. We have to stop this. Here and now."

"Traitor! Is this the way you reward a man for saving your life? How dare you, you miserable half-breed. You're nothing. You don't even have a name. You call yourself a name you made up."

"We've gone too far, Douglas."

"You fool," he hissed. "Is this what you call the Pawnee way?"

"No, it's my way," he cocked the musket.

"You can't kill me, Harmer, you know that. You can't kill Red Hair."

"Let him go, Douglas."

But Fairchild turned his back to Harmer. "Went-worth," he said to Tom, jerking his head back, making the skin taut and ready for his blade. "You've outlived your usefulness. Goodbye——"

All of a sudden his arm wouldn't move. His fingers clamped down on the handle of the knife and wouldn't budge. He was paralyzed by a great surging wave as the shot from Harmer's musket popped into his brain at the base of the skull. He turned around long enough to look back at Harmer, dazed and disbelieving, then, without a word, he slowly, limply crumbled to the ground, dead.

Immediately the Lewis and Clark men took advantage of the confusion to seize their weapons. They sharply raised them up to their shoulders and stood face to face with the renegades around the camp. Roxanna ran to Tom and embraced him, but every other person remained still, waiting to see what would happen.

Finally, after two long, agonizing minutes, Harmer lay down his gun and slowly walked through the grass toward Fairchild's body. Clenching his teeth, he reached down and lifted it up and held the stiffening corpse in his arms.

He looked around at the camp, at each man's face lit by the moonlight or by the glow of a fire. "This man saved my life," he declared in a clear but sad voice. "He saved my life and in return I took his." He looked down at Fairchild's face, warmer, more peaceful than he had ever seen it. With tears in his eyes, he looked up again. "Let the killing between the whites and the Indians, between the Americans and the British, stop here. Let it end here, now, this day!"

As he walked back with the body, Cathy Brussard came out to meet him. He paused, smiled at her but said nothing. She stepped up and held onto his arm as the two passed the line of Indians and proceeded into the clearing, headed back for their camp.

Slowly, deliberately, the Indians lowered their guns, uncocked them, and then, one by one, followed Harmer and the girl back into the darkness.

"Oh, Tom," Roxanna cried, holding Wentworth close to her body. "I was so scared. I thought at any moment—"

"So did I, Roxanna," he admitted. "I was beginning to see angels."

"You're hurt," she looked at his arm.

"Yes," he admitted lightly. "Every time I get around you, I get hurt. But I'm getting used to it."

"Well, you wouldn't get hurt if you didn't always insist on being so protective, Tom."

"Well, I do insist on it, Roxanna, so I guess I'll just keep getting hurt."

"Tom Wentworth, you're as stubborn as. . . ."

"As you are," he completed her sentence.

She laughed. "I guess so. I guess we are two of a kind, aren't we?"

As they were talking, the others drew close around them. Captain Lewis came up, holding his air gun at his side. "Are you all right, Tom?" he asked. "How serious are those cuts?"

"We're just fine," Tom smiled, squeezing Roxanna. "Now."

"That was close," Lewis sighed. "If Fairchild's man hadn't turned on him, I don't know where we would have been."

"It was too close for me, captain," Tom acknowledged.

"We found Private Craddock's body, Tom," Clark offered. "He'd been stabbed in the back."

"I'm not surprised at that," Tom declared. "That was what Fairchild was hired to do."

Lewis put his hand on Tom's shoulder. "I want you to explain all of this to us, Tom. After twenty months and a few thousand hard miles, to come this close to being wiped out. . . ."

Tom nodded. "I'll tell you all I know about it, Captain Lewis. But I don't know much. With Ned Craddock dead and Morton McKain and Buck Brussard missing, we may never know the whole story."

"Maybe we won't," Lewis mused. "But we might be able to piece it together. Somehow I have a feeling Mr. Jefferson will want to know not only *how*, but *why* the Lewis and Clark expedition almost ended in a massacre."

Chapter 22

Although the damp, heavy air was beginning to turn very cold when Tom and Roxanna returned from Harmer's camp, no one on the Lewis and Clark expedition seemed to notice. Everyone in camp was animated; all fifty men were moving about, packing food, clothes and tools, loading up the canoes on the river, dousing fires with buckets of water or smothering them with wet leaves.

Tom and Roxanna stopped on the edge of camp for a minute to watch the activity. Sacajawea, with Baptiste strapped firmly into the papoose cradle on her back, was meticulously wrapping Charbonneau's fishing gear into a Minnetaree blanket. Twenty yards beyond her, Sergeant Ordway was talking with Captain Clark under a pine tree, on the outer perimeter of camp while Patrick Gass laboriously carved his name into the trunk of a tree.

Captain Meriwether Lewis was stooped over his portable writing desk, his long quill racing across a page. He stood up graciously when they entered the tent. "Tom, Roxanna," he greeted cheerfully. "It's good to see you. Come in." As they settled in, he observed, "It's getting cold outside, isn't it?"

"Yes, it is," Tom agreed.

Lewis looked at them thoughtfully. They seemed uneasy to him. He cleared his throat. "I'm writing a letter to Mr. Jefferson," he told them after a minute. "I'm trying to explain to him how an official government mission managed to reach its destination and then end in violence."

"Captain Lewis," Roxanna squirmed, "I can't help but feel responsible for all this. If I hadn't insisted on coming—"

"If you hadn't insisted on coming," he interrupted her, "we wouldn't have made it this far to begin with. None of this was your fault, Roxanna. Don't reproach yourself for it."

"Captain Lewis," Tom queried, "is it absolutely necessary to report this to Mr. Jefferson?"

"Yes, it is," he answered. "The Lewis and Clark Expedition was his creation, Tom. He saw the need for it. He put it together. He got financial support for it. And he kept private interests out of it. I have to give him as much of the story as I can."

Tom nodded, understanding. "We can complete the story for you with what Harmer told us," he suggested. "And what the girl told us. It turns out she's Buck Brussard's daughter."

"His daughter!"

"Buck was out here looking for her," Roxanna explained. "And for Douglas," she added.

"Was Douglas Fairchild the one who abused the girl?" he asked.

"Yes, he was," she answered flatly. "I wish it wasn't true, but it is. I didn't want to believe he married me and stole my money and left me without a word, either. But he did. He was an evil man."

"Harmer says he hadn't always been that way," Tom offered. "His bitterness just gradually took control of him and made him into a monster."

"Bitterness over what?"

Roxanna sighed. "Over a woman. He was engaged to an American woman back in England. When he jilted her, she went to his family and exposed Douglas's many sexual escapades. He was publicly embarrassed, then disinherited."

"So," Tom deduced, "his hatred for that American woman led to a hatred of *all* American women, and then to Americans in general. Until it finally took control of him; he became insanely vicious."

Lewis nodded. "Sometimes society can make us more bestial than the wilderness can."

Tom rubbed his beard nervously. "What do you think Mr. Jefferson's reaction to all this will be, Captain Lewis?" he asked.

"President Jefferson is a reasonable man," Lewis admitted. "But the loss of life, no matter whose it was, will affect him deeply." He reached down, opened the lid of the writing desk and drew out a letter. "He wanted to avoid violence at all costs. He wrote this to me back in June, eighteen-oh-three: *'to your own discretions therefore must be left the degree of danger you may risk, and the point at which you should decline, only saying that we wish you to err on the side of safety, and bring back your party safe, even if it be with less information.'* "

He lowered the paper. "This wasn't exactly 'on the side of safety,' was it?"

"Captain Lewis," Roxanna persisted, "I know you have to tell this story to Mr. Jefferson. But couldn't you. . . ," she paused.

He searched her face. "Couldn't I what, Roxanna?"

"We were wondering, could you take us *out* of the journals and reports that the public will see?"

"Take you out?" he asked coyly.

"Yes. Couldn't you and Captain Clark delete all references to me, to Tom, Douglas—even Buck Brussard? Wouldn't that be possible?"

"None of us was really an official member of the expedition," Tom reminded him.

"No, that's true, you weren't," he agreed. "You and Roxanna joined too late to be on the Congressional list. But what about Ned Craddock?"

"He wasn't either," Roxanna pointed out. "He was working for Great Pacific Fur Company. He couldn't have been an official member of the Lewis and Clark Expedition."

Lewis scratched his chin. "To tell you the truth, Roxanna," he admitted, "Captain Clark and I have already talked about doing that."

"Then you'll do it?" she asked excitedly.

"Wait a minute, Roxanna," he cautioned. "To take all of your names out of the journals and reports would require several things. First, we'd have to get all the other men who are keeping journals to agree to do it."

"I'm sure they would, captain," Roxanna claimed confidently.

"Then we'd have to propose the plan to Mr. Jefferson, to see if *he* would agree to it."

"Do you think he would?" she wondered.

"Considering the international importance of the expedition, I think he would."

"Oh, Captain Lewis—"

"Now hold on, Roxanna. I only said I *think* he would. I can't speak for Mr. Jefferson."

"Yes, but he'll agree. I know he will."

"Now, even if he does agree, Roxanna," Lewis warned her. "He will have the whole story. That means it *will* exist."

"But if he agreed to deleting us from the journals," Roxanna reasoned, "surely he'd keep your letter secret."

"I'm sure he would, Roxanna. But secrets have a way of coming out—eventually."

"I certainly hope this one doesn't," Roxanna responded. "I hate to think what my descendants would think of me after this."

"Well, Roxanna," Lewis comforted her. "If someone does come across my letter to Mr. Jefferson a couple of hundred years from now and decides to tell the true story of the Lewis and Clark Expedition, maybe by then our society will have changed enough that people will be a little more tolerant and understanding about the presence of a woman on a great expedition of this sort."

"Even so, I hope no one ever finds it."

"In any case, you can't stay with the expedition," he told her.

She was surprised. "But you said you needed a nurse," she reminded him.

"I know I did. But I've taken care of that. While you were gone, Chillarlarwil brought us three women who seem to know what they're doing with the sick men."

"Oh," she mumbled, disappointed.

"So all we need to do now," Tom muttered, "is find a place to go."

Lewis was silent for a minute, then suggested, "Well . . . . as it happens, Tom, I have a place you might want to go."

"Where?"

He raised the letter from Jefferson to read again. "The President says here, when we reach the Pacific, we are to *'learn if there be any port within your reach frequented by the sea-vessels of any nation, and to send two of your trusty people back by sea, . . . with a copy of your notes.'* "

" 'Two people'—are you suggesting us?" Tom asked happily.

"Why not you? You're certainly 'trusty.' And who would take better care of these 'notes', this precious letter, to Mr. Jefferson?"

Roxanna's eyes filled with tears. "Captain Lewis—" she began, but couldn't finish.

He looked at her. "You'll have to take this letter to the President in absolute secrecy, Roxanna," he insisted firmly.

She nodded, sniffing.

"And you'll have to go to him properly, Tom," he hinted.

Tom understood. "We'll get the ship's captain to marry us," he promised.

"Captain Lewis," Roxanna wiped her eyes. "Buck Brussard was right. You are a great man."

"Well, right now I'm just a grateful one. I've been given a chance to lead an expedition into a magnificent new land. It's true we didn't find the Northwest Passage, Tom. But we found much more. Though it seems simple to say it, what we found was the other half of our country. And we've laid claim to it. Now, for the first time in its history, the United States will have the size and wealth and people to make herself strong enough to stand up and take her place among the great nations of the world."

At that moment, John Collins stuck his head into the doorway of the tent. "Captain Lewis? Captain Clark is ready."

"Thank you, John," he replied.

He led Tom and Roxanna out of the tent, across the grounds to where the whole assembly of men and Sacajawea had gathered around two huge pine trees, each stripped of its bark to eye-level. Hugh Hall was carving his name into the tree with a knife; there were at least fifty others above his.

When he had finished, he gave the knife to Clark. The captain glanced at Tom and Roxanna, then looked questioningly at Lewis. When the other captain shook his head, Clark understood that Tom and Roxanna were no longer considered part of the Lewis and Clark Expedition.

Clark raised his hands to quiet the crowd and spoke in a smooth, clear voice. The men paid him close attention. "Men," he began, "I know each one of you is anxious to move away from this infernal salty air and this constant roaring of waves and get ourselves back inland to the Netul River to set up our winter quarters. . . ."

"We don't mind the salty air, Captain Clark," someone called out. "But it is getting cold!" The others laughed.

Clark smiled. "I know it's getting cold. We're not going to wait for a ship any longer. We have to move out today. We need to get those cabins up by the first of January." He paused and looked around. "But before I put our official legend on this other tree," he continued, "I want to take this opportunity to announce publicly that Tom Wentworth and Roxanna Fairchild will be leaving this expedition shortly—"

The men stirred with the beginnings of grumbling.

"Now just a minute," he calmed them. "They are leaving—but they'll be leaving on another mission for Mr. Jefferson. A mission of great importance." He looked over at them fondly. "They'll be taking the news of our reaching the Pacific!"

The men cheered wildly and threw their hats into the air. "And now," Clark resumed, "this tree represents the point farthest west reached by the Lewis and Clark Expedition." He raised the knife and cut into the tree in deep, clear letters: *"William Clark, December 3rd 1805. By Land and Water from the U. States in 1804 & 1805."*

When he had finished, the men applauded vigorously until he brought them to order again and sent them back to the work of breaking up camp. As they dispersed, he came over to Tom, Roxanna and Lewis. "I'm happy it's working out this way for you."

"Thank you, Captain Clark," Roxanna smiled warmly.

Lewis turned to him, "They'll be coming back to the coast as soon as I finish the letter to the President.

They can catch the first ship that's going around the Cape. There should be one soon."

Roxanna was smiling through her tears. Impulsively, she reached out and embraced Captain Clark. "You're both great men. And I'm going to make sure Mr. Jefferson knows it."

"Roxanna—" Lewis murmured, but he dropped the sentence when she wrapped her arms around him and kissed him on the cheek. He flushed with embarrassment, but managed to hold her next to him and give her a fatherly hug. "William," he called sheepishly over her shoulder, "don't we have work to do here?"

Clark laughed. "Yes, we do, Meriwether. As the man said, it's getting cold."

Lewis wriggled gracefully out of Roxanna's embrace. "All right, then, captain," he spoke in a dignified voice, "let's do it. Let's go to work."

Tom and Roxanna clasped hands as they watched the two captains head back toward their tent. "It's strange," she observed to Tom. "We've been a part of this expedition all these months, and it's we who will be bringing Mr. Jefferson the news that Lewis and Clark made it overland to the Pacific; yet no one will ever know we were even connected with it. It seems so peculiar."

"I don't know," Tom mused, "I have a feeling that Captain Lewis was right—someday, maybe after you and I are dead and gone, Roxanna, the truth will surface."

She nodded and placed her head on his shoulder. "Maybe," she agreed.

The captains stopped and looked back at them. "Tom? Roxanna?" Lewis called out. "You're not on that ship yet. We can still use some help. Are you coming?"

Roxanna straightened up and took a long, deep breath. "We're coming, Captain Lewis," she smiled, looking up at Tom. "We're coming."

422